"A sweet and heartwarming second chance romance... I fell in love with the characters and the small fictional town, which Ms. Riley set in the Adirondacks in upper New York State... I know I didn't want to leave Emerald Lake and look forward to the next book in Ms. Riley's series."

— NightOwlRomance.com

Also by Bella Riley

Home Sweet Home

An Uncontrollable Desire

He found himself reaching out with his free hand to brush away the soap bubbles on her cheek.

He didn't just hear her swift inhale, he felt it reverberate through her jaw to his hand. And all he could think was how soft her skin was.

"You had some soap on your face." His words sounded strangled. Borderline gruff. He wouldn't have recognized the voice as his own if he hadn't felt them come up his throat.

"Thank you for cleaning it off."

Jesus, her breathy words did crazy stuff to his insides, had him thinking, wondering even crazier things.

Would her lips be as soft as her skin?

Would they taste like the first ray of sunlight in spring?

Sean had lived a perfectly controlled life for nearly twenty years. But in less than twenty-four hours this woman, his brother's ex-fiancée, was destroying that control. Without even trying.

Praise for
Home Sweet Home

"This wonderful visit to Emerald Lake is full of delightful characters. The struggles the heroine faces are understandable and the secondary story threads are a joy to read about."

—*RT Book Reviews*

"Author Bella Riley writes a beguiling story of living with past choices, sacrifice for love, forgiveness, and optimism for the future...a diverse hometown atmosphere...*Home Sweet Home* is an excellent read about family and community, filled with emotional drama and coming to terms with the past."

—RomRevToday.com

"This book was such a sweet read! I loved Andi right from the start, and I couldn't help but root for her the entire book...Nate is the guy every girl dreams about...If you want a cute book that makes you smile, then pick this one up! It feels just like home."

—GoodReads.com

"Warm, welcome story about old romances and new beginnings set in a lovely small town that will warm your heart."

—*Parkersburg News and Sentinel* (WV)

With This Kiss

BELLA RILEY

FOREVER

NEW YORK   BOSTON

This book is a work of fiction. Names, characters, places, and incidents are the product of the author's imagination or are used fictitiously. Any resemblance to actual events, locales, or persons, living or dead, is coincidental.

Copyright © 2012 by Bella Riley
Excerpt from *Home Sweet Home* copyright © 2011 by Bella Riley

Forever
Hachette Book Group
237 Park Avenue
New York, NY 10017

www.HachetteBookGroup.com

Printed in the United States of America

First Edition: March 2012
10 9 8 7 6 5 4 3 2 1

Forever is an imprint of Grand Central Publishing.
The Forever name and logo are trademarks of Hachette Book Group, Inc.

The Hachette Speakers Bureau provides a wide range of authors for speaking events. To find out more, go to www.hachettespeakersbureau.com or call (866) 376-6591.

The publisher is not responsible for websites (or their content) that are not owned by the publisher.

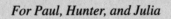

For Paul, Hunter, and Julia

Acknowledgments

This career has brought many wonderful people into my life—fellow writers, loyal readers, my agent, my editors, and fantastic cover artists. Thank you for the hard work you've put into my books over the years.

With This Kiss

Chapter One

You are such a beautiful bride."

Rebecca Campbell smoothed out the cuff of Andi Powell's long-sleeved silk wedding gown and smiled at her friend in the full-length mirror. Emerald Lake, still mostly frozen and lightly dusted with snow from last night's short storm, reflected through the large-paned window to the mirror.

Andi's eyes met Rebecca's in the mirror, full of excitement and anticipation for her wedding day. "I know I've said it a hundred times already, Rebecca, but thank you so much for everything you've done to help with my wedding. I could have never pulled this off so quickly, or so beautifully."

Rebecca was extremely pleased by how smoothly the wedding preparations had come together. Her final walk-through downstairs half an hour ago confirmed that the Emerald Lake Inn had been completely transformed into a tasteful, elegant wedding venue. She'd done it before, of course, but it meant more to her this time, knowing she was an integral part of Andi and Nate's special day.

Still, she had to tease her friend. "We both know you could have planned a dozen last-minute weddings in the past two weeks, Andi, and probably gotten a spread in *Brides* magazine while you were at it."

Andi grinned before tossing off, "That was the old me, before I decided to start playing with yarn all day instead."

Rebecca was happy to let Andi say whatever she wanted. After all, this was her wedding day. But both of them knew that moving back to Emerald Lake and becoming engaged to Nate hadn't changed the core of who she was. Andi had always been driven. Brilliant. And on top of that, she also happened to be one of the most loving, caring people Rebecca had ever had the good fortune of knowing. Business at Lake Yarns was more brisk than ever now that Andi had taken over the store for her mother and grandmother. Not just because Andi was a great businesswoman with a background in management consulting, but because she was truly passionate about knitting—and the women who patronized her store.

As Andi turned back to look into the antique mirror in the inn's "wedding prep" room, Rebecca noted that her friend seemed surprised by her own appearance. The wedding gown, the soft curls brushing against her collarbone, the pretty makeup.

"I never thought today would come," Andi said softly. "But I always wanted it." She lifted her gaze to meet Rebecca's. "I've loved Nate my whole life."

Rebecca blinked quickly to push away the tears that had been threatening to fall all morning just thinking about Andi and Nate's wedding.

"You deserve it." She could hear how scratchy her

words sounded. She had to work to swallow away the lump that had formed in her throat at Andi's soft confession of love. "You and Nate both deserve the love you've found again. Especially since this time it's forever."

She shot a knowing glance at Andi's slightly rounded stomach, the lump in her throat replaced with the joy of knowing there would soon be a new baby to cuddle and kiss and spoil.

Rebecca refused to acknowledge the envy that tried to steal through her as her friend's slender fingers automatically spread across the growing life inside her in a gesture of instinctive protectiveness and nurturing. But she couldn't hide from the concerned look on Andi's face in the mirror as she obviously noticed her heightened emotions.

"A little more blush," Rebecca said quickly, letting her long light-brown hair hide her face as she bent down to pick up the makeup bag.

She knew she'd just given too much away. She always did. Some people had poker faces, but not her. On the contrary, hers would cause her to lose everything in the casino because she didn't have the first clue how to play the game.

And it was true. Rebecca had never figured out how to play the game. Not with love, that was for certain. And not with jobs, until she'd landed here at the inn and realized she'd finally found something she was good at. Something she loved to do.

Even though they both knew her makeup was already perfect, Andi let Rebecca brush a tiny bit more powder over her cheekbones, just until she'd regained her composure.

But then, before Rebecca could step away again, her friend reached out and put a hand on her arm. "You know you can talk to me, don't you?" Her gaze softened. "My groom isn't going anywhere," she said with perfect confidence. "I've got all the time in the world."

Knowing the last thing she should do was dump her fears and hurts and baggage all over Andi on her wedding day, Rebecca was intent on finding a way to deflect her concern. "I always get emotional at weddings. You should have seen me at each of my sister's ceremonies. I cried buckets. The guests in my row were all wishing for raincoats so I wouldn't soak them." She smiled a crooked little smile, hoping to lighten the mood. "This time I've tucked some under the seats next to mine as a precaution."

But her friend, the woman she'd helped see through such a difficult time the previous fall, didn't so much as crack a smile.

"You don't have to pretend with me, Rebecca." Regret flashed across Andi's face. "Ever since I got pregnant, my brain has been fuzzy and I just want to sleep all the time. That's got to be why I didn't see it all more clearly before." She shook her head. "We shouldn't have scheduled our wedding for this weekend."

Andi's words were said softly, and while there wasn't pity behind them, Rebecca believed that was only due to the close friendship they'd forged during the last six months.

Unfortunately, there was no escaping the fact—not with Andi or anyone who was going to be downstairs at the wedding and reception—that Rebecca was supposed to have been the one about to get married this weekend. Instead of wearing the gown and saying "I do," she was going to be sitting in the audience, watching two wonderful people make their vows of love to each other.

The truth was that it hadn't been easy walking down Main Street these past three weeks, going to the grocery store, passing people she knew on the cross-country ski trails knowing they were whispering about her. Sure, they still smiled, still exchanged the same pleasantries. But she knew either they had to be feeling sorry for her...or they were trying to figure out just what horrible thing she'd done to make Stu call off the wedding.

And disappear from Emerald Lake the very next day without a word to anyone.

Only the women at Lake Yarns's Monday night knitting group had remained the same as always. Warm. Gossipy. And yet, utterly nonjudgmental. No matter how busy she was, Rebecca made sure to keep every Monday night open for drinking too much wine, and usually doing more talking and laughing than knitting.

She felt like she'd found her home in Emerald Lake, liked to imagine growing old on an Adirondack chair on a dock while she watched her future grandchildren playing in the blue water.

She hated to think that she'd only been accepted by the locals because she was engaged to Stu Murphy, whose family had lived in Emerald Lake for generations. She wanted to believe she belonged here on her own merit. Because people liked her and thought she contributed something valuable to the community.

But regardless of how off-kilter she was feeling, she absolutely refused to taint Andi's wedding in any way.

"You know I absolutely loved being able to put on this wedding for you and Nate. And really, it worked out perfectly. You needed a wedding venue right away and I had one all ready to go." Rebecca already had the tables and chairs and glasses and food ordered for her own spring wedding at the inn, so Andi and Nate were able to use them without having to try to pull together everything at the last second. "It was meant to happen this way. I'm certain of it. I absolutely love knowing that I'm a part of your happily ever after."

Anyone else would have stopped talking there, would have held something back, would have hidden the rest of her feelings. But Rebecca had never known how to do that. Especially when a dear friend was looking at her with such deep concern. Besides, she'd finally stopped lying to herself about her ex-fiancé three weeks ago. So what was the point in trying to hold back the full—painful—truth with anyone else now?

"You know Stu and I weren't right for each other. Not as anything more than friends. The truth is I enjoyed putting the finishing details on your wedding far more than I ever enjoyed working on it when it was my own." She shook her head. "I guess that should have been my first clue that something wasn't right. But it was seeing you and Nate together that showed me what real love was supposed to look like."

"You never told me that," Andi said, clearly surprised by what Rebecca had divulged. Awareness dawned suddenly in her brown eyes. "Oh my gosh. Three weeks ago. That's when Nate and I came in to ask about squeezing in a shotgun wedding here at the inn."

Rebecca nodded, feeling like she was a diary that had fallen open with a splat. "You two were supposed to be flipping through a booklet of cake toppers. Instead, your foreheads were together and you were staring into each other's eyes."

She hadn't been able to tear her eyes away from them, not even when Nate cupped Andi's cheek and gently kissed her.

That was what real love looked like. Deep and true love.

Forever love.

Just like that, Rebecca had known she couldn't go through with marrying Stu. Not just for her sake, not just because she wanted that kind of love for herself, but because it wasn't fair to Stu, either. He deserved forever love, too.

"I don't know what to say. I hate to think that I caused your breakup. But—"

Rebecca shook her head, wanting to still the remorse, the guilt that was emerging on her friend's face. "You didn't cause anything. You just helped me see the light." Finally. Long after she should have seen it on her own. "I'll be forever grateful to you for that."

Andi hugged her tightly and even though Rebecca longed to tell her friend more—it simply wasn't her nature to hold things back and the secrets she was keeping were eating her up inside—there was one thing she couldn't tell anyone.

Specifically, what had happened three weeks ago when she went to break her engagement to Stu after seeing Andi and Nate so in love.

She'd been so twisted up inside her head—and heart—on her way to Stu's suite of rooms that night that she hadn't thought to knock before opening the door. Rebecca could still remember the way she'd been frozen in place when Stu and John, a mutual friend of theirs from college, pulled away from each other so quickly that she almost thought she'd imagined their embrace. Although he'd always been closer to Stu, Rebecca had counted John among her friends, too.

Stu had cursed and come toward her, hands outstretched, his face ravaged with guilt. *"Rebecca, I can explain. I didn't want to hurt you. I swear it."*

She'd waited for betrayal to kick in, for anger to burst forth. Instead, a deep sense of sadness made her chest clench—along with a flood of relief. Because he didn't want to marry her either. Stu had been her best friend since freshman year in art college when they'd bonded over giggles during the nude-drawing class. They should have known better than to date and then actually go and get engaged to each other.

She knew she should have been shocked by Stu's kiss with John. Only, she wasn't. Not when all of the warning signs, everything that hadn't added up from the first time Stu had asked her out, suddenly made perfect sense.

After a lifetime of dating tall, dark, and mysterious men who made her heart race, men with a core of danger and secrets that she'd longed to heal and love, Stu had been safe. Gentle. A calm lake instead of a roaring sea. Their first date had been full of laughter, and even though the very few kisses that came in later months were nothing to write home about, she told herself fireworks were overrated. Lord knew she could live without the careening emotions that usually went hand in hand with her relationships.

Standing there in Stu's living room with John waiting

awkwardly by the window, she'd realized why their engagement had always felt so wrong to her: they'd both been desperately lying to themselves, both been wanting to believe in something that could never make either of them happy in the long run.

"Why didn't you tell me?" was what she'd finally asked him and when he'd said, *"I wanted so badly to make it work,"* in clear anguish, she'd tried to say, *"Everything's going to be okay."*

She'd thought her relationship with Stu was different from her previous relationships. She'd thought it was healthy. But she'd been wrong. Which was why she hadn't been able to force those false words out.

Stu was a blur of emotion. *"I thought I could marry you, but seeing John brought up so many old feelings. Feelings I thought had gone away. Feelings I'd convinced myself had never existed in the first place. I'm just so confused about everything. You must hate me. But I swear I didn't cheat on you. Just that kiss."* His tears, along with his confession, broke her heart. *"I'm sorry, Rebecca. So, so sorry."*

It had been hard to get him to listen to her, to understand that she'd come to talk to him to call off their engagement, too, that she was an equal partner in breaking things off. Ultimately, she'd accepted that nothing she could say was going to calm him down. Not that night, anyway.

"Please keep my secret, Rebecca." He gripped her hands so tightly that she'd found small bruises along the tops of them the next morning. *"I need to figure things out first. Please."*

She couldn't help but wonder how Stu could possibly ask her to keep a secret like that? Especially when he knew how big her honesty gene was, that she was terrible at holding anything back.

"*You know I'm no good at keeping secrets,*" she'd told him, but it was the fear, the pain, the confusion in Stu's eyes that had her finally promising to keep his secret despite her deep reservations...and the sure knowledge that keeping Stu's secret was only going to hurt everyone more in the long run.

Of course, she'd assumed he'd be there in the morning, had believed that once he'd calmed down they'd figure out a way to share the news that they'd decided to just remain friends.

Rebecca found his note in the morning.

I have to leave. I'm sorry. I need some time to think things through. I'll come home as soon as I can, but please don't come looking for me.

Mere minutes later, his mother, Elizabeth, burst into the inn's reception room gripping a similar letter in her hand. Tears were still fresh on her cheeks...and she hadn't bothered to hide the accusations in her eyes when she looked at Rebecca.

The church bells chiming loudly outside the inn's window brought Rebecca back into the present moment. Andi's look of concern had morphed into full-on worry.

How long has she been lost replaying her final night with Stu?

"Have you heard from him yet?" Andi asked.

"No. He hasn't been in touch with any of us. Not even his parents."

Rebecca turned her gaze out the window, as if she could somehow spot Stu out there on Main Street if she looked hard enough. But she sensed he wouldn't be back so soon. Even though she not only needed his help with the inn, but the Tapping of the Maples Festival was rapidly approaching and she was nearly running on empty trying to take care of everything by herself.

She understood that he was dealing with a lot right now, but every now and again she felt more than a little miffed that he'd left her here to deal with both the inn and the festival entirely on her own for who knew how long.

Andi gripped her hand tighter and Rebecca felt moisture tickling her eyes again.

No. This was Andi's wedding day. Rebecca hadn't cried once in the past three weeks, and she certainly wasn't going to cry for herself now as they put the final touches on Andi's dress and hair and makeup.

Firmly deciding that the only tears she'd cry today would be happy ones, she smiled widely and said, "I can't wait to see Nate's face when you walk down the aisle. He's going to be the happiest man alive."

After only the slightest moment of hesitation, Andi, thankfully, let Rebecca have her way in changing the subject.

"The church bells have chimed." Rebecca opened the door and held her hand out for Andi. "It's time."

Oh my. What a lovely wedding it was.

Of course, the bride was gorgeous and the groom was handsome. Pink and white and red hothouse roses were in bloom all over the room. But Rebecca knew Andi and Nate could have been standing in the middle of an open field wearing jeans and T-shirts and it still would have been one of the most beautiful ceremonies she'd ever witnessed.

The love between them was so strong it reached out to wrap itself around everyone in the room. At last, Rebecca didn't bother to hide her tears, not when pretty much everyone else in the room was dabbing at their eyes. Thankfully, she'd thought ahead and had put a small box of tissues at the end of every row of seats. The boxes were being passed back and forth as Nate's ten-year-old sister, Madison, reached into her basket of rose petals and threw them over her brother and new sister-in-law as they kissed and the crowd cheered.

Rebecca was on her feet clapping along with the rest of them. The new bride and groom walked down the aisle hand in hand and she had to put her hand over her heart, as if somehow that could keep everything she was feeling— and everything she was wishing for—deep inside.

Chapter Two

Sean Murphy heard the applause and cheers as he walked through the inn's front door. From the flower petals drifting out of the event room into the inn's entry, he could easily guess it was a wedding.

It instantly struck him as strange. Why would Stu schedule another wedding at the inn on the same weekend as his own? And how exactly had his brother planned to clean up this wedding party and still have time to set up for his own rehearsal dinner that night?

But those questions left his mind as quickly as they had entered, the noise coming from the event room digging at the headache Sean had been riding out all day. Frankly, all he really cared about right now was getting upstairs to his suite to take a shower.

The red-eye from China didn't usually take it out of him like this. But it had been a crazy three weeks of constant flights, of hotel rooms he'd barely had time to check in to before he was leaving for the next airport, the next meeting. Today, he'd hoped to have time to get back to his house in Boston to shower, to transfer clothes in his luggage, to flip through his mail before heading to Emerald Lake for his brother's rehearsal dinner, but his flight had been delayed. So he'd headed straight to the inn.

Sean usually made it a point to stay as far away from weddings as he possibly could, but he hadn't been home in so long that curiosity had him dropping his bags behind the check-in counter and walking across stray rose petals toward the large room that overlooked the lake.

Standing at a side door behind a large potted plant, he instantly recognized the bride and groom. Sean had been a couple of years ahead of Andi and Nate in school. As long as he remembered, they'd always been a couple. How was it that they were only just getting married? He would have thought they'd have gotten hitched a long time ago and popped out a handful of kids by now.

A moment later, Sean's gut inexplicably tightened at the sight of Andi and Nate kissing. Worse still, something that felt way too much like envy stole through him a beat later.

Despite his discomfort, Sean forced himself to keep his gaze on the happy couple so that he could dissect whatever it was that was putting these strange thoughts in his head.

In twenty years of dating beautiful women, he'd never wanted to get married, had never been even remotely tempted to get down on one knee and ask one woman to be his for eternity. As he watched two people he'd known as children make their vows to each other, Sean could see that Nate and Andi thought they were in love. And maybe they were.

For now, at least.

But it was what happened later—ten, fifteen, twenty

years down the road once they had kids and were supposed to be a cohesive family unit who all looked out for each other—that Sean had no faith in. In fact, the only thing he knew for certain was that the people who got hurt when love failed weren't just the man and the woman who had once made vows to each other on their wedding day. No, the net was cast much wider than that.

Pushing the rogue emotions away, he scanned the occupants of the room. It had been a long time since he'd been back to Emerald Lake but he recognized most of them. The old football coach. The owner of the general store. Several other people he'd gone to school with.

About to move away from the doorway, sure that a hot shower and a beer would go a long way toward unknotting the tightness in his gut, his eyes caught a flash of movement that held his gaze—and his feet—in place.

Long golden-brown hair was gliding like silk across a woman's back as she moved out from behind a tall elderly man. And then she turned her face toward him and his breath actually lodged in his throat as he looked at her. Her eyes were glittering with tears, her cheeks were flushed. She was biting her lip, and her hands were covering her heart.

And she was beautiful.

What was wrong with him? He'd never been drawn to a delicate woman like this who looked like she could sprout fairy wings and fly away. He always chose the women who shared his bed very carefully, making sure they were strong enough to never make the mistake of falling in love with him or thinking they could change him in some way.

But there was no denying his elemental reaction to this woman.

It was long past time to turn away, to go upstairs and take that shower he'd been looking forward to. Even more than that, he knew there were several documents waiting in his e-mail for his approval. He needed to leave. Right now.

But instead of doing any of those things, Sean Murphy simply stood right where he was and stared at the woman who wasn't only taking his breath away but who was making his heart beat faster, too.

Details had made Sean millions in the years since he'd left Emerald Lake. He never got them wrong. But now, as the sun came in through one of the large windows that looked out on the frozen lake and lit her up like a spotlight, he realized her hair was neither brown nor gold. Because as she shifted slightly and the silky curtain of hair moved, he saw clear flashes of red.

More than ever, he knew he needed to get moving before she saw him standing there gaping at her like an adolescent in the throes of his first major crush. But he didn't move, couldn't stop himself from running his eyes over her from head to toe.

She wasn't tall, but she wasn't short either. Her figure wasn't too slim or too rounded.

She was *perfect*.

Sean shook his head to try and clear the word away, but when he did, he just ended up back at *beautiful*.

He was renowned for his clearheaded assessments of not only companies but people, too. Sean forced himself to study the woman's clothes in an analytical manner so that he could put together a better, more accurate picture of her, one that had nothing to do with words like *perfect* or *beautiful*.

Her green dress was well-tailored, but not particularly flashy. The pearls at her earlobes and around her neck were elegant, but not at all intended to draw a man's eyes. Neither were her shoes, low-heeled and silver. He got the sense she wasn't the kind of woman who would ever try to draw attention to herself.

Even though she had every ounce of his.

The crowd was starting to file out of the room, following Andi and Nate, but the woman hung behind, bending over to pick up stray flower petals strewn around her seat.

Something jogged his brain, a prickle that was more than just a man's awareness of a beautiful woman, a warning that he knew her from somewhere, but he couldn't quite grab hold of it.

Finally, when the room was empty save the two of them and she was continuing to grab handfuls of flower petals off the floor, she faced him with a look of surprise on her face.

She was closer now, near enough that he could see just how delicate her features were, from her high cheekbones to her slightly pointed chin and the tiny indentations in each cheek as she smiled.

"Oh, hello."

In her surprise at seeing him standing in the doorway, a big chunk of the rose petals fell out of her hands and fluttered to the floor. She gave him a wry smile as she bent down to try and pick them back up, cradling the pile in her hands and arms.

"These smell good, but they're so messy."

Sean knew she was expecting him to say something, to tell her who he was or what he was doing staring at her like that, but for the moment, he was just enjoying listening to her speak. Her soft, melodic voice was another piece of the puzzle he'd been putting together from the moment he'd seen her silky hair glide across her back.

But most of all, her smile made him want to smile back.

Which was crazy.

She finally shook her head and said, with a small frown, "I'm sorry, you don't need to listen to me babble about roses."

But he did. Just as he hated seeing the frown replace her smile.

No, not just crazy. *Insane.*

Sharpening her focus on him, she continued with, "I didn't think anyone new was checking in today, so I wasn't monitoring the front desk." The welcoming smile on her face instinctively drew him closer to her. "Can I help you with something else? Are you visiting a guest at the inn, perhaps?"

Finally, he told her, "I'm Sean Murphy. I'm here for my brother's wedding."

In an instant, her smile disappeared. Her mouth opened slightly in surprise and her cheeks grew even more flushed.

She took a quick step backward and bumped into one of the covered folding chairs.

He waited for her gaze to drop to his scar and hold there, certain that was the reason for her sudden, too-strong reaction. But her eyes never left his, never once raked over the mark that bisected the lower half of his left cheek, from earlobe to chin.

"Oh my gosh. Of course you're Sean. I knew something about you looked familiar. I should have realized it earlier, but the wedding must have scrambled my brain."

All the while, as she spoke, she was blinking up at him,

her big green eyes stealing his brain cells away one at a time. It felt like a hammer was pounding away in his brain.

How did she know his name when he couldn't for the life of him think of hers?

She bit her lip, drawing his attention to their full, soft shape. For all the conservative nature of her dress and shoes and jewelry, her full mouth and silky hair seemed to show a deeper truth about her. A sweet sensuality she couldn't hide.

Half of him wanted to ask her how she knew his name. The other half wanted to ask her to say it again, to let her soft voice wrap itself around him like it had just a minute ago.

"Do you know where Stu is?" he asked, instead.

Her eyes grew even bigger. And, if he wasn't mistaken, more than a little horrified.

"You don't know what happened?"

The hammer pounded harder, joined by a warning bell inside his brain that told him something was definitely wrong. Hadn't he known it from the minute he'd walked into the inn and realized there was another wedding taking place?

Immediately worrying that something had happened to his younger brother, a brother he'd always looked after when they were kids but hadn't been around to check on much over the past few years, he said, "Tell me now. What happened?"

The woman's eyes were wide enough now that he saw how green they were, like fresh growth on bare trees in spring. She was clasping her hands together in front of her so tightly that her knuckles were turning white and the rose petals were getting crushed beneath her grip.

"I was sure he was going to tell you, that he was going to talk to you." She shook her head, tightened her hands more. "He should have told you. You're his brother."

He moved toward her then, worry for his brother making him put his hands on her shoulders before he realized it.

"Where is my brother?"

Her muscles and frame were surprisingly strong beneath her soft flesh. Her sweet scent wrapped around him, a faint blend of maple and vanilla.

"I don't know where he is."

Suddenly, he could feel her starting to tremble beneath his hands.

What was he doing manhandling a total stranger?

"I'm sorry," he said automatically. "I shouldn't have grabbed you like that." Sean started to lift his hands off her when he suddenly realized why she looked familiar.

"You're Stu's fiancée."

Stu had sent a picture of her when they'd announced their engagement and Sean's secretary had laid it out on top of the rest of his business correspondence. He'd been between meetings and had barely had time to look at the picture before it was filed away. But from what he recalled, while he'd thought his brother's fiancée had seemed pretty in the picture, nothing about her had drawn any special notice.

He could hardly place this woman before him to the one beside Stu in the staged photo. Same hair, same eyes, same face, same features, but totally different.

As if she'd somehow come into focus since that photo was taken.

"Yes," she said. "I'm Rebecca. I was his fiancée."

He couldn't miss the *was*.

She hadn't intended for him to miss it.

"You're supposed to be getting married tomorrow."

"Yes," she said again, but she was shaking her head even as she agreed with him. "We were, but—"

A door flung open and Sean heard his mother's voice. "Rebecca, have you seen my wrap? I think I left it at my sea—"

The words fell away as Elizabeth realized her oldest son was standing there. She was dressed in a long, sparkling silver dress and even though he hadn't seen her in the audience, he'd known she had to be at the wedding. Local weddings had always been a town affair.

She looked back and forth between him and Rebecca with surprise—and then a deep, confused frown.

Rebecca jumped out of his grasp so fast he swore he felt a blast of cold air in the spot she'd been standing.

"Sean?" His mother moved toward him, her gaze immediately going to his scar and holding there for several seconds. Finally, she pulled it away. "What are you doing here?"

"I'm here for Stu's wedding."

"I thought he would have told you," Rebecca said again.

But before he could return his focus to Stu's ex-fiancée, Sean's mother was exclaiming, "Oh, honey, I'm so glad you're finally home. It's all been such a mess. For all of us. Your father and I kept trying to reach you, but your secretary always said you were in a meeting." She lowered her voice. "I didn't want to leave such a personal message with a stranger."

"So there's no wedding?" He directed the question to Rebecca rather than his mother.

"No," Rebecca said. "I'm afraid not."

"Why?" Again, he directed the question to Rebecca, but this time she didn't answer. She simply stood there and stared at the floor.

His mother reached for his hand and gripped it hard. "Stu didn't say. He just left me and your father a note saying he needed to go away for a while to think about things and that the wedding was off. Isn't that right, Rebecca?"

Rebecca finally came unstuck and took a step forward. Her chin tilted slightly up to face his mother, who was several inches taller, and she said, "Yes," and for a moment he was struck by her surprising strength.

The impression deepened as she turned to Sean with her explanations. "Stu and I both agreed that the engagement and wedding were a mistake, but that we're still friends." Her words were soft but firm. "There are no hard feelings between us. None at all. We both just want what's best for each other." She paused. "Unfortunately, in the morning he was gone."

Rebecca's earnest words seemed genuine, but Sean wasn't satisfied with the explanation. Clearly, his mother wasn't either, as she said, "I just wish he'd come to tell me that himself, instead of disappearing in the middle of the night with only a note saying he'd left you in charge of the inn. I just don't feel right about it at all."

Yet again, the woman who'd trembled in his arms stood strong in front of his mother.

"Your son is a wonderful man. And I'm sure he'll be back soon to let us all know what's going on."

"When?" Elizabeth asked.

To anyone else's ears, Sean knew his mother's question was simply full of worry for her youngest child. But there was ice at its core. It didn't make sense that his first instinct was to protect Rebecca. But sense or not, the instinct was still there.

Fortunately, Rebecca didn't seem to need his protection. She simply shook her head and said, "I wish I knew. But I don't."

Again, Sean knew Rebecca was telling the truth simply because there was no hesitation behind her words. Only when asked why Stu had left had she stayed quiet.

She turned her face to his again. "Are you sure he didn't try to reach you, Sean?"

His name on her lips sent another jolt through him. Telling himself it was simply that he was feeling every one of the two hours of sleep he'd gotten on the red-eye— or rather, the twenty-two he hadn't gotten—he ran a hand over his face before answering. "Not as far as I know."

Damn it, if Stu was in trouble, why hadn't he come to his older brother? Had Sean done that bad a job of taking care of his brother these past years that Stu didn't know his door was always open? Stu was the one person he'd always loved with his whole heart. Stu was the only person he knew he could trust wholly and completely.

But now, out of the blue, his brother had done a runner. Not just on his fiancée and family. But on the inn as well.

Sean hated feeling that his trust had been misplaced. By absolutely everyone he'd ever loved.

"He left the rest of us letters," Rebecca said. "Perhaps yours got lost in the mail."

"I've been out of the country for three weeks. I came here straight from the airport. I'll have my assistant go through my mail tonight. If there's a letter waiting for me, she'll find it."

And hopefully if there was a letter, it would give them all more of a clue as to where his brother had gone.

The door creaked again and footsteps sounded on the old wooden floorboards. "Rebecca, I think I've got a tear in the seam of my dress and I was wondering if you could—"

Andi skidded to a stop halfway into the room, looking between Sean and Elizabeth and Rebecca.

"Sean, what a nice surprise it is to see you."

He forced a smile for the bride. "Congratulations, Andi."

His smile had been mostly teeth, but when she smiled back at him, she was so full of happiness he could almost feel it cutting a little hole through the frustration in the room.

"Thanks, Sean."

But then, as she looked from him to Rebecca and his mother, her smile fell away. "Rebecca, I really don't want to interrupt, but I think I'd better stitch my dress up before it turns into a full-on tear."

"No problem, Andi. I've got a sewing kit upstairs." Rebecca hurried to the bride's side. "I'll just run up and get it."

"Great, I'll come up with you."

A moment later, Sean and his mother were standing in a room full of empty chairs and hundreds of flower heads and petals.

"What exactly did Stu's letter say, Elizabeth?"

His mother's eyes flashed with hurt at the way he'd used her proper name. He hadn't called her Mom since he was fourteen. He wasn't about to start now.

"Just that he was sorry, but he and Rebecca had decided not to get married. And that while he was gone, he trusted Rebecca to run the inn as she saw fit."

She looked away too quickly and the hard knot in his chest tightened, the way it always did when he spoke with her. After all these years away from Emerald Lake, he'd believed he could be in complete control over himself during Stu's wedding weekend. But that had been when he'd thought it was going to be nothing more than a couple of parties.

Nearly certain that she was hiding something from him, he asked, "Is that all his letter said?"

His mother was an attractive woman, but as they stood together while the sunlight disappeared behind a cloud, she looked every one of her fifty years.

"I don't want to hurt you, Sean. Don't you know that? I've never wanted to hurt you."

He didn't say anything in response to her non sequitur. They both knew he couldn't say anything, not if she wanted him to continue keeping her secrets, just like he had for the past twenty years.

Her shoulders rounded ever farther as she sighed. "Stu said none of this was Rebecca's fault and that if anyone should take the blame, it was him." Her eyes were filled with tears as she added, "But you and I both know he wouldn't hurt a fly. He's always been such a good boy."

Another wave of exhaustion swept over Sean. "Don't worry," he finally told her, knowing it was what she wanted to hear. "I'll find out what's going on."

Looking relieved, her gaze went back to the side of his face. "Your scar looks much better. You must be using that cream I sent you. I know how much it's always bothered you."

No. He'd never really cared about the scar, but what

was the point in bothering to clarify things twenty years after the accident that had scarred his face?

"It's been a long day. I'm going to head upstairs to take a shower."

"Come with me to say hello to your father and grandmother first." He let his mother take him into the reception room. "Look who I found talking with Rebecca in the other room."

His father's face lit up. "Son, welcome home." Bill's arms were warm around his shoulders.

His grandmother, Celeste, was there a moment later, giving him a kiss on the cheek, then holding him still for a long moment so that her wise eyes could take in far more than he'd planned to give away. Just like she always did.

"You've met Rebecca?" He nodded and she smiled. "Lovely girl, isn't she?"

Something about his grandmother's smile shook him. Fortunately, his father asking, "You've heard about Stu and the wedding, I take it?" saved him from having to reply.

Sean nodded. "I'm heading upstairs right now to make some calls to his friends and see what I can find out."

"You can't stay at the reception a little longer?" his mother suggested, a hint of desperation at wanting to spend more time with him pulling at her words. "I know Andi and Nate would love to have you here."

As if the calls to Stu's friends weren't enough of a reason for him to need to leave right away, he told her, "I've got to contact my secretary to see if there was a note from Stu."

He was about to walk away when he felt his mother's cold hand on his arm. When he was a child, her arms had been warm, and he'd loved to sit with her while she read him books and told him fairy tales before bed. They'd once been so close.

But he hadn't been a child for a very long time.

And he knew better than to believe in fairy tales.

"It really is good to have you home, honey. We've all missed you."

He'd missed being home, missed the lake, the mountains, the clear air. But he hadn't missed the way the knot in his gut tightened, grew, whenever he was here.

He needed to find out where his brother had gone and bring him home so that things could go back to the way they were, as quickly as possible...and Sean could leave Emerald Lake again.

Chapter Three

"Was it kind of tense down there or was it just me?"

Carefully sewing the hole shut on Andi's dress, Rebecca pulled a pin out from between her lips and slid it into the strawberry-shaped cushion.

"Sean didn't know that Stu and I split up," she explained to her clearly confused friend. "He came here expecting there to be a wedding tomorrow."

Andi whistled softly. "And of course Elizabeth had to get right in the middle of it."

Rebecca bit her tongue. She might not be about to marry into the Murphy family anymore, but she still didn't feel right saying anything about how uncomfortable Elizabeth made her feel, even though Stu's mother had never been particularly warm and embracing.

"She's just concerned about her son."

"I know she is. We all are."

Rebecca was hoping Andi would drop it. But she'd come to know her friend well enough in the last six months to know better. Andi's laser focus had made everything she'd ever touched a huge success. Only love had eluded her for a decade. Thankfully, though, her friend had found true love in the end.

"I just don't get it," Andi finally said. "You're every mother's dream daughter-in-law, you know?"

The thing was, Rebecca had noticed Elizabeth acting strange around Sean, too. Completely different from how she behaved around Stu. His mother had always taken care of Stu, almost to the point of being overly nurturing. With Sean, she'd seemed tense. Worried.

Not knowing how to fake either a smile or an easy response, Rebecca pretended to be busy tying off the thread on Andi's silk gown instead.

"I haven't seen Sean in years," Andi mused as Rebecca finished up. "He and Stu were always close. I'm surprised he didn't know about the wedding being off."

"Me too," Rebecca admitted.

That was all she was going to admit. Not that her reaction to looking up and seeing Sean staring at her had been more powerful than any reaction she'd had to another man.

Ever.

Even realizing he was Stu's older brother hadn't been enough to stop feeling like fireworks were constantly shooting off in the middle of her stomach when he looked at her.

"He hasn't gotten any worse looking, that's for sure. Back in high school, pretty much everyone had a crush on him." Andi smoothed her hand over the fix-it job Rebecca had done with needle and thread as she said, "I swear the scar he got on his face after the car accident only made the girls want him more. Must have been all that danger and mystery swirling around him, I guess."

Rebecca had almost dropped the box of pins at the thought of Sean being in a car accident, even though she didn't know him at all.

"He had a scar?"

Andi shot her a strange look. "He still does."

"I didn't see it."

"It's on his left cheek. Lower down. It's hard to miss."

Rebecca tried to think back to those moments when he'd been holding her close, questioning her about Stu. But all she could see in her mind were his eyes staring into hers, all she could feel were those butterflies scooting around in her belly.

Not wanting to give away too much to Andi—who she'd learned noticed everything around her—Rebecca turned to put her needle away in her sewing box, making sure to let her hair swing over her face as she said in as light a voice as she could manage, "So was he a total heartbreaker in high school?"

"As far as I know he didn't date anybody at our school."

Rebecca couldn't think fast enough to keep herself from turning back to look at Andi in surprise.

Andi shrugged. "Sean's always been hard to read. You know how those mysterious good-looking types are. Women are always wanting to uncover their hearts. There's always some poor, delusional girl out there who thinks she's going to be the one to make him fall."

"Definitely delusional," Rebecca agreed. She knew firsthand all about girls like that.

Because she'd been one of them her entire life.

She'd wanted things to work out so badly with Stu that she'd actually accepted his proposal of marriage. And before Stu...well, she'd been even more delusional with her previous boyfriends. She'd seen only what she wanted to see.

And ignored all of the warning signs.

Never again. She'd never ignore those warning signs again.

Especially given that they'd started flashing bigger and brighter than ever before in the last thirty minutes when she'd been talking with Sean.

Her reaction to him had been beyond anything she'd ever felt before. One look at him standing there against the doorway watching her and she'd almost dropped the entire handful of flower petals.

Yes, just as Andi had said, he was incredibly good looking. Just Rebecca's type, in fact.

The very type that usually ripped her heart out from her chest and stomped all over it.

"Even though I'll be in the Bahamas for the next week," Andi said, "you can always reach me on my cell, day or night if you need me."

Rebecca gave her friend a warm hug. There was no way she was going to disturb Andi and Nate's honeymoon. She'd managed to survive the past three weeks of questioning looks—and outright questions from the people of Emerald Lake, especially Elizabeth.

Somehow, she'd find a way to deal with Sean's questions, too, without giving Stu's secret away.

Six hours later, Rebecca was rethinking her silent vow to survive whatever came her way alone.

"Such a lovely wedding, Rebecca. We're just all so sorry you won't be up there tomorrow with Stu."

Ugh.

"We're just so sorry for you, honey. It must be so hard at your age to have to start all over."

Double ugh.

"I know how overwhelmed you must be running the inn without Stu. I heard Sean was back home to help."

And no, Sean hadn't come back home to help her with the inn. God forbid. Ten minutes in the same room was enough to send her head spinning and her heart racing.

Working together would surely do her in completely.

In any case, she couldn't tell any of Andi and Nate's guests that Sean had no idea they'd called off the wedding until this morning when he'd arrived for the festivities. Given that it was impossible for her to disappear until everyone went home when there were so many details to take care of, she'd simply tried to look busier—which wasn't hard during a wedding reception—in the hopes that people would stop asking her questions.

Finally, after the guests had gone and she'd seen the bride and groom off on their way to sunny, sandy beaches, . she was back in her room. All she wanted to do was take a long, hot bath and read a good book. But first, she was going to relish the moment this dress came off.

It had looked so pretty in the store. Green satin that picked up the color of her eyes, with light ruching along the side, the knee-length cocktail dress played up the best parts of her figure and hid the worst. She hadn't told anyone that it was supposed to have been her rehearsal dinner dress.

Figuring it was better to get some use out of the dress after the amount of money she'd spent on it, she'd decided to wear it today. Strangely, it had almost felt like she was reclaiming something by putting it on this morning, the part of her that didn't want to look into her closet and always see a dress that meant a canceled wedding. Now the dress would always be associated with Nate and Andi's wedding instead.

Still, after ten-plus hours running around in it, she couldn't wait to get into a pair of leggings and a T-shirt instead.

But when she tried to pull the zipper down it wouldn't go. She tugged and pulled at it until her index finger was scraped sore by the small metal tab.

She desperately wanted to get out of the darn dress. Maybe, she thought, the dress was cursed. There had to be some alternative to cutting it off herself with a pair of scissors, didn't there?

Just then, the large window in her bedroom that looked out onto Main Street began shaking. She hadn't noticed the wind earlier in the afternoon—in fact, it had been strangely, ominously still out on the water—but she'd come to learn that the weather changed so fast in the Adirondacks that the sky could go from blinding blue to pelting hail in seconds.

Strangely, with some help from the moonlight she could see that the treetops weren't blowing. And the flag on city hall was limp. But the window was still shaking.

Stu had fixed up this suite of rooms high in the inn's attic especially for the two of them to move into after their wedding. Sixty years ago, this bedroom had been the honeymoon suite. A few years later, for some reason that no one seemed to know, it had been converted to storage.

Stu had insisted she move in a month ago and she'd agreed, glad to have the chance to make the rooms feel like home before the wedding, rather than returning from their honeymoon to an impersonal home. But as she stood in the middle of the bedroom, she felt cold, despite having turned on the heat earlier.

The small hairs on the back of her neck prickled and a rush of air moved over her, almost as if someone had walked by.

Spinning around, she saw that she was still completely alone.

Or was she?

The truth was, she'd always had a vague sense that something wasn't right about the bedroom. She'd even heard rumors during the months she'd worked at the inn that it had been haunted in the past. And even though she'd laughed it off, the truth was that over the past few weeks—since she and Stu had called off their wedding—she wasn't sure it was completely ridiculous anymore.

As goose bumps ran up her exposed arms, she suddenly wondered what on earth she was doing standing there thinking about ghosts and spirits. And as her stomach growled, she decided her bath could wait. First, she'd go back downstairs and have a snack. She knew there was leftover cake. Plenty of it. Considering she hadn't eaten much all day—and how rough the day had ended up being—she figured she deserved a big slice of cake.

Maybe two.

Besides, even though she'd sent her employees home, maybe if she was lucky a guest would be awake and reading in the common rooms downstairs and could help her unstick the zipper on her dress.

She just couldn't stand the thought of cutting it up. Not when that would feel like giving in. Like losing.

So the dress was staying on for the time being. Shoes,

however, weren't going to happen again tonight. The thought of putting her heels back on had her wincing.

Her feet bare, she left her living room and walked out into the private hallway. Well, not so private anymore, since Stu always kept a small suite here for Sean's visits into town—which had never happened until today. Not wanting to run into him again, she hurried past his door and down the stairs.

Picking up stray things as she made her way through the inn and moving them to their proper places, keeping an eye out for stray guests to help with her zipper but seeing none, unfortunately, it took her longer than it should have to get to the inn's kitchen. Her stomach felt like it was eating itself by the time she pushed open the door.

At which point she lost her appetite altogether.

Because Sean was sitting on one of the stools, tucking into his own piece of wedding cake.

And he didn't look any happier to see her than she was to see him.

Chapter Four

Oh hi," Rebecca said, wishing her voice didn't sound so breathy. "I didn't realize there was anyone in here."

Sean's eyes quickly took her in. The slightly wrinkled dress. Her bare feet.

For some reason, not wearing her shoes around him made her feel almost naked, even though she still had her dress on. It was too intimate.

Far more intimate than she ever wanted to be with Stu's brother.

"I got hungry and thought I'd come down to get a snack, but I didn't think anyone would be down here except maybe one of the guests wandering around the library or playing chess."

Oh god, she was babbling.

Stop talking, Rebecca. Just stop.

She clamped her lips shut and tried to lift her feet to back out of the room, but her feet were stuck like she'd just stepped into quick-drying cement.

Sean gestured to the cake. "There's plenty."

It wasn't exactly an embossed invitation to sit down

with him, but it didn't take a social genius—which she was not, by any stretch of the imagination—to see that if she ran now, she'd look guilty of something.

Like, maybe, breaking his brother's heart.

And, probably, single-handedly driving him out of town.

As if she needed any help from her stomach, it growled so loud Sean's eyes actually widened.

"When's the last time you ate?"

She shook her head, looking down to her wrist for a watch, but she'd already taken it off in preparation for the thwarted bath. "A long time ago."

She couldn't have been more surprised when Sean stood up, got a clean plate off the rack, and put a really large piece of cake on it. For her.

"Sit down, Rebecca. You were on your feet all day."

He'd noticed?

Oh. How sweet.

She tried not to flush. It was so embarrassing, but with her light coloring if she blushed it didn't just cover her cheeks. It also covered her chest. A chest that was on far better display in the green dress than she usually kept it.

Realizing she was still standing there in the most awkward way, she tried to put a smile on her face—and moved toward the cake.

And Sean.

Finally, her limbs obeyed her—unlike her heart, which was racing out of control again.

What was wrong with her? Why did Sean make her so nervous? Well, not nervous exactly, but kind of like she was buzzing on the inside.

She hadn't felt this way about a man since—

No.

No way.

All the things she hadn't wanted to acknowledge she had felt about meeting Sean when she and Andi had been talking upstairs earlier came to the fore. But even worse than the fact that she clearly had no self-control over her stupid feelings was that she was certain Sean could see her attraction to him written all over her face.

Her unfortunate reverse poker face.

Taking the stool to the far side of the one Sean had been using, she was pleasantly surprised again that he didn't sit down until she was seated. He was obviously a gentleman like his brother and father. It should have made her more comfortable.

Instead, her nerves ratcheted up a notch.

There was nothing quite like a man who looked like a bad boy acting the part of a gentleman. It tended to do all sorts of ooey-gooey things to her insides.

Okay, so she'd sit and eat as fast as she could and then she'd flee.

She was reaching for the fork when a pang landed in the pit of her empty stomach at the thought. Her instinct had always been to run. From bad jobs and bad boyfriends. Coming here, to Emerald Lake and the inn, brought her to the first truly solid place she'd ever had beneath her feet.

Why should she be the one to leave in a hurry just because Stu's brother had come home for a wedding that should have never been in the first place?

Three weeks ago when she'd gone to break it off with Stu, she'd vowed that she was going to change her life for the better. She'd started off by throwing herself into not just Andi and Nate's wedding, but something that was all hers: the Tapping of the Maples Festival. In two weeks she was going to put on her first big event in the Adirondacks. Even before Stu had left, she'd watched the details line up one after the other and knew in her heart just how great the festival was going to be for the entire town.

So, yes, she was uncomfortable, sitting in the inn's kitchen with Sean. But that didn't mean she was going to fold under the pressure. Just the opposite, in fact. Not only was she going to sit here and enjoy every single bite of her chocolate cake, but she was going to force herself to relax about Stu's brother. For years she'd listened to Stu's stories about his beloved older brother and she'd wanted to meet him. Finally, she was getting her chance.

"So," she said to Sean. "Stu said you were traveling?"

"I was."

While she waited for him to say more she finally took a bite of the cake. Oh god, it was good, half a dozen layers of chocolate cake surrounded by white and brown frosting. So good that she might have actually let loose a small moan of appreciation.

Closing her eyes to fully appreciate every single taste sensation of the cake, when she finally swallowed it down and opened her eyes back up, she was surprised to find a glass of milk in front of her.

After drinking half the glass in one gulp, she smiled and said, "Thank you. That was the perfect touch."

"You're welcome."

She swore one half of his mouth almost quirked up as he said it, but she couldn't have proved it for a jury. It was just a sense she had that he was loosening up a little bit.

"Where were you traveling, if you don't mind me asking?"

One of the things she loved most about her job was talking to the inn's guests about their travels. She very much wanted to visit all those wondrous places she'd heard about.

It was another vow she'd made to herself: one day would see the seven wonders outside of a book or cable TV program.

"I've been all over Asia these past weeks."

She could tell he was a big traveler, simply by the way he said it, like it was no big deal to visit Asia. If it had been her, she would have been gushing all over the place and pulling out pictures.

"I've always wanted to see that part of the world," she murmured after taking a second, smaller bite of cake. "Do you have a favorite country in the Far East?"

"Japan." He seemed almost surprised by his response. "Especially in the spring."

She leaned forward on her hands guessing, "Were the cherry blossoms in bloom when you were there?"

"Everywhere."

She closed her eyes, trying to imagine what it must have been like to stand beneath the pink blooms. "How lovely it must have been," she said, a smile on her lips at the vision in her head.

"Lovely," he echoed.

She opened her eyes and found his gaze locked to hers, a definite smile trying to form on his lips. His brown eyes were darker than she remembered them being a few minutes earlier. More intense. Which was saying something, because he was one of the most intense men she'd ever come across.

Wanting to go back to that space they'd just been in

where things had finally felt somewhat comfortable, she said, "Stu told me you own your own business."

His almost-smile disappeared. "I just sold it."

"Oh." She wasn't sure what she was supposed to say to that. Of course, she went for honest. Just like she always did. "Is that a good thing?"

"It was time to move on."

Yes, she knew about moving on. "Any thoughts about what you're going to do next?"

Feeling borderline comfortable again, she was about to take another bite of cake when Sean said, "Look, Rebecca, you seem like a nice person, but the truth is I don't understand what happened with you and my brother. Maybe you could explain it to me."

She nearly dropped the fork at his abrupt conversational switch. But really, how could she blame him for asking the question? They hadn't had a chance to talk much about it beyond her earlier, *"Yes, the wedding is off. And by the way, your brother has gone god-knows-where."*

"I'll do my best." She wanted to be as honest as possible with him, despite knowing she had to keep Stu's secret.

Ugh. This was going to be a hard conversation. The first of many to come if she wasn't mistaken.

She put down the fork on the side of the plate and pushed it away from her. She wasn't hungry anymore, anyway.

"You probably know that Stu and I have been friends for a really long time. Since college."

"He always said you made him laugh."

She smiled at the comment. "He made me laugh, too. Did he tell you the first time we met was a nude-drawing class?"

Sean's lips twitched a little bit again and she found herself wishing he would let himself smile. But, again, his mouth flattened out before that could happen.

"No."

Rebecca shook her head. "I probably should have known right then and there that I wasn't cut out for being an artist." She wrinkled her nose. "If it had been a naked woman then maybe I could have done it with a straight face, but a naked old man...Well, it was just so gross..."

He didn't say anything, simply raised an eyebrow, and she realized she was getting off track.

"Anyway, fast forward ten years later, and I needed a job." And an escape. From her mistakes. "Stu offered me one here at the inn." She looked around the inn's kitchen, at all the upgrades she'd helped make in the past nine months. "I love working here. I absolutely love it."

"Did you and Stu date in college?"

"No. We were just friends."

"When did that change?"

She dreaded this next part of her explanation. Because this was where it got sticky and didn't totally add up— even in her own mind. But she felt that she owed Stu's brother the fullest explanation she could give him. She would have told Stu's parents the same thing she was about to tell Sean, but they'd never actually come out and asked her. Unfortunately, it had been so awkward between them since Stu left town that she hadn't felt comfortable just blurting it out.

She had to take a deep breath before answering. "It didn't. Not really." She picked a chocolate crumb off the stainless-steel countertop with the tip of her index finger and absentmindedly licked it off. "That was the problem, in the end. I think we both were far more enamored with the idea of getting married and settling down than we were of each other."

Sean was silent for a long moment. "So you didn't love him?"

Rebecca didn't like the way he said it, like she'd set out to purposely hurt his brother.

"Of course I love Stu. I've loved him practically from the moment I met him." She was sitting straighter on her stool now, her shoulders back, her chin up. "But as a friend."

"How could it have taken you so long to realize this? You were engaged for months."

"When I saw Andi and Nate together," she admitted softly, "I knew I could never settle for anything less than that kind of love."

She couldn't believe she was saying these deeply personal things to a man she'd met only hours before. A man she wasn't sure liked her very much.

But Rebecca didn't know how to lie.

And the truth was, she didn't want to lie about her emotions anymore, about what her heart did or didn't feel.

Next time around the relationship block, she wanted love. Real love.

Not the false promises she'd let herself believe for so long.

"So when you realized this, you broke it off with him."

"I was going to, but he—"

She stopped, realizing what she'd been about to say. When Stu had begged her not to tell anyone he hadn't specifically added his brother's name to the list, but she'd made a promise to her best friend. And as hard as it was to keep that promise, by definition *anyone* included Sean.

"He what?"

She could see suspicion in Sean's eyes. He knew she was keeping something from him.

"He told me he'd just realized he couldn't marry me either. We agreed to call off the wedding."

"Okay," he said slowly. "So the wedding was off. But you were still friends, weren't you?"

"Of course we're still friends," she said, even though a little voice in her head couldn't help but wonder how a true friend could leave her to deal with not only the aftermath of their breakup but the inn and the Maple Festival all by herself.

"Why did he leave, Rebecca?"

Sean's voice was soft. Lulling. Coaxing. Mesmerizing, even.

Suddenly Rebecca realized that if anyone could get Stu's secret out of her, it was Sean.

This knowledge had her scooting off the stool, picking their plates up, and putting them in the sink. She could feel his eyes on her the entire time.

"Do you really expect me to believe that he didn't tell you why he was leaving? That he just left?" His voice was still smooth, but there was steel behind every word. Along with a determination to learn not only Stu's secrets... but every single one of hers. "Especially after you've just told me he's your best friend? Why wouldn't he have confided in you, even if you had both made a mistake about getting engaged?"

Rebecca turned from the sink and wiped her hands on a white dish towel. "I found his note in the morning. I thought we were going to have a chance to talk about things more in the morning. I thought we were going to be together to tell everyone about calling off the wedding."

"So he was just gone in the morning and you have no idea why?"

She hated this. Hated knowing without a shadow of a doubt that Sean was going to keep pushing and pushing and pushing at her until she broke.

She shook her head, feeling trapped in a terrible web. One that she'd help to weave.

Anger finally lit his features. "I'll never forgive you if he's hurt and you didn't give me the information I need to help him."

"I'll never forgive myself either," was the only thing she could bring herself to say.

"Then tell me, Rebecca."

She found herself looking desperately at the door. Not just as an exit, but with the hopes that if she was really, really lucky, Stu would reappear with a smile on his face and everything figured out so that he could give everyone the explanations they were looking for.

Too bad she knew better, wasn't it?

"It's late," she told Sean, feeling unbelievably weary. "I've got a busy day tomorrow and it starts early at the front desk."

She was halfway to the kitchen door, had almost started to believe he was going to let her get away for the night, when he said, "I'm not going to wait much longer for you to tell me the truth, Rebecca."

She whirled around, angry now herself. "How dare you accuse me of lying to you! Especially when I've just told you things you frankly have no right to know about my relationship with your brother."

But she could see from the hard, closed look on his face that he didn't care about what she'd told him. Only what she hadn't.

Didn't he realize how bad she felt about having to keep his brother's secret?

Well, no, of course he didn't. Which was why there was no point in her spending another minute down here with him. Forget the cake, she was going to go and finally take that bath she'd been dreaming of for hours.

Which was when she remembered her dress.

And the stupid zipper.

Of all the people to have to ask for help . . . she almost groaned out loud. But knowing it was either Sean or scissors, she turned around to face him one more time.

Wishing the earth would open up and swallow her whole, she made herself say, "This is really awkward, but I'm afraid I need your help with something." She lifted her right arm slightly. "The zipper on my dress is stuck. That's partly why I came downstairs. I was hoping to find someone who could help me. Since we're the only ones up, I'd really appreciate your help, if you wouldn't mind."

He didn't move for a long moment and then he was coming toward her. She shouldn't have felt like a lamb being stalked by a lion but—*oh god*—she did. And as he came closer, ten feet dissolving to five, then three, then a handful of inches, she had to firmly resist the urge to back up.

He'd touched her only once before now—when he'd grabbed her shoulders after the wedding to ask about Stu—and she hadn't been able to forget the feel of his hands on her yet. She didn't need round two to make things any worse.

"Lift your arm a little more," he said softly.

That was when she made the mistake of looking up at him and his eyes caught hers.

She'd heard what he'd said, but her brain couldn't seem to comprehend the meaning of it. Not when he was standing this close. Not when she could finally see the faint line of a scar that cut across his face, cheek to chin. Not when she was breathing in his intensely masculine scent, reminiscent of cedar chips and summer bonfires.

Finally, her brain registered his words and she lifted her arm. He held still just long enough for her to wonder if he was as reluctant to touch her as she was to be touched by him. And then she felt his fingers lightly brush against the side of her rib cage.

She could feel her body reacting to his nearness, heat creeping across her skin. Chills, followed by a rush of extreme heat, had no business swamping her system from nothing more than the lightest brush of his fingertips.

He worked the zipper slowly, steadily. Feeling light-headed, she realized she was holding her breath.

Breathe. She had to figure out a way to breathe.

"I see what's stuck, Rebecca. But I'm going to have to get at it from the inside."

The breath she'd been about to take caught inside her windpipe at the way he said her name, his low tones wrapping around the seven letters like velvet.

"From the inside?" she repeated pointlessly. He couldn't repair her dress through the thin safety of fabric? *She'd never survive this.*

"I'm afraid so."

How she wished Sean was like her brothers-in-law. They made her laugh, made her groan at their stupid jokes and irrational love of football, and she loved them because they loved her sisters, but that was it. There were no hidden currents. No reasons she wouldn't want to be alone with them in a dark hallway. And if one of them had had to reach inside her dress to fix a stuck zipper, even if they got a feel-up by accident, they would've simply laughed about it later.

But neither she nor Sean was laughing.

She had to stop thinking this way. There was nothing between her and Sean. And there never would be. He was simply Stu's brother.

Getting all weird about his fingers inside her dress was crazy.

"Okay," she said as firmly as she could manage. "Go for it."

She tried to think of something, anything but Sean's lightly calloused fingertips sliding over her skin. She focused on the problems they'd had getting the right silverware into the inn's dining room. She reviewed her mental files on the guest last week who'd "accidentally packed" the alarm clock. Heck, she went all the way back to the time when she was five and had the mumps so bad she could hardly recognize herself in the mirror.

But nothing, not one single thing she could think of, could distract her from the sensation of his warm touch on her sensitive skin.

Finally, the fabric from the inside of her dress shifted out of the zipper's teeth, and in one smooth motion Sean pulled it all the way down, then back up.

Abruptly, he pulled away. So fast that he half spun her around and she stumbled.

She'd just vowed—in triplicate—not to keep running. But if ever there was a time and place to run, it was now.

Because with only the slightest brush of his fingers across her skin, Sean had made her feel things no other man ever had.

She was upstairs and in her room with the door locked in record time.

Why hadn't she just used scissors to cut her dress off?

Chapter Five

What was wrong with him?

If he'd been the least bit in control of any of his senses, he would have gotten the hell out of the kitchen the minute Rebecca walked in. But every second he spent with her had his brain working on less and less of a rational plane.

Which was crazy, because he was always rational. Hell, he'd used his analytical mind to make millions of dollars.

She looked soft, warm, but finding out just how smooth her skin actually was, when she'd trembled at his touch, all he'd been able to think about was pulling her against him.

So close. He'd been so close to the edge. Almost all the way there, about to jump off into the abyss. She'd just told him she and Stu didn't love each other. That they were just friends. So there was no barrier there, not really.

But there were others. Big ones, like the fact that she wasn't telling him the full truth about Stu's disappearance. She hadn't actually admitted to knowing more than she was saying, but she'd quite clearly evaded his questions.

Yes, she seemed like an open book. It looked like everything she was feeling was written on her face. Hell, when she'd been talking about wanting love her wistful longing had almost gotten to him, to the heart he swore he didn't have.

Sean knew better than to be fooled by it, though. Not when everyone he knew held back as much as they could. Especially if it made them look ridiculous. And even though Rebecca gave off an air of not being able to hold anything back, he knew better.

She wasn't telling him the truth about his brother's disappearance.

Sean's early years as a venture capitalist had been exciting, but the past year or so he'd gotten tired of the scene, of dealing with people who were only in it for the kill. Just as he always had been. He'd come back to Emerald Lake for his brother's wedding and to prepare for his next career move, but now he realized there was a bigger reason he should have come back.

His brother had needed him. And he hadn't been there for Stu.

Sean wouldn't make that mistake again.

Just as he wouldn't make the mistake of falling for Rebecca's "look how honest I am" act, complete with big eyes and that sweet mouth that kept making him lose his train of thought like the idiot he'd sworn he'd never be for a woman.

Despite the late night, Sean was up early. Not as early as Rebecca, however. He found it hard to believe how fresh and bright she looked, considering how little sleep he knew she'd gotten the night before—and how hard she'd obviously worked putting on both Andi and Nate's wedding and keeping the inn running. He couldn't help but feel a grudging respect for her.

She was on the phone and there was a little frown between her eyebrows. The fact that his thumb itched to smooth it out made no sense, considering he didn't know her beyond their conversations the day before...and given that he didn't trust her.

From where he was standing, at the doorway to the inn's front room, he could see that she was on the phone and hear most of her side of the conversation.

"Mom, no, I'm fine." She frowned again, deeper this time. "Please stop worrying about me. I've told you before, it's not like I'm all alone out here. I have a lot of wonderful friends." She gave a little shake of her head, her long, silky hair moving around her shoulders. "Please don't come right now, Mom, and don't let any of my sisters drive up, either." She lifted her eyes to the ceiling as if she were looking for divine intervention. "No, it's not that I don't want you to visit. Of course, I do. But when you come, I want it to be for a vacation, so that you can relax on the lake. Summer will be a much better time for that."

Evidently, he wasn't the only one who didn't like seeing Rebecca look upset. Her mother was clearly beside herself at the wedding being called off.

"Besides, I have too much to do right now with the Tapping of the Maples Festival to spend time with you."

Tapping of the Maples Festival? What was that?

Finally, her lips curved up a slight bit at the corners. "It's going great. But I'm crazy busy trying to run the inn, too." Her smile fell away at whatever her mother said in response. "Stu would be here to help me with everything if he could, Mom."

It sounded like she meant it, but at the same time there was a thread of irritation there, whether at her mother or his brother—or both—he wasn't sure.

"I know I made another bad decision," she was saying into the phone, bristling now as she defended herself. "But I'm staying this time, Mom."

Another bad decision? What kind of woman had his brother been engaged to?

"No, I'm not waiting for him to come back." Rebecca's voice had risen and she was pacing the small area behind the check-in counter. "Even though things didn't work out with Stu, that doesn't mean I have to pack up all my things and leave my friends and my job." A pause, and then: "I really love being an innkeeper. And I love Emerald Lake."

He saw concern and remorse—and frustration—flash across her mouth as she said, "Of course, I love you all, too! But I've made my decision. I'm staying. Talk to you tomorrow. Give my love to everyone."

She'd been firm without becoming nasty. Yet again, she'd surprised him with her strength of will. In fact, she was a great deal firmer than anyone would ever guess, especially given how sweet and gentle she looked. It wasn't just her delicate angel's face that gave that impression; it was the picture of those pink painted toes he'd seen the night before that wouldn't leave his brain.

The inn was home to her. That was why she felt comfortable coming downstairs to the kitchen without shoes on. It was just what she'd told her mother.

Sean hadn't felt like he'd had a home in a very long

time. Although, in truth, the inn had a warmth about it that even managed to draw him in and made him want to stay in Emerald Lake when, previously, for years he'd barely been able to come back home without itching to get away again as soon as he could.

Why, he had to wonder, had her mother treated her like that? What else had Rebecca screwed up? And how badly?

Damn it, listening to her on the phone with her mother gave him more insight into her than he was comfortable with... and only made him want to learn more.

Being hit with yet another urge he didn't understand where Rebecca was concerned had him heading away from the check-in counter for the kitchen.

"Sean, well, aren't you a sight for sore eyes? I heard you were back but didn't get a chance to feast my eyes on you yesterday. Stand still and let me get a good look at you." Mrs. Higgins, the inn's head chef, grinned at him, her eyes twinkling. "I can see that you are still just as much of a heartbreaker as you always were."

Knowing better than to get into it with the woman who used to change his diapers when he was a baby, he said, "Are there any of your delicious scones left?"

She nodded to a tray beside her. "I just pulled a new batch fresh from the oven. How many, sweetie?"

Only Mrs. Higgins would call him sweetie. And, strangely, it was okay when she did it. Because he knew she was one of those very rare people who was just as nice as she seemed. No hidden shadows. No secrets.

"How about four?"

She raised her eyebrows. "Got a big appetite today, don't you?"

"I'd like to bring some out for Rebecca, too."

Her expression softened. "Such a sweet girl, isn't she? And so good with the guests. Although I've always thought there's a little bit of wicked waiting inside of her to get out." Not waiting for him to reply to her offhand comments, she said, "In that case, let me just add a pot of her favorite tea."

Sean could smell the roses from the leaves the chef put into the pot and something else that he was sure he was getting wrong.

"Is there maple syrup in that tea?"

"Oh, yes. It's a new tea she's been experimenting with. For the festival." She handed him the tray. "Her idea to launch the festival was a smart one, no question about it."

Biting back his questions for the time being, he thanked her and carried the tray back out to Rebecca. She looked up in surprise as he placed the scones and tea in front of her.

"Are you hungry?"

Given the way her mouth tightened at his question, he had a feeling that if she knew it was his idea to bring the scones out to her that she'd refuse them. He shouldn't care if she did. Then again, he didn't want his all-important innkeeper to faint from hunger at the front desk, either.

"Mrs. Higgins said these were your favorite."

"They are. Thank you," she said as she picked one up.

"I wanted to tell you, my secretary found Stu's letter."

"I knew he had to have contacted you," she said, clearly relieved to hear it. "Did he tell you anything about his whereabouts?"

"No." Damn it. "Just what he'd said in his note to my parents."

"I'm sorry. I know you were hoping for clues."

Sean felt a pang of guilt at what he wasn't telling Rebecca—that Stu had, in fact, said more. *"It's my fault. Treat Rebecca kindly, she deserves it."*

Reminding himself that he had nothing to feel guilty for and that she was the one who hadn't answered his direct questions last night, he forcefully returned his focus back to business for the time being. He'd quiz her on his brother again soon enough.

"How have things been going here at the inn with Stu gone?"

She poured two cups of tea and handed him one. It smelled surprisingly good, like being out in the large maple grove behind the inn.

"Good. Busy, but good."

"Mrs. Higgins mentioned a maple festival?"

Even though she clearly felt uncomfortable around him, Rebecca's face lit up. "Oh, yes, it's going to be wonderful." She reached under the counter and handed him a well-designed flier, putting the rest on a stack on the corner of the check-in counter. "It's going to be a day of nonstop maple syrup, maple cookies, maple candies." She lifted her cup. "Even tea. I've found some incredible vendors the past few weeks. I really think people are going to love being able to tap the maple trees themselves. I had someone come out and do a demonstration for me a few weeks ago and it was really fun." She tapped on a spreadsheet she had in front of her. "Just a few more details to iron out and the festival should be smooth sailing in two weeks."

Sean quickly scanned the flier. "How are you managing to run the inn by yourself and put on this festival at the same time? Especially with Stu gone?"

"Honestly," she said, "it hasn't been easy. But I've been pulling it all off so far." She gave him a little smile that made his heart do funny things in his chest. "Besides, who needs sleep? I figure I can do a little reverse hibernation after the snow thaws and the festival has passed."

"What are you going to do if a ball drops, Rebecca?"

She was about to take a bite of her scone when he saw his question register. Holding it halfway to her mouth she said, "Excuse me?"

"I understand that you've been managing to pull everything off thus far. But what's going to happen when you have a problem with one of your festival suppliers and you're needed to deal with an emergency at the inn? What if, say, two of the cleaning staff call in sick and you're needed upstairs as well as downstairs and you've got a vendor waiting for an answer to his question?"

Her flush disappeared as her face paled. He felt bad about poking holes in her plans, but looking for problems—and solving them before they happened—had been a big part of his career.

"I suppose I'll have to deal with that if it comes," she said slowly. "And hope that it doesn't."

He shook his head. "You should hire someone to deal with the festival and focus on your job at the inn."

She frowned at him. "No. No way. The festival is mine. It's the first thing besides running the inn that I've ever really felt proud of."

He couldn't believe the way she continually spilled her innermost thoughts and feelings. He would never—ever—admit to anyone the kind of things she was admitting. Was it some sort of trick to get him to back off on asking questions about Stu?

Telling himself it had to be a trick, that no one could possibly be this devoid of pretense, he said, "I'm afraid I don't see how the situation can continue for much longer. You're clearly exhausted. And I'd hate for the inn to suffer because you're focused on some festival."

Anger lit her delicate features. "First of all, Stu trusted me with the inn while he was gone. I would never let any part of it suffer. Second, it's not just *some festival*. The Tapping of the Maples Festival is going to do great things for this town and the inn. And third, considering Stu is the owner of the inn, I'm going to ask you to respect his wishes and let me run the inn as I always have, thank you."

Her strength surprised him, yet again. And the way her cheeks were flushing, her eyes flashing as she held her ground, made her even prettier.

Sean knew why Stu hadn't told her the full truth. He'd asked his brother to keep his involvement in the inn quiet. Just another half-lie to add to all the others.

Looked like it was time for there to be one less secret.

"Actually, Stu and I own the inn together. All these months, you've actually been working for both of us."

Chapter Six

Rebecca felt her eyes widen at the news. She narrowed them again as she glared at Stu's far-too-attractive brother.

It was just one surprise after another around here, wasn't it?

"Why didn't Stu tell me you owned the inn with him?"

She wished Sean looked guiltier about the way he'd sprung the news on her. He was clearly a very astute businessman, and yet he hadn't found a very nice way of giving her this information, had he?

"I never planned on coming back to run it, so it wasn't relevant."

Last night, he'd told her he'd sold his business and that he was looking for something new to work on. Is this what he'd meant? Oh, no, she wasn't sure she could work with a man like him bossing her around.

She dropped her untouched scone back onto the china plate with a loud clack. "No, I suppose it wasn't relevant to you," she said, not bothering to keep the sarcasm, or anger, from her voice. "Only to your employees who had no idea you were Stu's silent partner all these years."

A muscle began jumping in his jaw and she waited for him to defend himself, to point out to her that Stu was just as much at fault for not telling her the truth.

Instead, he said, "Now that the situation has changed, I'll need you to show me everything about running the inn."

She couldn't stop her eyes from widening at the thought of having to spend big chunks of time in close quarters with Sean, teaching him the ropes of the inn he owned but clearly never had any interest in learning about.

For the first time since Stu had left, she finally let herself be good and angry at him. How could he have done this to her, to Sean, giving them no other choice but to have to deal with one another?

Just then, a couple came down the stairs carrying a baby. "I hope we didn't keep anyone up last night," the woman said, an apologetic smile on her face. "Janie has some trouble sleeping out of her usual crib."

Her husband was trying to manage all of their bags and the car seat and bottles on his own, but Rebecca could see what a difficult time he was having, especially considering half of the bags weren't quite zipped all the way and a diaper was about to fall out.

She was incredibly glad for a reason to move away from Sean. "Don't worry about a thing. Your room was in the corner and I'm sure no one heard her crying. If it would help, I'd love to hold her for a moment while you get your things packed up and into the car."

"Oh, that would be wonderful," the woman said, fortunately not at all reticent about handing the sweet baby girl over.

Rebecca's heart squeezed as she looked down at big

blue eyes and a sweet little mouth. "Hey there, pretty girl. I hear you're quite the traveler."

The little girl started to fuss and the mother frowned and said, "I can take her back."

"I took care of three little sisters. I miss holding a baby. I miss making them laugh." As she spoke, she was quick to reposition Janie and get her giggling with funny faces.

The young couple were kneeling over their bags trying to do a quick reorganization while neither of them had their hands full when the phone behind the counter started ringing. Rebecca automatically shifted the baby to the crook of her right arm and picked up the line.

"Oh, yes," she said a moment later. "We'd love to be a part of your wedding plans in July. I'm a little bit tied up now, could I call you back in a few—" She paused, listened. "Oh, I see. You need to do it right this second?"

Sean was standing a handful of feet away, watching her on the phone with narrowed eyes. Feeling as if he was judging her performance—now that he was her surprise boss, and all—a devil landed on her shoulder.

Before she could stop herself she said, "I'd be more than happy to book it all with you right now. Could I put you on hold for ten seconds and then we'll get started?"

When they agreed, she put the phone down, walked over at to Sean, and handed him the baby.

"Could you take her back to her parents?" She looked over the couple, who had half of their things spread out across the rug and looked exhausted. "On second thought, I'm sure they'd be much happier if you could just keep her entertained for a few minutes."

Sean looked utterly, supremely uncomfortable. But,

amazingly, the little girl was snuggling in closer to him, her soft blond hair falling across his upper arms as she gave him an adoring coo.

Rebecca almost snorted at how quickly he had the baby caught up under his spell. Although, in some ways it did make her feel a bit better to know it wasn't just her. In any case, she didn't have time to wait for his answer before getting back on the phone and burying herself in wedding planning.

By the time she got off the phone, the couple and baby were gone. But Sean remained.

She'd never pushed at a boss like that, never deliberately gone and done something she knew would get her in trouble. But, for some crazy reason, he'd brought that out in her. A little bit of daredevil. It hadn't been on any kind of grand scale, but frankly, she was more than a little surprised to realize it was there at all.

And, even crazier, instead of apologizing for it and trying to start over on a better foot, another devil jumped onto her other shoulder and had her saying, "So, when do you want to start?"

He raised an eyebrow. "Start what?"

She didn't bother holding back her smile. "Your training."

Sean didn't like cute. He never had.

He wanted the people he worked with—men and women both—to be direct. To the point. But never teasing. And never, ever cute.

So then why was he constantly wanting to grin around this woman? Especially when he should have been focusing on the fact that she was keeping things from him.

Distrust had always been his fallback. Now was no time to change his MO, not when the welfare of his brother was at stake.

Looking just as wary as he felt, she explained, "When I first came to work here, I shadowed Stu for a few days," she told him. "Rather than trying to find snippets of time to sit down and try to tell you everything about the way the inn operates, it will probably be easier—and better—for us to work together."

Sean hadn't shadowed anyone since his first internship at a venture house in college. The thought of following Rebecca around the inn was laughable.

But given that he was considering an offer to acquire several more lakefront inns throughout the Northeast, he knew hands-on was the way to go. He'd need to understand the ins and outs of the business in order to have any true sense of whether he could run it at peak profitability.

"Sounds good to me."

He was pleased to see that she looked a little thwarted by his easy agreement. Had she been hoping to get to him?

"Fantastic," she replied.

Hmm, had that word come out from between her teeth? This time he was the one letting a grin loose. Despite how things had been left between them the previous night, his smile was there before he knew it was coming—or could stop it. He simply couldn't stop it from landing this time.

Her lips moved up in a little smile of their own. "I didn't think I'd ever see it," she said, so softly he almost didn't hear it.

He shouldn't be wanting to move closer to her. But some things were uncontrollable. Like his reaction to her, for one.

"What didn't you think you'd see, Rebecca?"

She looked back at him, her green eyes clear and purer than he thought he'd ever seen on a woman before.

"Your smile."

As thrown off his game as he'd ever been—and disliking the way her comment felt like a punch in the gut—he came back immediately with, "People don't say things like that."

Embarrassment shot across her face.

"I have no edit button," she agreed, but gone was the impish playfulness that she'd had on earlier. Instead, her mouth was turning down at the corners. "I obviously need one."

Right then, a woman who was probably in her early twenties came in. "I'm not late, am I, Rebecca? Last night's snow made it harder than I thought it would be to get into town."

He could still feel how embarrassed she was by what she'd said as Rebecca introduced him to Alice. Stepping away from the front desk, her cheeks were still pink as she met his eyes.

"Looks like you and I are free to head upstairs."

He'd gone over the line with her just now...and he regretted it. He hated the way the light had gone out of her eyes.

"I spoke out of turn, Rebecca."

As far as apologies went, it wasn't a great one, and she simply shrugged, trying to act like it was no big deal. But he could tell that it was.

Wanting, needing, to get them back on track, back to a place where business came first and emotions had no place at all, he asked, "What's first on your training agenda?"

There was no smile on her face as she said the one word guaranteed to strike fear into his heart...and to make sure he paid for the way he'd just spoken to her.

"Toilets."

"No one is ever going to complain about our standards of cleanliness," he told her a while later. "That's for sure."

Sean hadn't been this close to a toilet since his early teenage drinking days. He worked out daily, but he hadn't done this kind of awkward physical work for a very long time. The truth was he rarely even had to make his own bed. Either his housekeeper took care of it or he was in a hotel with service.

One thing was certain: he'd never leave a mess for them to clean up again.

And he'd be leaving *way* bigger tips in the future.

Rebecca didn't respond to his comment, but from her profile as she wiped down the bathtub, he could see a small smile on her face.

Her natural beauty was radiant enough that even with her hair pulled back into a ponytail and a smear of soap across her left cheek, he couldn't take his eyes off her.

Down on his knees in one of the inn's bathroom floors was just about as strange as it got in Sean's world. But, then, it got even stranger when he realized that the inside of his chest felt off-kilter. Like muscles that hadn't been worked in a very long time were trying to move again.

She looked over her shoulder at the toilet. "You're really good at that, you know."

He planned on making some sarcastic comment about his toilet-cleaning skills, but before he could even open his mouth, she was holding out a hand to help him up off his knees.

The touch of her skin against his stopped every synapse in his brain from firing. How could they, when electric sparks were too busy going off in every other part of him?

And as he pulled his gaze up from their joined hands to her beautiful eyes, he saw that her impish little smile was gone now, too. Her full lips had opened into a tempting *O* of surprise.

Maybe if he'd had any control whatsoever over himself around her, he would have located that sarcastic comment and put it out there between them. Maybe if he wasn't so mesmerized by the color in her cheeks from the hard work they'd been doing, he would have let go of her hand and gotten the hell out of the too-small bathroom.

Instead, he found himself reaching out with his free hand to brush away the soap bubbles on her cheek.

He didn't just hear her swift inhale; he felt it reverberate through her jaw to his hand. And all he could think was how soft her skin was.

"You had some soap on your face." His words sounded strangled. Borderline gruff. He wouldn't have recognized the voice as his own if he hadn't felt it come up his throat.

"Thank you for cleaning it off."

Jesus, her breathy words did crazy stuff to his insides, had him thinking, wondering even crazier things.

Would her lips be as soft as her skin?

Would they taste like the first ray of sunlight in spring?

Sean had lived a perfectly controlled life for nearly twenty years. But in less than twenty-four hours this woman, his brother's ex-fiancée, was destroying that control.

Without even trying.

She'd been his brother's fiancée.

His brain was finally starting to register sane thoughts again when Rebecca took an abrupt step back from him.

"Lunch. We missed lunch." Her cheeks were far more flushed than they'd been before they'd touched. She covered them with her hands as if she could somehow hide her reaction from him. "You must be starving. I'll go see what Mrs. Higgins can whip up for us."

She turned and fled the room. But Sean stayed exactly where he was.

For whatever reason, he couldn't think straight around her. Which meant he needed to get a grip right here, right now, before he joined her for lunch.

His reaction to her was unacceptable. Period. She was not only his brother's ex-fiancée, but she was also his employee. Sean had never mixed business with pleasure. He wouldn't start now. Not only did he need Rebecca to keep running the inn during Stu's absence, but working closely with her was the best way to learn the hotel business top to bottom. He needed more experiential data in hand before making any acquisition decisions for the inns he was considering purchasing.

Putting his hands on either side of the sink, he stared at himself in the mirror he'd cleaned with his own two hands.

Coming back to Emerald Lake had never been easy. He'd prepared himself for dealing with his family. With his mother, especially.

If only he'd known that the real person he should have prepared himself for was Rebecca. For sweet smiles. For charm that masqueraded as guileless honesty.

In the end, it was the most dangerous thing of all about Rebecca. He could protect himself from her beauty. Even from the attraction that sparked between them like a live wire.

But the seeming purity of her responses, the way she spoke every thought and feeling aloud regardless of whether it helped or hurt her... Sean hadn't believed there was a woman alive who possessed those qualities.

Despite how sweet Rebecca seemed, he still didn't.

How could he when she still hadn't come completely clean with him about Stu, and clearly had no plans to do so any time soon?

Not planning on beating around the bush another second, Sean slid into a seat across the table from Rebecca in the kitchen and said, "I've spoken with half a dozen of Stu's friends. None of them know where he is."

She stirred a spoon into her untouched split pea soup. "He obviously doesn't want to be found."

Sean couldn't argue with that. Still, he had to know. "I was surprised to find out that my phone calls are the first his friends have heard of his disappearance. They told me they knew the wedding was called off, via your e-mails, but nothing more."

He watched a whole host of emotions flit across her face. Regret. Frustration. And finally, resignation.

"I don't know all of Stu's reasons for what he did, Sean. But what I do know, I can't tell you. I'm sorry."

He jumped on the proof that she did, in fact, know more than she was telling him. His own anger and frustration lit a fire beneath his words as he told her, "If he's in trouble, I want to help him. I need to help him."

He watched her swallow, close her eyes tightly for a moment, the re-open them with a shake of her head. "He made me promise not to tell anyone his reasons."

Sean leaned in toward her, all but forcing her to look him in the eye as he said, "He couldn't have meant me."

She never broke his gaze, not even as she whispered, "I'm sorry, Sean. I promised."

"I'm his brother."

"I know." Regret hung in every word, in the faint lines around her mouth. "But he told me he needed time," Rebecca replied, as if it were really that simple. "I'm trying to give it to him."

They were sitting in a private back area of the kitchen, by a small window that looked out on the lake. It was a clear, bright day and he could see layers of ice on the surface of the lake starting to melt beneath the sun's warmth.

For all the power of winter's cold and ice, it could hold out for only so long against the growing heat of spring.

Not at all satisfied with her response—with any of them, no matter how genuinely upset she'd seemed as he'd poked and prodded at her to try and get her to break his brother's confidence—he said, "Why did you come here, Rebecca?"

Sean told himself he wanted to know the answer to this question simply because he was on a fact-finding mission on behalf of his brother.

She didn't answer for a moment. Finally, she said, "I was ready for a change."

There was nothing quite like hearing his words come back at him—and knowing them for the bull that they were. The previous night, she'd asked him why he'd sold his business and that was all he'd given her.

But now he understood, all too clearly, that if he was going to get any more out of her, he was going to have to give a little himself.

"Fair is fair," he said softly. "How about I answer you first? After fifteen years of launching new businesses for other people, I started to feel like I'd learned everything there was to know about venture capital. I woke up one morning and knew I was ready for a new challenge. I wanted my own business. That's why I bought the inn with Stu a couple of years ago. Because I knew it wouldn't be long before I'd be here learning the business, top to bottom."

And maybe, he'd started to think, he'd bought the inn because he wanted a reason to come back home one day.

"It's going to be your turn to answer my question soon," he said, but he didn't like that she hadn't so much as had a sip of soup or a bite of bread yet. "I want you to eat something first, though."

Her eyes narrowed as if she was getting ready for a fight. "I can take care of myself, you know. I didn't starve before you showed up here."

Liking that spark inside of her way more than he should have, Sean didn't let her snarky comment stop him from buttering a piece of bread and sliding it over to her.

"I've never had such good bread anywhere. Mrs. Higgins puts even Parisian bakers to shame."

Finally, she grudgingly reached for it and took a small bite of the delicious bread.

"Tell me about Paris while we eat."

It was clear that neither of them had forgotten she owed

him an answer to his question about why she'd come to Emerald Lake. But he wanted her to replenish some of those calories she'd burned off while cleaning the inn's bedrooms like the Energizer bunny first.

After all, he reminded himself yet again, she was a really valuable employee.

"The architecture is amazing. Every time I go back, I'm surprised all over again by just how much visual stimulation there is." He'd never been asked to put his feelings about Paris into words before, and he found that he was discovering his feelings at the same time as he was sharing them with Rebecca. "Throughout Europe, history is all around you, every moment of every day. Past and present, they all come together with perfect fluidity, from the ancient stone walls of the Louvre to the postmodern pyramid in the middle of the plaza."

Rebecca's eyes were lit with interest. "I've read so many books about Paris that sometimes I feel like I've been there. I've even dreamed about walking along the Seine, about standing in the middle of Notre Dame Cathedral looking up at the buttresses and stained glass, and then going for coffee at Les Deux Magots to see if I can hear echoes of the great writers in the walls."

Sean couldn't think of the last time he'd talked so much to anyone about something other than business.

"You could live anywhere, couldn't you, Sean?"

He certainly had the money and contacts to start a business anywhere. "Yes, I suppose I could."

"Emerald Lake must seem so small compared to everywhere you've been."

"It's small," he agreed, "but this part of the world is nice, too."

"Even compared to Paris? Or Rome?"

"There are so many beautiful places that if you tried to rank them you'd go a little crazy."

He could see the stars in her eyes as she tried to imagine all that beauty. It was obvious to him how badly she wanted to travel and see the world. So, then, why hadn't she? He knew plenty of people who could barely scrape together the money for plane fare, but that hadn't stopped them from traveling.

More questions were on the tip of his tongue but he was momentarily distracted by how beautiful she looked with the sun streaming in over her silky hair, her lips plump and soft from where she'd been biting them.

Upstairs in the bathroom he'd been schooling himself in how to proceed from here on out with Rebecca. He knew the right thing to do. Keep his distance. Don't get any closer.

Which meant keeping the rest of his questions—ones that had nothing to do with Stu's disappearance—to himself.

She put down her spoon and used a piece of bread to wipe clean her bowl before popping the bread into her mouth. She looked up and seemed startled to find him staring at her.

Her cheeks turning that lovely shade of pink he was liking far too much for either of their sakes, she quickly chewed and swallowed.

"I usually have much better table manners than that. Stu and I have known each other for so long, we're pretty informal with each other. I guess I forgot for a moment that you and I have only just met."

Something inside his chest grew warm at the knowledge

that she was comfortable with him. He couldn't remember the last time he'd felt that kind of warmth.

"Actually," he told her, "I think you're onto something." He grabbed the heel off the loaf and broke it in half, using it to clean his bowl just as she had.

Finally, she said, "You asked me at the beginning of lunch why I came to Emerald Lake and I don't want you to think I make it a habit of not answering direct questions."

To say that he was shocked to hear her actually admit to him that she wasn't answering his questions about Stu was a major understatement.

He was floored.

Her eyes continued to hold his as she said, "The quick and dirty answer is that I needed a fresh start."

"There are a lot of places you could have started over, rather than at an inn in the middle of the Adirondacks."

"Sometimes it's good to go where no one knows anything about you."

"You knew Stu," he reminded her.

"He'd told me about Emerald Lake for years and promised me if I ever came to visit that I wouldn't want to leave. Maybe that's what took me so long to finally come here. Maybe I was afraid to fall in love with some place that I couldn't easily pick up and run from."

Jesus, there she went again, saying things that most people wouldn't dare say out loud. Heck, most people wouldn't even admit something like that to themselves.

There were so many questions he still wanted to ask. But he knew better, knew that learning more about Rebecca would only draw him in deeper to the subtle web she clearly knew how to weave around people.

Yes, she was certainly good. He'd give her that. But no matter how genuine she seemed, how open and honest, Sean wouldn't make the mistake of letting her weave a spell around him.

"Alice will be leaving soon. I should probably check on the front desk, make sure nothing has come up that she needs me to deal with before she leaves. I'm sure you have other things to take care of this afternoon."

He got the picture. She wanted to get rid of him for a little while. And the truth was, he needed a break from her smile, from her fresh, sweet scent, from the way soft, silky pieces of hair had escaped her ponytail and were brushing against her chin.

Despite needing to remain on guard with her, he couldn't deny that she was very good at her job.

"Thank you, Rebecca. You've taught me a lot today."

Instead of accepting his compliment, she frowned. "Something tells me you already knew how to clean a toilet." She bit her lip. "The truth is, I might have been a little bit upset with you earlier today. I shouldn't have wasted so much of your time with cleaning the rooms."

"I appreciate you telling me that, but you didn't waste a single second of my time. I need to learn this inn from the ground up and that's what you were showing me. Most people wouldn't have the guts to hand me rubber gloves and a scrubber."

She cleared their plates from the table and put them in the commercial dishwasher. "Let me know if you need anything else today. Otherwise, I'll see you tomorrow."

He was looking forward to it far more than he should.

Fortunately, the one person guaranteed to help remind him to stay far, far away from the temptation that Rebecca presented was likely waiting for his report on Stu's whereabouts.

No doubt, dealing with his mother would be a fitting punishment for those few moments when he'd foolishly let himself enjoy being with Rebecca.

Chapter Seven

Rebecca had been too close to Sean for too many hours. There shouldn't have been anything exciting about bumping into each other as they made beds and vacuumed floors, but evidently even doing completely mundane tasks with him got her heart moving too fast.

She still couldn't believe how good he'd been about doing whatever she had tasked him with. He hadn't once acted too important for bathrooms or dusting. Even Stu had always complained about doing the cleaning on days when they were short staffed. But Sean had simply gotten to work and done a heck of a job. Maybe even a better job than she'd done, given how distracted she'd been by his nearness.

Okay, so she felt like a big coward for running, but how could she have stayed another second more without being able to take a full breath? She needed to clear her head. No, more than that, she needed to get it screwed back on straight.

Because the craziest thing of all was not so much that she could feel herself falling under his spell...but that moment in the guest room when he'd seemed just as captivated by her. As if he was surprised by his feelings, but couldn't help feeling them anyway.

Nearly at the front desk, Rebecca caught sight of herself in a hall mirror. Her eyes were bright, her cheeks were flushed, and her normally well-groomed hair looked like she'd been driving in a convertible with the top down all afternoon.

She must be crazy to think Sean was attracted to her, she thought as she pulled out her hair band and tried to quickly finger comb her hair back into some semblance of order. She didn't have to see pictures of the women he dated to guess his type. Polished. Highly educated. Perfect.

Not that it mattered. Because even if he was attracted to her, even if Stu's disappearance wasn't hanging awkwardly between them, she still wouldn't go near him with a ten-foot pole.

She knew darn well what her old MO would have been. Just like Andi had said, Sean's mysteriousness, the hints of darkness she saw in his eyes, along with fact that he was drop-dead gorgeous, would have had her giving herself over to him, like a modern-day beauty to the beast, turning herself inside out to win his love.

To save him.

Only, all the while, she'd end up losing herself more and more. Until the day he'd decide he was done with her.

Rebecca knew all about losing, about trying to rebuild herself back up into something whole again. Hadn't she already learned her lesson, darn it? Looking back into her relationship file told a clear-cut story. One darkly handsome, dangerously mysterious man after another. Stu had been the only deviation to the picture-perfect pattern, but that was simply because she'd been trying to swing as far as she could in the opposite direction.

She couldn't fall into the old trap again, couldn't repeat the same cycle she knew by heart.

Especially not when one Murphy brother had already left her in the lurch.

No question about it, the next time she fell in love, it was going to be with a man who didn't fall into either of those categories and was neither too sweet nor too mysterious. For once in her life, she was going to be strong and smart rather than letting her contrary heart lead the way.

Because, unfortunately, her heart hadn't been right one single time.

"Sorry I've been gone all day, Alice," she said as she approached the check-in desk.

"Don't worry about it," the young woman said with a smile. "Hey, did you do something to your hair? Or are you wearing different makeup?"

Rebecca stopped dead in her tracks a couple of feet from the desk. "No." She dreaded having to ask but she said, "Why?"

Alice shrugged. "You just look so pretty today, that's all."

Rebecca knew the right thing to do was to say thank you. But she was terrified that Alice would put two and two together and realize what—*who*—was responsible for her flushed cheeks.

God, she could only imagine the gossip in town if people thought she was drooling over her ex-fiancé's older brother.

"You know what? We're pretty low on fire logs. If you don't need me for anything else, I'll head out and grab some before you go for the day."

"It's really cold out there today," Alice said, "and we probably have enough logs to last the next couple of days."

But Rebecca was already shoving her arms through the warmest down coat she had in the back office. After putting on her snow boots and grabbing her bag, she headed outside.

The crisp, cold air shocked the breath out of her for a moment. But instead of turning around and heading back into the warmth of the inn, she was glad for the way the cold woke her up. She couldn't daydream about impossible happily-ever-afters in this kind of weather.

Crunching carefully through yesterday's snow, she was just turning around the corner of the inn when she looked up and saw the most breathtakingly beautiful sight.

The sun was just starting to set over the snow-dusted lake, a dozen spectacular colors radiated down from the sky to the icy treetops on the mountains that surrounded Emerald Lake.

For all that she longed to see the seven wonders and smell the salty scent of the ocean as it crashed on coasts all over the world, Rebecca was home. Emerald Lake would always be the place her heart longed to come back to, a haven for her soul, for her dreams.

Sean being here, Stu being gone, didn't change that. This small town, her friends, her career as innkeeper, they were all part of her new life.

One day she'd find the missing pieces: a husband who loved her as much as she loved him, and children to cuddle and play with and love the way that her parents loved her.

All would be well, she told herself as she started stacking wood in the small red wagon she kept by the pile.

Fortunately, she knew her own heart and mind this time. And she knew better than to go in and try and save Sean. Even though it went against every part of who she actually was, even if it ended up being the hardest thing she'd ever done, she was going to remain completely logical where Sean was concerned.

And for once, she was going to save her emotions for a man who was capable of returning them.

Besides, between running the inn and the festival, she had so much on her plate she couldn't possibly waste any time mooning over some guy. Lord knew, over the years, she'd put more than enough energy into men who were incapable of ever loving her.

Expecting his mother to be home and his father to be off working one of his contracting jobs, Sean was surprised to find his father at the house, lifting a heavy sander out of his truck.

"I've got the other side, Dad."

Neither of them said anything more until they'd carried the sander into the house and up the stairs to his parent's bedroom. Most of the furniture was out of the room. Only the bed frame and mattresses were propped up against the wall.

After they put the sander down, his father said, "I could use an extra hand with the bed, too, if you don't mind."

When Sean was a kid, he and Stu had loved to play hide-and-seek in the huge king sleigh bed. His father had made the head- and footboards out of a birch tree he'd cut down himself. Growing up, Sean had thought his father was the biggest, strongest man in the world.

Taking in his father's gray hair and slightly gnarled knuckles, he wondered when that had changed. He hadn't spent much time with his father since leaving for college and suddenly he realized it was one of the things he regretted most.

"I'm happy to help," Sean told his father.

Moving the heavy frame was definitely a two-man job. No question about it, Sean thought as his muscles complained at the weight, he definitely had spent too much time behind a computer these past years.

As a boy growing up on Emerald Lake, he'd spent most of his time outside. Boston had plenty of nice spots, but nothing compared to his hometown.

"Couldn't have done that without you," his father said when they'd completely cleared out the room. "I've been meaning to refinish these floors for a long time. Figured since work was a little slow this year, it would give me a chance to finally get your mother off my back. You know how she's been wanting me to redo these floors since you were in high school."

Sean was about to suggest they head down to the kitchen to discuss Stu's possible whereabouts when Sean's mother called up the stairs.

"Sean? Bill? Are either of you up there?"

Sean thought he saw his father's shoulders tense and his mouth tighten at the corners.

That made two of them.

Elizabeth was standing in front of them before either man could reply. "Oh good, I'm glad you're here, honey," she said to him, and then to his father, "I hope you didn't scratch any of the walls getting that bed frame out."

"We were careful, Elizabeth," Bill replied in a flat, borderline irritated voice.

Odd. Sean had never heard his father actually respond to his mother like that. He'd always just silently taken her jabs before.

What the hell was going on here?

First Stu had disappeared. And now his father was practically standing up to his mother. If Sean added in the way Rebecca kept getting under his skin, it was starting to feel like the earth was shifting on its axis.

His mother raised her eyebrows at Bill's curt reply before saying, "These floors have certainly waited long enough to be fixed up, haven't they, Sean?"

She'd asked him the question in a light voice with a smile, but Sean could feel the tension between his mother and father from where he was standing. Besides, didn't she know he had always been able to see past the smile and hear past the lightness?

"I'm sure they're going to look great," was his only possible response.

She reached out and put a hand on his arm. "When I saw your car, I was hoping you were here to tell us that you've heard from Stu."

Regardless of how he felt about his mother, the hopefulness in her eyes was difficult to see. Especially when he didn't have any good news for her.

"He did send me a letter. Similar to the one he left you." He ran a hand through his hair, using the movement as an excuse to shift away from his mother's touch. "Unfortunately, he didn't say where he was going or for how long."

Elizabeth's face fell. "How could he just leave us all like that? It isn't like Stu to do something like that."

Not having an answer for his clearly distraught mother, Sean continued to relay the information he did have. "I've spoken with several of Stu's friends and none of them have heard from him."

"I can't help but think that none of this would have happened if Rebecca hadn't come here. She's very sweet, but obviously things weren't good between her and Stu. Perhaps that's why he felt like he had to leave."

An instinctive urge to defend Rebecca rose up inside Sean. But before he could say a word, his normally mild-mannered, quiet father said, "That's ridiculous, Elizabeth. He adored Rebecca. Just like the rest of us do."

"Ridiculous? Adored?" His mother's color was high. "He was fine before they got engaged. Everything was just fine."

"No," his father said, "everything was not just fine. Instead of blaming Rebecca for hurting your son, you need to open your eyes and give her credit for single-handedly holding things together at the inn."

Blinking rapidly in surprise, Elizabeth finally turned to Sean for support. "Now that you're here, you can take over the inn for a while, can't you, honey?"

"I spent the morning working with her and can tell you firsthand that Rebecca is an excellent innkeeper. I have no intention of taking over for her."

Deciding to end the conversation—the whole poorly thought out visit, actually—Sean turned to head for the stairs. His father followed him, putting a hand on his arm before he could walk away.

"Thanks for the help, Sean. I'll be by the inn soon to

see if you need me to return the favor and to catch up on what you've been up to." In a lower voice that kept the conversation between the two of them, he added, "I know this might sound strange, but unlike your mother, I'm not too worried about Stu. It's occurred to me since he's left that sometimes you need some distance to see things more clearly. Perhaps that's all this is for him, a chance to finally see things for what they really are."

Too quickly, his mother was there again, following them down the stairs to the front door.

"Don't go yet, Sean. I've barely had a chance to talk to you since you've been back."

Bill's voice was firm. "Rebecca needs his help at the inn."

His father was right. Rebecca's workload was tremendous, especially after she'd spent the whole morning cleaning rooms with him instead of attending to her usual business.

He didn't want to take up any more of her day than he already had. At the same time, it was his inn. He was familiar with the finances—he wouldn't have bought the business blind, not even to help his brother—but there was a lot to be learned from going through a company's files. He'd spend the rest of the afternoon familiarizing himself with the back-end of the business—the high and low periods, the number of staff and their salaries, and the growth potential.

"I'm sure your mother is sorry about her outburst. Please don't say anything to Rebecca about it, Sean."

"Of course, I won't."

Hopefully an afternoon filled with facts and figures would help loosen the tight knot that five minutes with his parents had put into his gut.

* * *

"How dare you apologize for me!"

Elizabeth had never been so mad...or ashamed. She was allowed to have feelings, wasn't she? She should be able to speak her mind to her family, especially when she was a mother worried about her son.

Anyone would understand that. Except for her husband, evidently.

"Someone needed to apologize, Elizabeth. You were completely out of line."

She was too stunned by what felt like Bill's continued attack to say anything for a moment. Finally, in a softer voice, she asked, "Why are you speaking to me like this? I'm not the one who hurt Stu so badly that he felt he had no choice but to leave town."

But instead of helping to make Bill understand where she was coming from, she watched his normally cheerful, relaxed expression settle more firmly into disgust. At her.

"Whatever drove him away, it wasn't Rebecca. Couldn't you see how upset she was when she gave us the news that they'd called off their engagement—and that they never should have made the mistake of getting engaged at all? She has never been anything but honest with us—and everyone else in this town. She's barely holding it together without his help. He should have stayed to face the music with her."

Not understanding how he could possibly talk that way about their son, Elizabeth went back on the attack. "You should be worried about Stu, not some girl we barely know. What if all along she was seducing him into giving her control of the inn?"

Bill's bark of laughter at the word *seduce* shocked her.

How dare he laugh in the face of her fear. Her anger. Her worries.

"Seduce him? Are you kidding? There wasn't an ounce of spark between Rebecca and Stu. You had to see that. If you ask me, not getting married was the best thing for the both of them."

God, how she hated his talk of sparks. Way back when, the sparks had burned so brightly for her and Bill. Where had those sparks gone? For so long, she'd held out hope that they would come back.

But now that Stu was gone, sniping and fighting had replaced the heavy silences between them.

Leaving her almost all out of hope.

Chapter Eight

The next morning, Rebecca woke up shivering. The heat was on and she hadn't kicked off the covers, but her bedroom was strangely cold. In fact, ever since Stu had disappeared, the room had gotten colder and colder each night. She'd taken to wearing her long underwear and thick socks to bed.

She half expected to see her breath in the air as she reluctantly pushed back the covers and sprinted to the bathroom. Although the tiled floor should have felt like ice against her bare feet, it was much warmer in the bathroom than it had been in her bedroom. While she waited for the shower to heat up, she went back out and made a quick tour of the rest of her suite. The only cold room was the bedroom. All the others felt just fine.

She'd left the doors open to the living room when she went to sleep. The heat should have come into her bedroom. Instead, it was as if there was some kind of invisible barrier there keeping the warmth out...and holding the icy cold in.

Over the past nine months, she'd heard many stories

about the inn being haunted, but she'd discounted them all as small-town folklore. The thing was, ever since moving in to the newly redone attic suite, she'd started to wonder if they might possibly be true.

Of course, once she stepped into the shower and let the water warm her up the rest of the way, she had to laugh at herself.

The inn wasn't haunted. She was just tired from staying up and working on details for the Tapping of the Maples Festival long after everyone at the inn was asleep. With another big day ahead of her—one that was very likely to include more time training Sean—she forcefully brushed the remaining suspicions from her mind.

The past few weeks had been nuts. Between Andi and Nate's wedding and Sean's appearance, she felt like she'd been juggling half a dozen slick and slippery pins while balancing a plate on the tip of her nose.

Today was going to be better.

No, not just better. Great.

It was going to be a fantastic day. She'd make sure of it. Any challenges that came her way, she'd face head-on with a smile and courage. No matter what.

Sean knew he'd kept Rebecca from getting through her full workload the previous day. Deciding to finish going through all of the inn's paperwork before approaching her in the morning, he'd been working for a couple of hours in the small office behind the check-in desk where he had easy access to the inn's main files.

He'd heard Rebecca moving between the front desk and the dining room to oversee their guests' breakfasts for the past hour. She hadn't stepped into the office yet, and he hadn't gone out of his way to alert her of his presence, partly because he enjoyed listening to her chat with people as they passed through the inn's front room.

She was cheerful, but not annoying. Interested without being intrusive. All in all, the perfect innkeeper.

He had to hand it to Stu; his brother had done a great job hiring Rebecca to manage the inn. What she might have lacked in initial experience nine months ago, she'd certainly made up for in raw energy and sheer willingness to learn.

All night, he'd gone over the half a dozen reasons for him to keep his distance from her. Foremost among them was that it was a small town, she was his brother's ex-fiancée, and he didn't mix business and pleasure. But Sean knew better than to think that any of those were strong enough reasons to keep their attraction at bay. It all came down to the fact that he despised secrets of any kind. Yes, Rebecca's concern—and love—for his little brother shone through so clearly that Sean didn't doubt she was keeping the secret because she loved Stu and not because it particularly served her. If anything, he could see the way his brother's confidence weighed her down.

But she'd kept it anyway, even though Sean had told her over and over that he needed to know. And in the end, that was what Sean couldn't allow himself to forget.

"Rebecca." A man's low voice sounded through to the back office. "You don't know how much I've missed seeing your pretty face."

Sean put the file he'd been reading down on the desk. The man speaking to Rebecca obviously knew her as more than an innkeeper.

"Mark?" She sounded surprised. But not in a good way. "What are you doing here?"

"What do you think? I came to see you, baby. It wasn't easy to find this little town after a snowstorm, but you're worth it."

Sean barely held back a growl. First at the "baby" and then at the reference to Emerald Lake as a "little town."

"How is your wife?" Rebecca's voice held a sharp edge Sean hadn't heard before. But as she said, "And your children?" he realized the edges were dulled with pain.

He didn't know who the man was yet. But the sure knowledge that he'd hurt Rebecca had Sean's hands curling into fists, even though she'd certainly never asked him to be her protector.

"That's what I came here to tell you, Rebecca. My wife and I are getting a divorce. Now that it's almost final and I've been missing you so much, I couldn't wait any longer to come find you."

Sean reeled from the implications of what the man was saying.

Had Rebecca been seeing this man while he was married?

"You should have called first, Mark. I can't talk to you right now. Can't you see I'm working?"

"I know you're probably still a little mad at me," the man said in a cajoling voice. "But you've got to understand, I needed time to deal with my wife, with my family. And the truth is, I didn't realize until you were gone just how good you were for me. No one has ever taken care of me like you do."

What an asshole this guy was. Sean could barely remain in his seat. He wanted to rush into the entry and ram his fist through Mark's face.

But something held him back: the dark knowledge that

he couldn't listen to the conversation if he announced his presence to them.

And it wasn't like Rebecca had kicked the guy out yet.

Jesus, she wasn't going to go back to him, was she?

"It was always about you, wasn't it, Mark?" she finally said in a soft but firm voice that just barely carried into the back office.

"No, I've changed. I swear I have. I'm ready to hear what you need from me. I'm ready for you to tell me how I can win you back."

"Do you really want to know, Mark?"

"Yes, I really do, baby."

"Go back home. Go tell your wife you're sorry you've been such a terrible husband and father and hug your kids. You don't want me." She paused. "You only want what you can't have."

"Rebecca…"

Sean didn't like the edge that had crept into the man's tone. Instinctively wanting to protect her, he left the shadows.

"Is there a problem, Rebecca?"

Sean didn't waste much time looking at Mark, besides confirming that he was scum. Good looking and well dressed, but scum nonetheless.

Clearly flustered and embarrassed by the sure knowledge that he'd overheard everything, Rebecca said, "Sean, I didn't know you were in the office. I was just telling Mark that I needed to get back to work. Right away."

Mark's eyes moved between the two of them, narrowing before he returned his gaze to her.

"When do you get off, Rebecca? I'll wait for you so that we can talk privately."

Before he could think about what he was doing, Sean put a protective hand on the small of her back. Her warmth instantly permeated his hand.

Her entire body stiffened at his touch and she shifted to the side so that she was just out of reach. Sean knew he shouldn't have touched her so intimately, but he hadn't been able to stop himself. It had been pure instinct to want to protect her.

"Look, my schedule is really busy right now, Mark. I can't—"

"I came all this way, Rebecca," the man whined. "At least hear me out. Just let me take you somewhere private tonight to explain everything to you. To try and make you understand."

From his spot in the peanut gallery, Sean could see Rebecca reluctantly giving in.

"I have a meeting tonight, but I could probably spare a few minutes this afternoon."

He couldn't miss the triumphant look on Mark's face as he said, "Tell me when and where and I'll be there. Your terms this time, Rebecca."

"At four p.m. Follow signs to the public dock. I'll meet you out there."

Sean enjoyed the sight of Mark's eyes widening far more than he should have.

"Are you kidding? The public dock? It's freezing out there. Can't we meet somewhere warmer?"

"I thought you said they were my terms this time?"

The other man did a quick double take, almost as if he didn't quite recognize the woman standing in front of him. Or her strength.

"Okay," he said, putting his hands up. "You're right. I'll be there."

Rebecca held herself perfectly still until he had left the inn. Only then did she let her breath go in a slow exhale, her shoulders dropping slightly from her previous battle-ready position.

Sean half expected her to make an excuse about what had just happened. But he should have known better than that by now, shouldn't he? Because Rebecca didn't act like other people; she didn't seem to know how to brush awkward under the rug like anyone else would have.

"I'm really sorry about that, Sean," she said softly. "I'm just glad no guests came in while he was here."

Twenty years ago, Sean had learned how quickly things could change in fifteen minutes. How his mother could go from being the person he loved and trusted most in the world to a virtual stranger. Since then, he'd been careful to keep himself far out of the path of any emotions that might put him back in those teenager's shoes again.

Since meeting Rebecca, however, pushing his feelings away like he always had been had been a surprisingly difficult task. But now that he knew she'd been dating a married man, a man with children, he was glad he hadn't made the mistake of thinking she was a better person than she obviously was.

Instead of accepting her apology for what had just happened, he said, "I've been reviewing the inn's files. I have a few questions for you."

She raised her eyebrows at his abrupt change of subject and the hard tone of his voice. "Is that something they teach you in business school? To act like nothing happened when we all know it just did?"

No one had ever been this upfront with him about their

personal life. Especially not an employee. He had no business caring about whom she dated.

It shouldn't matter, damn it, even though she should have never messed around with a married man.

Wanting to make himself perfectly clear, once and for all, he said, "Your personal life is personal. And so is mine."

Her big, clear eyes went flat.

"Why don't you show me those files you were looking at. I'm sure I can clear any issues up for you. And then we can move forward with your training."

Any easiness that had been between them earlier completely disappeared and didn't make a return over the next hours as they pored over spreadsheets and files.

At four p.m. Rebecca looked up at the clock on the wall behind the desk and said, "I need to get going."

Sean hadn't liked the look of Mark and certainly didn't trust him. Rebecca going out into the cold to meet with him with no one around to make sure she was okay didn't sit right with him. Not because she wasn't strong enough to deal with the guy—behind her seemingly soft exterior was a core of steel—but because it would make him feel immeasurably better to stay close to her just in case the douche bag tried anything.

Which was what had Sean a breath away from grabbing his coat and demanding to go with her to meet her ex.

"I don't think you should go meet him this afternoon, Rebecca."

Her eyes met his, clearly irritated by his intrusion into her life. A personal life that he'd told her just hours ago he wanted nothing to do with.

"He's not dangerous. I can take care of myself."

He knew she wanted to believe that, but didn't she see how her kindness made people want to grab hold of her and never let go until they'd drained her dry? No wonder her mother wanted to come and drag her back home.

He caught his thoughts too late. How could he still be thinking any of that after what he'd just learned? She'd been the other woman. She was responsible for a marriage breaking up. What if one of Mark's kids had caught him with Rebecca?

It would have scarred them for life.

"If something happened to you, Stu would never forgive me."

"Ah. Yes. Stu." Each word was flatter, harder than the one that came before. "Well, he isn't here to stop me, is he?"

And clearly, thought Sean as she practically slammed the door in his face, he'd better not, either.

"He's watching us, isn't he?"

"I don't know, Mark. What Sean does is his own business."

For a moment there she'd thought he was going to insist on coming with her. She never would have let him do that in a million years... so, then, why did she appreciate knowing he was, in fact, watching over her? Especially because Mark's behavior did suddenly make her more than a little nervous.

"I don't like the way he looked at you," her ex said as if he had any claim to her at all.

Rebecca stared at him. Had she really been in love with him? Or had she just been in love with a fantasy of the perfect man?

It was almost funny just how imperfect Mark had ended up being.

Maybe next time around instead of searching for perfect she should look for imperfect so that things could only get better, instead of worse.

The thought had her mouth moving up into an unexpected smile.

"You're so beautiful, Rebecca," Mark said, brushing her cheek softly with the back of his knuckles.

A year ago, she would have nuzzled into his caress, rather than flinching and pulling away.

Things had changed.

"I need to get back to the inn, Mark. I just came out here to tell you that I'm not going to get back together with you."

Anger simmered in the eyes that she'd once looked to for approval. For what she'd thought was love. But he banked it and tried to give her a caring look.

"I remember the way you cried when you found out about my wife. You can't have gotten over me that quickly."

"I cried because I was ashamed of what I'd done."

He blinked, before recovering quickly. "Oh, baby, you weren't to blame for anything. Dating you on the side was the only way we could be together. But now we won't have to hide our love from anyone."

He was reaching for her again, but before he could touch her she backed even farther away. Sean had been right about one thing—coming here to try and talk some sense into Mark had been a mistake.

"I don't love you, Mark. How could I, when you don't even know what love really means?"

The wind whipped up around them and she pulled her jacket tighter around her.

"And you think you do?" His laugh was harsh. Mean. "I saw the way you looked at that guy in that podunk little inn. You think he's going to give you what you're looking for?"

His words almost made her stumble. They certainly had her heart filling with dread at the knowledge that what she already felt for Sean was big enough for Mark to see.

"Do you really think there's a man out there who is ever going to be able to live up to your fairy tale?"

Anger had her whirling around to face the man she wished with all her heart she'd never met, never wasted two years of her life on. "There's a big difference between lying about every single thing for two years and wanting a fairy tale."

Letting the wind whip her hair and her clothes around on the public dock, she let the anger drain out of her. The man standing before her simply wasn't worth it.

"Good-bye, Mark. Good luck with your marriage."

But instead of heading back to the inn, she walked across the park and headed for Lake Yarns on Main Street even though the Monday night knitting group wasn't meeting for another hour or so, and she didn't have any of her things.

She just couldn't go back to the inn. Not yet. Not until she'd calmed down. At least she had something to thank Mark for. He'd just reminded her of all the reasons to keep her distance from Sean. Facts were facts: she always fell for powerful, self-absorbed, cold men.

She wasn't going to do it ever again.

*   *   *

Sean kept his eyes trained on Mark until he got back into his car and sped away too fast on Emerald Lake's icy roads.

The whole time she'd been out there with that scumbag, he hadn't been able to breathe right.

Telling himself she was a valuable employee and he would have been just as concerned about another employee's well-being, he didn't realize his mother was standing beside him, following his line of vision out the window until she said, "Is everything all right, Sean?"

Hell no, he wasn't fine. He was thinking far too much, far too often, about a woman who shouldn't even be on his radar.

Having no intention of sharing any of that with his mother, he simply said, "The snow is going to melt soon."

He moved away from the window and she followed him over to the check-in desk. Only a coward would pray for a guest to walk in asking for help right now. And, unfortunately, only a lucky coward would see that prayer answered.

"I'm really sorry, Sean, about what happened over at the house yesterday. You shouldn't have had to see your father and me behave like that." She waved her hand in the air. "Bill is a little tense lately."

Not wanting to get anywhere near the middle of their relationship, he asked, "How's his business going lately?"

"Fine. Same as always."

"And your graphic design clients?"

"I'm still working for about as many as I did when you lived at home."

He could see how disgruntled she was when he refused

to pick up the emotional threads she was dangling in front of him. She should know better.

"We were hoping you could come to dinner tonight. It's been so long since your father and I got to spend some quality time with you. We don't know anything about your life. How your job is going." She paused, a hopeful glint in her eyes as she added, "If you're dating anyone."

"Sorry, I offered to work the desk tonight."

A smart man wouldn't have let her crestfallen expression crawl beneath his armor. But if his consistently inappropriate reactions to Rebecca were any indication, Sean had a feeling his smart days were long behind him.

"But tomorrow night will probably work."

His mother's smile was so bright, so big, it completely transformed her face. And despite himself, Sean saw just how beautiful his mother still was.

Chapter Nine

The minute Rebecca walked into Lake Yarns, she breathed a sigh of relief. At this point, she really needed a refuge from the emotions swirling around inside of her for a little while.

Carol Powell, Andi's mother, was busy helping a customer, and as Rebecca ran her fingers down a display of soft yarn, she was glad for the chance to focus on something other than the Murphy boys for a few moments.

She was a late convert to knitting but found it incredibly calming. Plus, she loved watching socks and blankets and sweaters take shape. She'd been toying with making new pillow covers for the couch in her living room, but just as she was about to grab a skein of blue worsted wool, her elbow knocked into another display. Super soft cashmere rained down upon her and she scrambled to catch the high-priced skeins before they hit the ground.

A short while later, Carol found her standing there with a dozen in her arms.

"Uh-oh, let me help you with that."

"Sorry," Rebecca said as she picked up a stray ball

that had rolled across the wood-plank floor. "I'm afraid I wasn't paying enough attention." Because she couldn't stop thinking about Sean, a man she shouldn't be thinking about at all.

Carol waved away her apology. "Andi always tells me I try to fit too much in a small space. And she's right. But I love all the yarns so much I can't stand to keep them in boxes in the back."

Rebecca adored Andi's mother. Carol's warmth and open smile made her long for her own mother, for the warmth of arms that had held her since she was a baby.

And yet, hadn't she just told her mother not to come visit for a while?

The problem was, Rebecca's mother saw everything. With five daughters, she had to. And Rebecca didn't want her to see how close to the edge of disaster her daughter was. As soon as she'd turned everything around, when the Tapping of the Maples Festival went off without a hitch, when Stu finally returned and Sean left the inn on another exotic trip somewhere on the other side of the world, that was when Rebecca would invite her mother and father and sisters and their husbands for a wonderful Emerald Lake weekend.

"We just got in the most delicious new pattern book," Carol said, drawing her attention to the photographs and patterns in a coffee-table-sized book. "Look at these."

Rebecca's eyes widened at the knitted lingerie, beautifully soft nightgowns and corsets. There were even bra and panty patterns. She felt herself blush.

"I'd love to knit up something from the book as a sample," Carol was saying, "but with Andi away on her honeymoon I'm backlogged enough as it is."

"I'll do it."

The offer was out of her mouth before she even realized it. Oh, no, how could she have just said that? She already had enough on her plate with the inn and the festival, but Carol didn't give her any time to reconsider.

"Would you really?" Carol looked positively gleeful at the prospect of some knitting help. "I just know this book will fly off the shelves if people can see one of the designs brought to life."

"The thing is, I—"

She was unable to get the words out. Everyone in Carol's family and store had been so kind to her since day one. How could she let her down on one small favor?

"I was looking for a new project anyway," Rebecca finally said. And it was true. She had been looking for something new to knit. She just hadn't planned on starting a new project while she had so much else going on. "I left my wallet at the inn, so I'll come back in tomorr—"

"Oh, no, Rebecca. You're helping me out. Everything is on the house."

This was exactly why she loved Emerald Lake so much. She'd known Carol less than a year, but she was treated like family. Somehow, she'd find the time to knit a sample for the store.

Plus, it was a perfect reminder why Rebecca needed to put a stop to any insidious feelings creeping in for Sean. She couldn't afford to have to leave another town because of a love affair gone awry. Not when she'd finally found the place she wanted to stay. And not when her broken engagement with Stu was already enough of a stain on her record.

"Why don't you have a seat while we wait for everyone

else to get here. You can thumb through the book to decide which pattern you might like to tackle. Although," Carol said, flipping through to a picture of a soft pink slip that was both sexy and sweet at the same time, "this is the one I keep going back to in my head."

"It's beautiful," Rebecca said, and the truth was she could already see herself wearing it, could feel the softness of the yarn as it skimmed over her curves like second skin.

Carol clapped her hands together. "Yay! I'll get you everything you need."

While Carol gathered needles and yarn for her, Rebecca got to work pulling out wine glasses for the group. Women were coming in now, one and two at a time. Ten minutes of small talk later, most of the regulars had arrived.

Rebecca was glad to see them all, but made it a point to sit next to Celeste, Stu and Sean's grandmother. She usually went by her cottage once or twice a week for tea, but she'd been so busy since Stu's disappearance.

"I'm sorry I haven't been over to see you more in the past few weeks," she said softly as she cast on her new project.

"Cashmere," Celeste said softly as she reached across to stroke the yarn between her thumb and forefinger. "My favorite."

Rebecca knew that conversations with Celeste didn't always go in a straight line. Some people found the gray-haired woman a bit eccentric because of this, but it was one of the things that drew Rebecca to her. As far as she could tell, Celeste lived her life according to her own rules and no one else's. After all, look at the construction business she'd built up and passed on to her son. For a woman who'd started back in the forties, her business success was nothing short of extraordinary.

"I'm going to be knitting up a sample from this book for the store."

Celeste's eyes went from the book to Rebecca and her eyes filled with a sudden gleam. "Yes. That should work out just right."

Hmm. Nothing should have been strange about that statement. And yet, it felt strange all the same.

"Could I ask you something, Celeste?" When the elderly woman nodded, Rebecca lowered her voice and said, "The old ghost stories about the inn...when did they start being told?"

"You've felt something, haven't you?"

Rebecca didn't want to come across like a crazy person, so she began her answer by saying, "You know how interested I am in the history of the inn," but when Celeste's gaze remained clear and patient, she added, "I'm sure it's nothing, but my new bedroom in the refurbished attic is so cold sometimes, even when the other rooms are perfectly warm. And a couple of times I could have sworn there was someone else in the room with me." She shook her head at her own foolishness. "Listen to me. Telling you I think my bedroom might be haunted." She smiled at the woman beside her. "Clearly, I've been working too hard lately."

But Celeste didn't smile back. Instead, the hint of loss, of sorrow that Rebecca had always felt was hiding behind her green eyes, rose to the surface.

"I knew this would happen. I told Stu not to refinish that room. There's a reason it's been shut down for sixty years."

Rebecca worked to hide her shock at Celeste's statement. "Stu never said anything to me."

Then again, there were plenty of things her best friend hadn't talked to her about, weren't there?

She was just about to ask Celeste what happened sixty years ago when Dorothy and Helen started telling her what a great job she'd done with Andi and Nate's wedding. Not wanting to be rude, she let herself be pulled into a conversation with two of her favorite people in town. Yes, they were two of the biggest gossips on the lake, but they were also two of her staunchest supporters. More than once, she'd overheard them deftly turn a conversation at Saturday's wedding reception away from her breakup with Stu to something far more mundane.

When she looked for Celeste a handful of minutes later to continue their conversation about ghost stories, Sean's grandmother was gone.

Sean could have left the front desk after dinner, but he figured it was just as easy to look through the final contracts that would turn over his venture business here as it was in the back office or bedroom.

And it meant he'd be certain Rebecca got back from the yarn store safely. Just because Emerald Lake was usually a safe small town didn't mean exceptions didn't happen. Especially if there was an angry ex waiting in the wings for a beautiful, delicate woman he thought should be his.

The inn's front door opened and he worked to keep his expression impassive, even though relief immediately swept through him head to toe that Rebecca was fine.

"Cold out there, isn't it?"

She jumped at his question. "Oh, I didn't expect you to be out here still." She frowned. "I should have told you that we don't usually man the front desk after everyone is seated for dinner."

The soft sound of her words fluttered across his skin as he drank in her flushed cheeks and the windblown silk of her hair.

He gestured to his paperwork. "I was fine working here."

She was in the process of taking off her down coat when her fingers stilled on the zipper.

"You were waiting up for me."

It wasn't a question. But he felt compelled to answer it, nonetheless.

"I had to make sure you got home okay."

Again, irritation lit her very pretty, cold-flushed face. "Do you always worry this much about your employees?"

She was up the stairs and gone before he could answer her slightly snarky, yet pointed, question... or deny the way the flash of fire in her eyes sent his heart to jumping around in his chest.

And made him want, more than anything, to claim her as his own, if only for one night, to know if her fire burned as hot and bright as he imagined it did.

Rebecca was exhausted, but even a long, hot bath and knitting row after row of the soft cashmere slip couldn't make her eyes want to close, or her brain turn off. She hated the horrible things Mark had said. And yet, somehow, most of those had washed off her like water off a duck's back.

No, what had her sleepless in Emerald Lake was that

even knowing how hesitant she should be to consider letting a man near her heart after that awful conversation with Mark, she couldn't stop thinking about Sean.

And that one perfect smile he'd given her earlier that day when he'd agreed to be trained on inn keeping by her.

One smile shouldn't have meant so much.

But it had.

Which was what made his obvious disgust over her relationship with Mark even worse.

And then, on top of all that, Sean was right about the burden of all she was taking on. She still had a great deal to take care of to ensure that the Tapping of the Maples Festival went off without a hitch. Just because the paperwork for the vendors she was approving and the contractual details between the inn and each and every one of the vendors had been making her eyes cross earlier was no excuse to slack off tonight. For the next couple of hours, as the digits on her digital clock flipped over from twelve to one and then two, she made progress. When she stabbed herself with a pen for the tenth time as she yawned, she threw it down and climbed up into her bed, turning off the lamp on the bedside table.

But she still couldn't sleep.

God forbid she wasn't at the top of her game tomorrow around Sean. Lord only knew how he'd manage to take advantage of her weakness.

Maybe he'd steal a kiss.

No! She sat up in the bed and turned the light back on. How could she sleep if that was the kind of garbage her brain was going to spit out at her?

She was most certainly not going to kiss Sean. Not tomorrow morning. Not ever.

Just as she was repeating the vow to herself, she heard an awful wailing sound. Her first impression was that she was listening to a broken heart come to life.

The practical part of her had her jumping out of bed to figure out where the sound was coming from. If one of her guests was in pain, she needed to help him or her.

But when she rushed out of the bedroom, the sound got softer. Frowning, she stopped and turned back to the bedroom. Her earlier conversation with Celeste playing around the corners of her mind, she took a few steps back toward the bedroom.

Yes, the wailing was definitely getting louder.

What on earth was going on here? A strange cold patch was something she could accept. But strange sounds?

No, that was just too weird.

It had to be an animal, probably caught up between her ceiling rafters and the shingles on the roof. She was just reaching for her jeans to put on over the camisole and boy shorts she'd worn to bed to go investigate further when she heard a key move in her door lock.

The door flew open and Sean rushed inside. "Are you okay?"

She'd never seen him in jeans, let alone without a shirt on. Oh boy. The sight of all those muscles along with his rumpled hair and the dark shadow of stubble on his face did funny things to her stomach.

"I'm fine," she said, but she wasn't sure he heard her because instead of stopping in his tracks and apologizing for barging into her—locked—suite, he had one hand on her shoulder and the other was running over her forehead, brushing back her hair as if he were looking for bruises.

"Sean, I'm okay," she said again.

At last, his eyes locked onto hers and he seemed to hear her. Obviously realizing that he was holding onto her like she was a breakable figurine, he dropped his hands and took an abrupt step back.

"I heard the noise and I thought for sure it was you. I was so afraid that someone was hurting you."

As irritated as she was that he hadn't even come close to starting to apologize yet for either the manhandling or the barging in, she couldn't deny that a little part of her was touched that he'd been so intent on making sure she was okay...and that she mattered enough to have him barely pulling clothes on and rushing to her suite of rooms.

"It freaked me out at first, too," she admitted. "I was worried it was one of the guests, but then I realized the sound is loudest in my bedroom."

She'd looked away for a moment to gesture toward her bedroom door and when she looked back at Sean his eyes were darker and filled with something that made her warm all over.

Suddenly she remembered he wasn't the only one who hadn't had time to pull on clothes. Every instinct she possessed had her wanting to run into her bedroom to throw on a thick, ankle-length robe, but she made herself remain right where she was.

Not only were her pajamas not overly sexy by any means—heck, she wore less on the beach during the summer—but Sean would surely think she had some sort of crush on him if she freaked out about what she was wearing in front of him.

"Stay in here while I go check things out."

She scowled at his back as he walked into her bedroom

without even asking if he could, then followed him and said, "I was thinking it might be an animal stuck in the ceiling."

Clearly more than a little irritated that she hadn't been a good little girl and stayed out of the way, he said, "Maybe. There isn't much space up there between the roof and the ceiling tiles." He looked around the room again. "Did you notice that the sounds seemed to stop when I came inside?"

She looked down at the keys dangling from his fingertips and raised one eyebrow. "That wasn't exactly the use I had in mind for the master set of keys when I gave them to you yesterday."

A muscle jumped in his jaw, but he didn't apologize. She wasn't surprised. She could already tell he was a man who did what he thought was right, regardless of the consequences.

Frankly, she was glad she'd been wearing any clothes at all. Imagine if he'd come in and found her naked.

She shivered at the thought she shouldn't have let herself have, a thought that made her feel much too warm in the usually cool room. Warm enough that she found herself saying, "Actually, my bedroom hasn't been this warm since I moved in. Not until right this second."

"You've noticed other strange things in here?"

Feeling slightly foolish for having said anything at all, she admitted, "It's been really cold at times, like the windows are wide open in the middle of a storm. But only in the bedroom. I mentioned it to your grandmother and—" She cut herself off, tried to think of a way to put it that didn't make either her or Celeste sound like they'd been eating straight out of a bowl of nuts. "She said this room had been closed off for sixty years. Did you know that?"

"I knew it hadn't been used in a while, but I didn't realize it was that long."

"Your grandmother would have been in her early twenties, right?"

Instead of answering her question about his grandmother, he finally noticed her festival paperwork spread out across the foot of the bed along with the slip she'd been knitting on top of the pattern book.

"Were you even asleep, or were you still working?"

She bristled at his accusing tone. Crossing her arms over her chest, she said, "Not that it's any business of yours, but yes, I was taking care of a few things."

"Don't you have enough on your plate already? You can't do it all, Rebecca. Not without things starting to fall apart here at the inn. With Stu gone and while you're teaching me the ropes, wouldn't it be easier if you let the festival go for now?"

Hating that he thought she would ever intentionally do anything to damage the inn, she called him on what was really behind his frustrated words. "This isn't about the festival. This isn't about the inn. This is about what happened this afternoon, isn't it?"

In an instant, she watched Sean shut himself down. He hadn't been thrilled with her before, but that was different from the way he literally pulled himself away from her now.

"Don't try to turn my concern for your well-being and the inn into something it isn't."

She knew she should let it go. That she should let him go. But she was sick and tired of men not telling her the truth. Especially this one, who claimed truth was everything to him.

"I saw your reaction to my conversation with Mark."

Instead of answering her direct question, he took another step away from her. "I shouldn't have been listening to your private conversation. And I shouldn't have barged in here tonight, either."

Beyond frustrated, she all but yelled, "But you were! And you did!" And the truth was that she hadn't been able to get his judgmental expression out of her head all night. "Why don't you be honest with me, for once?"

His mouth was tight, his eyes narrowed. "You broke up a marriage."

"I don't need to explain myself to you, but if I'd known he was married, I never would have—"

"You must have known."

Rebecca's eyes widened at Sean's accusation, at the way he'd actually voiced aloud the horrible things she'd already guessed he was thinking about her.

"He didn't wear a ring, he had his own apartment, he was free on evenings and weekends. There were no pictures of a family, no strange phone calls he didn't want me to hear."

But Sean clearly refused to take her explanation at face value. "There had to be signs, Rebecca. Signs you were ignoring. Times you couldn't call him. Places you couldn't meet him. But you chose to ignore all of them."

It would be so much easier to stay on the defensive, but the truth was his words were pricking at so many things she hadn't wanted to admit to herself. Was it true that she'd been more concerned with the fantasy than what was really right in front of her? And if that was the case, then wasn't she guilty of ignoring the reality about Stu, too? Along with the truth that a platonic life with him would have never worked out either?

"I didn't mean to hurt anyone," she finally said, exhaustion playing havoc with the extremely tenuous hold she had over her emotions. "And I'll never stop regretting the pain his wife and children must be in."

She waited for Sean to say "I told you so," or to hammer on her more, but all he said was "I'll check the roof and the water pipes tomorrow."

Even though a maintenance issue like this was something she would have passed off to Stu in the past, she was angry enough at the way it felt like he was judging her past to come back at him with, "Do you think I don't know what I'm doing here? Do you think I can't handle looking into those issues myself?"

For a moment, she thought he would argue with her, tell her again that she wasn't Superwoman.

Instead, he simply shook his head and said, "I know you can handle anything that comes your way, Rebecca. You've proved that to me in spades this week." The low rumble of his surprising words washed through her senses, making her powerfully aware of the attraction still coursing between them despite their angry words with one another.

It would be so much easier if she could pretend it was only the energy they'd whipped up between them in their frustration. But Rebecca knew that it wasn't.

Only, more than anything else, she knew exactly where tumbling into bed with Sean Murphy would get her. Yes, there'd be pleasure. She wasn't naive enough to think there wouldn't be. But there would be infinitely more heartache.

Along with an immediate search for a new job. In a new town.

But with her brain—and heart—still stuck on thinking of what his kiss would taste like, although she tried to find a response, before she could, like the ghost she was starting to believe really lived in the walls of her bedroom, he was gone.

Chapter Ten

The next morning, Rebecca knew exactly whom she needed to talk to about the sounds in her bedroom. She knocked on Celeste's door midmorning, but there was no answer.

She was turning to leave when she saw a small figure down on the beach. Squinting, Rebecca recognized one of Celeste's many hats. As she headed down to the sand, she wondered if she should take to wearing hats since Celeste's skin was incredible for a woman in her eighties. Yes, there were lines in it, but they were mostly around her eyes and mouth from smiling. Remarkably, she had very few frown lines between her eyebrows.

What, Rebecca wondered, had kept Celeste so young in so many ways? Case in point, with the same clear delight that a child would have exhibited, she was picking up pebbles from the sand and skipping them across a patch of water where the ice had melted.

Celeste waved a hand in greeting. "I'm so glad you came out to the beach to join me, Rebecca."

She stood there beside the older woman for several

long moments as she continued to skip rocks. But soon Rebecca could no longer resist picking up her own handful of pebbles that had washed in during the last storm. Feeling foolish at first, she wound up and threw her first pebble. It skidded off nearby ice and she winced at how bad her aim was.

"Just takes a little practice," Celeste said, as if reading her mind.

A few minutes and many dozens of throws later, Rebecca finally managed her first good skip. She couldn't help but cheer.

Celeste smiled at her fondly. "The wind is picking up. Why don't you join me for a cup of tea in my cottage."

"I'd love that," she said, but before turning away from the lake, Rebecca took another deep breath, letting the clean, crisp air fill her up and push away her lingering tiredness.

The Adirondacks were so lovely in all seasons. Having arrived at Emerald Lake the previous summer, it was a real thrill to experience her first spring in the small lakeside town.

"It really is lovely here," she said aloud.

"I never wanted to live anywhere else," Celeste told her as they walked together across the sand and toward the yellow-and-white cottage that sat just up from the beach.

"That's what I thought the first time I came to Emerald Lake," Rebecca admitted, feeling safer with Celeste than she did with almost anyone.

A few moments later, they were in the tidy, bright cottage and Celeste was fussing with her teapot and tray. A few minutes later, the two of them were having an incredibly elegant midmorning tea, complete with special butter cookies imported from England.

"This is marvelous, Celeste," Rebecca said as she sipped at her Earl Grey and nibbled at a cookie. In fact, she didn't know why she hadn't thought of it before: What if she did a special tea once a week at the inn? For both guests and locals? If it was successful enough, maybe they could even open up a tearoom off to the side of the inn, with teas from all over the world.

After saying as much, Celeste said, "You remind me so much of myself when I was younger. My brain was always spinning, always creating something new and exciting."

Rebecca flushed at the lovely comparison. "You built an entire company from scratch. I'm only managing the inn."

Celeste took a sip of her tea. "How have you been managing without Stu there to help you?"

Not wanting to say anything negative about Celeste's grandson, Rebecca carefully replied, "Well, my workload has certainly increased, but now that Sean is here I'm hoping to be able to have some breathing room soon. At least enough to make sure the Tapping of the Maples Festival is successful."

"What do you think of Sean?"

Rebecca worked like crazy not to blush. "He's very intelligent." She tried to think about him without remembering his hands on her, or how much she'd longed for him to kiss her. More than once. "He seems interested in everything around him."

Uncomfortable talking about Sean, knowing she was bound to give her ridiculous—and inappropriate—feelings for him away if they continued down that path, she said, "Last night at the knitting group when I asked you about the old ghost stories, you said something about my living in the attic rooms." Celeste, who had been so focused, so lucid only moments before, almost seemed to blur before Rebecca's eyes. Still, she pushed on. "What did you mean when you said you knew it would happen? What does *it* refer to?"

Celeste didn't answer right away. She took her time finishing her cup of tea, and then poured again for both of them. Rebecca worked to rein in her impatience. Celeste had always been a woman who lived by her own timetable. Something, she knew, that drove her daughter-in-law Elizabeth crazy.

Finally, Celeste put down her teacup and began to tell Rebecca a story.

Emerald Lake 1945

Celeste Farrington was the second daughter of one of the richest men on the lake. Evelyn was two years older; Rose two years younger. Celeste grew up in one of the biggest houses on the lake, content with her loving parents and sisters, although the past years had been bumpier than expected, what with the boys she'd grown up with going off to war ... not to mention all of the drama surrounding Evelyn and the man she'd fallen in love with.

Her older sister's happiness had been a long time in coming. Celeste was glad to see her sister happily wedded to Arthur—finally! But, selfishly perhaps, Celeste wasn't only happy for her sister.

She was happy for herself, too.

In the aftermath of learning about Evelyn's forbidden love affair with a man he deemed far below their family's station—and his precious daughter's love—their father had all but dropped prison bars around his three girls. Evelyn had been old enough—and especially bold after falling in love with Carlos—to still come and go pretty much as she pleased. But for Celeste and little Rose, well, they'd had to learn to live under a microscope.

Rose was fanciful enough that she could always disappear into her own world. But Celeste didn't like being stuck in a cage one bit. She longed to learn as much as she could about the world around her. She enjoyed female pursuits just fine and was an admirable knitter and sewer, but knitting was never going to become her passion, as it was for Evelyn.

No, what she really loved was building things. Even as a little girl she'd been happy to play for hours with blocks and her teachers had always remarked on her remarkable aptitude for math and science.

Still, she instinctively knew that no one would ever approve of her picking up a hammer or saw, so she funneled her interest first into her dollhouses and when she grew too old for those, she began to sketch first her father's house and then most of the other houses around the lake, big and small.

She especially liked the tiny cottages where happy families came to play in the summer. For years, she'd had a picture in her head of the cottage she was going to build for her own family. She could even see her babies playing on the sand, her sisters coming over with their own children.

The only thing she couldn't see clearly was the man who would be her husband.

She knew all of the boys in her classes at school
well. Too well to actually imagine marrying one of
them. And, of course, her father hadn't given her
much chance to get out and date anyone who didn't
live in Emerald Lake. Besides, with all that grilling
he subjected her dates to, any boy who dared ask her
out ended up sorely regretting ever looking her way
in the first place.

Fortunately, in the spring following Evelyn's
fall wedding, Celeste found more freedom at her
feet than she had in years. The weather was crisp,
but the sky was clear. Overly proud of her porcelain skin, she grabbed one of the many sunhats
she'd made over the years, one with large pink silk
flowers and a knitted rose-colored sash around the
brim. She slung her bag over her shoulders, left a
note for her mother that she was going to wander
the beach for a while, and then headed out in the
sunshine.

She walked for a long while, stopping now and
again when she found a patch of open lake water
amidst the ice that still mostly covered the water
to skip a pebble or two over the water. She knew
it was something a child would do and that she
was supposed to have grown out of the habit a long
time ago, but she couldn't see the point of giving up
something that was so much fun.

She was planning on sketching one of the new
houses that was being built about a mile down from
her house. She loved watching the foundations go in
and the studs go up for the walls. While she enjoyed
seeing the finished product, cozy or grand, cute or

historic, it was the internal workings of the building that truly captivated her.

For all her vanity, she couldn't resist turning her face up to the warmth of the sun. Storms had been battering Emerald Lake for most of January and February. It was only in March that the ice and snow had started to melt.

Dorothy, a friend from school, called out her name and Celeste realized she'd walked all the way downtown. She didn't usually come this far and she was thirsty. Fortunately she had some coins in her bag.

When she'd slowly made her way over to Dorothy, her friend was shaking her head. "Have I told you how much you remind me of a turtle?"

Celeste nodded. "Many, many times."

She just couldn't see the point of rushing anything. Perhaps it was because she was the second child. Evelyn had always been the one in a hurry. To walk, according to their parents. And certainly to fall in love. Rose was content to live in her dream world.

Celeste simply enjoyed the world around her. She loved the lake. Loved her family. Loved reading about all the places she'd travel to one day.

She wasn't worried that the day wouldn't come. She knew it would.

When the time was right.

And until then she'd soak up as much knowledge as she could, letting images and histories of Egyptian pyramids and French towers and Italian palaces fill up her imagination and heart until the day the knowledge transformed into a reality she could walk up and touch with her hands.

The two girls headed into the diner and drank hot chocolates while they chatted. Suddenly, Dorothy's eyes got big as she looked at something over Celeste's shoulders.

"Oh my. Now, there's a man."

Dorothy had a tendency toward being boy crazy, so Celeste didn't give much credence to her statement, not bothering to turn around and see whom she was talking about.

She was pulling out a few pennies to leave as a tip when Celeste grabbed her arm and hissed, "He's coming over here. Act natural."

Celeste had to laugh out loud at that. Of course she was going to act natural. She didn't care one way or another about some strange man.

Didn't care, that is, until the moment she heard him say, "Excuse me, ladies, could I intrude on your conversation for a moment to ask a quick question?"

His deep, rich voice had little goose bumps popping up one by one across the surface of her skin.

"Sure!" Dorothy chirped in an overly bright voice. Chalking up her goose bumps to the wind blowing through the diner's front door when someone walked in, Celeste knew it was up to her to act normal for both of them.

She slowly spun around on her stool. "How may we help you?"

It was fortunate that she finished her sentence before she lifted her eyes to the man's face.

He was beautiful.

She'd studied beauty and proportions for years both in books and with pencil and sketchbook in hand. But she'd never seen a face that held such symmetry. Only the slight bump across the bridge of his nose broke up the perfection. At the same time, she quickly noted that it was the imperfection that so well highlighted everything else.

Perhaps it was her father's lockdown during a formative period in her growth, or maybe it was just her natural personality... but Celeste had never learned the art of disguising her reactions.

Which meant that she simply stared wide-eyed at the stranger before them. It wasn't hard to do, considering his eyes had locked onto hers as well. Despite being in a crowded diner, in those moments they were the only two people in the room.

She'd been right not to search, not to worry that love hadn't struck her yet.

Deep in her soul she knew that the man she would marry was standing right in front of her.

At long last, the man cleared his throat. "My name is Charlie Murphy. I've come to Emerald Lake from New York City to meet with a Mr. Farrington this afternoon. But I'm afraid his business office on Main Street is locked. Do you have any idea where I might find him?"

Celeste didn't stop the smile from curving across her mouth at how completely fate took care of everything. If this man was already a colleague of her father's, she wouldn't have to invent a reason to be with Charlie, like Evelyn had done with her precious Carlos.

Smiling up into his light green eyes, she said, "He's my father."

Their courtship was short and oh-so-sweet. Just as Celeste had expected, her father was overjoyed by Charlie's attention to his middle daughter.

Celeste was overjoyed by it, too, even if she didn't always understand Charlie or the things he clearly seemed to think he needed to do to make her love him. He gave her so many gifts, expensive things that were pretty and fragile. She supposed she could have simply said thank you over and over again, but that felt like a lie to her. And Celeste didn't believe in lies.

"I don't need pretty things," she told him one night when he sat across from her at another fancy restaurant, another box sitting on her empty dinner plate. She lifted the box and gave it back to him. "If this is who you think I am," she said, pushing back her chair to stand, "then you don't know me very well at all."

She was out the door by the time she heard him say, "I know exactly who you are, Celeste."

The passion, the sincerity in his words—along with the fear she couldn't miss—had her stopping, turning around to face him.

"Prove it."

He blinked at her challenge. She knew what she'd said wasn't ladylike, that her father would be horrified to hear her speaking to one of his business associates like this, but she simply wasn't willing to continue to give her heart to anyone who didn't deserve it.

"You're a loving daughter. You'd do anything for your sisters. You'd risk a piece of yourself before you'd ever let one of your friends be hurt. You have no idea that you're the center of so many lives, that you're the lynchpin that holds them all together." He paused, looked down at the box in his hand. "And anyone who knows you, anyone who loves you, would never try to keep you in his life with stupid gifts. Do you know why, sweetheart?"

She realized then what he was feeling, why he'd been showering her with presents.

He was afraid.

Afraid of losing her.

"Charlie—" she began, but the look in his eyes had whatever words she'd been about to say turning to dust on her tongue.

"Because he would know that once you loved, it was forever."

She was in his arms a moment later, the word *forever* echoing on her lips just as she kissed him.

Three weeks after they first met at the diner, Charlie found Celeste by the lake, sketching. He hadn't needed to say a word to her, hadn't needed to announce his presence for her focus to shatter. Anytime he was in the same room, anytime he was near, she lost hold of anything but him, was literally unable to keep from smiling. And there was nothing more she loved than the look in his eyes when he smiled back at her, as if she was a perfect surprise, a gift he'd never expected would be given to him.

But although she'd smiled at him and reached out her arm for him to join her on the sandy shore, neither his serious expression nor his position changed.

"What is it, Charlie? Is something wrong?"

His eyes roved over her face. "What would a brilliant girl like you want with a man like me?"

She frowned, put down her drawing pad, and moved across the sand to him. She didn't have to think about her reasons. They were obvious. And very simple.

"I love you."

She put her hands over his and he lifted them to his lips in a gesture that seemed almost desperate. Something was wrong, but she didn't know what it was, didn't know what it could possibly be.

And then, almost as if in slow motion, she watched him drop to one knee on the soft green grass that bordered the sand.

"Charlie?" Her voice was strangely breathless.

"Marry me, sweetheart."

And later, after they'd gorged on kisses and whispered promises, when Charlie met with her father to ask for her hand in marriage, her father was as happy as she'd seen him since Evelyn's wedding day.

Their wedding day dawned sunny, the spring flowers all around the inn for the ceremony and reception.

Celeste's sisters were helping her with the finishing touches on her hair and makeup when there was a knock on the door. Rose went to answer it and her giggle told Celeste all she needed to know. Her baby sister's crush on the groom made her giggle incessantly whenever she was in the same room as Charlie.

Evelyn raised an eyebrow at Celeste, then ushered Rose out of the room to leave bride and groom alone.

"Celeste." He was staring at her as if he'd never seen her before. "You're beautiful."

She knew she was pretty at best. But around Charlie, when she saw herself through his eyes, she believed what he'd said.

A teasing smile on her face, she moved toward him in her wedding gown. "Don't you know it's bad luck for the groom to see the bride before the ceremony?"

But he didn't tease her back. "My luck changed the moment I set eyes on you, sweetheart." His arms came around her then and she barely had a chance to whisper, "Mine too," before he was kissing her with all the love in his heart...and she was kissing him back with just as much, if not more.

As she said "I do," Celeste realized that although she'd never felt incomplete, Charlie had completed her just the same.

At the same time, she savored every moment of their wedding night, from the sweet kisses Charlie ran all across her skin to his whispered words of love. Her mother and then Evelyn had both pulled her aside to warn her of what was expected in the wedding bed. She'd let them play their caring roles, never once telling them that she'd read enough books over the years to be well prepared to be naked with the man who held her heart.

And yet, nothing could have prepared her for Charlie. Not just the exquisite pleasure that he gave her on their wedding night, but for the depth of love in his eyes every time he looked at her.

When he finally stopped caressing and kissing her long enough for her to fall asleep in his arms, the last thing she heard around the beating of his heart beneath her ear was his low voice saying, "You'll have my heart forever."

Perfectly warm in the comfort of his arms, she fell into a dreamless sleep. She didn't need her old dreams anymore.

She and Charlie would make new ones together.

But as the dark of night turned into dawn, the warmth leached out of the bed, out of the room.

Out of Celeste.

Because she had woken up alone.

And Charlie was gone.

Rebecca's teacup clattered onto her saucer.

Not knowing enough about Celeste's past to know whether Charlie had come back or not, before she could ask, Celeste said, "Would you mind helping me clean this up, Rebecca?"

She flexed her fingers slowly, and Rebecca immediately worried that spending so much time out in the cold throwing pebbles had flared up Celeste's arthritis.

"Absolutely," she said, reluctantly accepting that she'd heard all she was going to from Celeste today.

It wasn't until Celeste was curled up on her couch under a warm blanket with a book and Rebecca was halfway back to the inn that a connection occurred to her: Had Celeste and Charlie celebrated their wedding night in her bedroom? And if so, could that be why it always felt so cold?

Rebecca longed to turn back and ask Celeste those questions, but she felt that she'd worn the lovely woman out enough already.

And the questions would certainly keep.

Because Rebecca had a feeling that if there really was a ghost haunting the inn, he or she wasn't going anywhere.

Chapter Eleven

It was all about holding focus.

Over the past weeks, Rebecca could have easily gone off the rails. First, when she realized her relationship with Stu was nothing but a lie. Next, when he left her to not only deal with keeping his secret but also with running the inn and putting on the maple festival all by her lonesome.

And then, of course, when big brother came in to survey all that was—shockingly—also his.

The thing was, she wasn't at all sure that she was sorry any of it had happened. Not when she'd learned something about herself in the midst of potential disaster: namely, that she was much tougher than she'd ever given herself credit for.

What's more, she had almost figured out how to turn twenty-four hours into twenty-five. Almost, but not quite, unfortunately. Which was why she was multitasking like crazy, having just finished dealing with inn business and turning over to final festival details while she manned the check-in desk.

Sean was bound to show up any minute and she could already see the expression bound to land on his face if he saw her festival papers spread out all over the place again.

Well, there was nothing he could do about it. She and Stu had agreed that putting on this festival would be a great thing for the inn. Regardless of what Sean had said to her in her bedroom last night, she had no intention of backing down.

Just as she had no intention whatsoever of ever acknowledging the attraction that had jumped between them in their half-dressed states as moonlight poured into her bedroom.

A gust of cold air blew in through the inn's front door and she looked up with a smile. A smile that didn't waver even when she saw who was coming in through the entrance.

She'd never had anything against Mr. Radin. Not until he'd stood up at that town hall meeting last fall and tried to tear Andi apart. Yes, people were entitled to their opinions about building codes in the Adirondacks, but it was the way he went after her friend that was truly horrible. He'd invoked her dead father's name, told Andi that he'd be ashamed of what his daughter was doing to his beloved town.

Rebecca had always forgiven too quickly. More than once, being able to hold a grudge might have helped her steer clear of personal disaster. But she still hadn't managed to forgive Mr. Radin for hurting her friend.

"Are you the person responsible for this Tapping of the Maples Festival?"

A warning bell went off in her head. He'd looked much the same that day at the town hall meeting.

"Yes. I'd be happy to answer any questions you might have about it."

He slapped down a thick folder. "You can't drill into Adirondack Park trees without the proper permissions. I've filed a halt petition with the preservation council."

Rebecca felt her mouth fall open, but at that moment she was powerless to close it. She stared at the papers, not wanting to touch them.

"I checked everything out with the park's agency before I started putting the festival together."

"The young pups at the agency haven't read the park codes any better than you have. The Adirondack Park is preserved for a reason, so that people like you can't come here from the big city and rape our trees."

Rebecca wasn't the kind of person who called people out on things as a rule. But some things were uncalled for.

"How dare you make some sort of claim that I'm trying to destroy the forest."

"We don't need more buildings and machines and people ruining our land. You're no better than that friend of yours with her condos."

She was glad for the anger that shot through her, if only because of the energy it gave her to stand up to this bully.

"You could have come and talked to me first, before filing this petition," she told him. "You should have given me a chance to address your concerns before escalating things to such a high level."

It had never occurred to her that someone would come in and try to stop her from putting on a small spring festival.

"All that talk just gets in the way of what needs to be done. I believe in taking action first."

She had to bite her tongue to point out how well that had gone for him. He was alone, grumpy, with virtually no friends in a small town that thrived on interpersonal connections.

"The festival is in two weeks, Mr. Radin," she said as calmly as she could. "Everything is in place with vendors. People have already made their plans to attend the festival and have booked rooms at the inn and all of the local B and Bs. Pulling the festival now would be a headache and a heartache for more than just me." She hated begging for things, but her festival was more important than her pride. "Please reconsider this petition. I'm not the only one who will benefit from this festival. It's not just going to be good for the inn. This entire community will reap the rewards of it. And I will personally make sure that none of the trees are harmed in the process."

When he didn't reply for a long while, a small flicker of hope rose up in her chest. Maybe the miracle of miracles was going to happen and he was going to be reasonable for once. Maybe, just maybe, he was going to think about someone other than himself.

"The preservation council will make certain of that," he said smugly.

The real shock didn't set in until he left, her festival spreadsheets still lying on the counter top.

Having no other choice, she picked up the petition and started reading.

Across the lake, Elizabeth and Bill were down on their hands and knees in opposite corners of their bedroom. He was sanding by hand while she worked to carefully finish the already sanded planks with a paintbrush.

Honestly, even though she'd practically had to beg Bill to let her help him with the bedroom floors, Elizabeth had never cared for work like this. Painstaking, patience-bending work had always been Bill's forte. Like his mother, he wasn't one to be rushed, and Elizabeth knew that was why his construction work was in such high demand. Elizabeth, on the other hand, liked seeing something go from idea to hear-and-see-and-touch reality as quickly as possible.

That was why she was so good at graphic design. There was a clear start and end to every project and loose ends didn't dangle forever. She heard what her clients wanted from a design, got a fairly clear image in her head, put it down on paper (now the computer, which she liked more than she'd expected), and then it was on to the next project. She supposed Bill's job wasn't all that different, but the day-to-day held so many tiny little details that everything hinged upon, and one big house around the lake could take him a year to see through from start to finish. She shivered at the thought of having to work on something for that long.

Still, she'd wanted—needed—to be in the bedroom with Bill, on the floor with a paintbrush, listening to the steady scratch of sandpaper. She dearly hoped working together on something they'd both wanted would bring them closer together. That they'd lie in bed when it was done and know that they could still be a team.

Perhaps it didn't make any sense to tie house renovation to a marriage, but their relationship felt so shaky lately that it scared her.

It wasn't just the thought of Bill slipping away that frightened her. It was all the thoughts that surrounded it. The thoughts she couldn't control, ones that had nothing to do with love and everything to do with irritation and annoyance.

Funny the things one didn't realize about someone when one was still in the first flush of new love. She'd loved how considerate Bill was, how seriously he thought about everything she asked him, rather than just giving her whatever answer she wanted to hear, like most men would. And if his mother, Celeste, drove her a little crazy in those early years, with the way she never seemed to answer a question directly, or even give a full answer until she was good and ready (which could take weeks, depending on the question), Elizabeth was content to know that her son was different.

But more and more, she'd come to see just how similar they were. Stu was like that, too, but he was her baby and therefore exempt from the rules Elizabeth expected everyone else to live by.

Whether he realized it or not, Sean was the most like her. She was glad he was coming to dinner tonight. She was making his favorite meal, pork loin and butternut squash. She looked down at her watch and saw that it was time to pull the cherry pie out of the oven.

Her back was stiff as she began to stand up. Before she could prevent it from happening, the can tipped over and lacquer poured out all over the boards Bill had worked so hard to sand to perfection.

She bent down to grab the can, but as she did so she accidentally stepped into a puddle of goo that had slid by her shoe. Slipping, she managed to catch herself on her palms before she could go down on a hip, thank god, but that was about the only good thing she could say about the whole situation.

"Betsy!"

Her husband was there before she could get her breath back. He had his hands on her, running them down her arms, checking for places she might be hurt.

It felt so good to be touched by him. When was the last time she'd felt his warmth? When was the last time she hadn't pushed him away because she was tired or grumpy or just plain preoccupied with something else?

"Does anything hurt?"

Just her pride. But she couldn't admit that, not even to her husband. Especially not to him, it seemed.

"No. I don't think so." She started to get up, but his hands were firm, holding her right where she was. A strange thrill shot through her at the proof of his strength, something she'd somehow forgotten, just as she'd forgotten his warmth.

"Stay put for a little while. Give your body a chance to recover from the fall." He finally looked from her to the mess she'd caused. The huge mess. "Well, that's something, isn't it?"

It was pure instinct for her to bristle, even though he hadn't outright blamed her for screwing up. She could hear it in his voice, the resignation that letting her help had been a bad idea right from the start.

"I didn't do it on purpose."

He didn't look at her, just shook his head. "I didn't say you did."

"But you were thinking it."

His chest filled with a deep breath, one that he let out before he said, "No, although I thought I was pretty clear about needing to close the containers before you went anywhere."

"What was I thinking? I should have known working together would be a bad idea." She pushed out of his arms, getting to her feet as fast as she could in the glop that covered her.

Bill was up on his feet just as fast. "Don't try and turn this around on me, Elizabeth." The moment where he'd slipped and called her Betsy like he used to was clearly long gone. "You're the one who's been pushing me to do the floors. You're the one who demanded to help. If you'd just let me do it the way I planned, none of this would have happened."

"You know what? We never should have started this renovation. We never should have tried to pretty up the past and make it look new again." Words flew from her mouth, one after the other. "You can't sand down and refinish something that's fundamentally broken and expect it to be like new again. To go back to the way it used to be."

It wasn't until she was done that she realized she'd said too much. Far more than she'd ever meant to say. Perhaps if she was more measured, like Celeste, she could have stopped herself in time, but Elizabeth had always been trigger-happy.

Unfortunately, this time she was very much afraid that she was holding the gun up to her marriage.

How many years had he tried to stay away from this conversation? Bill had loved Elizabeth so much that he couldn't let himself imagine a life without her.

More and more often he had to wonder if he'd been wrong.

If only they hadn't started this renovation. If only he'd

continued to put off fixing up their own home, especially their bedroom.

For years she'd been on him to redo the floors, but he'd always told her the same thing: that he didn't feel comfortable turning away business, especially as they got closer to retirement age and his body showed more signs of wearing out beneath the stress of hammers and electric saws and squatting in awkward positions.

But those had been only superficial reasons. In truth—and it was a truth he wasn't particularly comfortable admitting to himself—he'd been worried about spending so many hours in the house with Elizabeth. They seemed to manage best with evenings and weekends.

He should have been less surprised to see all of his fears had become reality, but he'd been practicing denial for so long that actually facing reality was a bigger job than hauling a hundred yards of dirt out of a muddy hole in the ground.

He could smell smoke and it was pure relief to leave the bedroom and rush down into the kitchen, even when he saw black smoke pouring out of the oven.

"Oh no, my pie!" Elizabeth tried to push past him to get to it.

He caught her arm before she could open the oven and burn herself with the steam that was itching to escape.

"Let me go!"

She was talking about the oven and her burned pie, but he had to wonder if "Let me go" was what she'd really been saying to him all these years. Only he hadn't wanted to listen.

"I can't let you burn yourself."

It didn't matter that he was angry with her, that she'd

hurt him deeper than she ever had before with what she'd just said up in their bedroom.

He simply couldn't stand the thought of Elizabeth ever being hurt.

Her eyes cleared and she stepped back. "You're right."

When she'd backed up out of the way of the smoke, Bill slowly, carefully, stood to the side of the oven and opened it. Just as he'd expected, sizzling hot smoke flew out of it.

The pie was a black lump of coal on the middle rack.

Elizabeth was opening windows to let out the smoke, but Bill knew the smell would linger long after this afternoon. Just as the words that had been laid between them would remain.

"If I start right now, I can probably get another pie made before Sean comes for dinner."

"I don't think dinner with Sean tonight is such a good idea."

"He's our son. We can't let our problems get in the way of finally getting a chance to sit down with him for a few hours tonight."

Damn it. She was right. He'd missed his son a great deal these past years that Sean had been out traveling the world making deals.

"Then you'd better make the pie. I'll go clean up upstairs and see if anything can be salvaged."

She winced at his words, even though he would have sworn he'd been talking about the floors and nothing else.

But he'd never been comfortable telling lies. Which would account for the unease that had been building up inside of him for so many years.

Because hadn't he been lying to himself about his marriage for nearly twenty years?

He wasn't a man who spoke without thinking. He needed some time to process what Elizabeth had said, to turn it around in his head and look at it from all angles. Most of all, he needed time to force himself to consider the reality of thirty-six years of marriage coming to an end.

"I'll put a bottle of paint thinner in the shower for you just in case the finish doesn't wash right off." Despite his efforts to the contrary, his voice was strained, rough around the edges where emotion was tearing away at him.

"Bill…"

He wasn't used to hearing a plea in her voice and that was what made him stop halfway out of the kitchen and turn around.

Elizabeth was the strongest person he knew. Even stronger than his mother. But now, for the first time in a very long time, she looked like she was about to break. Any other time, he would have been there holding her, caring for her.

"I didn't—" She paused to wipe away a tear falling down her cheek. "What I said upstairs, I didn't mean it."

But they both knew she had. That she still did. They'd been limping along half-broken for too long.

Knowing he was going to regret it, but unable to stop himself, he said, "Do you know why I finally decided to refinish the floors?"

His wife—still lovely after thirty-six years, so beautiful that she was still turning other men's heads at fifty—blinked at him from her post by the window. "Why?"

"Because I was hoping fixing the floors might fix us."

"Oh, Bill, I—"

He held up both hands to stop her. "But you're exactly right. Shiny new floorboards aren't going to heal what's broken between us. Not when one little mistake means having to rip them up and throw them away."

"What are you saying?" Her mouth was trembling and although there were no more tears rolling down her cheeks, her eyes were bright with them.

"I don't know yet, Elizabeth. I don't know. Let's have dinner with Sean tonight and take it from there."

"Okay."

But it wasn't.

Chapter Twelve

After a flurry of check-ins where she'd mentally been only half there while dealing with the inn's guests, Rebecca was finally alone at the front desk again.

She was surprised that Sean hadn't shown his face yet. Was he avoiding her after the weird day they'd had? Between Mark showing up and the strange sounds in her bedroom and then their almost-fight about her past... well, she supposed she wouldn't blame him for keeping his distance. Heck, wasn't that exactly what she'd told herself she was going to do?

In any case, she had plenty of other things to worry about besides Sean. She picked up Mr. Radin's petition and thumbed through it again, but she shouldn't have bothered. She already knew what it said by heart.

She was going to have to cancel the festival.

The Adirondack Preservation Council hadn't made a judgment against the festival. But the petition, at this point, was enough to put a halt to the proceedings until the council reviewed all of the arguments for both sides along with the current park policies.

And the next formal review session wasn't for three weeks...one full week after the Tapping of the Maples Festival should have already taken place.

She'd been trying to push away her broken heart over losing something that had meant so much to her personally all morning and afternoon. But given how absentminded she'd been as she'd checked in guests, making mistakes she'd never made before, like mixing up keys and forgetting names, she clearly hadn't been doing a good job of it.

All these weeks she'd thought she was doing such a good job of holding it together. Heck, hadn't she just been so proud of how strong she was becoming?

Right now she felt anything but strong.

Barely twelve hours ago Sean had pointed out—yet again—that she was being pulled in more directions than she could handle. She'd argued with him then, knowing how close she was to pulling off the festival, that there were only a few last-minute details to attend to.

But trying to convince the Adirondack Preservation Council to push her festival forward was way more than a last-minute detail.

It figured that Sean would finally make his appearance when she was feeling lower than low.

Frustration with Mr. Radin and his stupid petition, with Stu for leaving her to deal with everything alone, and with Sean for making her feel things she had no business feeling had her opening her mouth and throwing out a sarcastic "Guess what?"

Sean raised an eyebrow at her sharp tone as he put a tray down on the counter. She hadn't noticed that he was carrying a tray with cookies and two cups of coffee.

While she didn't need him to make sure she stayed fed and hydrated, she couldn't deny that there was something sweet about the way he always did it anyway.

"You'll be pleased to hear that the festival is off."

He frowned. "What are you talking about?"

She slid the petition across the counter. "This."

He looked at it with an incredulous expression. "There's a petition? Against your festival?"

"Growing up here, I'm sure you remember Mr. Radin."

He thought about it for a moment. "Wait a minute, is he the bored old man who likes to try to stir up trouble?"

She touched the tip of her nose with her index finger. "Bingo! He's filed a petition against my festival with the Adirondack Preservation Council." She pointed to the bound papers. "It's all right there in black and white."

He began to flip through the bound pages. "I can't believe he'd do this." He shifted his gaze from the papers back to her. "What are you going to do about it?"

She shrugged, all the fight from the previous night knocked out of her. It was time to be practical, rather than to try to hold onto the festival out of emotion, simply because she'd been so proud of what she'd done all by herself.

"In order to fight the petition I need to present my case at the next council meeting in three weeks. Even if the meeting had been early enough to attend before the festival date, it would probably be a full-time job to comb through all of the rules and regulations in the hopes of convincing the council." She couldn't read his expression as she continued with, "You were right last night. I can do only so much."

She reached out for a cookie as if their conversation

was no big deal, but the tremble in her hands gave her away, and she snatched her hand back before she touched the chocolate chip cookie. She couldn't have choked it down in any case.

She hoped he hadn't noticed the way she was falling apart, one little piece at a time. But Sean hadn't taken his eyes off her.

And she already knew that he noticed everything.

Finally, he said, "You didn't seem to think I was right last night."

Why was he pushing her? Why couldn't he just take his victory?

Instead of replying, she took a deep breath and said, "A contractor will be out soon to look at the pipes and roof."

It was clear that he knew she was changing the subject on purpose. She barely managed to hold his gaze when all she wanted to do was run up the stairs and feel sorry for herself. But she had a job to do running the inn.

She wasn't going to lose that too just because everything else had fallen apart.

After several long beats, he responded, "Good."

Still not wanting to talk about Mr. Radin or the petition or her now-lost festival, she said, "I've heard that they used to tell ghost stories about the inn. Do you remember any from when you were a kid?"

He almost smiled at that, and she longed—foolishly—to see him smile again. Just one more time.

"A few. When we were kids we used to scare each other around the campfire by sneaking up on each other and pretending to be the ghost."

She shouldn't have been able to picture Sean as a young boy playing pranks on his friends, but strangely she could.

"I just can't stop thinking about where those noises could have come from," she said, "and why my bedroom is always so cold." Except for last night, of course, when Sean had been there with her.

"You don't think there's a ghost in your bedroom, do you?"

Great, all she needed was for her boss to think she was losing her mind. She should have known better than to bring up the old ghost stories with him. Here's what she should do: she should open up her mouth and say, *"No, I don't think there's a ghost in my bedroom. How ridiculous."*

Of course, her horrible propensity of not being able to tell a lie had her shutting her mouth on the word *no* and saying, in its place, "What else do you think could be making my bedroom so cold? What else could be making those noises?

"Ghosts don't exist, Rebecca. But maybe you should move into another room until we resolve the issue."

"The inn is booked solid for the next week."

"In that case, I'll find another place to stay and you can use my suite."

But even though it might have made some sense for her to sleep in a quiet, warm bedroom, everything in Rebecca protested the thought of willingly leaving her rooms. She had the sense that it was a slippery slope. First, she'd be out of her suite. Next, she'd be out of the inn altogether, finding another innkeeper job in another small town.

And she'd never see Sean again.

The thought shocked her enough that she backed away from him and tripped over a box of fliers UPS had delivered an hour ago for her festival.

She didn't know how Sean got around the counter so fast, but his arms were holding her before she could knock her head onto something sharp and hard.

"Careful."

Any other time she would have jumped out of his arms and made sure that there was at least a handful of feet between them. But she was cold all over and his warmth was irresistible.

"I shouldn't have left the box there."

His eyes had shifted to her mouth as she spoke. "No, you shouldn't have," he agreed, but there was no censure to his words.

Neither of them said anything more, just as neither of them made a move to pull apart.

Suddenly, it all felt so inevitable, the kiss that was finally going to happen, and she didn't know why she'd even bothered to fight it for so long. Wasn't her life already a runaway train? Who did she think she was, trying to stop it before it hit a brick wall? Hadn't she learned yet that the train she was on always hit the wall eventually?

Sean's eyes grew even darker as he leaned in closer and she could almost taste his lips when the phone rang, loud and jarring enough for them to break apart so quickly that she almost tripped again.

She picked it up with a shaking hand. "Emerald Lake Inn."

Oh god, was that her voice, all breathy... and disappointed at losing out on a kiss she'd wanted so badly... but knew better than to take?

In any case, hearing Sean's mother's voice broke the spell that had been weaving itself around her and Sean so successfully that it was frankly impossible to dwell on how much she'd wanted Sean to kiss her just seconds ago.

"Yes, Elizabeth, he's right here."

She held out the phone and it shouldn't have mattered that Sean's fingertips brushed against her knuckles as he took it from her, but her body didn't seem to understand that.

It mattered.

"Hello."

She couldn't help but notice, just as she did every time she'd witnessed Sean interact with his mother, how still he became. As if he had to be prepared for disaster every second.

"Yes, I'll be there for dinner at six p.m. Will there be enough for one more?"

Jealousy lit through Rebecca so swiftly it almost buckled her already weak knees. Here she'd thought he was going to kiss her—that he'd wanted that kiss just as much as she did—when all along he had plans to go to dinner at his parents' house with another woman.

If hovering on the verge of believing in ghosts wasn't proof enough that she was off her rocker, the fact that she'd actually thought of Sean's dinner date as "another woman" was enough to make her certifiably loony.

Sean could see whomever he wanted to. He could kiss every last single woman in Emerald Lake for all it mattered to her. And the only reason she felt like she was going to cry was because it had been a hell of a day on top of a hell of a month.

Lie.

Lie.

Big fat lie.

And she hadn't thought she was actually capable of telling lies.

Good one. Where Sean was concerned, she was becoming a master at it with all of her "I won't fall for him" and "I'm going to be practical and stay strong" nonsense.

Truth: her foolish heart was already on the line.

Truth: Sean was sure to break it.

Truth: the mess of her life was only getting messier with every passing second.

A moment later Sean put the phone down. "Alice will be here at five p.m.?"

Rebecca nodded, not trusting her voice right that second. She didn't look up from the pile of bills she'd already gone through earlier, not trusting her face to do anything but give her jealousy away. Or her resignation over what she was feeling for Sean.

"Good. Because I'd like you to come to dinner at my parents."

Shock had her swinging her head around to him so fast that several strands of hair flew into her mouth and got caught on her tongue.

How was it that she always made herself look even more pathetic than she already was? It had to be her true gift. Especially when she was around gorgeous, perfect men like Sean.

"Me? You want me to come to dinner? With you?" Stop. She needed to stop babbling out questions. And still the words "Why would you want me to come with you?" slithered out.

"I think you could use something to take your mind off the festival. And"—she was surprised to see that hint of a smile on his lips again—"it's the only way I can guarantee that you'll actually eat something rather than work through your next meal."

For all that she was telling her heart to stop fluttering at his almost-smile, at his teasing, her mind couldn't deny how surprisingly sweet he was being. Sure, he'd come running to her rescue last night when they'd heard the horrible wailing. Still, they were so frequently at odds. Over her holding Stu's secret. And over the festival.

Wanting to go to dinner with him more than she should have, especially given that Elizabeth was far from her biggest fan, she said, "I thought you'd be happy about the festival being off."

"I honestly don't know what to think about it right now."

He never lies.

The thought hit her right between the eyes.

So many men had lied to her over the years—even Stu, by withholding the truth of who he really was—that she'd given up hope of finding one who didn't.

"I don't like the way Radin went about this, Rebecca. He should have come to you first, been upfront about his concerns, rather than weaseling in some loophole in the park's policies."

"That's what I told him."

His eyes lit up. "I would have liked to have seen that."

He almost sounded proud of her and her heart warmed despite herself. Even though he'd made it clear that he didn't want her to work on the festival, any more than Mr. Radin wanted it to take place.

She looked at the antique clock on the wall. Alice would be here any minute. The last thing Rebecca wanted was for the girl to witness this awkwardness between her and Sean. God forbid she read something into it.

"I really appreciate the invitation to dinner, but—"

"Please."

The one word had the rest of her sentence falling away.

God, she was such a sucker for a beautifully masculine face. For the heat she could feel coming at her from across the counter. And especially for the need she saw in his eyes, a need that held hints of desire, but was far more about the mysterious darkness she'd read in Sean practically from the first moment she'd met him.

Tonight. She could give him tonight. Besides, she'd been to dinner at his parents' house plenty of times before. It was no big deal.

"Okay."

He didn't smile, but she swore relief moved across his face. And as he left her with the agreement that they'd meet downstairs at five forty-five p.m., Rebecca knew one thing with absolute certainty: she was a fool.

Quite possibly the world's biggest fool.

Chapter Thirteen

You look beautiful."

Rebecca's heart, which was already beating too fast, jumped so hard behind her breastbone she was afraid Sean would see the front of her dress thumping to its beat.

She knew it wasn't a date, and had eaten plenty of meals with his parents, but that didn't mean she was any less nervous. The whole time she'd been trying on one outfit after another upstairs, she'd known she was being ridiculous. It didn't matter what she looked like tonight. But still, she ended up settling on a long-sleeved knitted dress and tights, and even put the blow dryer and her makeup bag through their paces.

Not sure she should trust her voice not to give away how nervous she was, she simply smiled her thanks. That silence lasted through the drive to his parents' house, and was only broken when they got to the front door.

Sean turned to her. "Thank you for being here with me tonight. Doing this alone would have been—" He shook his head. "Hard. Really hard."

Did he have any idea how much it meant to her that he

appreciated her coming tonight, even before they set foot inside?

"You're welcome," she said softly, wanting to reach out to take his hand and give it a squeeze. If he were any of her other friends, she would have. Only, she wasn't sure what they were, if friends was the right word for what was beginning to happen between them. "Just kick me under the table when you're ready to go, okay?"

She was rewarded with one of his rare smiles, one full of surprise and something else that wasn't quite as easy to define.

She shouldn't care if he liked her. She shouldn't hope that she could make him smile again.

But she did.

He was finally making a move to ring the doorbell when the door opened.

"Sean, what are you doing standing out here in the cold?" His mother registered Rebecca's presence a moment later as she stepped into the light. "Rebecca?" Elizabeth shot a confused glance at her son before quickly saying, "Come in you two."

Sean's father was far more welcoming. "Rebecca, what a nice surprise. I'm so glad you could join us tonight."

Rebecca managed a smile for Bill and let him take her coat. She could feel Sean's eyes on her, could practically hear him worrying that he'd brought her into the lion's den.

But these weren't her parents. They were his. And he clearly had problems with them, big enough that he'd needed to bring her here as a buffer.

Knowing exactly what it was like to need someone at her side to help her out, she shot him a brilliant smile along with the silent message not to worry about her. He looked like he wanted to pull her outside again to say something more to her, but then he was looking around the kitchen.

"Is something on fire in here?"

Rebecca sniffed the air. There was a distinct odor of smoke, but everything in the house looked okay.

"No," his mother said in a clipped voice.

"Your mother burned the first pie she made."

Elizabeth shot Bill a furious glance before saying, "I didn't hear the timer. It was a simple accident."

"I wasn't implying anything else," Bill said. But his curt tone said that he had.

"Well," Sean's mother said with a clearly forced smile that was all teeth with no real joy attached to it, "the second one I made looks much better."

Rebecca had never seen Elizabeth and Bill act like this with each other. Sniping and going out of their way not to touch as they moved around the kitchen getting her and Sean drinks. Things were so obviously strained between them that it was all Rebecca could do not to hold her face in a permanent wince.

A few minutes later, they sat down to a delicious-looking meal. The only problem was, her stomach wasn't exactly relaxed. It wasn't even Bill and Elizabeth who were making her nervous.

It was sitting so close to Sean that was twisting her insides up in knots.

She hoped that if she ate slowly no one would notice that she wasn't exactly mowing through her food.

Elizabeth turned to Sean. "How is your business doing, honey?"

"I sold it."

His mother's fork clattered on her plate and his father cleared his throat in surprise. "You did? When?"

"Just before I arrived in town."

"Why would you sell your business? You were so good at venture capital."

Bill didn't give his son a chance to answer before saying, "Maybe he was ready to move on, Elizabeth."

Rebecca swore she saw moisture flood the other woman's eyes.

Oh my god, what was going on here? Were Elizabeth and Bill having problems? She knew Stu's disappearance was difficult for them, but she'd assumed that it would draw them closer together.

Looked like she'd been wrong about that, too.

"I have a few other ideas I'm toying with," Sean said. "Rebecca has been teaching me the ropes at the inn."

Recovered now, Elizabeth said, "It's so nice of you to help out your brother with his inn while he's away."

Almost choking on her food, Rebecca couldn't stop herself from turning to look at Sean, a silent *Do they know?* passing between them.

He shook his head and she raised an eyebrow. *Come on, that's ridiculous. Why not?*

They stared at each other across the table for a long moment before he put down his fork. "When Stu decided to buy the inn, I made an investment in it, as well. I own half of it, actually."

"*You* own half of the inn?"

Sean nodded. "I do."

Elizabeth's face creased into a humongous smile. "That's the best news I've heard in a very long time, honey. I hope this means you're going to be staying here with all of us from now on."

Oh. Now Rebecca got why Sean hadn't told them. He didn't want to be pressured to stay in Emerald Lake.

"We'll see," was all he said.

Elizabeth's smile fell and she opened her mouth to say something more, but before she could, Bill interjected, "I agree that's great news, son. As for whatever you do next, we're behind you every step of the way."

The thing was, for maybe the first time ever, Rebecca actually was on Elizabeth's side.

Even though she knew better, even though she knew the odds were almost nil against it happening, she wanted Sean to stay.

And the way things were going with her foolish heart, odds were his mother's heart wasn't the only one that would be broken when he left.

Bill cleared his throat, looking a little nervous. "Actually, Sean, if you've got any free time, now that we've had what looks to be our last snowstorm of the year and the ice is melting fast, I was thinking about climbing the high peak in a few days."

Rebecca didn't see how it was possible for Sean to have anything against his father. Bill was a very, very sweet man. And yet Sean didn't exactly jump at the clear offer to spend time together.

"I'll have to see how my schedule looks."

Oh, the disappointment on his father's face was hard to witness.

Reluctantly giving up on his reticent son, Bill said, "How's the festival coming along, Rebecca?"

Rebecca should have known the question was coming.

After all, she'd been talking incessantly about her Tapping of the Maples Festival to anyone who would listen for a while.

"It was coming along fine, but—"

She wasn't at all sure how she should put things. Even though Mr. Radin had totally overstepped his boundaries, even though she thought he was a big fat jerk, she would never say anything nasty about him.

In lieu of pointing fingers, she opened her mouth to say something about park regulations cropping up, when Sean smoothly said, "We're currently dealing with some Adirondack Park regulations."

Rebecca lost sight of everything but the *we* at the beginning of the sentence. How many times had Sean told her to drop the festival altogether? She knew he wasn't happy about what Mr. Radin had done, but she thought he'd be happy with the result. No festival. No pull on her time and focus.

But Sean had just said *we*. As if they were a team.

"Is there some sort of problem?" Bill sounded concerned.

"Stu said everything was going well," Elizabeth added. "Before he left, in any case."

Ah, there was so much to Elizabeth's statements. First, that she'd never actually directly asked Rebecca any questions about the festival, had always gone through Stu. And, of course, there was a world of blame in those three words—*before he left*. Clearly the implication was that Rebecca not only was a master at driving away Elizabeth's sons, but she couldn't manage to keep her festival on track without Stu to guide her.

Rebecca's stomach cramped around the few bites of the delicious pork loin she'd eaten.

Yet again, it would have really come in handy to know how to lie, or to brush things under the rug. But she didn't have the first clue about how to do either of those things.

"I have to cancel the festival."

"Why?"

"It's a bit complicated." Sean's eyes were on her, dark and clearly concerned as she said, "It looks like there might be some problems with Adirondack Park rules and the preservation council."

"But you've worked so hard on it." Bill shook his head. "Is it anything I can help you with?"

"Can I get back to you on that?"

"Of course, Rebecca."

She thought some sort of silent message passed between father and son, then, but she was too mortified by having to admit her own failure with the festival to do much more than stare pointedly at her plate.

She was just about to ask if she could help clear the dishes when Elizabeth suddenly said, "I still don't understand what happened with Stu."

Everyone at the table went perfectly still. Rebecca wasn't actually sure any of them were breathing anymore. Especially her.

Funny how she kept thinking things were as bad as they were going to get.

And then they got worse.

"Someone doesn't just pack up and leave like that. Was there a fight? Did something happen that you haven't told any of us?"

With each word out of Elizabeth's mouth, Rebecca's face grew hotter and hotter. How could she possibly continue keeping Stu's secret under direct scrutiny?

God, she hated keeping something so important from his family. From his own mother. Especially when she knew how worried her mother would be if she disappeared one day, leaving nothing behind but a note.

"What happened between them is between them," Sean told his mother. "It's none of our business."

Rebecca didn't even come close to masking her surprise. Not only had Sean stood up for her, but he'd said more in that one sentence than he had to his parents all night long up to that point.

"He's my son," Elizabeth protested. "He's your brother. Don't you even care what's happening to him?"

Sean pushed his chair back. "I didn't ask Rebecca to join us for dinner tonight so that you could harass her and make veiled accusations. My mistake."

Rebecca was caught between Sean and his mother. She looked at Bill for help, but, clearly, he was just as stuck as she was.

No, she thought a split second later. The situation was far worse for him. This was his wife, his son, who couldn't get along. Who couldn't see eye to eye. Who could barely hold a civil conversation.

"Thanks for dinner," he said stiffly. "Are you ready to leave, Rebecca?"

She realized she had to make a choice. To stay with the Murphys. Or to go with Sean. The Murphys lived permanently in town and disappointing them would have long-term ramifications. Whereas Sean was planning to stay for only a little while.

Which was why it made no sense that she allowed him to pull her chair all the way back.

It made no sense to choose Sean.

But she couldn't have made any other choice. Not when he'd come to mean something to her in the past days they'd spent together. The little sweet things he did so unconsciously. The way he looked at her, with more heat than she'd ever known before. Plus, he'd defended her in front of his mother, had stepped in front of an out-of-control truck for her.

"Sean."

Bill's voice had both Sean and Rebecca stopping their progression out of the kitchen.

"Please stay for dessert. Your mother went to all the trouble of baking a second cherry pie after the first burned."

Leaving would be easier. So much easier than staying. But at the same time, Rebecca knew deep in her heart that although Sean desperately wanted to leave his parents' house, if he left like this it would only make things worse between them.

She put her hand on Sean's arm. "I do love cherry pie." She forced herself to hold his gaze, even though she suspected that was the last thing he'd wanted her to say.

Again, everyone was holding their breath. Rebecca was half expecting one of them to turn blue and pass out at this point.

Finally, he said, "Can the inn survive without you for a little longer?"

She didn't just want to squeeze his hand this time. She wanted to pull him down for a kiss. Because he was a good son.

And family meant everything to her.

"Absolutely." She turned to Elizabeth with a smile. "Do you have vanilla ice cream to go with that pie?"

The relief in the other woman's eyes nearly brought tears to Rebecca's own. "I wouldn't serve warm cherry pie without it."

The next twenty minutes were entirely made of small talk about the town, the weather, pro baseball prospects. Finally, they were able to leave without making a scene and they said their good-byes.

As they walked out to the car, Sean deadpanned, "I thought that went well."

His sarcastic comment was completely unexpected. And just what she needed to unravel the tension that had coiled up all of her muscles in his parents' house.

And for the first time all night—in days, possibly even weeks—Rebecca truly laughed, hard enough that tears came.

So many times she'd been on the verge of tears over the past weeks, but she hadn't let them fall. Until now.

All because Sean had made her laugh.

"Did you see that?"

Elizabeth was standing at the kitchen sink trying to wash dishes but her hands were shaking so hard a plate knocked into the porcelain and almost broke.

Bill saw the steam rising up and hurried over from the table that he was clearing to pull the faucet down and shut. "Jesus, you're going to burn yourself!"

But Elizabeth felt numb. Too numb to notice a little hot water.

"There's something going on between them." She turned away from the window where she was staring at the black night over the lake and looked at her husband. "Didn't you see it?"

"See what?"

There was annoyance in her husband's voice. He never used to talk to her like that. Even though she'd likely deserved it many, many times before now.

Only, couldn't he see how scared she was now? Couldn't he see how much she needed his support, more than she ever had before?

She knew she was irritable. She knew that she could be bossy. But she also knew that she'd never love anyone the way she loved Bill.

She used to think it was true for him, too. But now... well, she wasn't so sure anymore about that.

For twenty years she'd worked to convince herself that she wasn't afraid anymore of her horrible mistake coming to light. But then Stu disappeared and Sean reappeared and suddenly it felt like twenty years had been pulled away.

Leaving her just as scared as she once had been.

But she didn't want to think about her and Bill right now, couldn't possibly focus on the two of them, not when she'd witnessed something she'd never thought would come to pass in a million years.

Sean.

Rebecca.

Falling for each other.

Sure, like everyone else, Elizabeth thought the young woman was nice and did a good job running the inn. But Stu was gone. And as a mother, Elizabeth believed her younger son likely never would have run if not for Rebecca.

"Didn't you see the way Sean looked at Rebecca at dinner?"

Her voice was shaking now just as much as her hands were. Her skin felt tight and tingly from the hot water and steam that she had left them in for too long already.

"He likes her. Everyone likes her."

She couldn't hold back a snarl. "Are you blind? He could hardly take his eyes off her. And she blushed every single time he spoke to her."

"Fine. So maybe they like each other as more than just friends. What business is it of yours?"

She whirled around from the sink, water and suds flying all over the kitchen floor. "She already drove away one of my sons. I'm not going to let her drive away another. I'm not going to let her ruin their lives one by one."

"Whatever Stu's reasons for leaving, that sweet girl couldn't have driven him away."

"Stop saying how sweet she is!" She was yelling now, long past the point of being rational.

"Damn it, she is sweet. You say I'm the blind one. Now it's time for you to open your eyes. Can't you see that a woman like Rebecca is exactly what Sean needs?"

"You don't think I know what my own son needs?"

"No."

"And you do?"

"Love. He needs love. He needs a woman who will love him no matter what. Regardless of how hard things get. He deserves a woman he can love with his whole heart. A woman he isn't afraid to share anything with."

Oh god, he wasn't talking about Sean and Rebecca anymore.

He was talking about the two of them.

About what they used to have.

And about who they used to be.

Until she went and stupidly ruined everything in one weak and horrible moment that she'd regret for the rest of her life.

"Bill." She needed to tell him. She should have told him twenty years ago. She shouldn't have held it all inside. Because instead of the years making it seem less bad, every single year, every week, every hour had magnified her mistake a thousand times over.

But before she could tell him anything at all, he said, "Stay out of it, Elizabeth. Whatever is going on with Sean and Rebecca, let it be. If they've got something growing between them, it's their business and no one else's."

She knew he was right. She could feel it deep inside her torn-up heart. But the fear had her saying, "She was Stu's fiancée."

"If Stu and Rebecca were meant to be together they would be married right now. You read his letter. He didn't want the marriage any more than she did."

"But it isn't right for her to be with his brother. What will people think?"

"Hopefully, they'll think they're a beautiful couple. Hopefully, they look at the two of them and see love. Real love. Hopefully, all anyone will want is what's best for Sean and Rebecca."

With that, he got back to work loading the dishwasher and she was so tired, so weak—so scared—all she could do was sit down on a kitchen chair and watch him work.

How had she ever forgotten what a beautiful man her husband was? Thirty-six years after she'd met him, he was still muscular, with a wide chest, broad shoulders, and strong arms and legs. His brown hair was mostly gray now, but it looked great on him. She could see both of her sons in Bill: Sean's build, his hands and serious eyes, Stu's artistry, his ready smile, the way he could get along with absolutely anyone.

She wanted to say so many things to her husband, wanted to tell him how much she loved him, but she could see how angry he was with her. And how she'd only dug the hole between them deeper with her comments about Sean and Rebecca.

There was a time when they could have talked about the women their sons were interested in without fighting about it.

He closed the dishwasher. "Will the sander keep you up?"

"You're not coming to bed?"

"There's a lot of work to do still."

Just yesterday, he might have asked her to come upstairs and help him again. But she'd had her chance.

And she couldn't stand the thought of begging. Of being turned down.

Of knowing for sure that he didn't want her anymore.

She forced herself to stand up, to keep what was left of her pride intact. At least until she left the kitchen.

"Don't worry about me. I'll put my earplugs in."

She went through the motions of getting ready for bed in the guest room on the first floor where they were going to be sleeping while they worked on the master bedroom floor. She lay down on the bed, curling up on her side with her arms around her knees.

Even with her earplugs in she could feel the vibrations from the sander moving through her and was glad that they would keep her awake until Bill came to bed. Until

she could put her arms around him and say she was sorry
without actually having to say the words.

But even after the vibrations stopped, he never came.

And she had never been able to sleep without him in
the bed beside her.

Chapter Fourteen

Sean walked Rebecca upstairs to her door. The laughter had gone a long way to relaxing her, but she suddenly felt as skittish as a teenage girl on her first date.

Even though, as she had to remind herself again and again, no one in their right mind could have even remotely called that tense dinner with Sean's parents a date.

"Thank you for going with me tonight," he said again as they stood outside her door.

His eyes were even darker than usual, his jaw tighter. She wanted to make him laugh the way he'd made her laugh, but she didn't have the words. The smartest thing was just to say, "You're welcome" and go inside her suite and lock the door and be glad that she made it out of the night unscathed, without doing something as truly stupid as throwing her arms around Sean's shoulders and dragging his mouth down to hers for the kiss she'd been tasting in her dreams.

But, then, she couldn't say a word. How could she when she'd just made the mistake of looking up at him and getting lost in his eyes. A short lock of hair had fallen over his forehead and she reached up to brush it away before she could stop herself.

But even that might have been okay if it hadn't been for the slight way he'd turned his jaw into her hand before she forced herself to pull away from him.

He'd needed her already once tonight, as a buffer between him and his parents, and she'd given in to that need.

Now, right here, right now, just steps away from her bedroom, she knew he needed her again—whether he liked it or not, whether he wanted to feel anything for her or not. Only this time he didn't need her because he was the son of a difficult mother.

No, tonight he needed her for all the same reasons she needed him. Heat. Sparks.

Undeniable attraction.

Five seconds...they were less than five seconds from that kiss, and her heart was fluttering like mad. But then his heat was gone as he took a step—a large one—away from her, so that they were both backed up against the hallway walls.

"Don't be afraid to wake me up if you hear any more noises tonight."

Disappointment flared so strong within her at his husky words that she was unable to speak for a moment and simply had to answer with a nod.

"Yes." She cleared her throat. "Sure."

She blindly groped for her doorknob, somehow got her key inside, and said good night.

Rebecca didn't know how to feel. It wasn't a strange state for her. On the contrary, that internal confusion was precisely what got her in trouble all the time. And here she was, on the verge of trouble again.

Yes, Stu was still gone. And she was going to have to start making phone calls to vendors, to let them know the festival was canceled, very shortly. No question, both of those things sucked. Big time.

But surrounding all of that was Sean.

And the way he'd made her laugh.

He wasn't supposed to make her laugh, darn it. She could barricade her heart against the way he was always bringing her treats and continually kept her from knocking her head on something sharp and hard. Even the travel stories he told her, she could convince herself, weren't all that different from the stories that guests would tell.

But that laughter he'd yanked from her after what had to be the most awkward dinner *ever*...how was she supposed to fight the pure joy she'd felt from just being with him?

Stu's friendship had made her happy, but there was never any tingling, none of the heat that she had with Sean.

Amazingly, her bedroom was actually warm—semi-warm, anyway—and although she'd been certain she wouldn't sleep a wink, she got a good six hours.

By the time she woke and ate the bowl of oatmeal Mrs. Higgins had whipped together for her in the kitchen, Jean, another of her part-time assistants, was at the desk. With a few rare hours to herself, Rebecca knew they were hours she would have otherwise put to use organizing the festival.

But she still couldn't bear the thought of making the phone calls to call off the festival quite yet.

The sun was shining and she pulled on a coat, hoping some outside time would settle her down and get her to a place where she could deliver bad news to everyone who had been so excited about tapping the maples.

Rebecca had always been drawn to the maple forest. She'd never seen anything like it before, almost symmetrical rows of large trees. In the fall, the display of colors on the trees had been nothing short of mind-blowing. She hadn't expected the budding leaves of spring to even come close to matching that beauty, but amazingly, a few minutes later as she stood in the middle of the trees, their bare branches reaching out all around her, above her head, into the blue sky, she was overwhelmed by beauty. Growing up in Connecticut, she'd loved being outside, to go to the park or swim at the local pool, but being outside was different here. More as if she was part of nature, rather than just being witness to it.

Four months ago, as fall started to give way to winter, she'd conceived of the Tapping of the Maples Festival on a walk through this forest, as bright leaves fell to the ground all around her. She felt as if she could take root like one of the seedlings between the large trees, that the mature growth would shelter her from storms and let enough light through for her to grow and stretch and become strong.

Sap had been leaking from the trees, even then, and she'd reached out to brush some onto the tip of her finger.

The pure maple syrup had taste like magic. Like happiness.

She'd wanted to share that joy, that sweetness.

She still did. But now, with the petition...

She sighed and leaned against one of the maples, pressing her palm flat against it. Maybe there was a reason for all of this. For Stu leaving and Sean appearing and Mr. Radin trying to stop her festival.

What was it people always said? That when one door closed, a window opened up? That sometimes the best things in life sprang from the most difficult?

She'd always been optimistic. Some might say blindly so, given her track record with jobs and men. These past weeks were certainly doing their best to test that optimism.

Crunching over some pebbles on the way down to the beach, thinking of the way she'd been trying to skip them on the water the previous morning had her smiling in remembrance. But that was before she'd had a clue what was coming down the pike, that Mr. Radin was going to walk in and smash her festival to bits with a stack of official papers.

Her smile fell away, but she bent down and picked up the pebbles anyway. They were cold and smooth in her palm, and as she moved closer and closer to the water, her hand itched with the urge to let them all go, to see them rain down on the patch of blue water that was even bigger this morning.

Summer was coming; she could smell it in the air. And she was glad.

If only her heart would thaw out along with the ice and snow. If only everything would set itself to rights, instead of getting more and more jumbled up by the moment.

Without thinking, she wound up and chucked the pebbles at the lake.

Plop. Plop. Splash. Kerplunk.

"Now that's an interesting technique."

She turned to see Celeste at her side. More than once Rebecca had thought the woman was as silent as a ghost. One minute she wasn't there; the next she was. Or you'd be speaking to her, and in a moment's distraction, Celeste would be gone.

Rebecca hadn't forgotten their conversation from the previous morning, but she was wary of pressing her friend on such a sensitive subject. She knew the appropriate thing to do was to respect Celeste's privacy, to accept that she'd been told as much as she was going to hear for the time being.

But when Celeste chucked her own handful of pebbles a few seconds later, Rebecca had to laugh out loud.

Oh, it felt good to laugh. How long had it been since she'd really laughed like she had last night with Sean? Weeks, certainly. But even when Stu had still been here, even when they'd still been engaged, she hadn't really been happy.

It stunned Rebecca to realize that she hadn't really been happy for a very long time. And even though she couldn't possibly see how she could be happy now with everything crashing down around her, laughing with Sean and his grandmother was tapping into a part of her that felt really important.

And sadly neglected.

"You really remind me of Sean," she told Celeste.

Oh god, where had those words come from? She felt her face flush, prayed that Celeste would think it was the cold and sunshine making her cheeks turn bright pink.

"What a lovely compliment that is, Rebecca."

Rebecca nodded, knew she should shut up already. Instead, she had to say, "You both make me laugh."

Celeste raised an eyebrow at that. "Sean makes you laugh?" The gray-haired woman turned and stared out at the lake. "Well, then. That's certainly something, isn't it?"

Rebecca didn't know what to say to that. So of course,

what came out was, "I haven't been able to stop thinking about what you told me yesterday." There was no need to clarify, but there she was doing it anyway, off on her babble train because she was nervous. "About your husband, Charlie. And how he disappeared just like Stu."

Celeste, fortunately, didn't seem the least bit perturbed or upset by what Rebecca had said. "Well, there were quite a few differences, actually. You and Stu were never going to get married, for one."

Wait a minute. "How did you know that?"

Celeste laughed at that question. Actually laughed. "Oh honey, anyone with any sense at all knew that."

"Why didn't somebody tell me then?"

"Some things you need to figure out for yourself."

"A manual would be much better, thanks."

Celeste's delighted laughter had Rebecca laughing with her again. And then the two of them were picking up piles of pebbles and throwing them willy-nilly into the water like two little kids instead of twenty-eight- and eighty-four-year-old women.

"Now that we've gotten that out of our systems, I'm sure you'd like a cup of tea."

Celeste didn't wait for Rebecca to agree as she moved down the beach to her cottage. This, right here, was the beauty of Emerald Lake. She'd come out this morning feeling out of sorts and confused. It wasn't that she was any less confused now, but she felt lighter nonetheless for the blue sky and the beautiful lake . . . and a good friend.

1945, Emerald Lake Inn

Celeste waited for three days, through two more long and lonely nights for Charlie to come back.

She told no one that he was gone, knowing everyone assumed they were simply having a perfect honeymoon where they didn't even come out of their rooms for meals.

She picked the food up outside the door at every meal, and flushed most of it down the toilet so that no one would know there was only one person left in the honeymoon suite high in the inn's attic.

She stared out the window for hours, keeping watch for Charlie. But she needn't have bothered.

She'd know the second he was back, would feel it deep in her soul.

Every day the room grew colder. Every night as she dozed in the chair by the window she dreamed she heard crying coming from the walls.

The sun dawned on the fourth day and it was time for her to check out of the inn, to go off and start her new life as Mrs. Charlie Murphy.

She held her head high as she carried her suitcase downstairs, as she turned in her room key. She knew people had long thought of her older sister, Evelyn, as the strong one. But Celeste had hidden reserves of strength she'd never had to tap into.

Until now.

"I'll need to leave my things here until later," she told the innkeeper, a lovely young girl who was fairly new to town.

The girl's face had flushed. "Of course. Will your husband be back for them later?"

Celeste simply said, "Thank you," before turning and heading for the door.

She walked the mile to her father's house along the beach, but she saw little of the beauty around her, barely noticed the sun beating down on her back.

Her sister Rose saw her first. "Did you walk from the inn? Where's Charlie?" She stepped closer. "Have you been crying?"

Celeste put her fingers to her cheek. Oh. She hadn't known she was crying. She pushed the moisture aside.

"I need to speak with father."

"He's in the middle of a meeting with—"

Celeste was already moving past her sister. She'd thought the next time she walked through these doors, her husband would be beside her.

Where was he? Was he hurt?

Oh god, she prayed he wasn't hurt.

She headed straight for her father's study. He often took meetings in his house, rather than his office in town. In fact, the day that Charlie had come to town looking for her father, they'd ended up meeting right here.

"Father." She'd been told her voice had a lyrical quality, that she might have been a professional singer if she'd had any interest in it. Today it was flat. "I need to speak with you."

Three middle-aged men stood up quickly, their eyebrows moving up on their faces as they took in her clearly sleepless, tear-stained visage. Rose had been following her like a puppy but now she'd fallen back, leaving Celeste to stand all alone in the doorway to her father's dark wood and leather office.

Smoke from the men's pipes swirled and curled up to the ceiling.

"Gentlemen, this is my middle daughter, Celeste." Still gracious despite her interruption, he said, "I'm in the middle of a meeting. I'll come find you later, honey."

She lifted her chin. "I need to speak with you right away."

After three days in the inn's honeymoon suite, waiting and praying and hoping for the miracle of Charlie's reappearance, she'd decided that if her husband was, in fact, in trouble, she needed her father's help now, not later.

"If you'll excuse me, gentlemen, I'll be back shortly."

She could tell her father was upset by the hard set of his jaw, the tight way he was holding his shoulders.

He waited until they were out of ear shot. "You embarrassed me back there."

"Charlie's gone."

"What do you mean, gone?"

"I woke up the morning after our wedding and he had disappeared."

"He disappeared three days ago?"

"Yes."

"Why on earth did you take so long to tell me this?"

"I was waiting." Her voice was soft, small.

"You were waiting."

The sentence sounded strangled and she looked up to see myriad emotions cross her father's face. Empathy for his daughter, disappointment, confusion.

And, finally, anger.

"I gave him my money."

She nodded. Charlie had been about to start a new business in town.

"Have you checked the account?"

"No."

She hadn't thought about money. But now, she did. And she knew what her father would find when he went to speak with the bank manager.

But there was relief there, too. Because if Charlie had disappeared with her father's money, then it was less likely that he was hurt, wasn't it?

"Wait here."

She knew he was going into his office, that he was rescheduling his meeting. She stood in the same place, not moving a muscle as the three men filed out of the room and out to the front door.

"Come with me, Celeste."

He wasn't calling her honey anymore or even Cellie. No, she was a crisp Celeste to him now.

Thirty minutes later, all was confirmed. Charlie had come into the bank the morning after their wedding and withdrawn all of the funds but one hundred dollars.

Celeste silently followed her father out of the bank and down to the public dock next to the inn. On a cool spring day, despite the bright sunshine, they were the only two people out on the lake shore.

"You should have known better."

All of them had been taken in by Charlie, but she knew her father's pride would never live that down.

"We don't know why he took the money," she said, instinctively defending her husband.

"He took it because he's a crook."

But Celeste knew she could have never fallen in love with a bad man. "What if he isn't? What if he's in trouble? What if he needs our help?"

"That money he stole from me is the last help he'll ever get. He was a con man. You were his target." She knew exactly why her father was acting so awful, why he was sneering at her. It was because Charlie had pulled one over on him. "The perfect innocent little target. Just as I'd worried you'd be."

Only, although Celeste's heart was aching, she couldn't believe that it had all been a lie. Yes, she could accept that perhaps he might have come into their life as a con man; yes, she might have been his target, but by the time they had their wedding night, their love was real. There had to be a reason he'd left.

"We will have the marriage annulled right away," he father decreed.

"No." She wouldn't allow that.

She'd never talked back to her father before. Never really stood up to him either. But something had happened to her between that first kiss with Charlie and saying I do, between lying in his arms in the inn's honeymoon suite and waking up alone in an ice-cold room.

"I'm not a virgin anymore, father." Her father blinked in shock at her as she continued with, "Charlie will always be my husband, even if he never comes back to me."

Her father was silent for a long moment. "Char—" He stopped before getting her husband's name out, his face twisted with disgust. "Your new husband died in an unfortunate car accident."

"What? How could you know that?" No, she'd know if he was dead.

She'd know.

"From this moment forward, that is what happened. You will move back into our house and grieve your husband for an appropriate period of time."

Six weeks later, she threw up her breakfast. By the end of the week, her mother proclaimed it morning sickness.

Celeste was pregnant with Charlie's baby.

Chapter Fifteen

Rebecca hadn't thought she'd leave Celeste's cottage more shocked than she was the previous morning. She could hardly believe the man Celeste had loved with her whole heart and soul had conned her. That he'd left her pregnant. And alone.

Rebecca's tea had gone cold in her cup by the time she finally said to Celeste, "That's why my bedroom is haunted, isn't it?"

Celeste had simply stood up to clear the teapot and cups away, neither confirming nor denying the ghost—or its cause.

But Rebecca knew.

She *knew*.

Her head spinning, she headed back to the inn. She was due to start her workday in an hour or so, but she wanted to go up to her bedroom first and look around. See if it looked different now that she knew what had happened in that room to change everything.

True love had come.

And then disappeared.

And yet, she pondered as she took the back stairs so that she could be alone with her thoughts rather than bump into any guests, Celeste was clearly a strong woman who seemed happy with her life.

Sean's grandmother could have so easily given up at that point. How had she managed to survive—and push past—it all?

But that was a question for another day. A day when Celeste was good and ready to tell Rebecca more.

Knowing that day was certain to come made the wait a little easier.

Of course, when she got back to her bedroom, now that she was looking for clues to a ghost, now that she was waiting to feel the chill, to hear the horrible sounds, there was nothing to be found.

The bedroom was just like any other at the inn.

Still, Rebecca found herself pulling a chair up to the window, the same window Celeste had looked out for three days, waiting and watching for Charlie to return.

Despite all the signs to the contrary, Celeste hadn't given up.

Rebecca watched the cars slowly move from one side of Main Street to the other. She saw young mothers pushing their babies in strollers. Store owners unlocked their front doors and began the process of opening up for the day.

And she suddenly knew that she couldn't give up either.

There was a reason she hadn't started making those phone calls to cancel the Tapping of the Maples Festival: she was going to fight the petition.

Her sense of purpose back, Rebecca felt much better. How quickly she'd fallen into her old ways. How quickly she'd given up after hearing what Mr. Radin had to say. She'd thought she was changing, that she wasn't going to run scared from anything anymore, but when put to the test, she'd crumbled like a dry ball of dirt in a child's fist.

Her excitement about the festival came rushing back as she began to compile a list in her head of preliminary phone calls to make. She didn't know for sure if she could actually convince the Adirondack Preservation Council to give her a chance, but she sure as heck could give it everything she had.

She was going to take that life test again... and this time if she failed, at least she'd know that she'd tried her hardest.

Sean owed her.

Rebecca had thrown herself in front of an emotional bus for him last night at his parents' house. One way or another, Sean was going to give her back her festival.

Not only had he already made a dozen calls this morning, but he was quickly becoming intimately knowledgeable about the ins and out of the Adirondack Preservation Council. He'd spent most of the previous night after returning from the dinner at his parents' house—the less thought about that, the better—scouring the Internet for information about park policy.

And, more important, its loopholes.

His head legal counsel hadn't been surprised to hear from him this morning—they'd been on the phone constantly during the past few weeks as he'd sold his company—but Frank had clearly been caught off guard by what Sean was having him look into.

Sure, he knew Rebecca would be all right if the festival

didn't happen. She'd still do her job as innkeeper to the utmost. She'd still laugh and smile at all the right places with the guests. But none of those things were enough.

Because her natural sparkle had almost been extinguished yesterday after Mr. Radin had trampled all over her festival.

Sean Murphy had never cared about a woman's sparkle before. In twenty years, he'd done his best to stay away from serious relationships with women, and any flickers of sparkle he'd come across had been nothing more than a quick flash in a lover's bed.

But nothing he'd done, nothing he'd told himself, had made him immune to the power of Rebecca's smile. Seeing it fall, watching the sparks go out in Rebecca's eyes, was nothing short of heartbreaking.

Heartbreaking enough to make him start to wonder if he actually still had a heart.

An hour later, Rebecca's renewed excitement had pretty much fizzled out. She'd spent the past sixty minutes hitting one brick wall after another with not only the Adirondack Park's commission but the preservation council as well.

And for some crazy reason, the one person she wanted to talk to about it was Sean. He hadn't wanted her to work on the festival, initially, but hadn't he used the word *we* last night?

Maybe he would be willing to brainstorm some ideas with her.

She didn't want to give up this time, damn it!

She called his room, but there was no answer, so she went downstairs to look for him. Jean was checking out a guest when Rebecca asked, "Have you seen Sean?"

Jean nodded out to the front porch. "He's been outside on the phone for a while."

Rebecca's heart did a funny little flip before diving toward her stomach. She and Sean hadn't kissed last night, but there'd been a sensual tension between them that she could no longer deny. And every time she saw him, every time they spoke, that awareness, that attraction grew stronger.

Strong enough to scare her.

But she was done being scared, wasn't that what she'd just decided upstairs only moments ago?

Most important, he hadn't kissed her. Because he was still in firm possession of his self-control. And she had a feeling he rarely, if ever, lost control. Which meant it was perfectly safe to go outside and talk to him.

Sean wasn't on the porch, but she could hear his voice coming from the rose garden off to the side of the porch. In the summer and early fall, the arbor was the favorite place for brides to marry their true loves. In the thaw of spring, the sticks were still all bare, but Rebecca found the garden to be lovely just the same, with its promise of new growth and beauty.

He was standing beneath the arbor, looking out at the lake, and the sight of him standing in the exact spot where so many grooms had stood before had her breath catching in her throat.

Her brain started playing tricks on her, changing the scene so that Sean wasn't wearing jeans and a button-down long-sleeved shirt anymore. He wasn't on the phone. It was no longer spring.

Instead, she saw roses in full bloom all around him. He was wearing a tuxedo with a rose tucked into his lapel.

And he was waiting for her to walk toward him in a beautiful, long white gown...looking at her with more love than she'd ever seen in anyone's eyes.

Oh god. What was wrong with her brain? Why was it playing this trick on her? Why was it showing her a vision that seemed impossibly real? So real she could actually still smell the roses in the air, when she knew darn well there wasn't a single flower petal in sight.

Telling herself he clearly wasn't done with the phone yet—and that was the only reason she was leaving, not that she was running away again—she'd half turned around when a snippet of his conversation floated over to her.

"Will the entire council be there this afternoon?"

Council? Whom was he talking to?

Last night during dinner he'd used the word *we*, but that was when she hadn't yet decided that she was going to fight the petition herself.

Was he fighting for her anyway?

"Good," he said to the person he was speaking to. "We'll be there at four p.m."

Hanging up, he turned around and found her standing there staring at him.

"Rebecca, I was just about to come look for you. We have a meeting with the preservation council at four p.m. today to present the counterpetition for your festival."

She was stunned. Beyond stunned. "I've been trying for the past hour to get someone to talk to me there. How were you able to get them to see us?"

But she could see from his expression that he was going to tell her it was no big deal. Only, it was.

"I'm sorry for what I said yesterday. For the way I said

it." She'd been so mean with her, "*You'll be pleased to hear that the festival is off.*"

Only now, she knew for sure what she'd suspected since the start: beneath Sean's walls, the barriers he'd erected all around himself, he was a good man. Truly good.

"I don't want you to ever apologize for being honest, Rebecca. You were angry. I had told you to drop the festival more than once. You had every reason to assume I'd be happy about it."

She wanted to ask him why he was helping her, but the slope was already way too slippery where he was concerned. At this point, if he said even the slightest nice thing to her, she was liable to launch herself at him and plant kisses all over his gorgeous face.

Knowing that focusing on the festival would be her only savior at this point, she said, "We've got a lot of work to do before four, haven't we?"

He nodded, that hint of a smile playing around his lips. "Let's get to it."

At which point she forced herself to focus only on their work ... and not on how badly she wanted to turn that hint of a smile into a full one.

Sean couldn't believe it, but he simply hadn't thought things through.

He'd made a lucrative career out of thinking things through. He didn't make mistakes.

But somehow, Rebecca was changing everything.

He wasn't the least bit disappointed by her intelligence or by how hard she was willing to work. Heck, he would have liked to have had a few more people like her on his staff before he had sold his company.

But he hadn't realized—nor had he wanted to accept—just how hard it would be for him to keep his own focus on the job at hand. Especially when she was sitting so close. Close enough for him to breathe in her sweet scent. Close enough to reach over and curl his fingers around hers as they cruised down one of the back roads on their way to their meeting.

He could tell she was nervous by the way she was sitting ramrod straight in the passenger seat with her hands firmly clasped in her lap.

"Tell me about growing up at Emerald Lake, Sean."

He didn't like to think back on his childhood. And, perhaps, if she'd asked him another time, he wouldn't have told her anything at all, apart from the generalizations that anyone could assume.

But he wanted her to relax. And he knew talking about his travels was something she enjoyed. Only, this was the first time she'd asked him about his hometown, rather than some foreign locale she was longing to see.

The sudden urge to make that wish come true—to do so much more for her than help her get her maple-tapping festival back off the ground—hit him hard and fast. Harder so for all that it was unexpected.

"Stu said you and he used to sail every Sunday during the summer races."

"We did. Did he ever take you out in the *Flying Scott*?"

"Once."

"Only once?"

"I'm afraid I'm not much of a natural sailor. After getting his instructions about the mast or the stern or whatever it is backward, it nearly hit him in the head and we ended up tipping over in the middle of the lake."

"Beginners make that mistake every time. You didn't go out and try again?"

"I should have. It just seemed easier not to, I guess. You know, that way Stu could have a good sail without worrying about me."

He was on the verge of offering to take her sailing again once the ice on the lake melted. But he wasn't planning on staying in Emerald Lake that long.

He had to clear his throat before saying, "Our father taught us to sail. To this day he's still one of the best sailors I've ever met. Thirty knots coming at him and he doesn't even blink, just grins and hikes out into the wind."

"I like your father a lot."

He could hear the affection in her voice. "He's a good man," he agreed, his words gruffer than he had wished.

"Why don't you go hiking or fishing with him, Sean? He wants so badly to spend time with you."

Her hands had come unclasped now and she was turned to face him instead of staring so steadily out the window. He should have been upset that she was poking into his private life, but he found that he was simply glad to have helped her forget about their meeting for a few minutes.

And a part of him liked knowing that she cared.

He took a deep breath and blew it out before admitting, "My relationship with my father is complicated."

"He loves you. That's not complicated."

He knew what was coming next. She was going to ask about his mother. Thank god the preservation council building had just come into view.

"We're here."

* * *

Two hours later, Rebecca felt like a limp dishrag as she and Sean walked back to his car.

"I had no idea it would be like that." She slumped on the leather seat beside Sean. On the drive out earlier that afternoon, she'd been nervous about being in the small space with him. Now, she was too tired for nerves.

"Meetings like that call for one thing," he told her.

"A short rope and a tall tree to hang it from?"

Another time she would have appreciated his low chuckle, especially since she'd wanted so desperately to see one of his rare smiles turn into a full-blown laugh.

"A stiff drink."

She wasn't big on booze, but if ever there was a time for alcohol, this was it. The council had allowed them to say their piece. They had dutifully taken the documentation she and Sean had put together. They had asked approximately a zillion questions.

And they'd promised nothing.

Zilch.

Nada.

Ten minutes later, Sean pulled into the kind of roadside dive she never would have had the guts to come to on her own. A dozen motorcycles were parked outside and they were almost entirely surrounded by forest.

"I've driven past here a dozen times," she said, "but never thought to come inside. Have you ever been here before?"

Before he could answer, she heard someone call out, "Damned if I ever thought I'd see this day. Sean Murphy live and in the flesh."

Sean nodded at the heavily tattooed man behind the

bar. "Rebecca, meet Dick. We're in need of two of your specials."

Despite her shock that the two men knew each other—she'd assumed Sean lived solely in a world of suits—she couldn't help but smile back at the man who was grinning so widely at her.

"It's nice to meet you, Dick."

"Same here, pretty Rebecca." She blushed as Dick handed them their drinks. "Good to see you back home, Sean. You've been missed."

They headed over to a small booth in the corner of the dark room. "He seems nice."

"You like everyone, don't you?"

"Until I see a reason not to like them, yes."

"That trust is going to get you hurt, Rebecca."

"That's so cynical."

"But true."

More frustrated now by what Sean was saying to her than she'd been for the two hours they'd done their pointless song-and-dance for the council, she picked up her glass and took a huge gulp.

Her eyes were watering when she put it down. "My god, what's in this?" Surprisingly, she realized after the initial shock wore off, that it was quite good. Really good, actually.

"No one's ever been able to get Dick to give the recipe up."

She should have been angry with Sean for poisoning her with this way-too-potent, yet yummy, drink. Maybe she should have even been crying over the fact that their big shot at convincing the council to let her have her festival was a big goose egg.

Instead, she found herself laughing over the way everything in her life had spun so totally out of control. It was either laugh or cry.

She was afraid if she started crying, she might never stop.

"I'll be right back."

Amazed by how unsteady she felt on her feet after only drinking a few ounces of Dick's concoction, she was back sixty seconds later.

"Got it," she said, triumphantly.

"Dick told you what he puts in this?" Sean asked incredulously.

"I asked nicely," she said with an impish grin.

"Only you, Rebecca, could make a man spill a secret he's been holding onto for decades."

She took another smaller sip of the—really surprisingly delicious—drink.

"If you ask me, he was dying to have someone to tell, but everyone's been too afraid to ask him all these years." Bolder for the drink, she leaned across the table. "Now it's your turn to tell me a secret, Sean."

She wasn't expecting Sean's expression to change so quickly from teasing to deadly serious.

"This drink was a bad idea. I'm sure you want to get back to the inn."

He was pushing his chair back, about to stand as she put her hand on his arm to halt him. She wished she could be inside his head, wished she could understand what had cause this abrupt change in him when they were finally relaxing with each other.

But since she couldn't read his mind, she had to say, "I thought we were having fun. What did I do wrong, Sean?"

His eyes were dark, his jaw was jumping. She felt the air change, knew everything between them was on the verge of shifting, a split second before he said, "This, damn it."

And then his hands were in her hair and his mouth was on hers and he was kissing all of the air from her lungs.

Perhaps she should have been shocked, and maybe she should have pushed him away, but she'd wanted this kiss for too long to do anything but reach right back for him and deepen the sweetest, most sinful kiss she'd ever tasted.

And when he finally pulled away and she could figure out how to form words again, she whispered, "That was my secret, too."

Chapter Sixteen

After his abrupt loss of control, Sean made sure there were no more kisses in the bar or during their drive back to the inn. There was no more conversation either, not from either of them, as the miles ticked by slower than they ever had before.

He knew he should apologize to her for snapping like that, for taking something she hadn't offered. But how the hell could he ever be sorry about kissing Rebecca? Especially when she was softer, sweeter than any woman had ever been.

Only, the way she'd flat out asked him to tell her his secrets...well, it had cut straight to the core of him. Almost as if she knew things she couldn't possibly know.

He'd almost made it, had almost taken himself out of the path of temptation, when she'd touched him...and he'd lost it.

And kissed her the way he'd been wanting to kiss her since practically the first moment he'd set eyes on her.

"Sean?"

They were getting out of his car in the empty employee lot behind the inn. The moon was barely a sliver and it was dark. So dark he should have been safe stealing another glance at her beauty without being caught out as a thief.

"Are you sorry you kissed me?"

He should have known she would ask him something like that, the exact question that most people would never dare say aloud, but instead he found himself surprised every single time.

Sean worked to remind himself that she couldn't possibly be as much of an open book as she seemed to be, the same reminder he'd been repeating to himself for days.

Only this time, with the taste of her kiss still on his lips, even though he knew she still hadn't come completely clean about Stu with him, he just couldn't get himself to believe it.

He opened his mouth to say yes, they shouldn't have kissed.

But the lie wouldn't come.

"No."

"Oh."

The one word from her lips was more breath than letters. He saw the way the faint moonlight illuminated her shiny hair.

"Aren't you sorry you kissed me back?" he had to ask.

"I know I should be," she said softly, "but how could I possibly regret that kiss?"

It was too close to what he'd been thinking for either of their sakes and when she followed up with, "Could I ask you something?" he knew better than to do this.

They both did.

Because just as Sean didn't believe in ghosts, he had never believed in fate.

So then why did Rebecca feel inevitable? From that first moment he'd seen her at Andi and Nate's wedding he'd been inexplicably drawn to her.

And no matter how many times he tried to pull away, in the end he'd found he couldn't ever actually do it.

"What is it, Rebecca?"

She paused, and he swore he could almost hear her heart beating, that even the owls in the trees and loons on the lake were waiting for what she had to say.

"Would you please kiss me again?"

Sweet Jesus.

No one had ever asked him to kiss her like that. With such sweet need.

No wonder Dick had given up his drink recipe to her.

Rebecca was irresistible.

And then she was putting her hands over his shoulders and tilting her mouth up to his and the fact was that even the strongest man in the world couldn't have stopped himself from kissing her.

Her lips were soft and she tasted like a mixture of the sugar in her drink and something that was uniquely Rebecca. One kiss wasn't enough and so he kept going back for one more, had to see if anyone could really taste this good.

Only, with every moment that passed, with every kiss Rebecca so willingly gave him, images of his brother touching her the same way grew larger, bigger in his head.

Sean had never been a jealous lover. He'd never been possessive. But now, with nothing more than a few of Rebecca's kisses on his lips, all he could think was, *Mine.*

He dragged his mouth from hers. She was panting, and in the faint moonlight he could see that her mouth was faintly swollen from his kisses. He'd never wanted a woman this much, had never been on the verge of throwing her over his shoulder and carrying her upstairs to his bed.

"Did my brother kiss you like this?"

The vision sent him all the way over the edge, straight to a place he'd never gone before, hurtling to a place he knew he shouldn't go but couldn't possibly stop himself from heading toward.

Rebecca's eyes immediately widened with shock. "Excuse me?"

He knew he needed to stop, needed to take a step back and apologize for his jealous question. Instead, he did just the opposite.

"Was this how he held you?" He ran his hands down from her shoulders to the rise of her hips. Her hands had moved from his shoulders to his chest and she was pushing against him.

"You're acting like a child in a sandbox fighting over a prized toy."

He forced himself to release his hold on her. Damn it, he wasn't acting any better than her bastard ex-boyfriend had. But now that the dam had broken, now that they were admitting the truth of their attraction to each other, he could no longer deny that visions of Rebecca and his brother together had been playing around the edges of his mind all week. And they were visions that had his stomach clenching.

"I'm going crazy thinking about the two of you," he

admitted in a rough voice that he barely recognized as his own.

He was standing in the parking lot of his inn pleading with a woman who used to be his brother's fiancée, begging her to tell him she wasn't thinking of anyone but him when they were making out.

"He never kissed me like that. He barely even touched me."

Sean wanted so badly to believe her. But how could he when he knew firsthand that she was utterly irresistible?

"That's impossible, Rebecca. How could he have been with you and not touched you?"

"What else do you want from me, Sean? I just told you the truth and now you're saying you won't believe me."

"How can I believe you? You were engaged, Rebecca." Sean shouldn't have reached out for her again, shouldn't have let a silky strand of her hair thread through his fingers. "How could any sane man possibly keep his hands off of you?"

"I swear," she said in a raw whisper. "We barely even kissed in all the months we were together."

Sean knew he should have been ecstatic to hear it—and he was—but in some crazy way he was angry, too, on Rebecca's behalf. How could a woman this sensual, this passionate, have been on the verge of marrying a man who didn't desire her?

"How could you have accepted that? Didn't you think you deserved to be with a man who wanted you?"

She looked stunned, enough so that she wasn't moving any farther away from him.

"How long did you think you were going to be able to keep your desires buried?"

"Stu was kind. I knew he loved me. Maybe not as a woman, but as a person. It was more than anyone else had ever given me. I thought that dating a married guy was my stupidest moment, but I managed to up that by almost marrying a gay man."

She spun away from him and slapped her hand over her mouth. "Oh god. I promised him I wouldn't say anything."

"Stu." He needed to process what she'd just said. "Jesus, Rebecca, why didn't you tell me that the first time I asked you why he left, instead of letting me think he could be hurt somewhere?"

"He told me he needed time." She still looked horrified. "I shouldn't have told you that."

In some small corner of his brain, Sean knew there was some sense to what she was saying, but he wasn't able to heed that. Not when it felt like everything was splitting apart, breaking down, in his perfectly ordered world.

Beyond frustrated with his brother for running from them all when he should have confided in them instead, but unable to deal with Stu until he finally decided to reappear in their lives, Sean lashed out at Rebecca, instead.

"So you're saying you think it's okay for everyone else to give up their secrets to you without having to share yours with anyone else?"

Anger took the place of horrified as she whirled back toward him, her long hair flying behind her as she poked her index finger hard into his chest.

"You accused of me of hiding from the truth when I was dating a married man, but you did the same thing with Stu. How could you have missed the signs? You're Stu's brother; you've known him your whole life. You should know him far better than I do. He was afraid to tell your parents about his true feelings. He told me it would break them, though he wouldn't tell me why. But why is he so scared of you? Why do you make sure everyone is afraid of you? Why don't you let anyone get close to you? I see the way you barely say a word to your mother. I see how hurt she is when you keep pushing her away. Your father, too."

They were hard truths. Each and every one of them.

For all that he wanted to tell himself he didn't know about Stu, was that really true? Wasn't it more that Sean had been so caught up in his own life and business and doing anything he could to stay away from his parents, hadn't he been so damn busy telling himself it was better for everyone if he stayed out of their business, that he hadn't had even a minute to spare for his little brother?

And even after returning to Emerald Lake, hadn't he made sure not to get too close to anyone? He hadn't looked up any old friends. His mother had to beg him to come to dinner. His father was desperate to take an hour and go for a hike.

And all he'd done was work like hell to shut them out.

Rebecca watched him as he stood there silent before her. He wanted to say so many things, but he knew he didn't have the words.

Even if he did, he wasn't sure his pride would let him say them, anyway.

"I care about you, Sean."

Her words were soft, filled with that sweetness that he craved, sweetness that seeped deeper into his cells with every moment he spent with Rebecca.

"All week I've been trying to tell myself to stay away from you." She shook her head. "But you're a good man."

"How could you think that?"

"I've spent enough time with you, Sean, to know it. You didn't have to help me today, but you did because it was the right thing to do. You didn't have to stay to help with the inn. That wasn't your agreement with Stu. But you're here anyway. Even though you don't really want to be near your family, you've stayed to help. And—" She swallowed hard. "I want you." She was almost shocked by her soft admission. "Even standing here arguing with you, even when you're making me madder than anyone else ever has, I can't seem to stop wanting you."

"If I was a good man I would walk away from you so that you could find yourself someone better."

She blinked up at him. "You're not going to walk away right now?"

He slid his arms around her and lowered his mouth to hers and kissed her in a way he'd never kissed another woman. There was heat there, of course, but this time emotion trumped everything else.

A few moments later, he had to say, "How can I walk away from you, Rebecca?"

"You walked away from your family."

No one had ever called him on his bullshit like the one woman he couldn't stay away from no matter how hard he tried.

"You're right. I walked away from all of them."

"Tell me why."

"People lie, Rebecca." He stroked her cheek. "That's why I walked away. And that's why I can't lie to you. I can't tell you what you want to hear. I can't tell you that everything is going to work out, that this kiss is going to turn into a happily ever after."

He didn't know what he expected her to do, but she didn't flinch. She didn't pull away. Instead, she simply said, "Tell me the truth, then."

"I don't want to hurt you."

"Good." Her mouth moved into a small smile. "I'm sick of being hurt."

If he were smart, he would stop right there, make sure he didn't say anything else that would drive her out of his arms.

But, then, how could he possibly live with himself?

"Rebecca, I'm trying to tell you that I can't promise you anything."

He was surprised by another smile, a bigger one this time.

"Is this where I'm supposed to slap you and call you a cad for kissing me like you just did?"

This conversation wasn't going like he thought it would. Like it should. Any other woman would have pulled away and written him off.

But not Rebecca. She surprised him at every turn.

"You said it yourself," he forced himself to remind her. "You've been trying to convince yourself to stay away from me."

"Yup," she said, as blunt as he was being. "I've been working like crazy trying to stay away from you." She shrugged. "I also can't seem to help myself where you're concerned."

No, he wouldn't let her veer them back into another kiss. At least not until everything was laid out, clear and on the table, so that neither of them could ignore the truth of the situation.

"Your reasons couldn't have changed for wanting

to stay away from me." Suddenly he knew exactly what needed to happen. It was the only way to ensure he didn't hurt her. "Tell me your reasons."

"Seriously?" She frowned. "You want to hear why I should know better than to want you?"

"Here are mine: You were Stu's fiancée. You work for me." He paused before saying the most important reason of all. "And you deserve to be with a man who can give you everything you want."

She made a sound that was somewhere between disbelief and a laugh. "Mine is much simpler than that. You're the beast."

Whatever he'd expected, it wasn't that. "If it's so simple then how come I'm not following?"

"You know, like the beauty and the beast fable. Not that I'm all that much of a beauty—"

"You are."

"I'm giving a point to you for saying that," she said with a small smile. "But, see, I've spent way too many years finding broken men and trying to heal them." She shrugged again, but he didn't buy that there was anything that didn't matter to her in what she was saying. "Instead, I end up broken, too."

Wait a minute. "You think I'm broken?"

She met his eyes head on in the moonlight. "Aren't you? You barely speak to your mother. Your father is desperate for a relationship with you. And your brother has been keeping a secret from all of you his whole life. Did I miss anything?"

Damn, she made it impossible for him to say anything but "Sounds like you've got it just about covered."

"So," she finally said, "what do you think we should do

about all of this?" She pressed a finger to his lips and he couldn't stop himself from pressing a kiss to it before he covered her hand with his and moved it away from his face.

"Sleep on it, probably."

She thought about it for a second. "You mean separately, don't you?"

Jesus, that mouth—and the way she looked more than a little disappointed as she said *separately*—was definitely going to get her into trouble one day.

"You do know you're not supposed to say things like that out loud, don't you?"

"Only because you're always telling me so."

He shouldn't have broken out into laughter. But he'd never been able to help himself where Rebecca was concerned. And even though nothing had been settled, despite things between them being as confusing as ever, he couldn't help himself now, either.

She looked utterly delighted by him. "It's even better than I thought it would be."

No one had ever confused him as much as this woman. "What's better?"

"Your laughter. I've been wanting to hear it for so long."

"Come here and give me a kiss good night before we go back to our separate rooms."

"See, what did I tell you?" she whispered as she raised herself up on her tippy-toes and held her mouth a breath away from his.

Telling himself he was going to make sure this was the last kiss of the night even if it killed him to do the honorable thing, he was so dizzy with the desire to taste her sweet lips again that he could barely string two words together.

"What did you tell me, Rebecca?"

He felt her smile against his lips without needing to see it.

"You are a good man."

And then she kissed him.

Chapter Seventeen

As Sean and Rebecca lingered over the night's last kiss, neither of them saw the lone figure standing in the shadows.

Elizabeth had never spied on her kids before. She wasn't one of those overprotective parents who hovered and asked too many questions. And she certainly hadn't dropped by the inn tonight to catch her oldest son and her youngest son's ex-fiancée together. She'd simply come by to see if she could make some peace with her son, knowing too well that she'd done nothing but drive him even further away since he'd returned to Emerald Lake.

She desperately wanted to get back into her car and drive away, but if she so much as moved she was certain they would hear her.

She knew what it felt like to be caught. And even though she knew that Sean and Rebecca weren't actually doing anything wrong—when she'd cooled down the previous night, she'd had to admit that Bill was right and she should butt out of Sean's budding love life—she also knew they wouldn't appreciate knowing she was there watching them.

How, she wondered, as they finally made a move to go inside, could they not hear her heart beating? It had never sounded so loud to her own ears.

So many things were racing through her head, she didn't know what to focus on first.

Stu was gay. And that was okay. Of course it was. But why had he felt that he had to hide the truth from all of them? Why did he think it would break her and Bill? Of course, they'd made their fair share of mistakes—every parent did, she knew that—but had they really done such an awful job that he felt he couldn't trust them?

Unfortunately, Elizabeth was afraid she already had her answer in the list Rebecca had given Sean of the reasons she should steer clear of dating him. A list he'd agreed was accurate: *You barely speak to your mother. Your father is desperate for a relationship with you. And your brother has been keeping a secret from all of you his whole life.*

Elizabeth had failed both of her sons.

When she deemed it safe to move, she ran to her car and quickly drove away. Bill was waiting for her on the porch when she got home.

"I was wondering where you went," he said, and then, "Elizabeth, are you crying?"

"I went to the inn to talk to Sean. But he and Rebecca—"

Frustration flew across Bill's face. "I don't want to hear it. Whatever they're doing is their business."

It wasn't fair. She wasn't going to tell her husband about the kisses she'd witnessed. About how they'd taken her back to the first kisses the two of them had shared. Back to a time when neither of them had wanted to say good night either. Now they couldn't even be bothered to sleep in the same bed.

But where had her pride—and her mistakes—gotten her so far?

She forced herself to say, "You were right. Their relationship is their business."

Bill's eyes widened with clear surprise. "Then why are you crying?"

"Stu is gay." Realizing what it sounded like, that she was crying over her son's sexual orientation, she quickly clarified: "I accidentally overheard Sean and Rebecca talking about Stu and she finally told him why Stu left. He was afraid to tell all of us. He swore Rebecca to secrecy because he thought the truth would break us."

"My god, Elizabeth." Bill sat down hard on one of the porch rockers. "How could he have thought that?"

She wanted to say she didn't know, but snippets had been coming to her during the short drive home from the inn. Little signs, like the ones Sean and Rebecca had spoken of, things neither she nor Bill should have ignored.

"Didn't we always say that Stu was so different from Sean? That he reminded us of my brother?"

James passed away unexpectedly nearly twenty years ago from pneumonia. But the man they'd seen crying at her brother's funeral had clearly been more than a friend. He'd been her brother's partner. Only, her brother had never come out to her, either.

"I was such a wreck after James died. Stu must have thought he had to try and marry Rebecca to please us."

"And when he couldn't do it, he ran," Bill confirmed.

"I've ruined so many things." Her legs were shaking and she could feel them about to give way.

Bill was there before she could fall. Just like he always had been before.

"You're freezing cold. We need to go inside and sit near the fire."

She was grateful for her husband's warmth, for the way he cared for her even when she didn't deserve such caring.

And he was right. She was cold. But it was a cold that had hardly anything to do with the temperature.

Secrets were ripping her family apart. First, Sean had pulled away from her. And then, Stu had run.

Elizabeth needed to come clean about everything. Now. Tonight. Before the secrets ruined anything else.

Before the secrets ripped her husband away, too.

But as Bill continued to hold her by the fire and she reveled in his warmth and touch for the first time in far too long, fear of actually losing him kept the truth of what had happened twenty years ago locked up tight inside her heart.

Even though she could feel the barbs around that truth making them both bleed.

Rebecca had never been promiscuous. She wasn't a virgin by any means, but she'd never slept with anyone until they'd been dating for a while. Not because she was a tease, not because she was frigid, but because she'd never been able to let herself go, physically, without emotion tying her to someone.

Sean had changed everything, it seemed. Because even though he'd left her at her door like the perfect gentleman, even though she knew sleeping on their ridiculously hot kisses was the right thing—especially in light of all she'd revealed about Stu—it was taking every ounce of self-control she possessed not to grab her master key and unlock his door and offer herself to him, naked and more than willing.

Even stranger than the desire she couldn't seem to control—when there had never, frankly, been anything all that uncontrollable about her desire for any other man— was the way her bedroom had started out warm and now that she was done getting changed for bed was as frigid as it had ever been.

Almost as if it was trying to kick her out of it...or get her to invite Sean back in to see if his presence would warm it up again.

"I don't have the energy for you tonight," she found herself saying to the room at large.

Because if there was, in fact, a ghost lurking somewhere, she wanted it to know that she really needed to get some sleep tonight.

Thump!

In retrospect, she should have known better than to issue up a challenge like that. Because the sounds that started coming from the walls were less like the sad wails they'd been before...this time they sounded impatient.

Okay, so she was almost willing to believe that there was a ghost. Or at least some sort of spirit that hadn't been able to move on for some reason. But—and this was way too crazy for her to be willing to believe—did this spirit expect her to solve its problems? More specifically, had this bedroom been waiting sixty years for true love to set it straight after Celeste's honeymoon had ended in such tragedy?

Rebecca snorted at the thought. "If you're in here," she said to her bedroom walls, "and you're waiting for my love life to turn things around for you, I'll have you know you're going to be in for a much longer wait."

Thump!

Okay, that was weird. She could have sworn the wall was talking back to her, a loud banging that was akin to a foot stomping in frustration.

"Yes, I'm as frustrated about it as you are," she replied, even though she knew this conversation she was having with the walls of her bedroom was taking weird to a brand-new level.

Whatever. She was tired. Sean had kissed her senseless tonight. She was allowed a few minutes of weird.

"If I were you, I'd look toward one of the couples getting married at the inn. Trust me, you're bound to have better luck there. Besides, you've had decades to deal with this. Why now? Why me?"

And why did it have to be when she was so tired?

Not that she'd been too tired to stand out in the inn's parking lot and kiss Sean for ages, of course.

In any case, as soon as she could get away from the front desk for a few minutes tomorrow, she was going to hunt down Celeste and keep the tea pouring until she got the rest of the story out of Sean's grandmother. Maybe if she had some clues as to what had happened after Charlie left, then she could make whatever was going wrong in this bedroom stop.

Reaching into her bedside table, she pulled out two earplugs and jammed them into her ears. But less than sixty seconds later, she knew it was pointless. The knocking had gotten even louder—a *thump, thump, thump* that was sure to make that headache that had been forming in the back of her head come to full fruition.

And then she realized it wasn't the walls knocking.

It was someone at the door.

Sean had tried to do the right thing. He'd intended to say good night to Rebecca with one final kiss. But then he heard those sounds coming from her bedroom and how could he have possibly stayed away?

Now here he was, standing in front of her door again. He'd knocked once, then twice. The master keys were still on the coffee table in his room. He wouldn't barge in on her again, even if it meant catching another glimpse of her in her sinfully sweet pajamas.

Sean ran his hand through his hair as he waited in the hallway. Rebecca hadn't come to the door yet, possibly hadn't even heard him knock. He should get the hell back to his room. He should do everything he could to keep things from going from complicated to ridiculously messy with his most important employee.

If he didn't know better, he'd think there was some outside force pushing the two of them together. But even though Rebecca had spoken of a ghost, he still couldn't believe in anything he couldn't see and touch.

Which brought him right back around to where he was right now.

Dying to see her.

Dying to kiss her again.

Finally, he thought he heard footsteps and then the door opened.

"Hi."

Her smile had him smiling back. He simply couldn't help it. "Hi."

"You heard the sounds?"

"I did."

Her eyes were sparkling and if he'd seen any fear in them, he would have turned. Left her alone for good this time. Instead, there was excitement there and the same desire he knew he'd see in his eyes if he looked in a mirror.

"Want to hear it close up?"

He knew what she was asking him. And it had nothing to do with the strange sounds.

"More than you know."

"Oh, trust me," she said with another gorgeous smile that had his feet moving him all the way through the door, "I know."

"One day you're going to stop surprising me."

"I hope not," she replied. "You seem like the kind of man who likes to be surprised."

She was wrong. He hated surprises.

Or used to, anyway.

But there really was something so incredibly engaging about the way he couldn't predict what she was going to say next. Or do, apparently, because a moment later, she was cupping his jaw and moving to her tippy-toes to kiss him.

Sweet lord, the things she could do with that mouth of hers should be illegal. He tried to let her stay in the lead on their kiss, but he wanted her too much to follow through with that plan. Seconds later, he had his hands threaded through her hair, was wrapping his fingers around all of her soft hair so that he could tilt her head back and move his mouth from hers to the hollow beneath her chin.

She shivered as he began the decadent task of learning the taste of her skin, one inch at a time. And when their eyes met again, hers were a deeper, richer green than he'd ever seen them. He even thought he saw flecks of gold in them that he hadn't noticed before, almost as if her body was giving him proof of a too-long-latent heat of desire brought to life inside of her.

"Listen," she said softly.

Working to hear beyond the rush of blood in his ears and his overly loud heartbeat, it took him a few seconds to realize what she was saying.

"The sound stopped."

"I think our kissing is making the ghost happy."

He wasn't a man who kissed and laughed at the same time. Hell, he wasn't a man who laughed much period. But he couldn't contain it.

"Forget about the ghost. Kissing you makes me very happy."

"I like making you happy," she said, before proving it with another sweet, soft kiss.

But although he wanted nothing more than to pick her up and carry her into her bedroom, her sweet words hit way too close to home.

"I want you to be happy, too, Rebecca. But I don't think I'm the man who can do that for you. Maybe here, tonight, we can make each other happy. But not in the long run." Because he could never make the mistake of ever trusting anyone completely. Not even Rebecca.

She stroked her fingers down from his face to his shoulders and chest as if she couldn't resist touching him now that she finally had the chance. Through his thin T-shirt he could feel the heat of her.

He wanted to feel so much more, wanted to get so much closer, with nothing between them, but he didn't want it to happen with a lie. With deception.

He could tell she was thinking, knew that look, the way

her brows moved together slightly and her eyes focused on an imaginary point. For all that it seemed she was just blurting things out all the time, he knew she could be extremely thoughtful. She simply hated to hide the truth of her feelings from people.

He'd never known anyone like her. Suddenly, he had to wonder, if he had, would he be married with a family right now instead of resolutely single?

"It keeps occurring to me that a smart woman would be playing games to try and keep your interest."

She gave a small smile at his obvious surprise, the way his eyebrow went up at her blunt statement.

"I've never had the heart for games."

"I don't either." He tipped her chin up with his hand and held her gaze. "But I'm worried about your getting hurt, Rebecca. I would hate myself for causing your tears."

"Aren't you worried about yourself, too?"

There was no choice for them but to be painfully blunt at this point. They were way past the point of games.

"I'm not the one looking for someone to love me, Rebecca."

"Are you sure about that?"

Her whispered question shouldn't have made his chest clench. He'd thought she might flinch at the way he was throwing her earlier words about looking for love back at her. Instead, he was the one trying to hold steady.

"You were right in the parking lot," he forced himself to say. "This, you and me, we aren't going to end up like one of those fairy tales. You're beautiful, but your love isn't going to make me a new man."

Now she'd have to back down. Give up. She'd tell him to go. And he'd make himself leave her warmth.

Instead, she remained in his arms. "You don't need to become a new man, Sean."

He couldn't have been any blunter. He didn't want to hurt her feelings, but he didn't see how he had any other choice. It was either hurt them a bit now, or crush them later.

"Your love isn't going to turn the Murphys into one big happy family."

He watched for a flinch. It never came. Instead, her eyes flashed. With determination and something that looked—strangely—like humor.

"Darn it. And here I was thinking that sleeping with you tonight would do just that."

"Rebecca."

Her name was a warning on his lips. Here he was trying to be careful with her, and she was bound and determined to foil him at every turn. Didn't she know just the words *sleeping with you* were the proverbial straw that was going to break his vow to do right by her?

"Sean."

She mimicked his warning tone well. Too well. Well enough that some of that humor in her eyes almost seeped into his.

"I know what you want me to say," she told him. "You want me to say that I'm going into tonight with my eyes wide open. That making love with you won't change anything. That I won't hold you to more than a few sinful hours between the sheets when morning comes." She bit her lip. "See, this is where the games would be a really good thing. If I knew how to play them then I could just stand here and tell you a dozen different lies I know you want to hear."

"No." *God no, he didn't want to hear lies. Not tonight.*

"Okay, then, here it is: I can't promise you I'm not going to get hurt. And I can't promise you I'm not going to fall head over heels in love with you, even if you never let yourself love me back."

No other woman had ever talked to him like this. No one had ever had the courage to be so honest with her emotions. So up-front about the mistakes she might make.

He wanted to stop her from saying anything more, but she put one finger over his lips to keep him quiet.

"Right now, I'm sure of only one thing: I want you." She paused, lifted her mouth to his, slowly sliding her finger out from between their lips. "I'm absolutely certain that I want to make love with you tonight, Sean. Please stay."

On a groan, he captured her mouth with his and lifted her into his arms. Seconds later she was lying on her bed beneath him.

Their "last kiss" from the parking lot had nothing on this one, not now that he knew he wasn't going to leave, that he wasn't going to have to work like hell to tear himself away from her.

Part of him wanted to get right to it and try to quench his thirst for her right away, a thirst that had grown impossibly big and fast from that first moment he'd seen her. But the other part of him wanted to make this first time last, wanted to draw it out so that both of them were delirious with pleasure by the time they came together.

And in the end, despite his raging libido, he knew that Rebecca was a woman who should be savored.

Which was exactly what he was going to do tonight.

Chapter Eighteen

No one had ever kissed her like this, with such gentle desire, with such heat, with so much need.

All for her.

And, oh, she needed him just as bad.

So although she'd always been a woman who let men take the lead in bed, with Sean she couldn't stop herself from wrapping her legs around his waist and urging him to take anything—everything—he wanted from her.

But then, instead of answering her body's plea, he was pulling back, lifting himself up on his forearms to stare down at her.

"You're so beautiful."

His compliment warmed her even more. "Thank you."

"Ah," he said softly, running his fingertip gently along her hairline. Little tingles met his touch and she almost whimpered at the soft pleasure of it. "I don't think you understand quite what I'm saying to you."

His eyes were just as dark, just as unfathomable as

ever. But his tone was richer, filled with a depth of emotion he'd never let her hear before.

"Yes, I do. You think I'm pretty."

His smile was tinged with heat. "You're so much more than pretty, Rebecca." He pressed a kiss to the same spot on her forehead that he'd been lightly caressing. "Gorgeous. Stunning. Perfect. None of those words do you justice."

She'd expected goose bumps and heat and pleasure. She knew she cared enough for Sean to find emotion in their kisses and caresses.

But she hadn't thought there'd be such sweet words from a man who was so usually cautious with them.

He kissed her, then, a kiss that echoed his praise.

A kiss that made her believe what he was saying was real.

"Something happens when you kiss me," she admitted. "I feel beautiful."

"Never doubt that you are, not for one single second."

She felt like he was seeing all the way into her soul, into the hidden part where she'd tried to ignore the hurt from every man who had rejected her for not being exciting enough, for not being a risk taker. Even with Stu—especially with Stu—she'd lost hold of herself as a sensual woman.

One kiss at a time, Sean was giving that ultra-important female power back to her.

She still had her robe on and she wanted nothing more than to be naked beneath Sean, his powerful body pressing hers into the mattress. She reached for the sash, but before she could untie it, his hands were over hers.

"Undressing you for the first time is a pleasure I don't want to miss."

She actually whimpered before agreeing. "Okay. But could you hurry?"

That smile she loved to see so much played around his mouth. "No."

She groaned with disappointment even as her body heated up with increased anticipation. Along with the knowledge that she might not survive this night after all. Not if Sean was intent on driving her out of her mind before he finally took her.

"Pretty please?"

"So sweet." She watched his long, strong fingers slowly untie her sash. "And usually so good at getting what you want with that sweetness."

She was going to protest the "usually" when his finger-tips grazed the bare skin of her belly where her shirt had ridden up from her pajama bottoms. Instead of speaking, she sucked in a breath, her muscles trembling beneath his light touch.

"Such soft skin." He shifted on the bed so that he could press a kiss to that bare patch of skin and thrill bumps raced across her skin. "And so beautifully sensitive."

Another kiss followed the first, but before she could thread her hands into his hair, he was moving away again, putting his hands onto the lapel of her robe and sliding it off her shoulders.

With every bare patch of skin he uncovered there was another kiss. Places that had never been sensitive before responded to his slightest touch, to the brush of his lips followed by his fingertips grazing the new spot he'd marked.

Finally—*finally!*—he slid the robe all the way off her arms.

He'd seen her in fairly skimpy pajamas before, but even though there'd been attraction between them a week ago, it hadn't been this red hot. And neither of them had had any intention of acting on it.

But oh, were they acting now, as Sean slowly ran his fingertips down over the straps of her top.

"Just take it off, already!"

"All this time, I thought you were so patient," he said, a soft, heated chuckle underlying his words.

"In case you didn't hear me earlier," she said in a far more petulant tone than she could believe was coming out of her own mouth. "I said I wanted you." She waited until his gaze met hers. "Really, really, really want."

That won her a kiss, one that seared them both. With the few brain cells she had left, she tried to wriggle out of her clothes.

Sean's hands were there before she could pull her shirt any higher than the middle of the ribs.

"Not yet."

"Can't blame a girl for trying," she muttered, but then he was running kisses over her newly bared skin, exposing one inch at a time, and she had to admit that he knew exactly what he was doing.

"Lift your arms for me, sweetheart."

She was so bowled over by the endearment that she actually froze. She should have just let it slip by, should have locked it away in her heart for future cold winter nights, but how could she?

"You called me sweetheart."

"Arms up," he said again and she knew he was uncomfortable with what he'd just given her.

When her top was finally off, she should have been

focused on the fact that she was completely bared to his hot gaze. Soon, she would be lost to anything but Sean's touch, his kisses, the slow slide of his body into hers.

She felt shy as she looked up at him, and not only because she was partially naked and he was still holding her hands up above her head so that she couldn't cover herself. But when any other guy would have been ogling her body right now, his eyes hadn't dropped from hers.

He didn't think he was a good man. He didn't think he had a heart.

How could he be so blind?

She needed to let him know. "No one's ever said that to me before. I liked it. Say it again."

He kissed her. "You are so sweet."

She shouldn't need to hear it, knew better than to need the endearment. But when had she ever really known better?

"Sean. Please."

He'd barely lifted his lips from hers and the word came against her lips so softly that she might not have heard it if she hadn't been able to feel it, too.

"Sweetheart."

And as he kissed her again, and then began the long, slow process of kissing his way down her body, Rebecca knew she wasn't in any danger of falling.

She'd already gone and done it. Despite every warning he'd given her, despite every warning she'd given herself, she'd fallen for Sean.

Head over heels.

Sean wasn't a man who spouted poetry to the women he bedded. Sex had always been a silent affair, about taking care of physical needs. Sex had never been laughter, or teasing. Definitely not emotion.

And yet, Rebecca was drawing all three from him.

He knew what he should be doing, knew what was smart. Pulling away from her. Telling her he was sorry he'd come to her tonight. Saying this was a mistake.

The problem was, his brain was no longer in charge. If that was the only problem, he might have been able to dig into his self-control to leave before things went any further.

Something else was leading tonight with Rebecca... not just a body that desired her.

But a heart he didn't have the first clue how to control.

Drawing away from her to try and find the space, the air, to set himself back to rights, he made the mistake of looking down at her.

What he saw in her eyes humbled him.

And when she reached for him this time, he didn't have the strength to keep control of their lovemaking. He'd have to savor and prolong another night.

And in that moment Sean was forced to admit that control with Rebecca had never been anything but an illusion.

Her hands found his face again, and she turned her face to kiss both of his palms and then turned him onto his back so that she could lie over him. It was pure instinct to wrap his arms around her and pull her closer.

"Now."

The one word fell from her lips like nectar and he had to drink from her sweetness as she made surprisingly short work of his clothes and protection.

And then, in one seamless move, he was there, right

where he'd longed to be. Wrapped up in Rebecca, in her sweetness and her warmth.

He was happy. Finally, blessedly happy. And for one perfect moment in time, Sean Murphy knew not only pleasure... but peace.

Chapter Nineteen

Early morning over the lake was quite a sight, Bill thought as he watched mist drift up from the water to meet the rising sun.

His mother, Celeste, had gotten in the habit of rising early when he was a baby to enjoy the peace, the stillness and silence of the lake before even the birds woke.

Bill had enjoyed the walk over to his mother's cottage to help her with her kitchen sink. Now, even as he focused on the bolt he was loosening, flashes of blue and white and green through the kitchen window helped settle him.

"How is Elizabeth doing, honey?"

Bill looked over at his mother. Saying his wife was fine would be the easiest answer.

Unfortunately, it would also be a lie.

Slightly settled transformed to unsettled in a matter of moments. "She's worried about Stu."

Celeste nodded. "She's his mother. Of course she's worried. Has there been any word from my grandson?"

"No."

And now that Bill had more of an idea about why Stu

had left, he understood why his son had left Emerald Lake for a little while. It was a wonderful town. Small, nurturing, comfortable.

But a man needed to figure out some things for himself, far away from the people who were so sure they knew who he was.

There had been plenty of times Bill wouldn't have minded disappearing himself.

The one person he'd never had to hide from, fortunately, was his own mother. Celeste was simply one of the easiest people to be around. His mother wasn't a woman who pushed. Rather, she seemed to have infinite patience.

Appreciating the care his mother had always taken with him, he wanted to set her mind at ease about Stu. "He'll come back when he's ready."

Bill would let his son tell his grandmother his own truth at his own pace.

"Yes, I expect he will," his mother agreed. "This is home. For all of us."

Her comment had him asking, "Has Sean said anything to you about staying in Emerald Lake?"

"Announcements aren't his style." She laughed. "Neither is falling in love, however."

Bill almost dropped the wrench he was holding. "Love? He's in love?"

"Sean looks at Rebecca the way you once looked at Elizabeth."

Bill felt the muscles in his body tighten, one by one, until he was so stiff he couldn't move without being afraid that shards would crack off.

He and his mother never spoke about his marriage. Not once in thirty-six years had Celeste broached his relationship with Elizabeth. The two women had never been fast friends, but he'd accepted that they were different. One slow, one fast. One quiet, one loud. Both had a place in his life.

In his heart.

It was none of his mother's business, and yet Bill felt he had to say, "I still look at Elizabeth that way."

"Betsy."

He moved away from the sink to pick up a smaller wrench from his tool box. "Excuse me?"

"You used to call her Betsy. For years, you never used her formal name. She was always your Betsy."

His Betsy.

He'd woken up this morning, telling himself that everything was going to be okay. Stu would come back when he was ready. Sean had called to suggest a hike on the weekend. He and his wife had shared a bed again. They hadn't really touched, except by mistake, but at least they'd both been in the same place at the same time.

He shouldn't be surprised that it took his mother so few words to point out to him that everything was still broken.

Elizabeth. Betsy. They were just names.

But were they really?

Had his marriage finally gone past the point of no return? After all these years of trying to act like nothing was wrong, now that the door to unrest was finally open, did he have a prayer of getting it to shut again?

Or was there no way back? Was the only choice for him and Elizabeth to forge ahead without each other?

Did Stu have it right? Was leaving the only option?

Just as Bill's father had done.

A long forgotten pain—no, it wasn't forgotten, just pushed aside like so many other emotions Bill didn't want to feel—rushed at him. And this time, he wasn't sure he was capable of continuing to push.

His marriage wasn't the only thing Bill and Celeste didn't talk about.

They also didn't talk about his father.

All these years, he knew she'd been waiting for him to ask. And all these years, he'd told himself it didn't matter, that he'd had a wonderful childhood surrounded by family, by friends, that he loved the family he'd made, his career, his town, his community. He'd worked to convince himself that all of those things were more than enough for him.

But for all the other parts of his life that were good, for everything that made him happy, one truth always remained: he'd never had a father. Not for one single day of his life.

And all his life, he'd been haunted by one question.

Why had his father disappeared?

"Tell me what happened, Mom. Tell me about my father."

If not for her pregnancy, perhaps Celeste would have remained in her parents' house. It was certainly the easier path, to simply continue living the life she had before.

But Charlie had changed everything.

Most young women in her position would have been frightened. Celeste wasn't naive enough not to be scared. Of course having a child would be a big adjustment. A huge one. It wasn't even that Charlie's memory would now live on, whether or not he ever came back to her.

Having a baby of her own simply meant that now all of the love in her heart would have a place to flow to. She loved her parents. Her sisters. Her friends.

But this love was already different.

Different, even, from the love she'd felt for Charlie.

What she'd felt for her husband had been pure. True. But neither of them had truly depended on each other, and she would find her feet without him. She would have to.

This child would look to her for its health. Its happiness. Celeste would be there to give her baby, her child, all of that and more.

In the end, the one hundred dollars left in the bank account was all it took. She found a cottage on the beach, a small place where she could keep an eye on a toddler, with a beach where a growing child could run and play and learn to swim. Her parents tried to fight her decision, but the girl who everyone had always assumed was happy to follow others' lead had turned into a woman who finally knew just what she wanted.

A home of her own.

And a career with which she could not only support her child and herself . . . but that would feed her mind.

Those first months, most of the carpenters in town weren't sure if they were supposed to help her out to please her powerful father or if they should shun her to make sure she failed and had to move back home. She had to cobble together a workforce of newcomers to Emerald Lake, but they were all hard workers, and Celeste got in there with them whenever she could, wielding a hammer until her stomach grew too big.

Other women watched her, women she'd known her whole life, and while some of them were clearly aghast at what she was doing, many more of them told her that working for the war effort had given them a taste of something they wanted more of. Nights with her sisters, Rose and Evelyn, as they knitted blanket and caps and booties for her baby, sowed the seeds for Lake Yarns. The two Farrington daughters were the last girls the town would have expected to want to get their hands dirty with work.

But they were more like their successful, driven father than even he wanted to see.

It had been a struggle to get her construction business off the ground. But bigger than the struggle had been the joy of it.

She would miss Charlie forever. No other man could possibly replace him, but when the day came that her waters broke and the midwife made it to her cottage just in time to greet quiet, little Bill, Celeste was happier than she even knew was possible.

Years went by, one then two, and she had a chubby, laughing toddler to chase around at building sites and down the beach.

That was when the letter came, with the ticket to New York City.

A dozen different thoughts and emotions coursed through her one after the other. She was thrilled to know that his hands had touched these tickets, to know that he wanted to see her again. She was surprised that he'd reached out like this to her, and yet it was inevitable all at the same time because nothing had ever really been finished—the door had never been closed. She was scared about what she knew she'd have to tell him about how her life had changed since he'd gone. And she was nervous about what he'd do this time, if he could possibly be out looking for another profitable con.

But she never once thought about not getting on that train.

She never once considered not going to see him.

She had to see him.

Because this time, she was going to be the one to make the decision about the door opening up again...or closing forever this time.

Charlie was waiting for her at the station. His hat was pulled down low and he was thinner, so much thinner than he'd been before.

"Celeste."

"Charlie."

It wasn't awkward. They could never be strangers. And yet, Celeste knew, somehow, that keeping this distance was important.

Vitally important.

"You must be hungry after the train ride."

He knew enough about her to know that she was always hungry, and that she often got so caught up in what she was doing that she forgot to eat.

"I know a place just around the corner. A place we can talk."

Walking beside the man she loved so deeply, without touching him, without going to her tippy-toes and kissing him, was the most difficult thing she'd ever done. Far more difficult than telling her father that her husband had disappeared. Worlds harder than giving birth or raising a baby on her own.

"Yes," she said softly. "I would like to talk."

A table between them, coffee steaming from cracked white mugs, he simply sat and looked. She did the same, drinking him in.

"Falling in love with you was never the plan."

To keep herself from reaching out to touch him, Celeste had curled her hand around the mug, barely aware that it was scalding her skin.

"My father supposed that was the case."

"He was right. Money was what I was after. You were my target. I should have been pleased by how easy you were to woo, how much you liked to hear my smooth words, how quickly you agreed to marry me."

Just as she should have been going cold at her husband's frank admissions of why he'd pursued her, she knew that there were many different truths, weren't there? And only one had ever been important to Celeste.

"I loved you right from that first moment," she told him honestly, knowing there was no sense in pride here in this diner, sitting across from the man she still loved with all of her heart.

She watched his breath catch in his throat, remembered the taste, the scent of his skin on their wedding night. The one sweet night that had given them Bill.

"One day," he finally said in a hoarse voice, "I realized I wasn't simply saying what I thought you wanted to hear. I was telling you the truth. I loved you. I wanted a life with you."

She hadn't needed him to bring her here to say that. She had never doubted his love for one second. Well, maybe in the dark of night there had been a time or two when those doubts had crept in. But sitting here, across an old Formica table, surrounded by rough-looking strangers, she knew she would never doubt it again.

"And now you want me to know why."

"God, yes." His grip on his own coffee cup was so tight that the whites of his knuckles showed through his tanned skin. "I've barely slept since that night. Since I left."

She waited silently for him to gather the courage, the strength, to share the truth with her. Some things, she'd learned since leaving her parent's house and striking out on her own, took time. Growing a baby. Teasing out a smile from a toddler's tears. Building a business.

Speaking the truth.

"If I had been working for myself, I would have stopped. I would have given up my previous life for you. So many bad decisions led me to you, Celeste. So how can I regret everything in my past? I pulled myself up out of the gutter by working for the wrong kind of people. As soon as I fell in love with you I wanted to pull out of the deal I'd made." He closed his eyes. "But I couldn't. Not when it would have put your life, your family's life, at stake, too."

His hands were shaking, now, little drips of coffee spilling out across his fingers, running down to make little puddles on the tabletop. "I had to take the money. I had to leave, even though I knew that if I left I could never come back. I could never risk your life because I selfishly wanted your love for my own."

She'd been planning to tell him all along. Now, she said, "You have a son."

His mug of coffee tipped, would have spilled, but Celeste caught it before it could go all the way over. Her fingers brushed his, then, and she let them still over his hand.

Their eyes locked. Held.

"Bill is two and full of energy. He looks like you."

She pulled her hand back to reach into her pocket. She handed the photo to Charlie.

"My god." Tears were streaming down his face, the tears that she'd watched him hold back so forcefully from the moment she stepped off the train. "He's beautiful." His eyes lifted from the picture. "So are you, Celeste."

She could taste her own tears on her lips as she smiled back at him. And she could see, as clearly as she'd ever seen anything, that her husband wanted desperately to start a new life with her and his son.

Celeste would have risked herself in a heartbeat for Charlie's love. To be with him. But she could never risk her own son.

Not even for the only love she'd ever know as a woman.

"I will never regret my love for you, Charlie."

She pushed back her chair and made herself say, "Good-bye."

"My mother gave me a New York City paper the following year. Your father had passed away."

Bill was stunned by everything his mother had said. He knew he'd have to ask her to repeat it to him. Another day, when it wasn't all such a big shock.

"I never really understood what it was to have a father or lose one." Not until he'd become a father. Not until he'd realized the very last thing he ever wanted to do was fail his children.

Anger, that rare emotion that he'd been feeling more and more lately, came again. "The people he worked for stole everything from us!"

"Well," his mother said slowly, as was her way, "not everything. I still had you. You had me. There were siblings and cousins and grandparents and Elizabeth and Sean and Stu." She paused before adding, "And now, perhaps, Rebecca." Her kitchen clock clanged eight a.m. "Your men must be expecting you at the building site."

Knowing he was being dismissed—and how difficult telling this story had to have been for his mother—Bill forced himself to stand up.

"I'm not done with your faucet yet."

She smiled and it took a decade, at least, off her age. "I'll fix it myself."

Of course she would, as they both knew the only reason he ever helped her with anything around the house was rarely because she was too old to take care of it herself, but because it gave mother and son an excuse to be together.

"Besides," she continued, "you have plenty of things of your own to fix, don't you?"

She gave him a hug and he hugged her back tighter than he ever had before. His mother had been everything to him as a child, and she was still the best person he knew, along with his sons.

As he walked back down the beach, the sun was much higher in the sky now than when he'd walked toward Celeste's cottage earlier that morning, and it worked to warm him. The urge to take off his shoes and socks soon had him standing on the sand, feeling it between his toes. Amazingly, rather than being upset by his mother's story, he was filled with new hope.

His mother had no choice but to give up her true love.

But he had a choice.

Elizabeth—his Betsy—was still there. It was simply the love they needed help finding.

Chapter Twenty

Many times throughout the early-morning hours, Sean had tried to make himself slip out of Rebecca's bed. Finally, he gave in to her warmth, knowing he didn't have a prayer of forcing himself to leave.

Not when she was so soft.

Not when she was slowly waking and shifting in his arms to kiss him.

Not when her hands were sliding over his shoulders and the pleasure in her eyes was the sweetest thing he'd ever seen as he came into her again.

When, he wondered later as they lay panting in each other's arms after falling over the peak again together, would he be able to savor her? He'd need his control back for that.

Only, where Rebecca was concerned, his self-control was clearly in short supply.

"Good morning." Rebecca's first words of the day were husky. Lazy with fulfilled pleasure.

But he could hear the uncertainty in them, too.

Sean couldn't give her the words she needed to push

that uncertainty away, but he could kiss her again, just the two of them safe beneath the sheets even as the rest of the world waited outside her front door... a world full of people who would eventually find out about the two of them, even if they did their best to hide what was between them.

If control had been there, Sean would have felt confident in his ability to keep his feelings for Rebecca to himself. But given that he couldn't seem to look at her without wanting to touch her, kiss her—or just plain keep drinking in her beauty—he knew there'd be talk.

Questions.

That was why he forced himself to stop kissing her. And to say, "We won't be able to hide our relationship."

She reacted to his statement as if it were a bucket full of icy water poured over them both. Her muscles immediately went from loose to stiff and she scooted from his arms, pulling the sheet over her naked skin.

Did she have any idea how beautiful she looked sitting there, her silky hair tumbling over her shoulders, her mouth full from his kisses, her eyes big and so green they could have named Emerald Lake for her?

"Sean?"

He shook his head, trying to clear it. "I'm sorry. I got lost for a minute."

"Lost?"

He met her confused gaze, knew that he was a fool for saying it aloud, but there was no keeping it inside. "You're beautiful, Rebecca." At her flustered expression, he moved closer, picked up her hands, kissed them. "I've screwed up every second with you since waking up."

He was glad to see a small smile work its way onto her lips. "Not *every* second."

Sean knew the easiest thing would be to pull Rebecca back into his arms and make that flush of desire spread across her skin. And it was tempting, so damn tempting, to do just that.

But for all the pleasure it would bring him—the pleasure it would bring both of them—he'd spend the rest of the day hating himself for avoiding the truth. And knowing that he was a coward.

He'd never been so tempted to chuck everything in for sex. Still, despite how much he wanted her again, he knew this conversation was more important.

Sex would come again. It was inevitable given their attraction. Their physical connection to each other. But words, important things that needed so badly to be said... he'd learned so long ago that the longer one waited to have a difficult conversation, the more difficult it was to ever have it. Until the day when there was no way to talk anymore, at all.

"I've never been with anyone from town."

He watched as Rebecca took a deep breath. Finally, she said, "We're not together, Sean. We simply slept together."

It should have been what he wanted to hear. She wasn't trying to hold him down to anything more than physical attraction. So then, why did her words grate at him, at his heart more than anywhere else?

Still holding her hands, he tugged her closer, close enough that the sheet slipped and slid from her curves.

"I want to take you out. Tonight. On a real date."

"Why?"

Her blunt question had him smiling. If this conversation had been with any other woman, he'd be itching to get out of bed. To get on with the day. To get away from the woman's hopes. Her dreams.

Instead, he was the one asking for more. And making sure he got it.

"Why am I asking you out?"

"Yes. Why?"

"Because I like you, Rebecca."

So much.

Too much.

And she deserved more from a man than one night—and morning—of scorching sex.

Something flashed in her eyes as she murmured, "I like you, too, Sean."

His chest clenched at the simple words. Liking each other was perfect. Ideal.

Liking her would be enough.

It had to be.

"So we'll like each other during the day and have sex at night?" she asked. "For as long as you're in town?"

Telling himself, yet again, that he didn't want more than that, he nodded. "Exactly."

Rebecca slid from the bed, pulling the sheet with her. "You're right, you know. People are going to have a field day talking about us. You're Stu's brother and I'm his ex-fiancée. It's a gossip goldmine."

Her eyes, her expression, were clouding over more and more with each sentence. "It's one of the reasons I tried to stay away from you. But I couldn't." He blew out a breath. "I just couldn't."

Just like that, her pretty smile returned as she shrugged. "Who cares what people think? People are already talking about me. Might as well give them something fresh to gossip about."

She said it so easily, but he already knew her well

enough to know how sensitive she was. Strangers were simply friends she hadn't met yet. The urge to protect her from being hurt throbbed inside of him.

And the worst part of all was the sure knowledge that the person who was going to hurt her most of all wasn't a gossip . . . it was him.

Sean knew a hell of a lot better than to get involved with her. But then she was kissing him and it didn't matter what he knew.

He could focus only on what he felt. Not just desire, but the kind of peace he hadn't known for two decades.

When the phone rang, she pulled back, her eyes dilated, her breathing uneven. "It could be Alice. Downstairs."

"You have to get it, don't you?"

When she nodded, he reached over for the phone beside her bed and handed it to her.

"Oh, yes. Sure. Thanks for letting me know, Alice. I'll be right there." She gave him the phone to hang up. When he had, she said, "Your mother is waiting for me downstairs." Her voice dropped to a hush. "She'll know. She'll see me and know about you."

Sean didn't doubt that she somehow would. "I'll come meet her with you."

She jumped out of his lap. "No!"

"No?"

She shook her head. "Whatever she wants, you'll only make it worse." As if she realized what she'd said a beat too late, she grimaced. "I just mean that because the two of you don't really get along—" She pressed two fingers to her lips. "I'm going to shut up now and get in the shower so that I can meet your mother without looking like I've been having crazy sex all night long with her son." Her mouth quirked up on one side for a split second. "All morning, too, I guess."

But Sean couldn't stand the thought of their night together ending so suddenly. Especially not if his mother was the reason it had to end.

Standing up, he reached for Rebecca before she could lock herself in the bathroom. "Last night, this morning... they were perfect."

She blinked up him, before echoing, "Yes, perfect."

"You never gave me an answer about tonight," he reminded her, lightly caressing the pulse point at her wrist, dizzy with wanting her...even though he'd just had her. Surely there would come a day when he'd have had his fill of her sweetness, her smile, the silk of her hair between his fingertips as they made love. "Will you let me take you on a real date?"

Rebecca was silent for a moment before saying, "I like Thai food." She pulled out of his arms and was halfway into the bathroom when she turned back to him. "Just sex would be easier, you know."

He couldn't account for his response to that statement. "Just sex" should have been enough for him. He'd already told her he wasn't going to fall in love with her. They both knew he was leaving as soon as Stu came back and resolved things with everyone.

But Sean didn't like what she'd just said. Not one bit.

"Oh, Rebecca," Elizabeth said in a bright voice. "I'm so glad you're finally up and about. I didn't wake you, did I? Or interrupt something important?"

Rebecca had barely gotten to the bottom of the

stairs when Elizabeth stood up, looking as pressed and perfect as she always did. Even though Rebecca was by no means a messy person, she always felt like she should fix her hair or do her makeup better around Sean's mother.

"Good morning," she said. "No, you didn't wake me."

She fought the battle against blushing over the thought of precisely what Elizabeth had interrupted...and lost. Fortunately, apart from a slightly questioning quirk of her eyebrows, Elizabeth didn't seem particularly interested in Rebecca's too-hot cheeks.

"I had a thought about your festival this morning. And I think I know how we might be able to save it."

Utterly thrown off by Elizabeth's very unexpected statement, Rebecca fumbled for time to settle herself down. "Would you like to sit down in the dining room and have a cup of tea?"

The two of them went into the sunlit room. "You really have done a lovely job with the inn, Rebecca."

Hold on a minute. Was trying to help with the festival and complimenting her on the inn Elizabeth's way of apologizing for her behavior at dinner?

She studied Sean's mother's face carefully before saying, "Thank you."

Elizabeth held her gaze and Rebecca was sure she saw a silent *I'm sorry for the way I treated you* in them even though the words she actually said were, "You're welcome."

Alice popped by to take their breakfast orders and Rebecca was surprised to realize she was starving. Normally, sitting down with Sean's mother would have made her lose her appetite.

Then again, she'd probably burned off a ton of calories having all that sex.

With Sean.

Her eyes flew to the other woman's face and she couldn't stop her hands from covering her even hotter cheeks. Fortunately, Elizabeth wasn't looking at her. She was gazing around at the room.

"There is so much history here. So much beauty everywhere you look. The first time I came to Emerald Lake, I knew I wanted to stay forever."

Rebecca had never felt any real connection to Elizabeth. Until now.

The surprises just kept on coming.

"It was the same for me," she said softly. "I saw the lake, the mountains, this inn, and I knew."

Elizabeth turned her gaze back to Rebecca. "Have I ever told you how Bill and I met?"

Rebecca was glad that Angie came to them with the teapots and croissants right then. She needed way more time to gather her composure. Perhaps if she'd gotten more sleep, she'd be better up to handling this strange conversation.

Finally, she replied, "No, you haven't."

"We met right here. In this dining room. Bill was on a date with another woman." She chuckled, but Rebecca couldn't help but think there was some sadness behind it. "I didn't care, you know."

"Oh."

Really, what was she supposed to say to that? Especially when she was sleeping with her ex-fiancé's brother. Talk about stones and glass houses.

"I've shocked you, haven't I?"

She wanted to say no. Anyone else would have, darn it. Instead, that truth serum that she must have drunk at birth had the words "A little bit" coming out instead.

"Well, you know how gorgeous my sons are, so—"

Rebecca swallowed wrong and started coughing.

"Are you all right, honey?"

Honey? Had she gone to bed on one planet and woken up in another one—one where Elizabeth called her honey?

"I'm fine," Rebecca said, dabbing her watering eyes with the napkin as she tried to deal with the startling shift in Elizabeth's behavior toward her. "Sorry. Go on."

"As I was saying, Bill was quite something when he was younger. He still is." Elizabeth was silent for a moment. Pensive. Giving herself a little shake, she continued, saying, "My family was renting a house across the lake for one week that summer. It was our last night here." She pinned Rebecca with her gaze. "I had one night to win him so I pulled out all the stops, first in this restaurant and then later at the Saturday night bonfire that all the kids were going to."

"You must have dazzled him."

She expected Elizabeth to smile back at her. Instead, deep sorrow moved across the woman's face.

"Once upon a time I guess I did."

Rebecca wanted to say something to comfort her, but how could she? They weren't friends. And she had no idea what it was like to be married thirty-six years and to hit a rough patch.

"In any case, we were talking about the festival, weren't we?" Elizabeth said, suddenly.

Rebecca forced her brain to whiplash back to the

beginning of their conversation. "You had an idea for the festival?"

Elizabeth leaned forward. "Do you know what the land around the inn was originally zoned for?" She didn't wait for Rebecca to answer. "Agriculture."

"Wait a minute," Rebecca said slowly. "I thought the inn was originally a tycoon's summer house."

"It was. He got rich from newspapers, but what he really dreamed of doing was farming." Elizabeth gave her a wide smile. "I called a friend at the courthouse this morning and asked her to check their files. When the inn was turned into lodging, they added the commercial zoning. But they never took away the other zoning."

"So, it's still a farm?"

"Technically, yes. And maple syrup comes from maple tree farms."

In her excitement, Rebecca couldn't stop herself from reaching out and squeezing Elizabeth's hand. "Thank you for finding this." Now she and Sean could go back to the council with real firepower to ask them to pull the petition.

Sean walked into the room then and Rebecca felt Elizabeth's hand still beneath hers. Slowly, Rebecca moved hers away.

"Sean, honey," his mother said. "Join us."

"Actually," Rebecca pushed back her chair, "I need to take over from Alice at the front desk. You can take my seat."

She was afraid to look at him, knowing she was sure to give herself away in front of his mother. Sean might not be able to see that she was falling head over heels for him, but a woman would know it. His mother, especially, would know it. And Rebecca didn't think she'd be at all happy about.

Rebecca quickly said, "Thank you, again, Elizabeth," then left the room.

"What was Rebecca thanking you for?"

And why had the woman whose bed he'd just left been holding his mother's hand? No question, it was the last thing he'd expected to see.

"I think I've found a way around the festival petition."

Even though he'd been hard on the trail of loopholes, he wasn't surprised by how smart his mother's plan was. It was a stroke of luck, for sure, but one that might not have come about if not for Elizabeth's digging and knowledge of the Adirondack Park's history.

"That was nice of you to help her."

"I was thinking the same thing about you," she said softly. "You like her, don't you?"

"Everyone likes Rebecca. The guests. The locals. Even the babies stop crying when she picks them up."

His mother's eyes softened in a way he couldn't remember seeing. "Babies," she said softly. "I can't wait until the day I can hold your children." His stomach clenched even tighter than usual as she hit him with, "I saw you kissing her last night."

Sean felt every muscle in his body go still. Just as he'd told Rebecca this morning, he hadn't been planning on hiding their relationship. But he'd assumed it was their secret to tell.

"How could you have seen us?"

"I came by the inn hoping to see you. To talk about—" She paused, before saying, "Things. I was just out of my car when I realized I wasn't alone in the parking lot."

"And you just stood there and watched us?"

"No."

"You just said you watched us kiss."

"Yes. I did. But it wasn't like that, I swear to you, Sean."

He pushed his chair back to go, but she reached across the table and grabbed both of his hands.

"Please, honey, let me explain."

He'd heard enough of her explanations for one lifetime. He should have left, shouldn't have felt the least bit guilty about it.

But she was his mother.

And he couldn't walk out on her, no matter how badly he wanted to, especially with Rebecca's soft voice in his head, saying, *"Why don't you let anyone get close to you? I see the way you barely say a word to your mother. I see how hurt she is when you keep pushing her away."*

"You and Rebecca were sharing such a private moment. And even though I have to admit I don't know how I feel about the two of you having a relationship—"

"It's none of your business."

"I know that," she snapped back. "That's what I'm trying to say. I couldn't interrupt you, couldn't have possibly let you know I was there." Her eyes softened. Saddened. "I know what it's like to fall in love, Sean."

Fall in love?

No.

Hell no.

He'd come down here to talk to her about Stu, not to discuss his first kiss with Rebecca. A kiss that had turned into a night—and a morning—of the most wonderful lovemaking he'd ever known.

With the sweetest woman he'd ever had the privilege of kissing.

That was when he realized, a beat later than he should have because he could barely drag his mind away from Rebecca, what his mother's spying meant. "If you saw us kiss, you heard about Stu, too, didn't you?"

She took a shaky breath. "My poor baby. Why did he think he had to run?"

"He didn't think any of us could handle the truth. And it's true, isn't it?" he said softly. Deliberately. "Our family has never been able to handle the truth, has it?"

Knowing he'd said too much, that he'd already stayed too long at Emerald Lake, at the inn—that things were only going to get more complicated with his parents and Rebecca if he didn't shove out again soon—Sean slid his arms free of his mother's grip.

"I told Dad I'd meet him for a hike. I've got to go."

Elizabeth's mouth was completely dry, so dry she could hardly swallow. She picked up her teacup, but her hands were shaking so hard that she could barely lift it from the saucer without spilling it all over the table.

Sean had never spoken to her like that before. Never said something like, *"Our family has never been able to handle the truth, has it?"*

Fear and guilt rose up inside of her in equal measures.

Sean hadn't spilled her secret to Rebecca last night in the parking lot when the young woman had flat out asked him why he had such a fractured relationship with his mother. Elizabeth should have felt safe, knowing that if he wouldn't tell Rebecca—the woman who clearly held his heart—he wouldn't tell anyone.

But she didn't feel safe.

Not even close.

She'd come to the inn this morning to begin the process of making amends. Rebecca was easier to approach, of course, which was why Elizabeth had started with her. They didn't have a long history, and the truth was, the young woman was very sweet. Inherently likeable. The only reason Elizabeth had held herself back from becoming friends with Rebecca was because of her concern for her sons.

There was no point lying to herself anymore—just as Bill had said, it had been clear right from the start that while Stu and Rebecca obviously enjoyed each other's company a great deal, they were no love match. There were no sparks. Nothing that could possibly hold a family together through the ups and downs of life.

Elizabeth knew all about those ups and downs. The thrill of saying "I do" beneath the rose arbor outside the inn thirty-six years ago. Discovering she was pregnant with each of her sons and then giving birth to them, two years apart. The joy she'd felt when she held each of her children for the very first time, when she'd looked into their eyes and known only love, had been so intense she'd been stunned by the force of it.

But the flip side to all that joy had come when she'd lost her brother, when grief had propelled her into making first one mistake with a virtual stranger, and then another, even bigger one, with her son.

For two decades, she'd survived the fear, the guilt, but this morning she was suffocating under the weight of both. Her body felt heavy, as if moving, breathing were difficult things she'd have to find the strength to work up to.

Perhaps Rebecca would allow her to make amends for her chilly behavior over the past months, especially if her suggestion for saving the festival actually made a difference.

But would her son ever forgive her for making him carry the burden of her secret all these years?

And then there was Bill. Her husband had held her last night.

But she'd felt him warring with himself the entire time.

Sean and his father were climbing a steep, rocky section on their way to Echo Cliff. Rather than walking single file up a narrow trail, they were side by side, using their hands and feet to get up the wet rocks. The snow had melted almost all the way up to the top by now and icy water was streaming down the trail.

They'd been hiking in silence for several minutes, but although Bill was one of the most easygoing people Sean had ever known, it hadn't been a comfortable silence. How could it be when there was so much unsaid between them?

Sean had been close to his father until his teens and he knew Rebecca was right, that his father wanted to be closer to his son again.

But had she guessed just how badly the son wanted to be closer to his father again, too?

Deciding it was time to break the silence, at least where he felt he could, Sean said, "I need to talk with you about Stu."

"Your mother told me why Stu left."

Frustration bit at Sean. "He should have talked to me.

I'm his brother. He should have known he could trust me. With anything."

"His leaving, his keeping a secret from you, neither of those are your fault, Sean."

Suddenly it was hard for Sean to breathe. It had nothing to do with their climb. Nothing to do with the altitude. *Secrets.*

"I'm his father," Bill said in a rough, ragged voice. "If anyone should have seen his turmoil, should have guessed what he needed to get off his chest, it was me. You and Stu have always been the most important things to me. You know that, don't you?"

For all the distance between them, Sean did know it. "You've been a great father."

He could practically see his father's brain working, knew the question that was coming next: *So then why did you pull away from me so long ago?*

Needing to do something, anything, to cut that question off at the pass, Sean said, "So you also know that Rebecca and I are seeing each other." He left off the *while I'm in town* part of the sentence, because he didn't want his father to think that Rebecca was in any way cheapened by agreeing to a short-term affair with him.

"Good," was what he father finally said. There was no mention of Elizabeth seeing them kissing in the inn's parking lot. That wasn't Bill's way. "Rebecca is a truly lovely woman."

Sean realized he hadn't expected anything less from his father than complete and immediate support about his changed relationship with Rebecca. Bill had always been there for him.

It was his son who had turned away because he'd felt he had no other choice.

As the hill grew steeper, the rocks became slipperier.

Much like the way their conversation was going.

"Not everyone is going to take it as well as you," Sean told his father between breaths.

Out of the corner of his eyes, Sean could see Bill nod. "True. But Rebecca is worth surviving a little gossip for, isn't she?"

Of course, she was.

"I'm not worried about myself. I'm worried about Rebecca. I don't want her to be hurt. By anyone."

His father smiled. "You're in love with her."

Sean went still on the rocks. "I like her."

It was the same thing he'd told Rebecca time and time again. Like was an emotion he could recognize. Like was an emotion he could accept. Like would never cause anyone to cry.

Like would never tear anyone apart.

When his father didn't reply, Sean said, "I've known her only a week." Less than that, if he counted up the days.

"I knew your mother one night. That was all it took."

This was exactly the kind of conversation Sean couldn't have with his father.

Still, even though he knew better—so much better—he couldn't stop himself from saying, "Love at first sight doesn't always work."

A moment later, his father began to slip on the rocks he was standing on. Sean quickly scrambled across the rocks to grab him before he fell.

"Thanks, son."

But Sean knew his father didn't have a damn thing to thank him for.

They made their way to the top in silence, two men staring out at the Adirondack landscape...but neither of them was really seeing it.

Chapter Twenty-One

Rebecca was working hard on her knitting sample when Sean knocked on her door at six p.m. In the middle of a complicated section of the pattern, she called out, "Come in."

When she finally looked up at him, his dark good looks took her breath away just as they always did. But it was more than her lungs that were affected by Sean.

Her heart was there, too, beating hard. Hoping. Wishing. Longing...for something he'd already told her, flat out, that he couldn't give.

His eyes moved over her and the pleasure reflected in them had warmth filling her. No man had ever looked at her like this, like she was so beautiful he could hardly believe his eyes.

Finally, his gaze moved to the yarn in her hands. "I never asked you what you're making."

His voice was a little husky, reminding her of the way he'd sounded when they were making love not twenty-four hours before and he'd called her sweetheart.

A flush moved across her cheeks as she said, "Something from a new pattern book Lake Yarns recently got in. With Andi still on her honeymoon, Carol needed an extra pair of hands."

He picked up the pink, soft cashmere. Watching his large hands gently stroke the delicate fibers, the same hands that had brought her more pleasure that she'd known was even possible, she practically shook with wanting him.

"Is it a dress?"

"No. Not exactly." She tried to take a breath, but it got all caught up in her throat. "It's a book of lingerie. This is going to be a slip. To wear beneath a dress."

He lifted his gaze from the yarn. "Will you wear it for me when you're done with it? No dress. Just the slip."

On the verge of melting into a puddle right here on her carpet, she couldn't speak. All she could do was nod. And then he was kissing her—thank god, because she'd never needed a kiss more—and she had to put her hands on him. Dropping the needles, she wrapped her arms around his broad shoulders and pulled him closer.

The sound of the needles hitting the floor had him pulling back from her.

"Dinner. I'm taking you to dinner."

"I have food in the fridge."

She knew she sounded like a desperate woman, but she didn't care. She wanted him too much to care.

She saw in his eyes just how tempted he was by the thought of staying in tonight, of chucking in their dinner reservations and making a meal out of each other instead.

"You deserve more than just sex, Rebecca. So much more."

The horrible thing was, she knew he was right. Only, dinner wasn't what she was after.

Love.

She deserved love.

Too bad all Sean was offering tonight was dinner. And mind-blowing sex after.

Thirty minutes later they were in Wishing Lake, a pretty town that she hadn't had enough of a chance to explore on her rare days off.

It was one of those perfect nights in the Adirondacks. The sky was clear, the wind was still, and the air was sweet. Rebecca couldn't have set the stage any better for a romantic dinner.

Perhaps, she let herself think for a moment, luck was on her side for once. Maybe, just maybe, if she was really, really lucky, was there a chance that the love she felt for Sean wouldn't go unreciprocated?

"This is a real treat," she told him as they settled into their seats and the wine was poured. "I love Emerald Lake, but sometimes it feels like I never get a chance to leave town."

"The Adirondacks are definitely full of hidden jewels."

The way he'd phrased it had her asking, "Is that why we're at this lake? Are we hiding, too?"

"I told you I'm not going to hide our relationship, Rebecca, and I meant it. I just thought it would be nice to have our first date for just the two of us."

He was right, of course. If they'd gone to one of the restaurants in Emerald Lake, every eye would have been on them. Still, she couldn't help but feel that despite what he said, he might not actually be all that thrilled with being seen with her.

Her nonpoker face must have given her away, because he said, "Tomorrow morning, how about we walk down Main Street holding hands?"

A surprised laugh left her throat. Did he have any idea how sweet he really was?

"I don't know if we need to be quite that blatant. But thank you for offering."

"Once Stu returns, once he isn't afraid to share who he is with the people who've known him his whole life, no one will think twice about you having dated both of us."

"I suppose you're right."

Of course, there was a small matter of when Stu was actually going to come back. And what, exactly, he was going to do and say? Not to mention the matter of when Sean would leave...

"I meant to tell you last night about Stu's lover," she said, suddenly. "But I got distracted."

Sean reached for her hand. "Last night was about you and me. No one else."

For a man who had told her again and again that he wasn't right for her, that he wasn't going to stick around in the long term, he was surprisingly possessive about their time together.

She shouldn't like it. If he were any other man, she'd be remembering the lessons she'd learned from all her failed relationships. She'd be making sure he backed off, making sure he understood that she wasn't his to possess.

But with Sean, well, she couldn't help but like it. Because she couldn't help but want to belong to him.

Of course, she wanted him to belong to her, too.

She was thinking what a huge—and yet beautiful— mess it all was, when Sean said, "You were going to tell me about Stu's friend."

Oh, yes. She kept losing track around Sean, especially

when he was touching her, stroking his thumb across the inside of her palm.

"John is someone we've both known for a long time. He's a very nice person."

Sean's fingers stilled on the stem of his wine glass and she could see his mind working. Processing. Planning.

"Do you have John's phone number?"

"What are you planning to do with it?"

"I'm going to call him. I'm going to try to get Stu to come back home."

Rebecca knew Sean's heart was in the right place. He loved his brother. No one could doubt that for a second.

"Of course, I'll give you John's number. And I know how deeply you care for Stu, but please"—she paused, had to repeat—"please respect your brother's wishes. He asked us not to contact him. He told us he'd come back when he was ready."

She could see that Sean didn't like her answer. "Stu needs to know that I'm there for him. That we all are. We always have been."

"Deep in his heart, he knows that," she promised the incredible man holding her hand. "And when he's less confused and overwhelmed, he'll remember the love that's waiting here for him."

"How can you be so sure?"

"When Stu and I called off the wedding, my family wanted so badly to protect me, to come take me away from it all. But what I really needed was to figure things out for myself, for once. I needed to do it away from the familiar comfort of people who would swoop in and take care of everything for me. I didn't ask them to stay away because I don't love them, or think they don't love me.

I know how much they love me. I just needed to figure out how to love myself, all by myself for the first time. I needed to know that I was strong in my own right. That I'd been right when I decided Emerald Lake was home."

So many times over the past week, Sean had wanted to get to know Rebecca better. Each time, however, he'd forced himself to push his personal questions away, if only to keep them both away from getting too close.

Last night he'd been unable to resist his fascination with her body. Telling himself it didn't make sense to keep fighting his fascination with the rest of her, he asked, "How can you be so sure that you're home?"

"The first time I saw Emerald Lake, I knew it was where I was meant to stay."

"But you long to travel, to see the world."

She nodded. "I do."

"What if it turns out that Paris or Rome or Egypt is really where you're meant to be?"

She took a deep breath. "Well, I suppose the best answer I can give is that I hope I get the chance one day to see if that's the case."

"Why haven't you, Rebecca? I see the way you are with the inn's guests. You're not afraid of meeting new people. In fact, you thrive on it. And if money is an issue, I'm sure you know there are plenty of ways to travel cheap."

She lifted her eyes to his and he hated seeing the defeat in them.

"I'm afraid to fly."

Even as she confessed her secret to him, he knew he should let her be. Should stop pressing her. But it suddenly wasn't enough to know the taste of her skin, the way flecks of gold appeared in her green eyes when she was crying out her pleasure in his arms.

He needed to know everything.

"Why?"

She shook her head. "I don't know."

"There has to be a reason."

Budding anger replaced the defeat in her eyes. He didn't like knowing he'd made her angry, but he was glad to see the resignation disappear.

"Don't you think if I knew the reason that I would get past it, get on an airplane, and go somewhere?"

"Maybe," he said, and then, knowing he was sticking his opinions in where he shouldn't, he didn't stop himself from adding, "Or maybe it's easier to stay stuck right where you are."

Her eyes flashed. "Says the man who clearly found it easier to leave."

He should have seen that coming. But Rebecca's brain was incredibly quick.

And her heart was dead on target. Every single time.

"I had my reasons for leaving," he told her.

She stared at him for a long moment before saying, "You and I slept together last night."

"Yes, I know," he replied. "I was there, loving every second of it."

"We're probably going to sleep together tonight."

He had to smile at that. "I hope so."

"Me too." She paused again. "But here's the thing. I know you're not promising me love. You were really clear on that. But whatever it is that we're doing for however long we're doing it, there has to be a foundation of honesty between us. I know this is our first official date, and on any normal first date I'd be on my best behavior. But we're doing things a little backward." She paused, picked up her wine. "Wait a second." She took a large gulp. "Okay. Here goes. Why did you leave Emerald Lake, Sean? Especially when I can see how much you love it here. And that of all the places you been and seen, this really is your home."

He'd known that if he let himself get close to her, this question would come. But that didn't mean he was any better prepared for it.

"Something happened at home."

"Between you and your mother?"

"Yes."

"What did she do, Sean? What happened that hurt you both so much?"

Sean had never been so tempted to give away his mother's secret. But he couldn't bear to pass his burden on to Rebecca. Wouldn't ever want to put her in the position of having to face his father, or his brother Stu, with the knowledge of what his mother had done.

"Right after Stu left," he said softly, "when I asked if you knew the reason why, you told me you wished you could tell me. But you couldn't."

She shook her head, clearly remorseful over the decision she'd made. "You love him so much. I should have told you earlier."

"No, Rebecca, I can see why you didn't. Stu had your trust. It's like that, Rebecca. I don't want to keep you in the dark, but this isn't my secret to tell."

"Neither was Stu's, but I ended up telling you."

He suddenly realized she didn't yet know about what Elizabeth had seen. "My mother was there. In the parking lot last night."

Her eyes got big. Horrified. "She was...in the parking lot?"

"Yes."

"When we were"—she took another gulp from her glass—"kissing?"

"She heard our discussion about Stu, too."

"Oh, no. What have I done?"

"None of this is your fault." He realized he was echoing his father's words back to her.

"How can Stu possibly see it that way? He asked me not to tell anyone why he left. And here, I've ended up telling everyone."

Sean loved his brother, but the urge to defend Rebecca was strong. Strong enough that he told her, "He has absolutely no reason to be angry with you." Anger rushed him on her behalf. "He never should have asked you to keep his secret."

"But your mother asked you to keep hers, didn't she? And you've kept it. All these years."

He didn't know what to say to that. He felt Rebecca's hand cover his and finally remembered where they were.

"I'm sorry," she said softly. "We both know I should think more before I speak."

He hated the way she took the blame for his problems. He couldn't give her love, but he could work like hell to give her confidence. To fly. To travel.

And to believe in herself as much as he believed in her.

"You're perfect just the way you are, Rebecca."

He'd never kissed anyone in public before, had always been put off by displays of affection in inappropriate places. But tonight, with the moonlight shining in through the window, lighting up Rebecca's silky hair, he didn't care what was appropriate and what wasn't.

His mouth found hers soft and waiting for his kiss.

"I was planning to take you to my bed tonight," Sean said a couple of hours later when they were alternately kissing and stripping off each other's clothes inside her bedroom.

"Mine was closer."

After the heavy discussion that led off dinner, they'd settled into telling each other stories, each trying to make the other laugh harder. Sean had wild tales of elephants in India; Rebecca countered with tales of things that had happened at the inn, stories he had a hard time believing weren't fiction.

"My bedroom is only warm when you're here with me," Rebecca murmured into the crook of his neck as he lifted her up and carried her into the bedroom.

He lay her down on the covers and moved over her. "Go figure."

She giggled against his mouth, his kisses teasing, soft. And oh so potent. The ghost, or spirit, or whatever it was, was momentarily content. She could feel it in the energy of the room, the way it simmered at a low boil, rather than teetering on the edge of anger and pain.

Still, even as Sean began to kiss his way down her body and she instinctively arched into his touch, she knew that contentedness wouldn't last forever.

Lust, passion, was a good start.

But love was all that mattered in the end.

She shuddered as Sean's mouth found her sensitive spots, as she gave up her thoughts to pleasure. And, later, as she cried out beneath him, the words of love were right there on her lips, wanting so badly to be said.

Somehow, she swallowed back her *I love you* as she lost the thread of everything but the sweetness of his love-making, giving herself up entirely to him.

Neither of them noticed the room's temperature shifting back to cool again, or the glass in the windows clanging, or the chilly air shifting and swirling around them as they reached the peak and jumped off together.

Feeling her shiver despite the heat they'd created together, Sean pulled the covers over them. Rebecca threaded one hand through his, putting the other over his heart, falling asleep to the steady beat beneath her palm.

Sean remained awake. He needed to think. Needed to make a plan and stick to it. He'd meant it when he'd said she deserved more than sex, but he'd told himself that a few dates, and some laughter, would be enough.

For a man who never lied, he had to wonder if he was, in fact, doing a hell of a job of it.

Rebecca shifted closer to him in the bed, so soft, so sweet. His guard should have been going up even higher. But he was safe here, with her sleeping, wasn't he?

For just a few hours, couldn't he let his walls drop?

There was enough moonlight coming in through her window for Rebecca to see Sean's features relax into sleep. But it was more than sleep he was giving in to. She could feel it deep in her soul.

They hadn't had sex tonight.

They'd made love.

But he'd been tense afterward and she'd been so afraid that he was going to leave.

Only, he hadn't left.

He'd stayed.

With her.

She heard it then, a low moan coming from the walls, the windows, the floor. And despite knowing she should feel safe in the protective curve of his strong arms, she felt that moan of despair deep in her own heart.

Whether or not he'd intended to, Sean had made love to her tonight.

But that didn't mean he was ever going to let himself love her.

Chapter Twenty-Two

The next morning when she heard Sean turn on the shower, Rebecca picked up the phone. "Hello, this is Rebecca Campbell. Yes, I was in to see you last week. But I need to see you again as soon as possible because I've recently learned something really important about the inn's zoning." She was smiling as she said, "Noon? Yes, I can be there by then."

With bells on.

She was on the phone with Catherine at the town hall saying, "If you could please print out those zoning maps, Cat, I'll be right over," when Sean walked out of her bathroom with a towel wrapped around his waist.

She actually lost the thread of her thoughts as she took in his tanned skin, his muscles, and the heat in his dark eyes.

"Sorry, what was that, Cat?" she said into the phone. "Thirty minutes is perfect. Thanks."

She hung up the phone, tried to find her breath as she said, "Good shower?"

"Lonely shower."

The breath she was about to take caught somewhere in her windpipe. "Oh. You don't mean you and I could have—"

He moved closer, said, "That's exactly what I meant," before bending down for a kiss. He pulled back and said, "Sounds like you were hard at work."

She stared blankly at him. His mouth on hers, along with the way he was showing more skin than he was covering, combined to make her brain go completely blank.

"Work?"

He brushed a lock of her hair away from her cheek and his touch sizzled through her.

"You were checking on the zoning?"

Her brain finally snapped back into place. "My friend Catherine in the county clerk's office confirmed what your mother told me."

"Good. I'll call the council while you shower."

She stood up, put her hand on his cheek. "I already did." She kissed him softly. "Thank you for offering, but I was hoping you could cover for me here for a few hours."

He looked surprised. "You already set up a meeting?"

Rebecca loved Emerald Lake's community. His mother's suggestion to look into the zoning was wonderful. And, of course, Sean's support for her festival touched her deeply.

But some things a woman had to take care of on her own.

This was her idea. Ultimately, it was up to her to fight the final battle. If she succeeded, if she failed...either way, she was twenty-eight years old, and it was finally time to find out what she was made of.

"I don't want you to feel left out after all of your help,"

she said softly, but before she could finish her sentence he was tipping her chin up with his hand.

"Give 'em hell."

"You're not upset that I'm going alone?"

He smiled at her, that beautiful smile that made her insides gooey.

"After seeing the way you played Dick at the bar, I've been wondering if I was standing in your way with the council that first time."

"You were great with them, Sean. You're so good at that sort of thing, so much better than I'll ever be at meetings like that."

"Don't underestimate yourself, sweetheart."

The endearment had her heart skipping a beat every single time he said it.

"I'm trying not to," she said, and then he was kissing her again, and she was on the verge of forgetting all about the zoning maps and the council meeting.

"I've got an inn to run," he said when they finally came up for air. "And you've got a festival to save."

From shower to dressing, to heading out to the clerk's office to driving through the winding Adirondack roads to the preservation council building, Rebecca didn't stop smiling.

"Ms. Campbell," the pretty middle-aged woman at the front desk said with a smile. "They're all expecting you. Are you ready to go in?"

Previously, when Rebecca had been standing in this light-filled entry, she'd been shaking with nerves. She'd been unsure of so many things—her feelings for Sean, along with her chances at convincing the council to let her festival go forward.

And even though not very many days, or hours, had passed, so much had changed.

One sweet kiss with Sean in a roadside dive had turned into so much more.

Sean's mother had approached her almost as a friend would have, or at least as an ally of sorts.

And Rebecca had decided to stop giving up.

From here on out, if she wanted something, she was going for it. Because she'd finally learned that the worst anyone could say was no.

And for the first time in her life, she was banking on yes.

"Yes," she told the receptionist. "I'm ready."

Finally.

"The festival is back on!"

Rebecca had been bursting to tell someone her good news. She'd assumed Sean would be the first person she'd tell, but then, strangely, she found herself driving to his mother's house instead and knocking on the door.

"Rebecca, what a nice surprise." Sean's mother looked like she meant it. "I was just putting together something for lunch. Would you like to come inside and have something to eat?"

"That's a lovely invitation, but I really need to get back to the inn to make sure Sean's okay holding down the fort all alone. I just had to come and say thank you first."

"Why don't I come with you, then? I haven't had lunch at the inn in a while."

Rebecca couldn't refuse the company. After Elizabeth quickly put away the food on her counter, and they walked out to Rebecca's car, Rebecca was simply bursting to share her good news.

"So my suggestion about the zoning was—"

Rebecca interrupted with, "Brilliant."

"I'm glad," Elizabeth said. "I always thought your festival was a great idea. I don't know why no one had thought of it before now, actually. Maybe it takes someone with a fresh eye on the town to see something new."

Rebecca didn't know what to say to that compliment, apart from, "Thank you. That means a lot to me."

"By the way, your fliers and posters look very good, but if you need any help in the future, please don't hesitate to ask."

Elizabeth would have been her first choice, but Sean's mother had never really seemed to like her so she hadn't thought she'd get a yes. "I'd love to work together, but I'm pretty sure we can't afford your graphic design skills this year."

"Nonsense," Elizabeth said with a wave of her hand in the air. "I do pro bono work for local events all the time. Besides, my sons own the inn and the festival directly benefits their business. Of course, I want to help them in any way I can."

Up until that moment, everything had been so good, but the reminder of Elizabeth's fraught relationship with her sons—and the fact that she knew all about her kiss with Sean—made Rebecca glad when they pulled up to the inn.

She should get out of the car. Not open her mouth and mess up the first really good conversation she'd had with Sean's mother.

But, oh, she had no idea how to do the right thing, did she?

"Elizabeth, I wanted to come thank you for helping me

with the festival, and I also—" She had to pause, had to stop to try and find a way to say what she needed to say about Sean. About how much she cared for him.

"You're just what Sean needs, Rebecca."

Rebecca gulped down whatever words had been about to spill. "I am?"

"Yes."

Tears pricked at Rebecca's eyes. It was a day of miracles. First the thumbs-up on her festival and then the same from a woman she'd never even thought really liked her.

"I care deeply for both of your sons. Stu will always be one of my closest friends, and Sean is..." Her words fell away as she looked up at his mother.

"He's very special," Elizabeth said softly.

When they headed into the inn, Sean was clearly surprised to see them back again, but as Elizabeth excitedly shared the good news with him, he didn't hesitate to reach for Rebecca in front of his mother.

He kissed her and whispered, "I'm happy for you," against her lips.

Shocked that he'd embraced her in front of his mother, Rebecca was amazed to find that all of her worries had been for nothing. First, she'd been worried that she'd never get her festival back on track, and then that dating Sean was the equivalent of banging on a locked door.

But for the first time since the door on her almost-marriage to Stu had slammed shut, she wondered if she'd found something even better than an open window to crawl out of. She'd found a clean, clear lake to swim in. A tall mountain to climb.

And a wonderful man to kiss...at least for a little while.

*   *   *

The next few days were a blur: keeping the inn running while going back and forth with the preservation council and parks commission during the day and making love with Sean into the late hours at night.

Rebecca was equal parts exhilarated and exhausted. Plenty of people had seen her and Sean at city hall looking at records. She'd seen their confused glances, the way they were trying to tell themselves there couldn't possibly be anything going on between them. And then Sean would put his hand on the small of her back, or lean in to kiss her forehead, and the "nothing going on" illusion was shattered.

"You do it on purpose," she said to him the dozenth time he stroked a hand over her hair after they'd picked up two cups of coffee at the Moose Café.

"What do I do on purpose?"

His tone was full of innocence, but she saw the wicked truth in his dark eyes.

"You touch me. Kiss me."

"I like touching you. I love kissing you." He backed up his words with a light stroke of his thumb across her lower lip, his mouth on hers.

"You like shocking them all, don't you?"

He pulled back at that, stared at her for a long moment. "I'm proud of you. Proud to be with you."

"I know you are," she said, trying to stop herself from adding, "At least for now," and failing.

She regretted the words as much as she'd thought she would, hating to see the way his mouth tightened, his jaw jumping once. Twice.

"You were clear from the start about what you can

give. It's just sometimes," she said, barely above a whisper, "I find myself wanting more."

She knew how important honesty was to him, but she'd just told a lie. Straight to his face.

Because she didn't want more *sometimes*.

She wanted more *all the time*.

She knew she had his respect. She knew he appreciated her. That she made him laugh when few others could.

All of that was great.

But she wanted his love.

She'd hoped she could go into this relationship knowing the score, knowing what was possible, and come out on the other side having had a taste of something sweet and lovely. But Sean had known better right from the start, hadn't he?

He'd predicted her broken heart.

And then he'd kissed her...and those predictions hadn't seemed to matter as long as he was close.

Sean started his car and pulled away from Main Street. The air was tense, filled with her longing and his reticence. He hadn't told her where they were going, just that he had a surprise for her. She assumed it had something to do with the festival.

They were driving through the heavily forested part of Route 10 when he pulled into a narrow gravel driveway.

"Where are we?"

"My property."

She shifted in her seat in surprise. "I didn't know you owned property on the lake."

"I bought it a few years ago."

She should have guessed, knowing how much he loved Emerald Lake, that he'd always planned on coming back here one day. For all the problems he had with his family, how could he resist?

Despite the earlier awkwardness, hope moved through her that maybe, just maybe, he'd make that full-time move back here sooner rather than later. If he stayed in town, and they continued to date, it wasn't completely impossible that he could fall in love with her one day, was it?

Knowing her heart was running away with her brain again—in a tremendously stupid and pointless direction, no less—she was just on the verge of vowing not to let it happen again when the trees opened up.

"You have a plane?"

The first hint of a smile came back to his lips. "A float plane."

She swallowed hard, felt all the air begin to press and squeeze out of her lungs.

"Oh." She worked to get control of her lungs, to get her stomach to stop cramping to absolutely no avail. "Your plane takes off and lands on the water?"

"Now that the ice on the lake has melted, I was able to have it delivered." Sean's hand was gentle on her chin as he turned her face to his. "Come up in it with me, Rebecca."

She blinked at him. "This is your surprise."

"I want to take you flying."

"I—" Her mouth was dry, so dry her tongue was stuck to the roof of her mouth. She closed her eyes, whispered, "I can't."

"Rebecca, look at me, sweetheart."

She made herself open her eyes, tried not to see the plane in front of them, floating there at the end of his dock, taunting her.

"You are strong. Determined. Something like getting in a float plane shouldn't break someone as full of resolve as you."

"It will."

"It won't. I know it won't."

"How can you know that?"

"Do you trust me?"

More than she should.

With everything, including her heart.

Still, she could barely get the word out. "Yes."

"We'll just climb in. Get used to the feel of the seat, the belts, the way the world looks from a front-row seat in the sky."

"You make it sound so easy."

"It will be."

And then he leaned over and kissed her, softly at first, but the passion that burned between them was never far from the surface. Her nerves, her fears, all started to melt away as their tongues danced. She reached for him, threaded her hands into his dark hair, and somehow he pulled her onto his lap and she was lost to everything but how much she wanted him.

Before she realized it, he'd opened the door and she was standing on the sand in his arms. He took her hand in his to lead her over to his plane.

"How am I supposed to think straight after a kiss like that?"

"You're not."

"You tricked me."

He didn't look the least bit guilty as he maneuvered them across the sand and toward the dock.

"I did."

And then, just that fast, he had her sitting in the passenger seat of the small plane.

"See. It's not scary at all."

Even though she didn't want to believe him, he was right. The console had a lot of buttons and switches and gauges, but she supposed it wasn't all that different from sitting in Sean's expensive car.

And yet, she still didn't think she could do it.

She could feel him staring at her, taking in her panic. Finally, he said, "I wait all day long to make love with you. Do you know why?"

Oh god. No one had ever spoken like this to her. She couldn't get her mouth to form the word *why* but Sean didn't let that stop him from telling her his reason.

"I've never seen anything as beautiful in all my life as you are when you let go in my arms."

The remaining tension pooling in her gut, her limbs, melted away as he said, "Ever since we met, I've seen how much you love learning new things. How you love adventure. Even fighting for the festival has been fun with you." He looked into her eyes, held her gaze. "Maybe it's just me being selfish. But I want to see you up in the air with me. I want to see the wonder in your eyes when you see the lake from the clouds for the first time."

If this wasn't love, she wasn't sure she knew what love was.

She took a deep breath. And said, "Go."

He didn't wait another second, didn't give her time to change her mind.

They started to glide across the water and she let out a little squeak as they suddenly climbed into the sky.

Just as her lungs were shutting down again, Sean

reminded her, "One breath at a time. Just one, Rebecca. Just give me one."

She could do that, couldn't she? Just one breath. And then another when she was done with that first one.

She wanted to pinch her eyes shut, wanted to pretend she was anywhere but in an airplane, but the dark blue of the water, the light blue of the sky, the faint wisps of clouds, the dark greens of the forest were all starting to make their way into her brain.

Snippets of beauty came at her like a flashing video screen, one after the other, so magnificent that she could still hardly breathe.

And that was when it hit her: she was up in the clouds in a tiny plane . . . and she wasn't dying.

Instead, she was more alive than she'd ever been before.

"Thank you."

She hadn't realized she was crying until she said the two little words.

Trying to take it all in—the magnificence of the lake and mountains and sky—her words were blurry with her tears of joy as she agreed, "It's even more incredible than I imagined."

Sean was silent beside her, but she could feel that something had changed inside the small space. Turning to him, she saw that he was looking at her with such tenderness, such wonder, her heart actually skipped a beat.

"No one has ever cared this much about me," she told him then, as they flew through the sky. "No one has ever made me face my fears like you just did."

She was stunned that he understood her so well, that he knew she'd not only survive the flight but would relish it so completely.

In so many ways, Sean knew her better than she even knew herself.

No one had ever had so much faith in her before. She'd trusted him with her embarrassing secret, that she was too much of a wimp to get in a plane, and instead of turning it against her, instead of finding her weak, he'd found a way to help get her through it.

His tactics might have been unorthodox—no one had ever kissed her fears into submission before—but it had worked. Mostly, anyway, she thought as she gripped the door tightly and tried not to think about falling out of the sky.

How could she possibly let him know that she had faith in him, too? And that he could trust her with his pain?

"Are you scared now?"

She took a breath, looked around her again, then smiled. "Yes."

He frowned. "You are?"

"I am. But it's a good kind of scared."

"A good kind of scared?"

"I'm scared that I've wasted too much time. I'm scared that there are too many beautiful things out there for me to possibly fit into one lifetime."

She gathered up all of her courage to say one more thing.

"And I'm scared about what I'm feeling for you."

Chapter Twenty-Three

Neither Sean nor Rebecca said anything else during the rest of their aerial tour of Emerald Lake. She held her breath during the landing, but it was just as smooth as the takeoff. Rebecca knew she was spoiled by having Sean as her personal pilot. She trusted him in a way she'd never trusted anyone else.

He helped her out of the plane, his hands on either side of her waist. They stood together like that for a long moment, staring into each other's eyes, before he had to move away to secure his plane to the dock.

She was waiting for him on the beach, sitting in the sand with her legs curled up beneath her arms.

"You belong here, Rebecca."

She felt it, too, such kinship with this small town deep in the Adirondack Mountains. That was why it had hurt so much when Mr. Radin accused her of trying to destroy the land with her festival.

"I feel like I should warn you," she said when he sat down beside her in the sand. "Since you decided to take me on that flight, I've decided it's time to have a really serious talk. Just in case you want to make a run for it through the trees."

He didn't smile at her comment, but she wasn't smiling either. "I'm not running, Rebecca."

She reached over, took his hand in both of hers, turning it in her hand so that she could trace the lines in his palm.

"I never expected you to come into my life. All those years I knew Stu, all the years he spoke to me about his amazing older brother, I never realized just what you would mean to me one day." A thousand times more frightened than she had ever been of flying, Rebecca had to force herself to look Sean in the eye. "I've fallen for you." She sucked in a shaky breath. "Hard." Fear had her saying, "I know you warned me not to but"—she laughed with the air she had left in her constricted lungs—"you sure make it hard for a girl to keep her heart to herself."

"Rebecca."

She squeezed his hand with hers. "No. Please. I didn't just say all of that because I think it will get you to say it back to me. I just—" She brought his hand to her lips, pressed a soft kiss to them. "You've become my best friend, Sean. And I need to tell my best friend that I've fallen in love."

Women had claimed to love Sean many times, but never like this. No one had ever bared her true soul to him.

And no one had ever put her heart in his palm and given him the chance to crush it so easily. So completely.

Unbidden came a flash of what it'd be like to have Rebecca by his side from this moment forward. As a wife, in his arms every night. As a business partner, running lakefront inns across the Northeast together. As the mother of their children. She'd be warm and loving . . . and a fierce protector—and proponent—for all of them.

He brushed away the tears that fell down her cheek. No one had ever meant as much to him as this beautiful woman sitting beside him.

Her eyes searched his face. He was afraid she was looking for something neither of them would ever find.

God, he hated hurting her. Hated it with every fiber of his being.

"All my life I've looked at things I want from every angle and only when it made sense did I go out and get it. But the way I've wanted you has never made sense. Not when you'd been in a relationship with my brother. Not when you wouldn't tell me why he left or where he was. Not with you working for me. Not when I know you're looking for something I can't give you. But in the end, all that seems to matter was how much I want you, Rebecca."

"And you got me."

"No, sweetheart. You're so much more, so much bigger than any one man could possibly hold on to."

"How can you call me sweetheart in one breath and tell me not to love you in the next? You want to love me, don't you, Sean?"

More than anything he'd ever wanted.

And still, he couldn't say the words.

His heart was twisting in his chest as she said, "I taught you how to make the inn's beds. Maybe I could teach you how to love me, too."

Sean wished it were that easy.

He kissed her, had to kiss her, then, because she was so sweet. And so honest in every moment. Even the ones where she could be hurt the most.

Especially those.

If he couldn't give her the love she deserved, he at least owed her an explanation why.

"When I was fourteen years old, I found my mother in bed with someone. Not my father."

Rebecca didn't gasp. She didn't exclaim. She simply reached for his other hand and moved them both to her heart.

"I should have been in physics class, but I'd forgotten my football helmet and had aced the quiz the day before, so the teacher let me skip out for a few minutes."

He'd never said these words aloud to anyone. All these years, he'd thought it was because he had to keep his mother's secret.

Now, for the first time, he realized that the reason for his silence went far deeper. A part of him had hoped that if he never said the words aloud, somehow his silence could help erase the past.

"Elizabeth probably thought there wouldn't be anyone home for hours. I didn't find them actually having sex."

"Thank god."

"She was wearing her robe and telling him it was a mistake. That they couldn't tell anyone what had happened. That she hadn't been thinking straight. She told him to put his clothes on and leave. That was when she walked into the hall and saw me."

He'd never forget the look on her face. She'd already been crying; he could see that, and he could see the self-hatred, the guilt already ravaging her face at what she'd just done.

In a split second all of that was replaced by fear.

"She stood in the hallway, her hand over her mouth,

her face white. That was when he walked in." Rebecca hadn't asked who the man was, but he didn't want to tell her only half the story. "He was the architect my father worked with. It was pretty much a joke in town that he'd screw anything in a skirt. He still lives in town. He's married now. Has a couple of kids." Sean had to clear his throat before continuing. "She told him to go. To get the hell out, and then she came to me, begging me, pleading me not to tell my father what I'd seen."

"How could she?"

"My father loved her so much. She was everything to him. I don't know how she could have cheated on my father."

"How could any mother ask her child to do something like that?"

"She had no other choice."

"She damn well did!"

He'd never heard Rebecca talk like that. She didn't swear. And she didn't yell.

He pulled Rebecca onto his lap, had to have his arms around her, had to try and soothe her by stroking a hand down her back as she asked, "Has she ever tried to talk to you about it?"

"No." *God no.*

It was easier—better—just not to talk at all about anything more than the weather.

Rebecca reached up to touch his face, her skin so soft and cool against his. "Have you ever told anyone before now?"

"No. But everyone had to know something bad happened in our family. I couldn't listen to her begging anymore. Couldn't stand to look at her and see that fear. So I grabbed the car keys to get the hell out of there. I didn't have my license yet, but I shouldn't have been driving anyway. I think I hit the tree on purpose, like somehow I could punish her by crashing her car. Instead, the car got put back to normal and I ended up with the scar on my face."

He moved Rebecca's fingers over it, made them trace the slightly jagged skin under his cheekbone.

"You've never said anything to me about my scar."

"I never see it."

Her eyes were big. And so full of love he almost felt as if they were reaching into his soul.

"I see only you, Sean."

He kissed her again, because he couldn't not kiss her... and because he was afraid of what she'd see in his eyes.

Against his lips, she said, "I wouldn't want to love someone again, either, if that had been me. If I had been through what you've been through all these years."

Wait a minute. "Isn't this where you're supposed to tell me it's all in the past? That my relationship with my mother doesn't have anything to do with my relationship with you?"

"But it does. How could it not?"

"It doesn't."

But they both knew that it did.

She leaned closer, pressed a kiss to his scar. "Are you ever going to talk to her about it?"

"No. Never."

"Never?"

"Rebecca." He heard the warning in his voice, knew it had no place in a scene where she'd just told him she loved him so sweetly. But none of that could stop him from saying, "Promise me you'll never say a word to her about it."

"Sean..." She licked her lips. "Didn't you hear what I said? About how I'm in lo—"

He had to cut her off, had to try and stop the panic from chasing through him.

"Promise me. Not a word. Not to her. Not to anyone."

She stared at him, her eyes big and bleak. Time stretched out between them on the beach, the sun moving down behind the tops of the tall trees.

"I love you."

His chest squeezed, his throat clogged with emotion. Still, he had to hear her say it. He had to know she wouldn't ever speak of what had happened to anyone.

"Promise me, sweetheart."

Her whispered "I promise" floated away from them and out across the lake.

Chapter Twenty-Four

That night, Andi's arms were around her the moment she stepped into Lake Yarns. "Rebecca!"

She'd been clutching her knitting bag to her chest as if it were armor, but she needed both her arms to hug her friend, so she let it drop to the floor.

"You look so tanned and gorgeous," she told her friend when they pulled apart. "And happy."

Andi's grin could have lit up the yarn shop all by itself. "I am," she said softly. "So happy." She picked up Rebecca's bag and leaned in close to whisper, "So...is Sean as good of a kisser as it looks like he'd be?"

Rebecca had been so wrapped up in her thoughts—going over and over what Sean had told her, and the promise she'd made—that it took her a long moment to even process her friend's words.

A flush came first. "He—" She licked her lips. "I—"

"Well, that's a yes if I've ever heard one. Come over here, I've staked out a quiet corner so that you can tell me everything."

A good fifteen minutes late to the Monday night

knitting group meeting, Rebecca returned hellos and smiles. She took a glass of wine and silently reeled at how much had changed in one short week.

Finally sitting down beside Andi in the only truly private spot in the crowded group of knitters, who were all thankfully back to their gossip and laughter, Rebecca pulled out her knitting.

"Oooh," Andi said, reaching out to slide the yarn between her fingers and then hold up the almost finished slip. "This is sexy."

Rebecca grabbed it back. "Please, I don't want everyone to see it."

Andi's eyebrows went up. "Mom told me you were working on the pattern for the shop." She took in Rebecca's flushed face, her bright eyes. "But I think you should keep it."

"I couldn't."

"Hmm." Andi thought about it for a moment. "Looks like you should be able to finish this tonight."

With only a couple of rows and a bind-off to do, Rebecca said, "I suppose so."

She shouldn't hate the thought of parting with the cashmere slip without ever even trying it on. After all, she'd known all along that she was making it for Carol and Andi and Evelyn to hang in their store as a sample next to the pattern book. Still, she hadn't forgotten the way Sean had looked at it—and her—when he'd said, *"Will you wear it for me when you're done with it? No dress. Just the slip."*

"At least promise me you'll wear it once." Andi had a wicked glint in her eyes. "Tonight."

As Rebecca's mouth gaped open, Andi picked up her glass of wine from the table and handed it over.

"Here."

Rebecca didn't even bother saying thank you. She simply tilted her head back and drank.

"Just to make sure I've gotten it all straight, I got married on Saturday and then you and Sean started kissing on…"

Rebecca's took another drink from her glass, emptying it this time. "Thursday. But we should talk about your honeymoon."

Andi snorted. "That wasn't even a good try. So the kiss was Thursday." She scanned Rebecca's face for clues. "That night, huh?"

All Rebecca could do was nod. And say, "I love him."

Andi's arms were warm as her friend moved closer. "You would have never slept with him if you didn't."

Rebecca tried to blink back the rush of moisture at her eyes as Andi said, "Stu is going to be happy for you. For both of you."

Only a true friend would understand, without being told, just how much hearing that—believing that—meant to Rebecca.

More than anything, she wanted to confide in Andi, to ask for advice on how to help the man she loved heal his heart. Holding Stu's secret had been hard, too, but at least she knew that Stu would eventually resolve his situation.

Sean, however, would always be broken, as long as he held onto his mother's secret. As long as he carried the burden of keeping his parents' marriage together on his strong shoulders.

And he would never really trust a woman, never really let himself love anyone until the day came when he could let go of his mother's secret.

But she'd promised. He'd made her promise. So instead of saying any of that, she simply said, "He can't love me back."

Andi frowned. "Did he say that?"

"Even before that first kiss, he warned me. But I would have loved him anyway."

She waited for her friend to tell her to run. To get the heck out of a relationship that wasn't ever going anywhere.

"I know exactly what you mean. Even if Nate couldn't have loved me back, I wouldn't have been able to stop myself from loving him." Andi instinctively put her hands over her slightly rounded stomach. "I wouldn't have wanted to."

From the first moment she'd met Andi in this very knitting group the past fall, Rebecca had felt a kinship with her.

"Thank you for understanding."

"You don't owe anyone explanations or thanks," Andi said, her expression fiercely protective. So much like the way Sean had looked when she'd told him about Mr. Radin's petition.

Rebecca had always known she was loved by her family, but neither Andi nor Sean was a blood relative. They didn't have to care for her.

But they did, anyway.

Andi gently put the needles back in Rebecca's hands. "I really, really think you should finish this tonight."

"I'm not sure my head is in the right place. I'd hate to mess it up right at the end."

"How about this, while you work on those final rows I'm going to tell you all about the Bahamas."

Andi knew how much Rebecca longed to travel,

that she could listen to travel stories all night long, and Rebecca had to ask, "Will Nate be upset if I kiss his new bride?"

Andi answered her with a smacking kiss on her lips.

"Sean is a lucky man," Andi joked in a soft voice before shooting a pointed glance at the yarn in Rebecca's lap. "And about to get luckier."

And as Andi began her delicious tale about sun and sand, Rebecca made one stitch and then another and then another, until she finally realized she was relaxed for the first time in hours.

A while later, Rebecca bound off the last stitch and looked up to find Andi smiling at her.

"It's beautiful."

Rebecca had to nod. "It really is."

A voice called out, "Elizabeth, it's so nice to see you."

In an instant, Rebecca felt her entire body go tense. She steeled herself to try and stay calm before she looked over at Sean's mother.

Andi's gaze went from her to Sean's mother. "Rebecca? Are you okay?"

She shook her head, tried to say something, but no words would come out.

"Can you help me with some boxes in the back room?" Andi said in a voice loud enough to carry through the group.

Rebecca was almost too shell-shocked to catch on. Were it not for her friend tugging her to her feet and grabbing the slip and her bag, she might have missed her escape route.

Running. She was still running, she thought, as they quickly made their way to the back of the store.

"Did something happen between you and Elizabeth? Did she say something to you about your dating Sean?"

"No." Thank god that was the honest answer. "But I need to leave."

"I meant what I said at the inn on my wedding day. I'm here for you. Anything you need, anything at all, I'll be here to help you. I don't need to know the reasons if you don't feel you can tell me what they are."

Rebecca hugged her friend. "Welcome back home, Andi. I'm so glad you're back."

Seconds later, she left out the back door, into the rain that had just started to come down. Making sure her knitted slip was safe in her bag, she ran across the street. Back to the inn.

Back to Sean.

Elizabeth wasn't a huge knitter, but she'd come to the Monday night knitting group enough over the years to know that there was usually comfort to be found there.

All day she'd felt like her skin was on too tight, like something inside of her was about to explode. To burst into a thousand little, messy pieces.

It didn't make sense. Apart from Stu's continued absence, things were better than they'd been in a while. She and Bill were both making an effort to be kinder to each other, to appreciate each other again. She'd made him dinner the night before and then they'd gone to sit out on the end of their dock to watch the stars. His hand had moved across to hold hers.

And she'd let him.

What's more, Rebecca was bringing her closer to her son. Now that she was involved with the Tapping of the

Maples Festival, Elizabeth had a reason to go by the inn at least once a day. It was such a pleasure to see Sean, to speak with him for a few minutes. They weren't saying anything important, but she hoped that would come eventually. At least he wasn't running anymore.

So then why did she have such a deep premonition of doom?

And why did her secret—her lies—loom bigger than ever?

Elizabeth let Helen and Dorothy, two elderly women she'd always thought were a hoot, settle her onto the couch with fat needles and thick, soft green yarn that reminded her of the budding leaves on the trees.

"We haven't seen you in months. Since the end of summer, isn't that right?"

Elizabeth knew Rebecca was here every Monday night and that had been part of the reason she hadn't been in since last fall. But now that they were starting to forge a friendship, there was no reason to stay away.

"Bill and I have been fixing up our house," she said by way of an explanation.

Helen raised her eyebrows. "Working on the house with my late husband made me want to take a hammer to his head. My hat is off to you, Elizabeth."

It should have made her feel better to know that most husbands and wives didn't get along all of the time. It should have pleased her to note that people saw a loving partnership when they looked at her marriage.

Instead, she felt like it was one more lie added to all of the others she'd been telling for so long.

She looked around the store. "Isn't Rebecca usually here on Monday nights?"

Andi handed her a glass of wine. "She just finished her project and had to leave."

Elizabeth took the wine, her usually steady hands on the verge of shaking. "I'm sorry I missed her."

Realizing too late that half a dozen eyes were on her, assuming they must all be wondering how she felt about Sean and Rebecca dating—if she was angry or felt that Stu had been betrayed by his ex-fiancée and brother—she quickly changed the subject.

"How was your honeymoon, Andi? You look fantastic."

Elizabeth smiled at all the right places, made appropriate comments when necessary, and she even knitted a few rows of a simple baby blanket pattern Helen got her started on, but coming to Lake Yarns hadn't made her feel any better.

On the contrary, she felt more tense—more scared—than ever before. The weight of her secret had never been heavier. And she knew deep within her heart that she couldn't possibly expect Sean to keep it for her forever. Not if she ever wanted to have a real, loving relationship with him—and the family he would surely have one day—again.

Soon.

She needed to tell Bill the truth soon.

Chapter Twenty-Five

Sean had been tempted to wait at the front desk for Rebecca to come back from her knitting group, but the last time he'd done that, she'd thought he didn't trust her to take care of herself.

He did trust her. In a way he'd never trusted anyone else.

And that was why he forced himself to head upstairs to his room, to open his laptop and wade through e-mails that should have been answered long before tonight.

Concentrating had never been a problem for Sean. It shouldn't have mattered that he hadn't been getting much sleep. Heck, in the past, a circus could have been going on all around him and he would have been focused on his task. On his goal.

But tonight he didn't have a prayer.

How could he when he was checking the clock on his computer or the watch on his wrist every other minute? When he was holding his breath waiting for footsteps outside his door, for the moment when Rebecca came back to him, warm and pretty and so damn sweet he never wanted to let her go.

Sean pushed away from the couch and walked over to the window that looked out on Main Street. He hadn't been planning to stay in Emerald Lake. Even if he decided to buy a string of inns, he'd been planning to run his business from Boston or New York City, close to funding and opportunities and partners.

Only, he couldn't take her from Emerald Lake. She was as much a part of the land, the water, the mountains as anyone whose family had been here for generations. And the thought of leaving Rebecca behind had every muscle in his body tightening.

Again and again he found himself thinking back to their flight, to their conversation on his beach...to what she'd told him: *She loved him.*

And what he'd told her: *He trusted her.*

Their first kiss had been more than a little unexpected. The sparks that ignited between the sheets blew his mind every single time they came together. But Sean had had good sex before. Not anywhere as good as it was with Rebecca, but what he used to think was good enough.

So it wasn't sex that had him rethinking everything.

Rebecca's love—and the way he trusted her—were two things he'd never seen coming.

The rain was coming down, a spring shower that would turn buds to leaves, dirt to grass, ice to lake water. The dark street was empty, the lights all along Main Street making it look like a movie set for an old film like *Singing in the Rain.*

That was when he saw Rebecca running across the street, through puddles, a bag clutched to her chest. A half-dozen emotions ran through him. The desire that had been there from that first moment. A surge of protectiveness, the knowledge that he would sweep the sky of rain if he could keep her dry and warm.

But strongest of all was the one emotion he never thought he'd be able to feel. Or recognize. But it was there, so strong, so powerful, he had to grip the edges of the window frame to steady himself.

Love.

He loved her.

Rebecca hadn't promised Andi anything. She hadn't said she'd actually wear the slip tonight. But when she finally got back to her rooms, stripped off her wet clothes and hung them to dry in the bathtub, her knitting bag's pull was too strong for her to resist.

She'd just try it on, simply to find out what it felt like against her skin this once, and then she'd put it away.

In any case, she knew she needed to calm down before going to Sean tonight. Seeing his mother had yanked up all of her anger, all of her fury at what he'd been through over the years because of what he'd seen.

Because of what his mother had made him promise.

For all that Sean tried to act like he wasn't tapped into emotions, he was. If he pulled her into his arms and looked at her with those dark, heated eyes while she was so out of control, she was afraid of what he'd see. He'd see a love she couldn't control. And he'd see how much she wanted to strike out at his mother on his behalf.

She didn't want to scare him away because she cared too much. He already knew she loved him, but since he didn't love her back, she knew better than to smother him with that love.

With trembling fingers, she picked up the cashmere slip and put her arms and head through the top of it.

The knitted fabric was so soft it took her breath away. As did a thought: *Sean would love to see her in this.*

And she would love to wear it for him.

Like magic, there was a knock at the door.

She'd never loved anyone this much, enough that it made everything hurt, from the inside out. She wanted so badly to heal him, to give him everything he hadn't allowed himself to have for far too long.

But just as she'd known better than to fall for him in the first place, just as she'd known better than to kiss him, just as she'd known better than to take him to her bed, just as she'd known better than to confess her love to him out on his beach this afternoon...she knew better now than to go to the door wearing this slip, where her feelings for Sean were in every soft stitch she'd made.

But where Sean was concerned, her mind clearly had no power over her body.

Or her heart.

That heart was pounding hard and fast as she walked from the bedroom, through her living room, to her front door. She'd opened it for Sean so many times in the past week.

But this time everything was different.

Standing before her, his eyes held on hers for a long moment, like he was drinking her in after a long, long absence—even though it had been only a couple of hours.

Finally, he looked away from her face and realized what she was wearing.

"My god, Rebecca."

He didn't move from the hallway, didn't come toward her, but the look on his face told her everything she needed to know.

Before she knew it, she was in his arms and he was kicking her door shut.

He carried her into the bedroom and then laid her on the bed as if she were the most delicate porcelain. Rebecca had never been looked at this way, as if she were the only person on earth who mattered.

All her life she'd been happy to blend into the background, the quiet girl who wasn't the least bit interested in taking center stage. She waited for embarrassment to flood her at the intense way he was looking at her, but there was such warmth—such emotion—in Sean's gaze that all she could do was bask beneath it.

"Kiss me, Sean," she said, and then he was gently, slowly moving to her, over her, his mouth warm and alive and sweet.

His kisses were always spectacular, but this one was different. Almost like the kiss was merely a beginning to something more.

Finally, he pulled away and the next thing she knew he was sitting up and she was on his lap.

He brushed another kiss against her forehead, down to her cheekbones, before stopping at her earlobe. "I can't believe you're real, that you're here with me." He continued in a low voice, "I can't believe you love me."

She wanted to say she'd be there for him forever, but she forced herself to swallow back the one word sure to push him away.

Still, as thrill bumps chased up and down her skin at the feel of his mouth on her earlobe, his teeth lightly scoring the sensitive skin, she couldn't stop herself from admitting, "I never had any other choice."

A moment later, he'd threaded his hands into her hair, holding her still. She expected a kiss. She even knew to expect the heat in his eyes.

But she was thrown completely by the emotion there.

He'd never looked at her like this. Not even a few seconds ago when he'd been taking in the way the knitted slip draped over the curves and valleys of her otherwise naked body.

"Sean? What is it?"

But he just kept staring.

"You can say anything to me. Anything at all."

His eyes crinkled at the corners for a split second. "I know I can. But this—"

He stopped, took a breath, actually closed his eyes as he steeled himself for whatever he was going to say to her.

Her heart was racing out of control.

Please. No. Don't let him say this is the end. That he is getting ready to leave again.

His eyes opened again, the deepest, richest brown she'd ever seen them as he gazed at her as serious, as passionate—as loving—as she'd ever seen him.

"I love you."

She thought her mouth might have fallen open, knew she was having a hard time finding enough oxygen to pull into her lungs, but before she could get a handle on anything—anything at all—he was kissing her.

The kiss that followed the three words she hadn't thought she'd ever hear Sean say turned her brain to mush. He wasn't the only one who could hardly believe this was happening between them. Her brain was a lost cause... but her heart needed to know for sure.

She dragged her mouth from his. "Sean?"

It wasn't until the corners of his mouth moved up that she knew for sure that she wasn't dreaming.

"Do you want me to say it again?"

She'd asked him to do just that the night he'd called her sweetheart for the first time and she loved how he obviously remembered every word between them.

"Yes," she whispered, tracing her fingers over his jaw, along his cheekbones, over his lips.

He held her hand there, pressed a kiss to her fingertips that had her shivering with desire.

With love.

"I've never trusted anyone the way I trust you. I've never admired anyone the way I admire you." He moved her hand from his lips to his chest, holding it steady right over his heart, beating steady. Strong. "And I've never, ever loved anyone the way I love you."

She wanted to remember every single moment of the night, the way his love wrapped around her along with his strong arms, but when pure passion turned to love, it was all she could do to try and keep up with the pleasure, the sweetness.

It should have been harder to tell Rebecca how much he loved her. But she made it easy. Her eyes shining down at him as he moved his fingers beneath the thin shoulder straps of her slip.

God, she was gorgeous. Her skin was so soft, so pretty as it flushed beneath his every touch and she gave herself over to him.

Body and soul.

For so long, for his entire adult life, he hadn't believed in love.

But now, here, tonight, love was all he could feel. For these few, precious hours with Rebecca in his arms, he could forget everything but her. Nothing else needed to matter.

And in the morning, when life, when reality came rushing back, he'd start to try and figure out how to balance what he knew to be true about the world with this new love that he couldn't deny.

He pressed a kiss to the center of Rebecca's chest, wanted to feel her heart beating beneath his lips. Her hands moved from his shoulders to thread through his hair.

"Sean?"

He lifted his head and instantly read her desire. But there was something else there, something that had his heartbeat hitching in his chest.

"I want you so badly, but—"

She shifted, and for a split second, he was afraid she was going to move away. Instead, thank god, she pressed herself more tightly against him as if she were trying to take shelter in his arms.

"I'm scared."

He would have expected her to be scared the other times they'd made love, when he'd flat out told her he wasn't going to make a commitment to her. Why now?

She answered him before he could ask the question, saying, "When I thought you didn't love me back, I knew I had to be prepared for...for this to all end. I kept telling myself that I didn't have expectations. Even though

I knew I was falling for you, it was easier somehow to know that it went only one way. I know it sounds strange, but it was safer. For me. For my heart. But now, if something happens—"

He kissed her before she could finish her sentence.

"I love you, Rebecca. You love me. Whatever comes, we'll figure it out. Together."

But even though she whispered her love again, even though he lay her back on the bed and stripped the slip all the way off before moving into her waiting arms, even though the peak they reached together was higher, and so much sweeter than it had ever been before, Rebecca's words *if something happens* were waiting for him in the back of his subconscious.

And the bedroom was growing colder.

Chapter Twenty-Six

During the next week as Rebecca worked to make sure the Tapping of the Maples Festival came together as well as she'd envisioned it would, Sean helped her when she needed it, gave her enough kisses through the day to fry what was left of her brain cells, but otherwise was on the phone working on his own business.

She didn't want to pry, or try to listen in on his private calls, but she couldn't help hoping that he was following through on his idea to acquire more inn's throughout the Northeast—and that this new business would keep him here, at Emerald Lake. She would never want her love to be something that boxed him in. Still, she couldn't help but hope that she was important enough to him that he'd factor her into his future plans.

And that she wasn't the only one with visions of long white dresses and babies with his eyes.

Every night, when she thought she was too exhausted to do anything more than sink into a bath with a glass of wine, just being in Sean's arms was enough to chase away all thoughts of sleep and baths—unless he was in there with her doing deliciously wicked things to her.

But she knew it wasn't just how hard she was working; it wasn't just her lack of sleep at night that had her so off-kilter during the busy week.

It was the secret he'd trusted her with.

The secret he expected her to hold forever.

Sean had never trusted a woman enough to let himself love her. Not until her. She couldn't stand the thought of betraying his trust. But she couldn't stand being near Elizabeth, either. Not knowing what she knew.

Not knowing how badly the woman had hurt her own child.

Every day that frustration, that anger on Sean's behalf grew bigger and bigger. Rebecca was very much afraid the day would come when she wouldn't be able to hold it all inside anymore.

"Your work crew has arrived!"

Rebecca turned to see Nate and Andi, Nate's eleven-year-old sister Madison, and Andi's mother, Carol, walking in through the inn's front door. She'd been so busy this week she hadn't seen Nate since they'd returned from their honeymoon.

Forcefully pushing her thoughts about Elizabeth aside, she gave him a hug. "Thanks for coming to help, you guys."

"This is exciting," Madison said. "My friends are all dying to tap a maple."

Nate grinned. "We've been practicing making the perfect pancakes to eat the syrup on all week."

Surrounded by her friends, warmth flooded Rebecca. Emerald Lake was beautiful, but that wasn't the only reason why she'd fallen in love with this town. She'd fallen for the community almost as quickly as she'd fallen for the natural surroundings.

But she'd fallen even faster for the man who was walking into the room. Her body was attuned to Sean so that she could always feel his presence before she saw him coming down the stairs.

He was smiling as Carol called out a greeting, and Andi shot Rebecca a surprised glance.

Rebecca had almost forgotten that he hadn't smiled when he first came here. It was still one of her greatest pleasures to tug a grin or, even better, a full-blown laugh out of him.

A few moments later, he was standing behind her and his arms were around her waist, pulling her against him, pressing a kiss to the top of her head.

Rebecca almost laughed at the way Andi's eyes just about popped out of her head. Nate and Carol simply looked pleased.

Looking at her friends who were waiting to help her, she realized that all along, while she'd looked at putting on this festival as hers alone, she'd been so wrong. Andi and Nate and Madison and Carol—just a few of the people she'd come to love so much in Emerald Lake in such a short period of time—reminded her that the work she'd done had all been for the community.

A community she was absolutely thrilled to belong to.

"Now that everyone's here, why don't we—"

The words dried up in her throat as Bill walked in the inn's front door... followed by Elizabeth.

A burst of anger came so swiftly that Rebecca's hands actually fisted. She knew it had all happened twenty years ago, but she had just found out the truth about what Elizabeth had done, and Rebecca felt raw inside. How could she help but be protective toward the man she loved?

It was only when she felt Sean tense behind her, and pull her tighter to him, that she snapped out of her haze.

Bill was smiling as he asked, "Can you use a couple extra pairs of hands?"

Rebecca hoped the smile she gave Bill wasn't as shaky as it felt. "Absolutely. Thanks for coming."

It was a relief to bury herself in details, to get everyone off and running. Andi, bless her heart, ran interference with Elizabeth, so that Rebecca didn't have to deal with the woman face to face.

The problem was, she knew she couldn't keep her distance forever. One day she was going to have to figure out how to sit down at a dinner table with Sean's mother... and not throw a sharp knife at her chest.

When everyone else was out putting up tents and moving the tapping equipment into the spots she'd marked on her map, Sean reached for her hand.

"Come here, sweetheart."

It still gave her the shivers every time he called her that. Every time he said *I love you* felt brand new, like she was hearing it, feeling it, for the very first time in her life.

"You're tired."

He kissed her eyelids, first one then the other, and she let herself sink against him. Just for a moment and then she'd get back out there and run around some more getting everything that needed to be done, done.

He pressed a soft kiss to her mouth before saying, "Everything is going according to plan. The festival is going to be a hit."

After everything she'd been through to get it off the ground, not once, but twice, she knew she should be ecstatic.

"I hope so."

"I know you have a lot of work to do, but I want to show you something first." Sean led her by the hand, out the front door of the inn and over to the gazebo.

She looked out across the lake, over to the maple forest, then back at the inn. "What is it? Is something wrong?"

"No, nothing's wrong."

She didn't get it at first, but then as he wrapped his arms around her again, her back to his front, and she felt his strength, his steady heartbeat against her skin, she took one deep breath. And then another.

Finally, she saw what he'd brought her outside to see.

In the span of the few short weeks they'd known each other, the trees had gone from bare to budding to bright green leaves just starting to grow. The roses that had been hiding during the freezing days were more than ready to show off their pinks and whites and reds and purples in the sunlight. The mountains were no longer white and brown, but every shade of green.

"It's going to be summer soon."

She'd always thought she was so in tune with the seasons, but it had taken Sean to remind her that she was missing the miracles taking place right before her eyes.

"As soon as the water's warm enough, I'm going to take you sailing," he said. "And when we tip over, we're going to get right back up."

She knew what he was trying to tell her: he was going to stay.

"I love you," she said softly as she turned in his arms and slid her hands around his neck.

And as they stood there, forehead to forehead, in the place so many brides and grooms had stood before, Rebecca felt more love for Sean than she ever had before.

Bill couldn't take his eyes off of Sean and Rebecca. "Remember the day we stood in that gazebo?"

Elizabeth looked up with surprise from the table that she was trimming with fabric. "The gazebo?"

She followed his gaze to the inn where their son and his girlfriend were holding each other and looking out at the lake.

"Of course, I remember," Elizabeth said softly. "Our wedding was one of the best days of my life."

Bill took in the wistful expression on his wife's face, the clear longing for what had once been.

He longed for it, too, had been trying for days to find a way to take them back to that place they'd been so many years before. But Elizabeth had returned from Lake Yarns on Monday night distant and clearly out of sorts. He hadn't been able to push past her walls, and he was, frankly, getting tired of trying.

Not when it felt like he'd been trying for so long. And where had it gotten them?

But seeing Rebecca and Sean, so obviously in love with each other, gave Bill hope to try again.

One last time.

"Mine, too," he said, putting the staple gun he was holding down onto the table.

He took Elizabeth's hands in his. They were cold and, if he wasn't mistaken, trembling.

"Betsy," he said. "I love you."

Her eyes were big. Wild. "I love you, too. So, so much."

Her words were just right, but there was a desperation behind them that worried him.

"Tell me what's bothering you. Let me try to help."

Oh god. She couldn't keep her hands from tensing in his.

This was her chance to tell him the truth. To confess everything, to lay her soul bare and hopefully wash it clean.

Only, Bill was clearly trying so hard to reconnect. He'd been doing sweet things for her all week, picking freshly bloomed flowers for the vase in the center of the kitchen table, coming home with her favorite fresh-baked bread from the bakery when she couldn't get away from her computer.

Holding her at night when she was tossing and turning.

If she told him about her affair, he'd pull away.

He'd hate her.

She moved closer, loving the way his arms wrapped around her.

She couldn't give this up.

She just couldn't.

"I was just thinking about Stu," she finally said.

It was true; she'd been thinking all day that her son should have been here helping along with everyone else. Thinking Stu should have never run in the first place. That he should have been brave enough to face them... and to remember that they all loved him, no matter what, no matter whom he loved.

"I wish he'd come home."

Bill was silent for a long moment, and she got the

distinct sense that he knew she wasn't saying everything she had to say.

Finally, he said, "I wish he was here, too. He belongs here. With his family. His friends."

She felt him shift, knew he was looking back toward Sean and Rebecca again.

"Looks like there's going to be a wedding, after all, doesn't it?"

Tears pricked her eyes. She was so glad her son had found the love he deserved.

And she prayed that nothing would come between Sean and the woman he loved.

"Yes," she said, feeling Bill's heart beat against hers. "It does."

Chapter Twenty-Seven

The morning of the Tapping of the Maples Festival was full of sun and bright blue skies. The wind was still, the birds were chirping, and the flowers were blooming.

Everything was perfect.

At ten a.m. the festival opened its "doors" and there was no doubt in anyone's mind that it was a huge success. Hundreds of people had come from all around New York to celebrate a new ritual of spring at Emerald Lake.

Rebecca had worked toward this day for months. She was glad to see what fun everyone was having, both young and old, as they learned to tap the maple trees. Mr. Radin was conspicuously absent, of course, but she wouldn't have expected anything else.

But instead of basking in her success—and Sean's, too, as she couldn't have possibly pulled it off without his help—her gut churned.

Because all the while, as she stood beneath the clear, blue spring sky, as she kept an eye on the festival proceedings and dealt with a handful of issues throughout the morning, she couldn't push away her memory of watching

Sean sleep last night, the hard lines of his beautiful face softening as he relaxed into her arms. She'd never loved anyone the way she loved him.

And she simply couldn't stand beside him every day, couldn't lay with him in her arms every night and know that a promise he made continued to tear him apart every second of every day.

Confident that everything was under control with her festival, she was glad for a few minutes to walk away from the crowds. Somehow, she needed to figure out how to take a full, deep breath through her clenched and tight lungs. She was doing just that when she felt a buzzing along her spine and saw Elizabeth Murphy coming toward her.

The breath Rebecca had been taking exploded in her chest.

You promised him you wouldn't say anything.

Elizabeth gave her a wobbly smile as she approached, but Rebecca couldn't smile back. Not yet, not until she'd done a better job of swallowing down everything that was still bubbling up.

Twenty years. That's how long it had been since Sean had caught his mother in a compromising position with another man. Rebecca tried to remember that everyone had willingly stuffed it down, pushed away the ramifications of a promise made under duress. It was up to them to change things, not her.

"I'm so glad the weather is cooperating for your festival today, Rebecca."

She hadn't spoken with Elizabeth since Sean had told her his secret. Not trusting her voice, Rebecca simply nodded her agreement.

Sean's mother looked tired, more worn than Rebecca could remember seeing her in the nine months she'd been in town. With any other person, Rebecca would have asked if everything was all right, if she could help with anything.

But she didn't dare say those words to Elizabeth. Not when she knew others might follow, harsh words that weren't her place to say.

You promised not to say anything, she reminded herself again, the words playing over and over in her head as she tried to get herself to heed them.

"You're angry with me, aren't you, Rebecca?"

Rebecca's breath caught in her throat. Oh god, what was she going to say to that?

She needed to lie, needed to tell Sean's mother that everything was fine.

But she simply didn't know how to do that.

She turned to face Elizabeth, looking her square in the eyes. "Yes, I am."

Sean's mother looked terribly fragile as she nodded her acceptance of the truth. "I'm sorry. So very sorry for the way I've behaved."

Rebecca felt as if she'd stepped into the twilight zone again with Elizabeth, one where everything had turned topsy-turvy. Because, if she wasn't mistaken, this was a woman who rarely apologized to anyone for anything.

Desperate to keep her vow to Sean, Rebecca chose her words very carefully. "You don't know how much it means to have you say that, to know that you plan on fixing things."

Elizabeth gave her a strange look, one tinged with confusion ... and fear.

"Yes, Rebecca, I want to fix things between us. I've never treated you as well as I should. I was too protective of Stu." She paused. "And then Sean. I wouldn't let myself see you for who you really were because I was afraid you were going to hurt my sons."

Rebecca barely kept her mouth from falling open. *This* was what Elizabeth was apologizing for? For being somewhat cold and unwelcoming to her?

Blood rushed in her ears again, louder this time, and her hands were tight fists by her side. She needed to turn away, needed to back down from confronting Sean's mother. But, damn it, he'd borne the pain of his mother's deep betrayal for nearly twenty years already. One more second was one second too long.

"I'm not the one you should be apologizing to." Her words were flat and so much colder than Elizabeth's had ever been to her.

Elizabeth flinched. "Rebecca? What are you talking about?"

Rebecca said only one word. "Sean."

She wasn't glad to see his mother turn a nasty shade of white-green. She wasn't doing this because she wanted to see his mother put in her place. It was simply instinctive to protect the man she loved from the one person who'd hurt him the most. Not just once, but again and again with her continued demand for his silence.

Elizabeth wasn't saying anything. She wasn't pretending she didn't know what Rebecca was talking about. She wasn't defending herself, either. Instead, she was standing there looking completely broken, tears sliding from her eyes one after the other.

Rebecca knew how soft she was, that she'd never been

able to hold a grudge, that the sight of tears always made her give in.

But this time, she was immune to Elizabeth's tears, even to the woman saying, "I was such a mess. My brother had died and I wasn't thinking. I should have never had the affair."

Rebecca shook her head, even though she wanted to put her hands on Elizabeth and shake her instead. Everything she'd told herself she needed to keep inside to hold on to Sean's trust broke through the dam...and came spilling out.

"But you did. And when he caught you in the act, instead of being brave and owning up to your mistake, you asked a child to be your partner in crime. For a crime he didn't have any part of. You hurt him, Elizabeth. You changed him. You taught him all the wrong things about relationships. About women. And he's paid for your mistake his entire adult life." She all but bared her teeth at the crying woman. "You're not going to let him pay any longer."

"Oh god." Elizabeth's hands were over her mouth and she was sobbing. "The accident afterward was all my fault. That's why he has that scar."

"The scar on the outside doesn't matter. That's the one that healed. But you could never stand to see it, could you? Not when it reminded you of everything you did wrong."

Elizabeth's shoulders moved up and down and the tears continued to fall.

"You shouldn't have worried about the scar on his cheek. It's the one on the inside of Sean that never healed, Elizabeth. He loved you. God help him, he still does, despite what you did. But the lies you made him keep for you from the father he loves ripped a hole inside of him that's never even come close to closing."

"He won't talk to me."

"Of course, he hasn't wanted to talk to you," Rebecca said bluntly. "Why would he when every conversation is lined with betrayal. With secrets. With lies."

"Oh god," Elizabeth said again.

"But if that's ever going to change then, you're going to have to try again and keep trying." She paused, let her fists unclench from where her fingernails were digging into palm. "Start now, Elizabeth." She could feel her own tears coming. "Love your son. Please just love your son."

"I do love him. I've always loved him."

"Then go find him. If the only thing you can say right now is 'I love you,' that's a hundred times better than continuing to say nothing at all."

"How have I been so wrong for so long? About everything?"

Rebecca had done things that were wrong, too. But she was starting to see that it wasn't the past that should be holding any of them back. It was the future they should be looking forward to.

And every single beautiful moment in the present that they should be cherishing.

Just like she'd cherished every moment with Sean. Every single smile. Every kiss. Every time he held her in his arms.

"I know you've lost so many years," she said in a low voice that came out at barely above a whisper, for the huge lump in her throat. "Don't lose any more, Elizabeth. Please try. Please just keep telling him how much you love him. Even if he doesn't want to listen, even if he pushes you away, he needs to know that you're sorry. And you love him."

"I was going to tell Bill today. I swear I was."

Rebecca didn't know what was going to happen between Sean's parents. Of course, she hoped they'd work through their issues, but she said, "Your son needs you first."

Elizabeth took a breath, one that shook her entire frame. "I know."

And then, she was turning and running toward the inn, to find her son, to find the son who needed her love now just as much as he'd needed it when he was fourteen.

More, even.

And in that moment as Rebecca stood on the edge of the maple forest with people laughing all around her, with small children playing tag and cuddling in their mother's arms, as she wiped away her own tears, she had a moment of pure, sure knowledge.

Sean was going to leave her.

And it wouldn't matter that she'd broken her promise to him out of love.

In his eyes, a promise broken was a promise broken.

Sean was more important to her than any festival. He was more important to her than her job at the inn. If it meant helping him, she was willing to risk losing him in her life, was willing to risk her job, and any future she could have had in Emerald Lake.

All her life, she'd thought she was such an open book. But now she realized that she'd always been holding something back. Sean had cracked the final part of her shell open and she now loved more purely, more wholly than she ever had before. When she had to start over somewhere new, at least this time around she'd know that she hadn't held any part of her heart back.

Which was why she had just risked it all.

For love.

She hadn't confronted his mother with the truth because she was trying to find a way for Sean to be able to love her back. No, she'd done it simply because, in the end, she couldn't *not* do it.

Sean deserved true happiness, the kind that would never come until he and his mother were honest with each other. It might not all happen today, but the painful silence he'd kept for two decades would end today. At least with his mother, the person he'd been the most alienated from all these years.

Still, for all Rebecca's clear-cut reasons for what she'd done, despite how much she believed in each one, she could feel her own heart breaking, one painful beat at a time.

She knew Sean. And she knew, without a doubt, that by her own actions, the man she loved was already gone. Even if he didn't know it yet.

But he would as soon as his mother found him.

"Sean, honey."

He looked up from the check-in counter where he'd been reviewing contracts on the new inn he'd been working to acquire.

In an instant—an instant in which everything in his life changed, just as it had that afternoon when he was fourteen—he knew.

Rebecca had told his mother what she knew.

He'd told himself he could trust Rebecca. That if there

was a woman on earth that he could hand his heart, his fears, over to, it was her.

But he'd been wrong.

"We don't need to do this," he said.

He had been playing this game with his mother for long enough to know that his only chance to get out of the big emotional scene she wanted to have in order to assuage her own guilt was to nip it right in the bud. To act like it didn't matter to him.

Because it didn't, damn it. He was over something that had happened when he was fourteen years old.

She stopped, faltering as she came toward him, her arms that had been outstretched falling to her side. She shook her head, opened her mouth, but nothing came out. And he thought maybe, just maybe, he was safe.

But then, she closed her eyes, put her head in her hands, and for the first time he saw her age. Instead of the woman who had always seemed so strong, almost ageless, he saw the frailty of her shoulders.

Shoulders that were shaking from fear. From sorrow.

Sean shouldn't be feeling pity for her. He shouldn't be feeling anything at all. But Rebecca had changed him. He'd let himself feel, had let his heart lead him, for the first time in nearly twenty years. And he couldn't figure out how to close down the pathways to his heart this fast.

Soon. He'd take care of it soon. But for this goddamned moment, he wasn't nearly as cold as he needed to be to protect himself.

His mother lifted her head, looked directly at him, holding his gaze with such focus he couldn't pull his away.

"I love you." Her mouth wobbled and fresh tears came.

"I love you so much, Sean. I always have. From the first moment I held you in my arms when you were a baby. When I watched you grow up from such an incredible child to a young man."

She took a step toward him and he couldn't contain his flinch.

Seeing it, she almost crumbled to the ground, catching herself on the side of a chair a split second before he leaped to her aid.

He might be angry with her, she might not have been a great mother to him, but he would never want anything to happen to her. He would never want to see her hurt.

"Sit down, Elizabeth." He tucked a pillow behind her shoulders, made sure she was steady before he stepped away, putting much-needed distance between them.

"I remember the first time you called me by my name instead of Mom. You were in the hospital after the car crash and they told me you were awake. All night long I'd prayed for the chance to rewind time, to take back what I'd done, to make it so you wouldn't see what you'd seen, but when I saw my baby lying there in the hospital with bandages over part of your face I knew none of those prayers were ever going to be answered. Your father was there. You called him Dad, just like you always had. And then you said my name instead of Mom. And I knew you would never forgive me."

He hadn't moved far enough away, because she reached out and grabbed his hands, holding them so tightly he couldn't let go.

"I knew what I did was wrong. Every minute of every single day I've known it, but I was so scared. So scared of losing everything. But I lost everything anyway, didn't

I? You. Your father's love. And any self-respect I might have had."

What did she think he was going to say to that? Did she think he was going to absolve her of everything just because Rebecca had confronted her?

Into his continued silence came, "I ruined your life, Sean. I'm so sorry."

He hated the thought that she could have possibly had that much power over him. "You didn't ruin my life."

"I taught you about lies. I taught you about secrets. I've seen you with women over the years, the way you hold yourself back from them. The way you never let any of them touch your heart." She paused, and he knew what was coming. "Until Rebecca."

He couldn't keep his fingers in her grip any longer. "If you want to talk, fine. We'll talk. But keep Rebecca out of it."

"She loves you."

"What the hell do you know about love?" Years of repressed anger banged and bumped up against the walls he'd built to contain them.

It was the first time he'd ever spoken like that to her and she looked shocked, but then, instead of falling apart even more, she actually straightened up a bit in the chair.

"I can take it, whatever you've got to say to me," she told him. "You must be so angry with me."

"It all happened a long time ago." Even though when he closed his eyes he could see the whole scene with his mother and Roy, the architect, in the compromising position like it was yesterday.

"I love you, honey."

There it was again. Love. Coming at him from all

directions. From Rebecca. From his father. And now, from the most unexpected place of all. His mother.

"Please, Sean," she begged. "I'd rather you yell and scream at me than continue to look right through me."

"I'm not the one you should be apologizing to. I'm not the one you should be coming clean with."

He left her sitting on the chair...alone. Just the way he'd been since he was a teenager.

Just the way he was going to be again once he undid the mistake he'd made with Rebecca.

The mistake of thinking he could let himself trust her.

And love her.

Rebecca hadn't moved from her spot by the maple tree on the farthest corner of the forest. She was glad she was wearing a bright red jacket over her sweater and jeans. She wanted it to be easy for Sean to find her. Not because she wanted to get their break up over with faster (that wouldn't make it hurt any less, she wasn't nearly stupid enough to believe that), but because she knew how much he must be reeling right now.

Easier. She just wanted to make life a little bit easier for him. Now. In the future. And then one day, maybe he'd wake up and realize that he missed her.

Or maybe he wouldn't.

She watched him as he approached her, her heart breaking even further apart with every step he took closer, his expression proving, without a doubt, that she was right.

Not that she'd ever doubted it for a second. But maybe, just maybe, there'd been a little bit of hope that magic would strike and turn her dreams into reality.

Unfortunately, since that wasn't going to happen, she now had less than thirty seconds before everything ended. Half a minute to try and pull herself together. And even though she needed more like thirty years to accept that Sean was already gone, she'd use every last store of strength she had for what was coming.

The last thing Sean needed was one more woman crying. One more woman begging for his forgiveness.

Besides, she wouldn't let herself be sorry about giving her heart for his.

And then, there he was, close enough that she could reach out and touch him. Close enough that he could pull her into him and kiss her. Close enough that he could tell her everything was going to be okay.

Instead, he just stared at her like he didn't believe what he was looking at. She hated the pain she saw, the way his eyes were full of not only the memories that he'd pushed away for so long, but also the way she could tell he was berating himself for ever trusting her in the first place.

"You promised to keep what I told you between us."

She wished he could see into her heart to understand why she'd done it. But he couldn't. And she understood why.

"I know I did." She paused, made herself say, "I made that promise to you because I thought I could keep it." A tear fell before she could fight it back. "But I couldn't."

"You're the first woman I've trusted since I was kid."

"I know that, too...but I love you too much to have kept that promise."

Her words were soft, but they didn't waver. Regardless of all she'd lost as a result, hopefully the person she loved most in the world would only benefit from here on out. Hopefully Sean would find a way to patch things up with his mother and finally let all that love he was holding inside out.

"If you really loved me, you wouldn't have said anything to her."

But that's where he was wrong and she knew she'd already lost so much that there was no point in stopping herself from telling him. "That promise you made to her has hurt you from the first moment you made it. I held Stu's secret for only a little while, and even that was too much. It was too long. And it took something out of me that I shouldn't have had to give up. Just like your mother shouldn't have ever asked you to give up a piece of your soul for her mistake."

"You should have respected my wishes. Period. It doesn't matter what your reason is."

She knew what he was doing, that all he wanted was for her to stop loving him, that he wanted to finish putting up all those walls she'd thought were coming down, and walk away.

And even though she knew it was the last thing he wanted her to do, she reached out, took his hand, and held it. She couldn't stop her eyes from closing at the pleasure of feeling his warmth, of knowing his touch this one last time. Every second with Sean had been precious. She would never regret a single one, regardless of the way it was ending.

"Sometimes loving someone enough means breaking a promise that will only hurt them if it's kept." She steeled herself to reopen her eyes, to hold his gaze, to keep the tears back. "You're more important than any promise I could ever give you."

Where there had once been warmth and love in his eyes just hours ago, there was nothing. Not even anger.

She finally let go of his hand. But she had to say it one more time, while he was still standing with her.

"Whatever you think, Sean, I love you. I think I loved you from that first moment I saw you at Andi and Nate's wedding." She made a sound that could have been a laugh, but not now. That was impossible now. "I was crying then, wasn't I?" She wiped them away. "At least I make consistent first and last impressions, don't I?"

She knew she was back to that babbling open book she'd always been, and she hated it. Hated that she'd never been able to hold back with Sean. That she couldn't do it now even if it was the difference between saving what little strength she had left to move forward.

She took a step away, had to let the cold penetrate not just her coat but her flesh, her bones.

Her heart.

"I won't make you choose. This is your home. You should be able to find someone to run the inn in a couple of weeks." She looked over his shoulder at someone struggling with their syrup tapper. "I think someone needs help with a machine. I'll have a report for you on the festival attendance by the end of business tomorrow."

And then she forced herself to move past him, to squash the part of her praying he'd call her name out, come after her, and tell her not to go.

She knew that was never going to happen.

And it didn't.

Chapter Twenty-Eight

Rebecca had wanted to run, to flee, to hide. She'd been tempted—so very tempted—to leave the festival grounds and lock herself in her bedroom to curl up on her bed and cry for all she'd just lost.

Instead, she'd forced herself to stay. To follow through on what she'd set out to do.

Working on saving the festival had helped bring her and Sean together. Now, even though her actions had ripped them apart, she had to see her vision through... and hope that keeping her focus on the festival would help to save her, that being busy taking care of a million and one details today and tonight would help her get through to tomorrow in one piece.

Even without Sean's love.

She was standing a hundred yards from the bustling activity, working to open a cardboard box of empty maple syrup containers when she heard, "Rebecca!"

Her entire body tensed at the voice she'd been longing to hear for weeks. How was it, she thought at she turned to face Stu, that he'd managed to not only come back in just as an abrupt way as he'd left, but that his timing couldn't be worse?

"It's so good to see you, Rebecca."

He looked like he was going to open his arms to her for a hug, but something in the way she was looking at him—doing a quick scan, head to toe, of the man who had been her best friend for so long to make sure that he was okay—had him laying his arms back down by his side.

"I'm sorry for leaving like that."

An hour ago, perhaps, she would have simply accepted his apology. She would have told him not to worry about it, that he'd had to do what was right for him.

But this was one apology too many from the Murphy family.

"You should be sorry. You left me here to deal with everything. To run the inn by myself." She gestured to the crowd of happy people with a jerk of her arm. "To get this festival off the ground."

"You're my best friend, Rebecca. I shouldn't have treated you like that but"—he gestured to the festival, the inn—"everything looks like it's going so great. You pulled the festival off beautifully, Rebecca. Just like I knew you would."

Maybe another time she could have appreciated his compliment, the faith he'd always had in her. But right now, she was being hit by a second burst of anger.

First mother, then son. Her whole life, she'd held herself apart from anger, tried to convince herself that she didn't ever feel it.

God, what a liar she'd been. And those lies had allowed the anger to eat up her heart, one piece at a time. Only

Sean had been able to sew it back together, to get it beating strong again.

"Do you really think that's all you left me with, Stu? Just the festival? Just the inn?"

She could see his surprise at her harshly asked questions. She'd never spoken to him like this, had never really let loose on her true feelings with anyone until Sean. With him, she simply hadn't been able to hold back the love she'd felt.

Rebecca suddenly realized how closely linked love and anger were. And that giving way to one meant letting the other in, too.

"You left me to deal with telling everyone the wedding was off," she began. "I thought you were going to be there beside me, that we were going to tell everyone together."

She could see the flush even beneath his tanned skin. "You're right. I was a coward. I wasn't thinking about anyone but myself."

She waved her hand in the air. "But dealing with people whispering, wondering about me wasn't the worst. Even the way your mother looked at me, talked to me like I'd driven her baby away wasn't the worst." She paused, tried to gulp in air as a swift hit of pain nailed her in the chest. "Your brother came home, Stu. He didn't get your letter. He didn't know that the wedding had been canceled."

"Oh shit." Stu grimaced. "I told him it was my fault, that he shouldn't take it out on you, but if he didn't get the letter..."

"Emerald Lake was supposed to be a safe haven for my heart." Words were falling now, one after the other, with no way to hold them back...or to stop them before she admitted absolutely everything. "If I could have stopped myself from dreaming those dreams again, I would have."

"What dreams, Rebecca?"

"I love him."

Stu blinked at her, obviously more confused now than ever. "Rebecca? What are you talking about? Who do you love?"

"Your brother." She wiped away a rogue tear. "I love your brother with all my heart."

"Sean?" He ran a hand through his dark hair, leaving it standing on end. "You're in love with Sean?"

"You know me," she said sarcastically, "always falling for those dark, mysterious types."

"No," he protested. "Sean's not like that. I mean, he is, but down deep inside he's not like those other guys you dated. He's a good man. One of the best I've ever known."

"You don't need to tell me how good he is. I know."

So good that one day when he could finally let himself love again, the woman, the children he loved, were never going to doubt his love for a single second.

How she envied them.

And how she longed to know that kind of love for herself. Just once.

There had been moments when she was in Sean's arms that she'd thought he was almost there, when he'd looked into her eyes and she'd seen clear into his soul, when he'd said, "I love you."

But his love for her had never been whole. Because he wasn't whole.

"I should have known," Stu was saying slowly, softly. "If anyone could reach my brother, it would be you."

"Wrong." She couldn't disguise the raw pain behind the

one short word. "He doesn't love me back. Do you want to know why?" She didn't wait for him to reply. "Because I suck at keeping secrets. His." She paused, guilt knocking into her as she admitted, "Yours, too."

Stu paled.

"I trusted you, Rebecca."

Now it was her turn to say, "I'm sorry. I tried to keep it from him, but in the end, he was so worried about you. He loves you so much his fear for you was tearing him apart." Her words had fallen to a faint whisper. "And I simply loved him too much to keep any secrets from him at all."

She waited for Stu to be angry with her, like Sean had been, for spilling his secret. Instead, he pinched his eyes closed with his fingertips. "Jesus. Talk about screwing up. I should have never asked you to keep that secret, Rebecca. I know it's no defense, but when you found John and me, I was flat-out panicking."

The way he immediately owned up to the complications he'd caused softened Rebecca's response. "I know you were."

Finally, she gave into the instinct to throw her arms around him. They hadn't aired everything yet, but she knew there would be time to completely clear the air in the future. First, she needed to ask, "How are you feeling about everything now?"

He smiled down at her, that gentle, sweet smile that she'd always loved from the first time she'd looked across the drawing class and found a kindred spirit who thought the whole thing was goofy.

"Better. So much better. I'm not going to hide anymore, Rebecca. I'm not fooling myself into thinking it's going to be easy with everyone, but I don't want my life to be a lie."

She finally found a smile for him. "Good. We all love you, Stu. Everyone in your family. This town. And especially your best friend, who wishes you had confided in her a long, long time ago. And you need to know, your mother overheard my conversation with Sean, the one where I told him your secret. Your parents both know. And they both love you."

Relief blanketed his face and he covered her hand with his own. "Thank you, Rebecca. For everything. For being my friend all these years. For being my friend, even now that I've made things so difficult for you."

A baby cried in the distance. A cloud moved to cover the bright sun. And a wave of exhaustion hit her hard, sweeping through her from head to toe.

"I'm happy you're home, Stu. And I'm even happier that you're happy."

She saw Dorothy and Helen over his shoulder, knew they'd spotted Stu. Rebecca couldn't stand here while everyone in town exclaimed over his return. But she couldn't leave the festival, not when the responsibility for its success—or failure—was resting entirely on her shoulders.

"I've got to check on things," she said, then headed for the biggest group of strangers she could find and hoped—prayed—for them to need her help with something.

The inn's dock was strangely empty. Sean knew everyone was in the forest at the festival. He was going to head back in a few minutes, couldn't live with himself if he let Rebecca shoulder the responsibility of the event all by herself. But he'd needed to get outside, get away, just long enough to pull himself together.

He quickly untied the nearest rowboat. The oars were cold and squeaky from a winter and spring of non-use. These past three weeks that he'd been home, the ice had melted from the surface of the water, with only small patches left floating here and there.

Sean's heart had been like this lake when he'd arrived for Stu's wedding. Frozen solid, but for so much longer than one winter and the beginning of one spring. Rebecca's smile, her gentleness, her love, the heat of her kisses, the way she gave herself over to him so completely when they were making love—they had all been more warmth than his ice could combat.

He pushed away from the dock, the cold water enveloping the hull of the wooden rowboat. The town got smaller. The water got colder the farther he went out on the lake.

He let the larger and larger chunks of ice envelop him.

But after fifteen minutes of hard rowing, he had to face facts.

This time around, he couldn't seem to close himself off, wasn't having any luck making a decision about what he would and wouldn't feel and simply following through on it.

Everything that had worked for him in the past was failing him this time around.

Because he loved Rebecca.

Secrets. Trust. He'd thought those were the most important things of all.

But now he knew better.

Only love mattered.

And he'd thrown it away.

*   *   *

Stu stood on the edge of the dock and watched his brother come back toward him. His big brother had always been larger than life. He'd always looked up to him.

When they were teenagers and Sean ended up completely changed by that car crash, Stu had always wished he could have the brother back who had been so happy, so much fun when they were kids. But he'd been holding too tightly to his own secrets to dare ask anyone else for theirs.

Rowing into shore with his back to Stu, Sean didn't see him until he was at the dock and Stu was helping pull him in and tie up the rowboat.

"Son of a bitch. Where the hell did you go, Stu? I've been trying to track you down for weeks."

"Now that I'm back, I promise I'll tell you everything you want to know."

But Sean didn't look particularly happy about that vow. "You should have told me everything a long time ago."

Stu understood why Rebecca loved his brother. But he also knew the reasons she'd be frustrated with him.

"I know you're angry with me, but—"

Sean all but jumped out of the rowboat to face Stu down on the dock. "Do you think I would have cared that you're gay, Stu? Do you think that would have bothered me even the slightest bit? Don't you realize the only thing that could possibly bother me about it is that you kept something so important from me for so damn long and I couldn't be there to support you?"

"I was confused, Sean. And I didn't want to put you in the position of having to lie to Mom and Dad." Stu tried to explain everything he'd been forcing himself to dissect for the past three weeks. "Don't you remember how Mom was after her brother died? And then when they found out it was AIDS? She didn't get out of bed for days and she was so fragile for so long after that. I didn't want her to worry about me going the same way."

"I would have helped you figure things out, Stu. We used to be so close. Didn't you know I'd always be there for you? Don't you know that I still am, even now when I'm so angry with you that I can hardly see straight?"

"I'm not the only one who screwed up." Stu loved his big brother enough to finally go out on a limb. The limb he should have gone out on a long, long time ago. "You've been making excuses and pushing all of us away for way too long. I know you're angry with me for disappearing the way I did, but I'm mad, too. You're upset that I didn't confide in you. But you didn't confide in me either! I know I wasn't brave enough to ask you for answers when we were kids, but neither of us is a kid anymore."

He watched his brother carefully, knew that the time had come to find out the truth.

"I've been gone for three weeks, Sean. But you've been gone for nearly twenty years. What happened between you and Mom when we were teenagers?"

Finally, Sean told him the truth of what he'd seen when he was fourteen... and of the promise he'd made and the secret he'd held for so many years.

Chapter Twenty-Nine

Elizabeth found Bill in one of the smaller barn buildings hammering on the leg of a wooden table that had broken off beneath the weight of the tapping equipment. So much had changed these past weeks. Stu leaving, Sean returning. Love forming between Rebecca and his oldest son. Along with what Bill hoped was the beginning of a new, better, closer relationship with his son.

The hammer landed square on the head of the nail he'd selected from a tin can of old, hammered-straight nails. If only he could straighten out his marriage, then everything would be perfect.

But it was all so much more complicated than that.

He felt his wife's presence before he saw her, had always known when she entered a room simply by the way the air changed and sparked around her.

"Bill."

His name shook, fell from her lips.

And he knew.

The time had come for the final secrets, the final lies, to be revealed.

"I had an affair. Twenty years ago. After John died. With Roy."

His wife looked ragged. She was crying, but he could see that she'd clearly been crying before now.

"I know."

Her shocked gasp resonated through the room. "But you never...you never said anything to me." Her words came at barely above a whisper. Raw and ragged. "You never did anything that made me suspect you knew."

"You might not remember the past very clearly anymore, but I do," he told her, his own voice shaking now from the force of emotions pushing up from his gut, his chest, through his windpipe. "Your twin brother died and you went from being the strong, capable, loving woman I'd married to a brittle shell. I did everything I could to try to help you, but you were lost to me. To your sons. To everyone who cared about you."

"I never meant—" A sob choked her words short. "He didn't mean anything to me."

"I know that. Just as I knew it then. Being with people who loved you hurt too much. So you jumped into the arms of a man who didn't care about anything more than his next orgasm." It hadn't been hard for him to piece two and two together—and to get Roy to tell him the truth over one too many whiskeys at the local tavern. For so long he'd waited for her to tell him the truth. But then, when she hadn't, he'd tried to convince himself that it was because she was afraid of losing him. "And I know it never went beyond that one time." He tried to smile at her, wanted to reach out to her, but it was too difficult. "I forgave you a long time ago."

In all the ways he'd thought this conversation would

play out over the years, he'd never imagined that he'd tell her she was forgiven and she'd break down and cry harder.

"Sean..."

He could barely make out his son's name. "What about Sean? Is something wrong?"

Her voice was shaking so hard, he had to concentrate hard to hear her say, "He saw me. I made him promise not to tell you."

Bill tried to focus on his wife's face. Thirty-six years ago he'd taken one look at her and known that he would love her forever.

Only, no one could have told him forever wasn't nearly as long as he'd assumed it would be.

He'd loved her enough—so damn much—that he'd tried to convince himself it was enough. For nearly twenty years, he'd told himself one version or another of that lie.

But his love could never be enough. He saw that now.

Just as he finally saw all the anger, the frustration, the hurt that he'd forced himself to push into the background for nearly two decades.

"I loved you." He heard the past tense at the same time she did. "How could you, Elizabeth?"

She flinched at the way he said her name. Even when he'd recently stopped calling her Betsy, he'd never said her given name said so coldly.

She reached out her hand, tried to stand and come to him. His heart broke looking at her, but he wouldn't let himself go and pull her into his arms. Even though every cell in his body screamed at him to do just that.

No. He knew how it would turn out. He'd forgive her again, hope for their love to return to the way it used to be, all the while knowing how fruitless that hope was.

"Bill. No. Please."

His feet moved toward her despite knowing better than to go to her. To let himself touch her.

To let himself hope.

Barely a foot from her, he pulled from what was left of his anger and stopped where he was. She was still standing there, her arm outstretched.

"I thought I could look the other way when you came back to me. But it was always between us." He looked down at her hand, her diamond ring still gone from where she'd taken it off when they were sanding the floor. Watching her take that ring off three weeks ago had been a prophecy of doom. "Even though I forgave you a long time ago for cheating, I kept waiting for you to tell me the truth. To let go of that secret."

"I wanted to tell you so many times, but I couldn't risk telling you. I didn't want to lose you."

"I know why you cheated, Elizabeth. I even told myself I understood. But I'll never understand how you could ask a fourteen-year-old boy to keep a secret like that." He took a step closer to her. "I'm his father, for God's sake! You forced him to lie to me! You made it so he couldn't look me in the eye."

Incapable of holding anything back, his voice boomed at her, his breath blowing her hair back from her face. Strands that were damp with tears clung to her cheekbones.

He'd always thought she was the most beautiful person he'd ever seen.

He wasn't sure he'd ever be able to see her beauty again.

"The affair was forgivable. What you did to our son isn't."

*　　*　　*

"Sweet girl, come here."

For hours, she'd been on autopilot, running the festival. Now, Rebecca knew her grief, her exhaustion, was making her hear things.

But the arms pulling her close were warm. And real.

"Mom."

She breathed in her mother's familiar scent and closed her eyes as she let herself be held by someone she knew would never desert her.

She looked up from her mother's shoulder and saw, through her tears, her father and four sisters and their husbands and kids.

Her family had come, after all. They'd waited weeks for her to clean up her messes just like she'd asked them to.

And yet, here she was, even more of a mess than she'd ever been.

She knew what they were going to say. That they were going to tell her to come home with them to let them all take care of her the way she'd always taken care of them.

And this time, the temptation to give up every stride she'd taken to become a strong person over the past months was big.

No.

She forced herself to pull out of her mother's arms, to dry her eyes as best she could.

"I'm so glad you're all here," she said to her family. "Come, I'll show you around and introduce you to my friends."

Her sisters and their husbands looked at each other in surprise. Her father came to kiss her on the forehead.

"We're proud of you. We always have been."

And that was when she knew: she wasn't going anywhere. Emerald Lake was her home. She'd never stop loving Sean, but this time she wasn't going to be the one running.

Ruffling the soft hair on one of her nephew's heads, she said, "You guys are going to love tapping a maple. Come with me and I'll show you how."

Chapter Thirty

Sean had left his brother standing on the dock, obviously reeling from what he'd told him about their mother. Sean was glad his little brother was finally back home, even more glad that everything was finally out in the open between them. He hoped neither of them would see the need for secrets in the future. If they got confused and started to fall back on their old ways, he hoped with every last piece of his heart that Rebecca would be there to set them straight.

And to love them both despite their failings.

"Man the inn," he'd told his brother. "I need to take care of Rebecca."

He thought he saw his brother smile, but he was already heading down the dock toward the forest.

Toward the woman he loved.

He'd quickly spotted her, working steadily to help families with small children get situated behind the maple syrup tapping equipment. A young child fell and she knelt beside him, brushing the dirt off his pants, talking animatedly to him until he'd stopped crying.

The child's parents looked at her gratefully, but she wasn't at all aware of them. She was wholly focused on the little boy's welfare and happiness.

Just as she'd been wholly focused on Sean's.

God how he loved her. Since that first moment he'd seen her standing at Andi and Nate's wedding with tears streaming down her face and her hand over her heart.

Loving someone means breaking a promise if you know keeping the promise is going to hurt them.

His beautiful Rebecca. So sweet. So wise. And so much stronger than anyone ever gave her credit for being. Especially him.

He'd give anything to share her life, to be strong for her and let her be strong right back. With their children. With his family, even the mother he wasn't sure he could forgive.

Here he'd thought he wasn't afraid of anything, when all along, she was the truly brave one. The dragon slayer who would face down the hottest flames, the sharpest teeth, to protect the people she loved.

He wanted to call out her name, wanted to beg her to forgive him, to take him back, right then and there. But she needed his help more than she needed his pleas.

As he attended to various issues that cropped up throughout the rest of the afternoon, at first she gave no outward sign that she saw him. But he could feel her warmth wrap around him, just as it was wrapping around everyone else she came in contact with.

Still, for the rest of the day she made sure that they were on opposite sides of the festival, moving away from him whenever he came too close.

At one point, he saw her with a large group of people and quickly realized they must be her family. He wanted so badly to meet them, to thank her mother and father for raising such an incredible woman. But he knew better than to do it today.

Rebecca was hurt. Angry. And she had every right to be.

He'd been a complete asshole.

He'd gotten everything wrong.

Everything.

As night began to fall, Sean made sure every last festivalgoer got back to their car all right in the dark. Just in case it rained, he wanted to make sure the tapping equipment was put away and covered for the rental company to come pick up Monday morning.

But Rebecca was already there, kneeling down beside one of the tappers, wiping it down with a wet rag.

He couldn't stop himself from watching her. And from wishing he'd realized what love was really all about before he went and threw it all away.

Rebecca's hand stilled on the equipment as she realized he was standing behind her. The moon was bright enough that he could watch her slowly pull air into her lungs and then let it back out.

"Thank you for your help today."

He'd gone and stomped on her heart and she was the one thanking him for helping with the festival? He didn't even come close to deserving her.

"You don't need to thank me for anything, sweet—"

The endearment was halfway out when Rebecca's flinch came ricocheting out to him, piercing straight through his heart.

He knew she wanted him to leave her alone. But how could he bring himself to leave her? And how could he ever let her go, if that's what she really wanted from him now?

He tried again, saying, "Your family came."

Her mouth almost tipped up into a smile. "They wanted to surprise me."

"I'm glad they were here for you, Rebecca."

For the first time in their conversation, she met his gaze. Her chin was lifted, her shoulders were back. This was the strong woman who had fought the preservation council, who had believed in herself and her festival. This was the woman who had always been such a big part of his brother's life. This was the woman who so many people in town cared for and wanted to see happy.

This was the woman he would never stop loving.

"I am too. I've missed them."

She looked pale. And tired. But still so beautiful he could hardly believe his eyes.

"Have you eaten today?"

She covered the tapper, then stood up and wiped her hands off on her jeans. "You don't have to take care of me," she said softly. "I already know how to take care of myself. I've always known, but I haven't wanted to make the hard decisions about when to stay. And when to go."

It killed Sean to stand there and let her walk away. He couldn't do it.

"Rebecca, I—"

She stopped, looked at him over her shoulder. "Nothing has changed. Not between you and your parents. And not between you and me." She paused before saying, "Stu is going to cover for me for a few days. I've got some things to take care of."

All he wanted was to run to her, to beg for her forgiveness.

But he knew now that wasn't enough.

Rebecca wasn't leaving because their broken relationship was beyond repair. She was leaving because of problems that had nothing to with her and him...and everything to do with the way he had dealt with his family for so long.

He was surprised to realize that she wasn't the only one who hadn't wanted to make the hard decisions about when to stay and when to go.

He'd done exactly the same thing.

And in that instant he understood that there was only one way he could possibly prove his love to Rebecca, only one path to having a solid, loving relationship: he needed to deal with the demons that had been eating away at him for nearly twenty years.

His gut clenched, tightened even further, at the thought of seeking out his mother.

Soon. He knew he'd have to speak with her soon.

But first, he'd go make his apologies to a man who had only ever wanted to love his son.

Sean found his father in his workshop, surrounded by saws and hammers but not using any of them.

"I'm sorry I pushed you away. I didn't know what else to do. I thought if I was around you too much, one day her secret would slip out. You loved her. Stu and I both saw how much. I didn't want to be responsible for anything happening to your marriage."

His father looked crushed. Shaken.

Bill walked across the workshop and pulled Sean into a hug. And Sean, rather than fighting it, found that he didn't want to pull away. Not when he and his father had twenty years of lost hugs to make up for.

Finally, his father said, "I wish you hadn't felt like you needed to protect me. But you've always been so honest. Such a good person, even when you were a little boy you were helping the other kids at school, protecting your little brother from bullies." He grimaced. "I always knew, Sean. If only I had confronted her right away then it would have all come to light and you wouldn't have had to live with her secret for so long. Will you ever forgive me?"

"There's nothing to forgive. You're the best father I could have ever asked for."

"No, I'm afraid I wasn't. But I'd like to be if you will let me try again. Very, very much."

"What is going to happen with you and Elizabeth?"

His father's face, which had been so open, shuttered. "I don't know." He sighed, deep and long. "I don't know. But the one thing I do know is that no matter what happens, I don't want you to feel responsible in any way for my marriage. All I want is for you to be happy, son."

"I'm going to talk to her."

Both of them knew he wasn't talking about Rebecca, that he was finally going to have a long-overdue discussion with his mother about what had happened twenty years ago.

"I don't know that I deserve to," his father said, "but can I give you a piece of advice?"

"Please. I'll take whatever you've got."

"Every time I build a new house, somewhere in the middle of it all, I look around me, at the mess and disarray. But do you know what I see? I see the potential for what's coming. The new building that will soon stand tall. Proud. This is when clients worry that everything's going wrong, that we'll never be able to turn the piles of wood and shingles and cement and tile into a home. I soon learned there was no use in trying to placate them. It was better to be honest. To tell them, yes, things were messy, bordering on being out of control. But that I was sticking to my vision anyway...along with my hope that with focus and determination, all was going to go well.

"You're focused, Sean. And you're determined. Let yourself be honest, too. Getting things out in the open won't necessarily make them any less of a mess. But at least everything will finally be laid out on the table."

His mother was in the house, standing at the kitchen counter, staring out the window above the sink into the darkness. When Sean walked in, she turned to him and he could see she was crying, the tear tracks fresh on her cheeks.

Black. White. That was the way he'd seen the world since he was fourteen. He'd never been a person who looked for the shades of gray. Even as a child, he'd liked what he liked, and disliked what he didn't. Stu had been his exact opposite. Happy with whatever came, willing to find a way to like things.

But standing in the kitchen of the house he'd grown up in, the same kitchen where his mother had asked him to promise he wouldn't tell anyone what he'd seen, for the first time in years, Sean wondered if things really were completely black and white.

Yes, his mother had still cheated on his father. Yes, Sean had still gotten in that car and crashed into a tree to try in a foiled, childish effort to forget what he'd seen.

But if he'd known that one day in the future he'd find a love like Rebecca's...well, then maybe it would have all been worth living through, just to get to her.

"Sean?" His mother's voice shook on his name.

The truth. His father had advised him to simply tell the truth.

"I don't really want to forgive you," he told her. "But I'll do anything for Rebecca, even put what happened behind us with the hope that forgiveness will come someday."

"I'm so sorry."

He nodded. "I know."

And, for the first time, he truly did.

He wasn't going to solve things with his mother today. But they'd just made a start. Finally.

Sean made it back to the inn just as Rebecca was leaving. She was carrying a suitcase.

He already knew that she'd arranged with Stu for a few days away from the inn.

From him.

She stood before him on the inn's front porch, and the delicate beauty he'd been so aware of from the first moment he'd set eyes on her was made even more beautiful by the moonlight that illuminated her features.

"I'll be back to help with the wedding this weekend."

She'd answered only part of his question. Yes, he now knew she'd be back by Saturday. But then what? Would she leave again?

And the next time, would it be forever?

"I talked with my father tonight. About—" The words choked in his throat, but he made himself push them out. "About everything."

Her expression softened. "That's good." The edges of her lips moved up, almost making a smile. "Really, really good."

"I also talked to Eliz-...to my mother."

Rebecca's eyes widened at that news and in the moonlight he could see tears about to fall. A moment later, as she blinked, two tears moved from her eyelashes to her cheekbones.

"Sean."

She whispered his name and there was so much love in it, he could feel it wrap around him, warm enough to almost chase away the chill of the wind blowing across the lake.

Sean had never begged a woman for anything. Not for attention. Not for love. Until now.

"Please don't go."

When she didn't put the suitcase down, he said, "Earlier today, you said nothing had changed, that you couldn't stay until I worked things out with my parents. I'm trying, Rebecca. I swear to you, I'm trying."

He watched myriad emotions moving across her pretty face: hope, longing, love.

"Why, Sean? Why are you trying?"

He didn't have to think about his answer. "Because I love you. I don't want to lose you, Rebecca."

A cloud drifted in front of the moon, making it impossible for him to see her expression.

"Stu knows to call me with any problems while I'm away this week." She moved her suitcase into her other hand. "Good night, Sean."

And as she walked away, the only thread of hope he had to hold on to was that she'd said good night.

And not good-bye.

Chapter Thirty-One

After packing her bags the evening of the festival and leaving Emerald Lake, Stu had called her cell early the next morning. At first, she'd thought he was calling to ask for help with something at the inn. But he never even brought the inn up.

Her friend said one thing, and one thing only: "He loves you."

"You asked all of us to let you go away for a while, to let you think about your life and what you wanted from it. Now I'm asking you for that same thing."

Only, Stu had continued to call. And Rebecca knew why: her friend cared about her. He cared about his brother. He wanted to see them happy. And, preferably, together.

After that first conversation, Rebecca let Stu's calls go through to voice mail. She had a lot to think about. Namely that she'd been running her entire life when things got too complicated, not because she was weak nor afraid or unable to take care of herself.

But because she'd never had a reason to stay.

And she'd never had anything important enough that she didn't want to lose.

Sean was important, had been important right from the first moment he'd spoken to her, touched her, looked into her eyes and connected with her despite all the reasons not to.

This time around he'd been her reason to run...but he was also her reason to go back.

And to stay.

She returned to Emerald Lake early Saturday morning just in time to witness the first outdoor wedding of spring. Rebecca was happy for the couple, who had just said their "I dos" and kissed in front of their applauding family and friends. And still, she was crying, just like she always did at weddings, whether she knew the couple saying their vows or not.

There was nothing she loved more than a happy ending.

Even if she hadn't yet gotten one for herself.

As the bride, groom, and their guests all moved inside for the reception, Rebecca was just stepping beneath the roof and onto a wooden floor covered in rose petals when she heard her name on the lips of the man she'd fallen so deeply in love with.

"Rebecca."

Slowly, she turned to face Sean. He was staring at her and she couldn't read his expression.

After all, he'd told her he loved her, had begged her to stay, and she'd left, anyway.

Because she'd had to. Because she'd needed a little time by herself to really think things through. And to make sure that she knew her own heart.

"I missed you," he told her, not moving from his position twenty feet away.

Rebecca stood in the center of the gazebo where *forever* had been declared so many times before. She'd never known how to lie. She didn't know how to lie now.

"I missed you, too."

She could almost feel his relief, could certainly see it on his face. She was about to tell him everything she was feeling when he spoke first.

"You were right, Rebecca."

Her heart was thundering in her chest. "About what?"

"To go." Sean crossed the distance between them, coming close enough that she knew he'd catch her if she fell. "I gave you a million reasons to leave me. A million reasons to stop loving me. All I wanted was to try and find one to make you stay. Just one." He ran a hand through his hair. "You were the only reason I went to talk to my mother that night. Because I knew you wanted me to. Because you thought I needed to. Because I knew you'd leave if I didn't. But you left anyway."

Her chest had never felt so tight, so constricted. "I didn't want to go. Leaving you was the hardest thing I've ever done."

"When I was a teenager, I didn't understand that loving someone meant sometimes having to break a promise. I've made and remade that mistake over and over for twenty years, but you were wise enough to know better than to keep a secret that was going to tear someone apart. The first time I saw you, I thought you looked so delicate. But you're the strongest person I've ever met. So strong that you'll sacrifice anything for the ones you love. Even yourself."

She felt the tears start to come again, but she didn't want anything to blur her vision of the man standing before her.

"It was a hell of a week," he said softly. "Probably the worst one since I was fourteen. But all I could think was that maybe, just maybe, if I kept at it, if I kept trying to forgive her a little more, then somehow you'd know and you'd come back."

"I told you I was coming back."

"Not just for the weekend, Rebecca. For good." She was surprised to see a hint of a smile on his lips. "But somewhere along the way, I realized I wasn't just talking with my mother for you anymore." He paused. "I was trying to fix things in my family for me, too."

She couldn't stand apart from him another second longer. Dropping the basket to the floor, she reached for him, wrapped her arms around his broad shoulders.

He held her even tighter. "You were gone, but I could feel your love was behind me every step of the way, sweetheart."

She didn't bother to try and stop her tears as she pulled back. "It still is."

She felt his hands move across her shoulders and down her arms, until he was holding her hands in his. And then he was getting down on one knee and looking up at her.

"You taught me to trust, again. And to love with all of my heart. Please stay in Emerald Lake, not only because you love your job and your friends and this town, but because you want to live out forever with me."

She had to join him on her knees. She didn't let go of his hands. "You say I taught you so many things, but what about everything I've learned from you? For so long I was afraid to trust my heart, but it led me to you. You showed me a world I've only glimpsed from the outside, that I was too afraid to explore, and that day out on your beach, with your plane, you gave me your hand and asked me to trust you one more time. Because you believed in me in a way no one else ever has."

"You would have eventually gotten into an airplane, even without me."

"Maybe, but it wouldn't have been nearly as special. Nothing is as good without you, Sean. When I'm with you, everything is brighter, sweeter." She smiled a small smile. "I spent the week planning a trip I should have taken a long time ago, because being with you has shown me that I can't put off what I want—what I need—another moment longer."

She intercepted the pain moving across his face by placing his hands over her heart. "I want you, Sean. I need you."

"But you just said you were leaving."

"You know how I'm always saying and doing things no one else would? Well"—she shrugged—"turns out I couldn't give up on hope when anyone else would have, either." She couldn't hold back her smile any longer. "I bought two round-the-world tickets. One for me. One for you." She smiled even wider. "Looks like we're going to have to see a whole lot of stuff real fast, before my legal name changes and my ticket isn't valid anymore."

Sean's eyes were shining as he tested out her future married name: "Rebecca Murphy. I like the way that sounds. So is that a yes?"

Rebecca whispered, "Yes."

She leaned in close to seal it with a kiss.

Epilogue

Two weeks later

Stu threw them a heck of a going-away party at the inn. Rebecca and Sean's bags were packed and they were due to fly to London that night on the red-eye. For the next several months, the world was theirs, ready to be explored hand-in-hand.

Rebecca looked around the room at her friends, then out the window at the lake. "All this time, I've been wanting to see the world. So then why do I wish we could just take our bags back upstairs and stay right here?"

Sean smiled at his fiancée. "It will all still be here when we come back," he promised her.

It wasn't just a promise; it was something he knew from experience. He'd tried to leave Emerald Lake behind, but he'd never succeeded. Rebecca was going to love the Eiffel Tower, the Tower of London, the beaches of Thailand, but nothing would ever take the place in her heart that this small Adirondack town held.

He wanted to say all of this to her, but before he could, his mother approached them. His parents were currently living apart. After the Tapping of the Maples Festival, Bill had moved out of the house he'd built. He was now renting a cottage on the other side of the lake. Bill had come in earlier to say his good-byes, but he'd left before he and Elizabeth could run the risk of bumping into each other in the inn's event room.

"I was just telling your brother what a lovely party this has been." It was easy to see the sorrow behind her smile. "I'm so happy for both of you. We all are."

Sean and his mother had been meeting every few days for coffee out on her porch. He knew how glad Rebecca was to see them trying to forge a new relationship. And he was glad, so glad, to see her face his mother with none of the anger that had been eating her up before.

He pulled Rebecca closer as she thanked his mother.

Suddenly, Elizabeth turned her gaze to him and said, "Your father and I have been talking. Not a lot, but more than we were last week." Rebecca squeezed his hand as his mother added, "I'm hopeful that we'll be able to make a new start. One day soon."

Before either Sean or Rebecca could reply, she seemed to shake herself, putting on another smile all of them knew she didn't really feel.

"Be sure to send me postcards," she said, her hidden meaning of *Please let me be involved in your life in some way* not at all hidden.

Celeste came to say good-bye next, kissing both him and Rebecca on the cheek before saying, "Promise me something, Rebecca."

"I'll take good care of your grandson."

Celeste smiled. "I never had any doubt of that," she said in her serene way, as if she had expected them to fall in love all along. "At every shore, throw a handful of pebbles and think of me."

"It's already on my list," Rebecca told his grandmother. "Thank you for sharing so much with me, Celeste."

Her new grandmother-in-law took both of her hands and squeezed them. "Just like you, I never regretted loving with all my heart."

Rebecca was blinking back a rush of tears as Stu moved into their small circle and pointedly looked at his watch.

"Time to go, lovebirds."

He was their chauffeur for the night, having offered to drop them at the airport on his way to visit John for a couple of days. Rebecca had been training April and Jean to share innkeeper duties while she was gone and this was their first trial run by themselves.

After hugging everyone good-bye—with Rebecca solemnly promising Andi and Nate she was going to come back home with plenty of time to spare before they had their baby—the three of them headed off down the winding forested roads to the Albany International Airport.

During the drive, Sean and Stu kept Rebecca laughing with their stories of growing up on the lake. There was nothing Sean loved more than seeing her smile, knowing he could make her laugh; everywhere, including the bed they shared.

Stu was just pulling up to the curb to let them out at departures when he said, "I forgot to tell you guys. That contractor who came out to look at that problem you've been having with noises and cold in your bedroom finally got back to us."

Sean and Rebecca looked at each other before she said, "It's been silent and warm for the past two weeks."

She smiled and Sean knew what she was thinking: the problems with the bedroom had all gone away when they'd declared their love to each other, a love with no secrets in the way the second time around.

"What did he tell you was wrong?" Sean asked his brother, sure that there was a logical explanation for it all.

"Nothing."

Rebecca laughed. "Did he say anything about a ghost?"

Stu clearly didn't know how to respond to that. "Uh, no. Should he have?"

Rebecca hugged him. "Thanks for everything."

Sean could hear Stu say, "I'm happy for you," before he moved from Rebecca to Sean, the two brothers hugging each other out on the airport curb.

When his brother had driven away and it was just the two of them, Rebecca's eyes were sparkling.

"I'd rather have you than a ghost, you know." Her smile had always made him want to smile right back, just like he was doing right now. "But it's much more fun knowing I have both."

With that, she turned, flipping her silky hair over her shoulder as she headed into the check-in area. And as Sean followed her inside, grinning widely, he gave his own silent thanks that he'd been given the precious gift of unexpected, extraordinary love.

Andi Powell's job brings her
back to the hometown she's tried
so hard to forget—and to the man
she never could . . .

Home Sweet Home

Please turn this page for an excerpt.

Chapter One

Home.

Andi Powell couldn't believe she was back home.

During the five-hour drive to Emerald Lake from New York City, Andi had felt her stomach tighten down more and more with each mile she covered, each county line she crossed. She'd pulled up in front of Lake Yarns on Main Street five minutes ago, but she hadn't yet been able to get out of the car. Instead, she sat with her hands still tightly clenched on the steering wheel as she watched people on Main Street. Mothers pushed strollers, shoppers moved in and out of stores, and happy tourists walked hand in hand.

Through her car window, Andi could see that the warm days of summer had already given way to a crisp, cool fall. She would have had to be blind not to notice that the thick green trees around the waterline were transformed into a dazzling display of reds and oranges and yellows.

No wonder why everyone on Main Street looked so happy. Utterly content. Emerald Lake was picture-perfect: the sky was blue, the lake sparkled in the sunlight, and the white paint on the gazebo in the waterfront park looked new.

But Andi wasn't here to become a part of *picture-perfect*. She had a job to do. Which meant it was time to unclench her chest, to untangle the knots in her stomach, and to get down to business.

The sooner she dealt with Emerald Lake, the sooner she could head back to the city.

Pushing open her car door, she grabbed her briefcase and headed toward her family's store. The Lake Yarns awning was bright and welcoming, and the Adirondack chairs out front welcomed knitters to sit for as long as they had time to spare.

She smiled her first real smile of the day, thinking of how much love and care her grandmother and mother had put into this store over the years.

The shiny gold knob on the front door was cool beneath her palm, and she paused to take a deep breath and pull herself together. Entering a building that had practically been her second home as a little girl shouldn't have her heart racing.

But it did.

Opening the door, the smell of yarn was what hit her first. Wool and alpaca, bamboo and silk, cotton and acrylic all had a specific scent. Although Andi hadn't touched yarn in almost two decades, somehow the essence of the skeins lining the walls, in baskets on the floor, knitted up into samples throughout Lake Yarns had remained imprinted in her brain.

She hadn't come back to Emerald Lake to play with yarn, but as Andi instinctively ran her hands over a soft silk-wool blend, thoughts of business momentarily receded. The beautiful blue-green, with hints of reds and oranges wound deep into the fibers, reminded her of the lake and mountains on a fall day like today.

From out of nowhere, Andi was struck by a vision of a lacy shawl draped across a woman's shoulders. Strangely, the woman looked like her.

"Andi, honey, what a lovely surprise!"

Andi jumped at her grandmother's sudden greeting, dropping the yarn like she was a thief who'd been about to stuff it into her bag and dash out the door.

What on earth had she been doing thinking about shawls? This creative world where women sat around and chatted and made things with their hands had never been hers.

She let herself be enveloped by her grandmother's arms. At barely five feet, Evelyn was eight inches smaller than Andi. And yet it never ceased to surprise her how strong her grandmother's arms were. Warm, too. They were always warm.

"Your father's commemoration isn't until next weekend. We didn't expect you to come home a week early." Her grandmother scanned her face for clues as to why she was back in Emerald Lake.

Andi forced a smile she didn't even come close to feeling. Lord knew, she certainly had practice pretending. In the year since her father's sudden death, she'd been going into the office every day with that same smile on her face, working double-time to make sure her work didn't suffer in the wake of her grief.

But it had. Which was how she'd found herself about to lose her biggest client ever in a meeting a week ago.

The Klein Group wanted to build beautiful vacation

condominiums in the perfect vacation town. They'd shot down every single one of her proposals—Martha's Vineyard, Nantucket, Cape Cod. Her boss, Craig, had been frowning at her the same way for three months, like he didn't think she could hack it anymore, and as panic shook her, Andi's mind had actually gone completely blank. That was when her phone had jumped on the table in front of her, a picture of Emerald Lake popping up along with a message from her mother.

It's beautiful here today. Makes me think of you.

Before she knew it, Andi was saying, "I have the perfect spot."

Just that quickly, the old energy, the excitement she used to feel during pitches, rushed through her as she pulled up one beautiful picture after another of Emerald Lake on her computer in the middle of the meeting.

No pitch had ever been easier: The condos would have a spectacular view. There was an excellent golf course close by. And best of all, their clients would be only hours away from New York City, close enough to take a break from the stress of their real lives but far enough removed to get away from it all.

Andi would never leave the city, but that didn't mean she didn't see how magical Emerald Lake could be for the right kind of people. The Klein Group had agreed.

The previous Wednesday, she'd been ecstatic, but now that she was back in her hometown, all she could think was, *What have I done?*

In lieu of going into a detailed explanation about her sudden appearance, Andi asked, "Where's Mom? I was expecting her to be in the store with you."

"Carol had some errands to run in Saratoga Springs

and won't be back until late tonight. Will you be able to spend the night before heading back to the city? I know how much your mother would love to see you."

What a huge understatement that was. Andi's mother would be heartbroken if her daughter came and went without seeing her, but Evelyn had never believed in guilt. She had never once pressured Andi into coming home more often or sticking around for longer on the rare occasions when she did visit. When Andi heard her coworkers talk about how their families were forever pressuring them to move back to their hometowns, she was glad her own family was so hands-off with her. They would never try to convince her to come back to the small town she'd grown up in. They respected her goals and plans too much to ever bombard her with hints that they missed her.

Wasn't she lucky to be so free?

"I'll probably be here a week. Maybe two." And then she would leave again, returning back to the city life she'd chosen as soon as she'd graduated from Emerald Lake's small high school. "It's a bit of a working vacation actually."

Fortunately, her grandmother had never been interested in talking business—yet another way they were different.

"Two weeks?" Evelyn looked like she'd won the lottery. "What a treat to have you here, especially when we're having such a beautiful fall."

As a sharp pang of guilt at not seeing more of her family settled in beneath Andi's breastbone, she followed her grandmother's gaze out the store's large front windows to the lake beyond the Adirondack chairs on the porch.

"Fall was always my favorite time of year at the lake," she admitted softly.

Andi's career as a management consultant in New York City meant she'd barely been back to Emerald Lake for more than a weekend, even over holidays. Growing up watching her father do such great things for so many people as senator had fueled her to want to follow in his footsteps. Not as a politician, but as someone who worked hard, cared deeply, and felt joy at a job well done. After graduating from Cornell University with both an undergraduate degree in economics and then an MBA, she'd chosen Marks & Banks carefully based on their commitment to the environment and the fact that they did more pro bono work than any other consulting company out there.

Her father had always encouraged her to "go for the brass ring," and even if some nights she fell onto her bed fully clothed and woke up the next morning with mascara smudged around her eyes and her stomach empty and grumbling, that was exactly what she'd done for the past ten years far away from her teeny, tiny hometown. Emerald Lake was barely a speck on the map, a blue stretch of water surrounded by rolling mountains.

Andi pulled her gaze away from the sparkling lake. "The store looks great, Grandma."

Evelyn frowned as she scanned the shelves. For such a tiny woman with a sweet, pretty face, her grandmother could be one of the most blunt people Andi had ever come across. The polar opposite of Andi's mother Carol, actually, who simply didn't believe in confrontation. But they were both small and gently rounded. Andi had always felt like a giant around the tiny women in her family.

"I just don't know about the changes your mother made."

Seeing the way her grandmother hated to move even a couple of skeins of yarn from one side of the store to the other had Andi second-guessing her project for the Klein Group again.

Why couldn't she have blurted out any other Adirondack town than Emerald Lake? Still, she was glad for her grandmother's unintended warning to tread carefully. The condos were bound to be more change than this town had seen in fifty years at least.

Taking the time to notice the changes in the store, Andi said, "Actually, I think the changes help liven up the place." And then, more gently, "It's still your shop, Grandma. Just a bit shinier now for the new generation of knitters."

"That's exactly what your mother said. Two against one."

Andi didn't want her grandmother to think they were ganging up on her. Just as she would have approached a potentially disgruntled client, she took another tack. "What have your customers said?"

"They love it."

Andi had to laugh at the grudging words. "Good."

"Well, since you're going to be home for so long, I'll be expecting you to finally pick up the needles again," her grandmother shot back.

Barely holding back an eye roll, Andi said, "We both know that isn't going to happen, Grandma."

"You used to love to knit when you were a little girl. I'm telling you, it's not natural to quit knitting one day and not miss it."

"Are you calling me a freak of nature, Grandma?" Andi teased. Only way down deep inside, joking about not belonging didn't really feel like a joke.

Instead, it felt like a reality that she'd tried to pretend hadn't hurt all her life.

Evelyn picked up a few balls of yarn that were in the wrong basket. "I'm saying I think you must miss it." She looked thoughtful. "Perhaps it's simply that you haven't found the right reason to start knitting in earnest yet."

"I just don't like knitting, Grandma. Not like you and Mom do." Andi hadn't thought about knitting, hadn't been into another yarn or craft store for nearly two decades. Clearly, the yarn addiction hadn't passed through to the third generation.

"You know, my mother tried to get me to knit for years before I really fell in love with it."

"You're kidding me?" Andi assumed her grandmother had been born with knitting needles in her hand. "What changed?"

Evelyn sat down on one of the soft couches in the middle of the room. "I met a man."

"Grandpa?"

"No. Not Grandpa."

Andi's eyes went wide with surprise as she sank down beside her grandmother.

Evelyn reached into a basket beside her seat and pulled out a half-finished work in progress. As if she was hardly aware of the movements of her hands, she began a new row.

"Everyone was doing their part for World War II. I wanted to help the soldiers, and I was always good with knitting needles. I knew our socks and sweaters were giving joy and comfort to men, strangers I'd never meet, but who desperately needed a reminder of softness. Of warmth."

Andi thought about the tiny caps and booties her grandmother had always made for the new babies at the hospital. Andi had made them, too, when she was a little girl. She'd loved seeing a little baby at the park wearing something she'd made. But her grandmother was right. That hadn't been enough to keep her knitting.

"So it wasn't just one man who made you love knitting," Andi said, trying to keep up with her grandmother, "but many?"

"I knit for the cause, but that's all it was. A cause. It wasn't personal. Not until *him*. Not until I made his sweater." Evelyn's eyes rose to meet Andi's. "Every skein tells a story. As soon as a person puts it in their two hands, the mystery of the story is slowly revealed."

Andi's breath caught in her throat as her grandmother said, "Hold this, honey." Since she didn't know how to knit anymore, Andi laid the needles down awkwardly on her lap.

"Those fibers you're holding can become anything from a baby blanket to a bride's wedding veil," Evelyn said softly. "But I've always thought knitting is about so much more than the things we make."

Andi looked at her grandmother's face and saw that Evelyn was a million miles away.

"Sometimes yarn is the best way to hold onto memories. But sometimes, it's the only way to forget."

Andi found herself blinking back tears.

This was exactly why she never came back to the lake. There were too many memories here for her. Memories of people that had meant so much to her.

The walls of the store suddenly felt too close, the room too small. She needed to leave, needed to go someplace where she could focus on work. And nothing else.

"Grandma," she said as she stood up, "I need to go." The needles and yarn fell from her lap to the floor.

Frowning, her grandmother bent to pick them up, but suddenly she was racked with coughs. Fear lancing her heart, Andi automatically put an arm around Evelyn and gently rubbed her back as if that could make the coughing stop.

Her grandmother tried to say, "I'm fine," but each word was punctuated by more coughs.

Evelyn Thomas was a small-boned eighty-eight-year-old woman, but Andi had never thought of her grandmother as frail or fragile. Until now.

As her grandmother tried to regain her breath, Andi couldn't believe how translucent her skin had become. Evelyn's hands had always been one of the most impressive things about her with long, slim fingers and nails neatly rounded at the tips. So strong, so tireless as she quickly knitted sweaters and blankets, the needles a blur as she chatted, laughed, and gossiped with customers and friends in Lake Yarns.

"You shouldn't come to work if you have a cold." Fear made Andi's words harder than they needed to be, almost accusing. "You should be resting."

Mostly recovered now, her grandmother waved one hand in the air. "I told you, I'm fine. Just a little coughing fit every now and then." At Andi's disbelieving look, she said, "Things like that happen to us old people, you know."

Andi hated to hear her grandmother refer to herself as

old, even though she knew it was technically true. It was just that she couldn't bear to think that one day Evelyn wouldn't be here, wouldn't be living and breathing this store, the yarn, the customers who loved her as much as her own family did.

A twinge of guilt hit Andi even though there was no reason for her to feel this way. Her mother and grandmother had always run Lake Yarns perfectly well by themselves. Nothing had changed just because Andi was going to be in town for a couple of weeks.

Still, she couldn't help but feel that she should have been here before now. What if something had happened to her mother or grandmother while she'd been gone? Just like it had happened to her father.

"Have you seen Dr. Morris yet?" Andi asked, immediately reading the answer in her grandmother's face. Sometimes Evelyn was too stubborn for her own good.

Andi grabbed the cordless phone and handed it to her grandmother. "Call him."

"I can't leave the store unattended."

"I don't care about the store, Grandma. I care about you. That cough sounded awful. You need to get it checked out, make sure it isn't something serious."

When Evelyn didn't take the phone, Andi decided to take matters into her own hands. "Hello, this is Andi Powell. My grandmother Evelyn has a terrible cough and needs to see Dr. Morris as soon as possible." After a moment of silence, where she listened to the friendly receptionist's questions, Andi shot Evelyn a look. "She isn't calling herself because talking makes her cough. Yes, she can be there in fifteen minutes." She put the phone down on the counter. "He's squeezing you in."

"I won't put a closed sign up in the middle of the day on my store. I've been open rain or shine for nearly sixty years."

Andi found her grandmother's purse behind the counter and forced her to take it, just as Evelyn had forced her to take the needles and yarn. "I'll watch the store."

"You?"

Evelyn's disbelief was right on the edge of insulting. "Yes, me. How hard can it be?"

One neat eyebrow moved up on her grandmother's pretty face, and Andi realized how insulting her response had been.

"I didn't mean it like that, Grandma. Look, the register is the same one you had when I was a kid. I couldn't have forgotten positively everything about knitting. If I don't know something, I'll figure it out. I promise."

"Well, if you think you can handle it for an hour..."

The challenge in her grandmother's voice had her saying, "After your appointment, I want you to take the rest of the day off. I'll close up."

But after Evelyn left, the bells on the door clanging softly behind her, Andi stood in the middle of the store wondering what the heck she'd just signed up for. With all the money Andi made in skyscrapers and on corporate campuses, she had absolutely no idea what she was doing in a place like this.

Still Andi told herself there was no reason to panic.

Anyone with half a brain could run a yarn store for a few hours on a Monday morning.

A few seconds later, the front door opened and a gray-haired woman walked in.

"Hello," Andi said in an overbright voice. "Welcome to Lake Yarns."

"Thank you. I've heard such good things about your store that I drove all the way from Utica to come take a look."

Andi's eyes widened. "You drove an hour and a half to visit this store?"

The woman gave her a strange look. "Yes, I did. Several of my friends simply rave about your selection and customer service."

Andi hoped she didn't look as horrified as she felt. This woman had traveled one hundred miles to shop here…and she was getting stuck with someone who didn't even know how to knit.

Sorely tempted to run down the street to call her grandmother back, Andi told herself she was being ridiculous. How much help would someone need in a yarn store? If you were a serious knitter, shouldn't you already know everything?

With another wide smile, Andi finally said, "Be sure to let me know if you need anything."

She stared down at the ancient register, not really remembering how to use it at all, and wondered if there was an instruction booklet somewhere under the counter. She didn't want to look like an idiot in front of her first customer.

"Excuse me?"

Andi straightened up from her fruitless search for a manual. "Yes? Is there something I can help you with?"

The woman held up a skein of yarn. "It says this is superwash, but I'm a fairly new knitter and I don't know whether I should trust the label or not. Can you tell me how this actually washes? Does it pill or felt if you leave it in the dryer for too long?"

Andi carefully studied the label as if "100% Superwash Merino Wool" meant something to her. If she said she had no idea how it washed because she didn't knit or know the first thing about any of the yarns in the store, the woman would be—rightly—disgusted. But if she lied and said it would wash well and then it didn't, Lake Yarns would have lost a customer for life.

She'd never thought she'd have to think so fast standing in the middle of a yarn store.

How wrong she'd been.

Quickly deciding the truth was her best option, Andi said, "Actually I've never used that particular yarn."

The woman frowned. "Is there anyone here that has?" she asked, craning her head to see if there was some yarn guru hiding in the back of the store.

"I'm sure there's some information online about that brand. It will just take me a minute to look it up."

Thank god she never went anywhere without her tiny laptop. Unfortunately, it seemed to take forever to start up. She felt like she was standing in front of one of her clients who wanted answers about their project and wanted them now. Andi usually worked double-time not to be put in this kind of position.

But her grandmother really had sounded terrible. Watching the store was the right thing to do.

"I'll just find an Internet connection and then—"

Shoot. All of the nearby wireless providers were locked tight with passwords. Working not to let her expression betray her, Andi reached for her phone. But after what seemed like an eternity of trying to pull up her search page, all she got was a message that said, "Cannot connect."

She couldn't believe it. She was being beaten by a yarn store.

Shooting her clearly irritated customer a reassuring smile, she said, "I'll have the information for you in another few moments," then picked up the cordless phone and local phone book and went into the back.

Flipping through the pages, she found another yarn store in Loon Lake and quickly dialed the number. "Hi, this is Andi Powell from Lake Yarns. I have a quick question for you about—" The woman on the other end of the line cut her off. "Oh yes, of course, I understand if you're busy with a customer. Okay, I'll call back in fifteen minutes."

But Andi already knew that fifteen minutes would be way too long. Desperate now, she walked out the back door and held her cell phone out to the sky, praying for bars.

"Thank god," she exclaimed when the word *searching* in the top left corner of her phone slowly shifted to the symbol that meant she had a wireless connection. Typing into the web browser with her thumbs, she actually exclaimed "hooray" and pumped her fist in the air when the information she'd been looking for appeared.

A moment later, greatly relieved to find her customer was still in the store, she said, "Good news. It seems that everyone who has used that yarn is really happy with how well it washed. Plus it evidently doesn't itch in the least."

The woman nodded. "Okay."

Uh-oh. That was less than enthusiastic.

Hoping that talking about the woman's intended

project might reengage her earlier enthusiasm, Andi asked, "What were you thinking of knitting with it?"

"A baby blanket for my new granddaughter."

The woman pulled a picture out of her purse. The baby was chubby and bald and smiling a toothless grin.

"She's beautiful," Andi said softly.

The woman nodded, her previously irritated expression now completely gone. "I learned to knit for her."

Just like that, Andi suddenly understood what her grandmother had been talking about: this baby was the reason this woman was falling in love with knitting. As Andi instinctively ran the yarn's threads between her thumb and forefinger, a shiver of beauty, of sweet, unexpected calm suddenly moved through her.

At long last, the knot in the center of her gut came loose, and she told the woman, "I think it will make a really beautiful baby blanket."

Andi wasn't trying to sell the woman anything anymore.

She was simply saying what she felt.

THE DISH

Where authors give you the inside scoop!

From the desk of Stella Cameron

Frog Crossing

Out West

Dear Reading Friends,

Yes, I'm a gardener and I live at Frog Crossing. In England, my original home, we tend to name our houses, and the habit lives on for me. Some say I should have gone for Toad Hall, but enough said about them.

Things magical, mystical, otherworldly, enchanting— or terrifying—have occupied my storytelling mind since I was a child. Does this have anything to do with gardening? Yes. Nighttime in a garden, alone, is the closest I can come to feeling connected to the very alive world that exists in my mind. Is it the underworld? I don't think so. It is the otherworld, and that's where anything is possible.

At night, in that darkness, I feel not only what I remember from the day, but all sorts of creatures moving around me and going through their personal dramas. I hear them, too. True, I'm the one pulling the strings for the action, but that's where the stories take root, grow, and spread. This is my plotting ground.

In DARKNESS BOUND, things that fly through tall trees feature prominently. Werehound Niles Latimer and widowed, mostly human, Leigh Kelly are under attack from every quarter by fearsome elements bent on tearing them apart. If their bond becomes permanent and they produce a child, they can destroy a master plan to take control of the paranormal world.

The tale is set on atmospheric Whidbey Island in the Pacific Northwest, close to the small and vibrant town of Langley, where human eyes see nothing of the battle waged around them. But the unknowing humans play an important part in my sometimes dark, sometimes light-hearted, sometimes serious, a little quirky, but always intensely passionate story.

Welcome to DARKNESS BOUND,

Stella Cameron

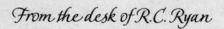

From the desk of R.C. Ryan

Dear Reader,

Ahh. With QUINN I get to begin another family saga of love, laughter, and danger, all set on a sprawling ranch in Wyoming, in the shadow of the Grand Tetons. What could be more fun than this? As I'm fond of saying, I just love a rugged cowboy.

There is something about ranching that, despite all its hard work, calls to me. Maybe it's the feeling that farmers, ranchers, and cattlemen helped settle this great nation. Maybe it's my belief that there is something noble about working the land, and having a special connection to the animals that need tending.

Quinn is all my heroes wrapped into one tough, rugged cowboy. As the oldest of three boys, he's expected to follow the rules and always keep his brothers safe, especially with their mother gone missing when they were children. In tune with the land he loves, he's drawn to the plight of wolves and has devoted his life to researching them and to working the ranch that has become his family's legacy. He has no need for romantic attachments...well, until one woman bursts into his life.

Fiercely independent, Cheyenne O'Brien has been running a ranch on her own, since the death of her father and brother. Cheyenne isn't one to ask for help, but when an unknown enemy attacks her and her home, she will fight back with everything she has, and Quinn will be right by her side.

To me, Cheyenne is the embodiment of the Western woman: strong, adventurous, willing to do whatever it takes to survive—and still very much a beautiful, soft-hearted, vulnerable woman where her heart is concerned.

I loved watching *the sparks* fly between Quinn and Cheyenne.

As a writer, the thrill is to create another fascinating family and then watch as they work, play, and love, all the while facing up to the threat of very real danger from those who wish them harm.

I hope you'll come along to share the adventure and enjoy the ride with my new Wyoming Sky trilogy!

R. C. Ryan

www.ryanlangan.com

♥ ♥ ♥ ♥ ♥ ♥ ♥ ♥ ♥ ♥ ♥ ♥ ♥

From the desk of Bella Riley

Dear Reader,

When my husband and I were first married, one of our favorite things to do was to go away for a romantic weekend together at a historic inn. We loved to stay at old inns (the Sagamore on Lake George in the Adirondacks), or windswept inns on the Pacific Ocean (the Coronado in San Diego), or majestic inns made of stone in the middle of a seemingly endless meadow (the Ahwahnee in Yosemite Valley). Now that we've got two very active kids, we have slightly different requirements for our getaways, which are more boisterous and slightly less romantic…although I have to say our kids put up with "Mommy and Daddy are kissing again" pretty darn well! Fortunately, my husband and kids know that my favorite thing is afternoon tea, and my husband and son don't at all seem to mind being the only males in frilly rooms full of girls and women in pretty dresses.

As I sat down to write the story of Rebecca and Sean in WITH THIS KISS, I immediately knew I wanted it to take place in the inn on Emerald Lake. With those pictures in my head of all the inns I've stayed at over the years, I knew not only what this inn looked like, but also the many love stories that had been born—and renewed—there over the years. What's more, I knew the inn needed to be a large part of the story, and that the history in those walls around my hero and heroine would be an integral part of the magic of their romance. Because when deeply hidden secrets threaten to keep Rebecca and Sean apart despite the fireworks that neither of them can deny, the truth of what happened in the inn so many years ago is finally revealed.

I so enjoyed creating my fantasy inn on Emerald Lake, and I hope that as you're reading WITH THIS KISS, even if you aren't able to get away for a romantic weekend right this second, for a few hours you'll feel as if you've spent some time relaxing…and falling in love.

Happy reading,

Bella Riley

www.bellariley.com

♥ ♥ ♥ ♥ ♥ ♥ ♥ ♥ ♥ ♥ ♥ ♥ ♥ ♥ ♥

From the desk of Jami Alden

Dear Reader,

Who hasn't wished for a fresh start at some point in their lives? I know I have. The urge became particularly keen when I was starting high school in Connecticut. Not that it was a terrible place to grow up, but an awkward phase combined with a pack of mean girls eager to point out every quirk and flaw had left their scars. Left me wishing I could go somewhere new, where I could meet all new people. People who wouldn't remember the braces (complete with headgear!), the unibrow, the glasses (lavender plastic frames!), and the time my mom tried to perm my bangs with disastrous results.

In RUN FROM FEAR, Talia Vega is looking for a similar fresh start. Granted, the monsters from her past are a bit more formidable than a pack of snotty twelve-year-olds, and the scars she bears are physical as well as emotional. But like so many of us, all she really wants is a fresh start, a new life, away from the shadows of her past.

But just as I was forced to sit in class with peers who remembered when I had a mouth full of metal and no idea how to wield a pair of tweezers, Talia Vega can't outrun the people unwilling to let her forget everything she's tried to leave behind. Lucky for her, Jack Brooks, the one man who has seen her at her absolute lowest point, will do anything to protect her from monsters past and present.

And even though I got my own fresh start of sorts

when I moved across the country for college, I sure wish someone had been around to protect me from my mother and her Ogilvie home perm kit. I don't care what the commercial says—you CAN get it wrong!

Jami Alden

www.jamialden.com

Find out more about Forever Romance!

Visit us at
www.hachettebookgroup.com/publishing_forever.aspx

Find us on Facebook
http://www.facebook.com/ForeverRomance

Follow us on Twitter
http://twitter.com/ForeverRomance

NEW AND UPCOMING TITLES

Each month we feature our new titles
and reader favorites.

CONTESTS AND GIVEAWAYS

We give away galleys, autographed copies,
and all kinds of exclusive items.

AUTHOR INFO

You'll find bios, articles, and links to personal websites
for all your favorite authors—and so much more.

GET SOCIAL

Connect with your favorite authors, editors, and
other Forever fans, and share what's important to you.

THE BUZZ

Sign up for our monthly romance newsletter,
and be the first to read all about it.